$\mathcal{V}$OICES OF THE $\mathcal{S}$OUTH

TAKE ME BACK

ALSO BY RICHARD BAUSCH

Real Presence
The Last Good Time
Spirits and Other Stories
Mr. Field's Daughter
The Fireman's Wife and Other Stories
Violence
Rebel Powers
In the Night Season

Take Me Back

A NOVEL BY

Richard Bausch

LOUISIANA STATE UNIVERSITY PRESS

Baton Rouge

07 06 05 04 03 02 01 00 99 98   5 4 3 2 1

Library of Congress Cataloging-in-Publication Data
Bausch, Richard, 1945–
    Take me back / Richard Bausch.
        p.   cm. — (Voices of the South)
    ISBN 0-8071-2331-5 (pbk. : alk. paper)
    I. Title   II. Series.
  PS3552.A846T34   1998
  813'.54—dc21   98-23623
                                                    CIP

The paper in this book meets the guidelines for permanence and durability of
the Committee on Production Guidelines for Book Longevity of the Council on
Library Resources. ∞

FOR

Robert Carl Bausch
Helen Simmons Bausch
Bob and Geri Bausch
Wesley, Emily, and Paul

And because of Karen

All love

I beg pardon for this sad spectacle I've had to present before all you ladies and gentlemen to remedy the evil which, without wanting, without knowing, you are doing this unhappy woman—with your compassion.

LUIGI PIRANDELLO,
It Is So! (If You Think So)

Book One

I

ONE EVENING—it was in the first week of June, in Point Royal, Virginia—a man sat out on his back patio, part of a newspaper in his lap, and watched a girl walk in the gravel lot just beyond the strip of grass that bordered the apartments behind him. The girl pushed a stroller with a baby in it, the baby sitting there like a sleepy dauphin, though the pinched face was smudged, cheeks blue, as if bruised, with jelly or grape juice or whatever it was. The day had been airless and hot, and the man swatted at flies, watching the girl and watching, too, the drifting haze that moved like the heat itself along the tops of the trees beyond. His name was Brinhart; he had just eaten dinner and drunk one beer and now he sat here, uncomfortably full, while his wife prodded his stepson.

"Eat," she said. "Will you concentrate and eat." Brinhart heard this through the screen at his shoulder, but he did not turn around. He was watching the girl.

On a radio somewhere a man was talking about the air-quality index, photochemical mists; everyone was to stay inside and run the air conditioners, but there were brownouts, and the air conditioners blew fuses, broke down. The newscaster wondered what would happen in July, when real summer settled in. Brinhart concentrated on the girl, who moved in an arc around to the edge of the grass before him and on, walking slow, her hair tangled and sweat-matted across her forehead.

She had come out of the trailer court, from the path through the hedgerow which, on this tail end of the Winston Garden Apartments, was fitted like a T square to the lot, and served as a demarcation of sorts between apartments and mobile homes, the one being slightly higher in the scheme of things than the other—at least according to the owners of Winston Garden. ("It's unfortunate," the real estate agent had said, "but we didn't think we'd have to build this far. That's why the rent on this apartment is lower." Brinhart hadn't minded: he might've taken anything at the price. And Katherine, his wife, for all her objections, had relented finally. "Where will Alex play? What sort of people live in trailer courts?" "Rock 'n' roll singers," Brinhart had said, but he had meant to be funny. "You go to hell," said Katherine.)

Now she was after the boy again: "Eat, I'm telling you. If you think I'm going to let your grandfather take you to a ball game—eat."

"Katherine," Brinhart called over his shoulder, "the old man said he was thinking of coming up. He might not come up."

"If he *does* come," Katherine said, "dammit."

Brinhart looked at the girl, who had turned, was coming back. She stopped, bent over to coo in the baby's ear. The child's mouth, as if functioning separately from the rest of the face, emitted a froth of spit in a sloppy farting sound, and the girl laughed, sent the laugh at the sky. Her neck gleamed; she had a good tan. She wore a white halter-top, jogging shorts. She couldn't have been more than eighteen, if that. Her slender hands toyed with the baby's fat arms, and then she was pushing the stroller again, back around the lot. She had been making this walk almost every evening now for some weeks, and Brinhart had found himself looking forward to watching her—a harmless and private pleasure, at a peaceful time of day. But there was no peace now: Katherine's voice, discordant and shrill, admonished the boy about baseball.

"Do you think he'd like it if I took him to see the Orioles?" the old man had asked. "I mean if I decide to come. Is he interested in baseball?"

He is obsessed with baseball.

Brinhart looked at the section of newspaper in his lap: the sports page, and Alex had marked up the box scores again, figuring the changes in averages. He folded the newspaper, looked out at the lot. The girl had turned back toward the hedgerow, the path. Beyond the hedgerow two or three windows were already showing light; the trailer court looked like an aggregate of railroad cars with a wild growth of TV antennas growing out of the metal. They were all old and slightly run-down—some of them even sagged a little—and the grass grew so tall between them and behind them that the whole area looked abandoned. What his father would say about this view if he saw it: That was what bothered him now—that the old man might really come after all. Brinhart hadn't asked him, had merely said, "Sure. Well, give us a call and let us know." "Katherine," he said now, "I'll bet he doesn't come. He's probably trying to get us to go down there again."

"Honey, will you come in here if you want to talk?"

"That's all right."

"What?" She was moving dishes now.

"I said, that's all right."

"I don't care whether he comes or not, Gordon."

"You were pretty excited when I told you he might."

"I can't hear you."

He listened to the dishes clattering. He wanted a beer, and now he stood. The girl had stepped into the path. He watched the little glimpses of white and red cloth through the leaves of the hedgerow, then he turned to the screen in the patio door. It was sliding glass with a sliding screen, and it never worked right. Now there were perhaps twenty flies on the screen and around the aluminum edges. He folded the newspaper, tried to get a few; but the newspaper was too thin and he only stirred them up. He stood waving the folded newspaper through the air, hearing Katherine letting dishes down in the sink: she had a way of rampaging through her cleaning and ordering, as though something pursued her and might strike if she paused for anything before she was finished. Brinhart put the newspaper down, looked through the screen at her. She stood there, her back to him, across the space of the living room and dining area. Alex sat quietly at the table, his plate before him, some pieces of bread in coagulating gravy, a half glass of milk.

"Could you not break anything?" Brinhart said. But she had just let a handful of knives and forks down, and his voice was lost in the noise. "Katherine, for God's sake."

She turned. "What?"

"Lay off it, will you?"

"Lay off what. If he comes, he is not taking this boy to any baseball game. Period."

Brinhart looked at the boy. "Eat," he said. "Eat, eat, eat, eat, eat."

"I'm so tired of waiting for him to finish."

"Eat," Brinhart said.

"Just forget it," said Katherine, rattling the silverware in a fast foam of water from the tap. "Go back to your newspaper."

"Oh. You want help with the dishes?"

"I can't hear you, Gordon." Her hands were in the water.

"I said, you want help."
"That would be nice."
Brinhart sang:

"If you want me, honey, I'll come by,
I'll do anything you want.
You can be my honey pie,
And I'll be your debutante."

Turning to the table, Katherine smiled, though he could see that she had tried not to. The boy took some of the milk, which had warmed enough to leave a chalky stain of itself on the glass. "All the great baseball players eat good, kid."
"Sure, Brinhart."
"I've told you before," said Katherine, "I don't like that. Dad. You say Dad."
Brinhart winked at the boy.
"Dad," the boy said.
"Want to go for a walk?" Brinhart suggested.
"No," Katherine said.
"Want to play guitar?"
Katherine stopped, but she did not look at him.
"Just kidding, sweetheart."
She began to work quickly and noisily, as though alone.
"Sweetheart."
Nothing. The boy looked at him as though to ask what was wrong. Brinhart shrugged, turned back to his chair. Maybe it was trouble again. He did not want any of that—especially if his father were coming. The old man would pick on anything and say he had known all along—or he would think it if he didn't say it. As he would think himself right about college and so many other things, looking at this apartment complex and the trailer court and Brinhart still working a job he planned no future in, passing through toward something better, not settled yet. And now

Brinhart experienced an old, familiar unease. It was a feeling that he vaguely connected to the last hour of daylight; it always made him long for midnight, past sundown, morning. It did not happen often—sometimes not for months—but when it did, it happened with the intensity and the familiarity of any chronic trouble, and there were times when he believed it gradually weakened him, as though it were the preliminary of some more serious barrage yet to come, for which he would have no adequate defense. This idea always slightly unhinged him, and for a long time now he had sought relief by having a drink of something stronger than the usual beer; there were periods during which, sensing that the anxiety or the dread or whatever it was might be hovering near, he had drunk whiskey to ward it off.

"Whiskey again," Katherine said, scrubbing a plate, "You had beer with dinner." Her smooth wrists were flecked with suds. She did not wait for an answer. "You left the screen open."

"I'm going right back out."

She seemed not to have heard him.

"You want to join me?"

"I'd like to talk to you, yes."

"Talk," he said, dropping ice cubes into a tumbler, opening the whiskey. He poured it straight into the glass, without measuring, and he was aware that she watched him. "I'm listening."

She dried her hands quickly, not looking at him, and walked out of the room. As she did so, in a strange shift of his mind, he remembered coming half awake the night before and hearing her walking around in the living room. He took a gulp of the whiskey.

"Katherine?" he said. But then he could hear her in the boy's room. Yes, she had been up last night; he remembered clearly now the pacing steps, back and forth. It was hard not to see the signs, even now, even knowing how much she hated his seeing them, and believed that his vigilance—as she called it—predicated things. As he crossed toward the open screen, drink in hand, he heard her give a deep sigh, almost like a gasp, in the hallway. He paused, looking for her there. He heard her complaining to Alex about daydreaming—there was a crumpling of paper, the boy's soft, apologetic voice. Katherine muttered the word *closet*.

"You want help?" Brinhart called, and when there was no answer, but only a pause, as if Katherine and the boy were listening for him, he called again. "Want help?"

"Go out and close the screen, please," Katherine answered.

He did so. He sat down in his chair and sipped the whiskey, gazing out at the patches of yellow light on the coming dark: the windows of the trailer court, in one of which the girl might show herself. Not that he looked for her. He saw her in his mind and wondered what dreams she might have, what she might want for herself, hope for, love. He had begun to feel the whiskey, but the uneasiness still clung to him. He drank again, looked at a heavy cloud, like a barge, floating across the hazy moon. The sky was a sick, low burning red screen, without stars, though before him the shadows had merged everywhere, colors fading into one smoky shade. It was a little cooler now, a humid stillness that smelled faintly of exhaust. To his right a long file of squares and rhomboids of light shone on the grass from the neighboring apartments, illuminating the trunks of trees with their coats of moss on into the dark up that way. It was ghostly; there wasn't a soul moving anywhere and the mountainous shadows of maple and oak and sycamore seemed to close him off. Two patios away, someone had lighted charcoal in a grill, and the fire licked up into a space that seemed darker for the yellow-blue brilliance of the flames. It was very quiet. Brinhart could not hear Katherine anymore, and now it dawned on him that he had been hearing her: those sighs that were like gasps, her displeased talking to the boy, who was put to bed and who, no doubt, was going over his baseball in the semidark of his room. Brinhart listened, letting an ice cube out of the glass onto his tongue, sucking the whiskey from it. He would have a little more when this was done and he would be cheerful and easy with Katherine and she would not accuse him of looking for signs. He would not tease about the rock 'n' roll. Or no, he would, because if he did not, she would interpret that. What he would do, he would make love to her.

There was a cry, somewhere far-off in the night—animal or human, he could not decide. Then he heard a faint voice—the professional singsong of television or radio. He looked at one of the lighted windows in the trailer court. In a moment he would definitely fix himself another whiskey; it had already set a sweet glow in him, and for a fleeting instant now he lost any sense of who he was or what had bothered him; it was a red twilight and he was a pair of eyes, watching. Slowly, as the whole evening crept back to him where he sat, the uneasiness entering his blood, he realized that Katherine stood behind him on the other side of the screen. He swallowed the dregs of the whiskey, turned, and, seeing her there, her eyes blazing—or seeming to in that odd fire-tinted light from the burning charcoal yonder—experienced a moment of something like horror: somehow she was much closer, much larger than he had pictured when he had decided that she must be there.

"Coming out?" he said.

She opened the screen, paused a moment, as though studying her own movements, then stepped out, turning all the way around to close it.

"Here," he said, rising, "Just let me get another drink."
She stepped aside.

When he returned, she was standing at the edge of the patio, arms folded, gazing out at the moon. "Scary," she said. "Amazing."

He sat down. "The moon is beautiful, but covered with gas." He laughed.

"It's not really funny," she said.

"No. Suppose not."

"The awful thing is that it's beautiful."

Brinhart took a little of the whiskey.

"It's so quiet out," she said.

"Peaceful." He watched her turn and sit down in the chair across from him. She sighed, looked beyond him, putting her hands down in her lap.

"I'm dead, Gordo."

"It's this air—takes it out of you. And Alex—Alex too."

"He was no more trouble than usual, today."

"Drink?" he said. "Just a tad? Calm your nerves."

"No drink."

They both watched a man step out onto the patio where the charcoal burned. The man was enormous: all hip and thigh and calf.

"I don't know anybody here," Katherine said. "Isn't that amazing? We've been here two years and we don't know who lives next door."

"Everybody moves away. You get to know them and they move away."

"If your father comes—you'll be at work all day. I mean, what will I do with him—say to him?"

"He's probably not even coming," Brinhart said, "Don't let it get to your nerves. I don't want you all fucked up again. Especially if he is coming."

"That's it," she said. "Say just the right thing." She tried to laugh.

"Come on, honey."

"This just isn't the right time for him to come."

"He didn't say he was coming *now*. He said he might come sometime—"

"I *know* what he said."

Brinhart waited a moment. "Besides, you've convinced him that you're not the wild rock 'n' roll queen he thought you were when I brought you home."

"It's not *him*, Gordon. I can't stand anybody staying here right now."

"Relax," he said, because that was all he could think of to say. He drank the whiskey, and for a long time they were quiet. The haze had lifted a little. Two other people had joined the fat man on the other patio, and there was polite laughter, someone being witty. The fat man was pouring drinks.

"I just don't want anybody now," Katherine sighed.

"Just relax; don't worry. Take things easy."

"Stop talking like that."

"Just trying to soothe you a little."

"Well, don't. All right? Let's pretend that I never had any trouble and I'm just in a bad mood."

"You never did *really* have any trouble. You only imagine you did."

"Let's just leave it alone," she said.

Someone dropped a glass on the other patio; it shattered, and there was a general commotion. Brinhart gazed at his wife in what was now almost pure dark, her features only vaguely discernible, and he remembered—it was truly as if he had to remember it, as if it were so akin to the quality, the feel, of memory as to seem somehow in the past—that he loved her.

"I just want you to be happy," he said gently.

"I have to be happy," she said. "Because if I'm not happy, you think I'm nuts."

"No," he said. "No."

They were quiet again. He wished his father had not called, he was certain that this was what had set her off. Momentarily, as though a segment of film ran through his mind, he saw Katherine in a din, at the center of pounding noise and amplifiers, her fingers running up the neck of the guitar and light shattering everywhere, as though from the electric explosion of the music, her voice high and clear and perfect over it all. He had finished the whiskey and now held an ice cube between his tongue and the bridge of his mouth.

"Gordo, why don't we get out of here?" Katherine said. "Why don't we go somewhere out in the country so we can breathe?"

"You never took to moves very well, honey, and you know it."

"I want out," Katherine said. "Look at that sky, will you? It's like Mars. I want to get where I can breathe. Just look at it. It looks like the end of the world."

"It'll pass," he said.

"Maybe this time it won't," she said. "Nobody really knows for sure. Suppose it doesn't go away?"

"Then that's the end, I guess. But we'll get some rain and it'll go away, you'll see."

After a moment she said, "I mean it, I don't want Alex going to any baseball game with him if he comes."

"He probably won't come."

"Baseball is the last thing Alex needs—he's a zombie about it now."

"He's a kid—"

She broke in: "It is not healthy. It's very unhealthy."

"It's a phase, Katherine."

"Would you say that if he was acting this way about sex or drugs or weird methods of execution? I don't care what you say. It's morbid. Look up 'morbidity' in the dictionary."

"Okay," Brinhart said, "easy. Just calm down."

"You're so anxious to be the good-guy stepfather. That stuff—calling you Brinhart. What is that?"

"Listen to yourself, Katherine. You sound like—" But he didn't know what she sounded like. He got up and went inside and made himself another whiskey. Then he went into Alex's room, coming from the light of the hall, unable to see clearly at first. "Hey?" he said, opening the door wide. There was always the sense, when he entered the boy's room, that he might find him doing something private, might catch him looking at dirty pictures or masturbating.

The boy lay in a ball under the sheet. He insisted on being covered with a sheet, no matter how hot it was. The room smelled of his dirty clothes and his body. "What do you want, Brinhart?"

"You asleep."

"I'm asleep, Brinhart."

"Dad."

"Dad," the boy said.

"Thought we might talk a minute about you and the baseball."

Alex cradled his pillow. "She's already let me have it. Dad."

"Don't be smart." Brinhart sipped the whiskey. "You're a smart fart for an eleven-year-old kid."

"Takes one to know one."

"That's original."

"I saw you tonight," Alex said.

"Saw me what?"

"Looking at that girl. So did Mom."

"What girl?" Brinhart raised the whiskey to his mouth. "Me?"

"Mom said she thought she was pretty. The girl. She said she was parading."

"She did."

"Do you think she's pretty as *she* thinks she is?"

"She, she. Who she."

"The girl."

"Do *you* think she's pretty?"

"I don't know," Alex said, "and I don't care."

"You're above such things."

"Maybe."

Brinhart sat down on the bed. "Your mother says you're in a daze. You've got to show her you're awake more."

"She gets crazy."

"Oh," Brinhart said, "we're all crazy."

"Sure."

"For instance, it's crazy to figure what Pete Rose is hitting before the National League does."

"Maybe."

"Sure it is," Brinhart said, drinking. "Sure it is." In the past ten years there had been ARCO and National Savings and Trust and Texas Bill Ford and John Bennings Chrysler, and now it was Iowa Life Insurance; there had been the old house (his father's) and a converted garage and a stream of apartments—Winston Garden the latest—and little hope of ever really settling in anywhere, of ever buying a house. Brinhart, all that time, barely holding on, trying to keep even, to make things smooth and the same —somehow he had always wanted to keep things the same. They had been at Winston Garden two years now—two years and not an extra penny in the bank and Iowa Life Insurance was getting old and the old man might come or he might not come and here was this boy, and now Brinhart almost laughed, an odd, desperate sort of elation rising in him as he looked at the many pictures on the walls, of men cradling sticks as though some deity resided there, of whole teams, of queer birds and painted sox and Yankees. For a moment he didn't recognize any of it. Jesus Christ, he thought. "We just have to try to get along," he said.

"Yeah." Alex closed his eyes.

"We buddies?"

"Sure."

"You sound really committed to the idea."

"I'm sleepy now, Brinhart."

Outside, Katherine was as he had left her.

"Just talked to Alex," he said. "We got it straightened out."

"I hope your father comes," Katherine said.

"A switch." He sat down, watched the people on the other patio going inside. "What changed your mind?"

She leaned over and touched his knee. "Don't drink any more, honey. Please?"

Brinhart nodded. "Last one."

"I guess I'd like to see him," she said, leaning back. Then she sighed. "I hate summer."

"We'll get through it," he said. "We'll take a couple of trips to the ocean. We'll swim and get healthy and be together. Just us, all right? We'll rent a cottage and stay there a week, and if the old man comes up, he can go with us. Maybe I can get a place right on the beach so we can hear the surf at night, and we'll sit out on a screened-in porch and play cards or something—you and I can take long walks. Wouldn't that be nice?"

"He probably won't come," she said.

"Then it'll be us. We'll have a ball. You won't be nervous."

"Nervous," she said, standing. "Quit harping on that." She opened the screen and went inside.

"Close the screen," he called. As soon as he had spoken he understood what the reaction would be. She came back and stood there in the opening, her face a white, grimacing mask. "Damn you," she said, "you're doing it all on purpose."

"No," he answered. "I'm sorry."

She closed the screen and was gone. He listened for her crying, half hoped to hear it in some cold little corner of his spreading intoxication, but there was no crying. There was no sound at all. He looked up at the other patio, saw that it was dark, empty, the coals sending off a dim red glow. He drank the rest of the whiskey, poured the ice out onto the grass, standing unsteadily at the edge of the patio, feeling quite lonely and now heavily drunk: sodden, sluggish, depressed. He thought of the walking girl and her baby, and his depression deepened. Up the row a light went out. There was never any way to predict when or even if Katherine's trouble would start up again. It had been almost four years since the last time. Self-destructive spite, he thought, giving up the music. Like this: He threw the glass out into the lot. Astonishingly enough, it did not break. It rang like a tinny bell, an omen, not breaking, rolling among the stones. He walked out to fetch it. When he had done so, he stood looking at it: no cracks—it hadn't broken. "I'm just drunk, honey," he said. The night was coming to sound again—the chirruping of crickets, the buzzing of locusts, moths everywhere, June bugs, the hot, thick air stirring in the leaves. He thought he heard, from one of the lighted windows in the trailer court, the faint, wild streaming of a guitar. He went inside, put the glass down in the sink, sat on the sofa in the living room and tried to look at the TV listings. Nothing. Somehow the glass had not cracked or broken. He was drunk and it was quiet again and he knew Katherine was awake in the bedroom. He turned the lights off and went down the hall, opened Alex's door, and looked in. The boy was asleep, sprawled out on the bed among the hundred souvenirs of baseball. Brinhart closed the door quietly and walked into the bedroom, where Katherine sat propped against pillows, smoking a cigarette and watching the portable TV. He did not speak to her. He undressed and got into bed and kissed her cheek, and then he went to sleep.

II

THE BOY AROSE EARLY, as usual, and fixed himself cereal and milk. He did not like eggs, and since his mother always fixed eggs, he had found this way of avoiding the problem: He could tell her he had already eaten. He could leave the signs—the empty bowl with the coin-size pad of milk and sugar at the bottom, the two or three white drops on the rubbery tablecloth—and go out to the field beyond the trailer court without having to worry about being called back for breakfast. He ate the cereal mechanically, without really tasting it, and there was only the sound of his eating. Before he could finish, Brinhart came in from the bedroom, already dressed.

"Sneaking cereal again," Brinhart said.

The boy did not answer.

"Ty Clob's lifetime batting average."

"It's *Cobb*, Brinhart, and you know it."

"Okay—Cobb."

"Three sixty-seven."

"You're amazing." Brinhart took a bowl from the cabinet, poured himself some cereal.

"Why're you up so early?" the boy asked.

"Work." Brinhart sat down across from him, yawned, ran his hands through his hair, sniffed loudly. "Got to make a buck."

"It's *Saturday*," Alex said.

"Don't talk that way. You sound like a—well, just don't say *Saturday* like that, through your nose that way."

They were quiet for a moment.

"Don't know how you eat this crap," Brinhart said.

"Beats eggs."

"Hell it does. Froot Loops. Jesus."

"Why are you working on Saturday?"

"I got work to do."

"Mom won't like it."

"I don't like it either."

"Then," Alex said, chewing, "it seems illogical to go."

"Hey," said Brinhart, "can you maybe try not to sound like—well, like a kid who's figuring out a new number system?"

"What is that supposed to mean?"

"Listen to you," Brinhart said. "For Christ's sake. 'What is that supposed to mean.' What is that? You're eleven years old."

"What do you mean, 'Figuring out a new number system'?"

"Nothing. Forget I mentioned it."

The boy was silent.

"Indubitably," Brinhart said.

"You're all screwed up, Brinhart."

They ate for a while, without looking at each other. Alex gazed out the window at a bird on the lawn. He could see the tennis court across the way; it was empty. The sky was beginning to clear, whitening with sun.

"Remember," Brinhart said, "you're supposed to call me *Dad*. And if the old man comes, he's Granddad."

"Daddy," Alex said.

"It's for your mother, kid. That's all. We have to work together and make her feel good."

"Okay, so lay off me."

"Look, do you want to fight or something? Because if

you do, it might be good to remember that I'm a hell of a lot bigger than you are."

"I don't want to fight," Alex said. "I'll call you *Dad.* Even when she's not around."

"Don't say *she* like that. That's your mother."

"All *right*. Just—lay off."

"Okay," Brinhart said, "I'll lay off."

Alex filled his mouth with cereal, staring down into the bowl. He was almost finished.

"Kid in school," Brinhart said, swallowing, "named Alan. Funny—they all seemed to be named Alan, or Norman. Every one of them. Super smart. Ahead of everybody else, and they wore glasses and got beat up a lot. You get beat up a lot?"

Alex set his spoon down.

"Do you?"

"You wouldn't know if I did."

"I'd know *now*. If you told me."

"Why do you want to know?"

"Let's say, so I can kick the asses of every one of your enemies, or friends, as the case may be."

"Yeah," the boy said.

"Yeah, you get beat up a lot?"

"No."

"You don't."

"No, I don't."

"But you're not popular."

"What *is* this?" Alex said.

"*Are* you popular?"

"How popular are you, Brinhart?"

"Oh, shit," Brinhart said, "I've got millions of friends. Millions of them. I don't have enough time for everybody."

"Sure. Right."

"But we were talking about you, weren't we?"

"This is crazy," Alex said.

"There're kids here. Why don't you play with them?"

"Because I don't like them."

"They bore you."

Alex nodded.

"They don't like baseball."

"They play down at the park sometimes—"

"*You* don't like baseball."

"Not to play."

"You're too smart for it."

The boy said nothing.

"All right. This kid—because your mother is worried about you. Losing sleep." Brinhart took a bite of the cereal, shook his head chewing.

"This kid—this Alan I was telling you about. Wore the glasses. Talked like that—*Saturday*. All that—well, inflection. You know what 'inflection' means, right?"

Alex nodded.

"Figured so," Brinhart said. "So this Alan got beat up a lot, and I used to lay in bed at night and thank God I wasn't Alan, you know? Ever think there may be kids who lay in bed at night and thank God they're not you? Because this Alan was a real bimbo, and what I remember about him is that he was always working on making up a new number system, as if we needed that. Always, this kid was feverishly working on that thing. See, he really loved numbers, ate slept walked drank breathed numbers, like a machine or something. Brilliant with them, he was. But he was a dumb kid, really, because nobody liked him worth a damn, and it was because of the numbers and he knew it, but he didn't change. Man, all he wanted in the world—can you imagine, in this great big beautiful world with all there is to see and do and all those people out there—all he wanted was those damn numbers. I mean, there's something wrong with that."

"So?" Alex said.

"So, do you get beat up a lot."

"I already told you no."

"Because you can tell me, you know." Brinhart leaned toward him, his eyes wide and hard. "And maybe we can do something about it."

"I'll tell you if I do."

"Good."

And now it seemed to the boy that Brinhart might suddenly upset the table or begin to shout. "Look. Be good to her today. Do something besides daydreaming about the fucking baseball."

"Okay," Alex said. Brinhart was looking at him with those hard brown eyes, seemed about to say something else. "I'll be good today, really."

"I've let you have pretty much what you wanted," Brinhart said. "Haven't I?"

Alex nodded.

"Your mother's a little upset, see, so we have to pull together. Like we always do."

"That's right."

"So, are we buddies?" Brinhart asked.

Stay home, Brinhart, Alex wanted to say. Stay home, man. But he only nodded, while Brinhart shook his hand, as though they had made a bargain.

"I'll be home as early as I can."

When Brinhart was gone, Alex put the cereal bowls into the sink; then he put his shoes on, being as quiet as he could, and stepped out front. Before him was the tennis court, another row of apartments, a swing set near the end of the hedgerow on this side, its spoon-shaped worn places in the grass below each swing. The clouds had gone. The sun blazed in every surface of the cars in their neat rows up to the entrance. To his right were the maples and oaks that surrounded the field, and the shade there was black. A mailman, bent under the weight of his brown leather sack

—even the sack gave off a dull reflection of the sun—walked past, whistling; and above his whistling was the distant hum and rattle of traffic. The mailman's shadow followed him like spilled ink on the grass.

Alex walked out to the edge of the curb. Across the way, just entering the tennis court, a heavy woman dropped three yellow balls from a can. She wore white, and her legs were white, thick, corrugated around the thighs. Alex watched her for a while, then ambled down to the swing set, where he sat without swinging, and kicked at the red dirt beneath him. In a little while the tall boy, James, would come out of his apartment wearing the dark-sleeved baseball shirt, carrying the glove oiled to a black sleekness. James was the star of the Point Royal High School team, and there was talk in the local newspapers about a contract with the Orioles. He had never spoken to Alex—though occasionally he would wave carelessly as he passed. Alex knew who he was through the newspaper. Almost every morning, at about the same time, this boy, this major leaguer of the future, would come out of his apartment and walk down past the swing set, through the hedgerow into the trailer court and beyond, to the high school a mile and a half away, where he would hit baseballs over the fence and boys like Alex might sneak over there to watch him and dream. Alex had done so three or four times, and had planned to do so this morning; but he had told Brinhart that he would be good, that he would not trouble his mother today. So he waited a little forlornly, hoping only to see the other boy. From the tennis court came the sound of the tennis ball being slapped into a green plyboard on the fence. Above the oaks two crows circled, like shadows. James did not come. Alex waited a little longer, then wandered through the hedgerow, into the eastern end of the trailer court. Beyond the last mobile home on this end was the field, which descended to a choked creek. On the other side of the creek the ground rose almost straight up, in a cluster of bent trees, and then flattened out toward the highway there, and the shopping mall. At night the neon from the mall was visible through the trees, a confusion of multicolored, broken light and the shapes of branches thick with leaves.

Alex started across the gravel-and-dirt road, on either side of which the mobile homes were ranked like boxes. He was on his way to the field, but then he heard high, rich laughter nearby, a woman's laughter, and someone said, "Where do you think you're going, kid?"

He turned. There was an open van before one of the larger trailers. Seated in the back, legs swinging out over the bumper, fanning herself with a magazine, was a girl, who laughed again—that laugh—and tipped her head slightly to the side, looking at him as if something in his walk or his clothes or his presence amused her. As he was about to go on he saw a wide shape in the doorway of the trailer. In the next instant he realized that it was the bottom of a chair. The girl laughed again, and the chair bounced through the door, revealing a thin, balding man, who groaned, lifting it, bending suddenly to get more of his weight beneath it. "Damn," he grunted, "woman." He stepped down from the portable stoop, and the upper part of his body pitched forward, the chair coming down hard in the burned grass. Then he slowly straightened, pulled a handkerchief from his back pocket, wiped his forehead. "Blanche," he said. Then he shouted: "Blanche!"

The girl stepped away from the van, having pushed off from her perch with both hands. She kicked the red dust, approaching Alex. "My mother doesn't want the chair anymore," she said. "We lugged it with us all the way from New York, and now she decides that she doesn't want it."

Alex said nothing.

"What's your name?"

"You moving out?" he asked.

"Moving *in*. I told you, all the way from New York."

"Moving in," the man said, folding the handkerchief and running it over his bare arms. He wore a sleeveless undershirt, soiled and darkened with dust and his sweat; it hung loosely on him. "We're moving in, if you can believe it."

"Mom got one look at the chair in that tiny living room, and out it goes."

"Yeah," said the man. "It's easy to *say* out it goes—when you've neither moved it in, nor are you going to have to move it out."

"What's your name?" the girl said, smiling. Her skin was very white and her eyes were large. Alex told her his name.

"Alex what?"

"Brinhart."

"Burned heart," said the man.

"What?"

"That's what it sounds like," the girl said. "Daddy likes to do that—say things how they sound. Don't you, Daddy?"

"Yeah, sure." The man seemed suddenly out of breath. "My God, it's hot."

"Say something that sounds like something, Daddy. Show him."

"Anchors away, bankers . . ." The man hesitated. "Ah, I can't think, honey."

" 'Burned heart' isn't very good."

"No, it's not."

"Mommy can do better than that, I'll bet, can't you, Mommy?"

And now Alex saw another figure in the door—a woman so big that her cheeks were like white balls under her eyes. She stepped out and down with some difficulty, and Alex looked at her wide, dimpled arms. The arms tapered to small hands, from which the fingers seemed blown as from the ends of a balloon; they seemed not to have nerve endings or musculature.

"It ain't getting any cooler, Stan," she said. Then she laughed. It was precisely the same laugh Alex had heard from the girl. "Well," the woman said, "we have a neighbor here." She turned her great body toward Alex.

"Hello," he said.

"His name is Alex," said the girl.

"Hello, Alex. You and Amy want something cold to drink?"

"Yes'm," Alex said.

"The only problem is, I don't have any ice yet."

"Then you don't have anything cold to drink," said Stan.

"I have tap water." The woman's voice seemed to tumble up out of that enormous padded chest.

"Who wants tap water?" Amy said.

The woman looked at Alex. "No, thank you," he said, and began to edge away from them. The girl stepped to his side.

"You-all don't get too far away now," Blanche said.

"Ever see anybody as fat as my mother?" Amy whispered.

They walked past the end trailer, which was closed, and white-curtained and quiet, and into the field; the field was all knife grass, cattails, ragweed, and wild flower. It was bordered on one side by the tag end of the hedgerow, and on the other by tall maple and oak. There was a path, a cut line through to the beginning of the slope downward; this was worn thin in a wide patch, like hair at the crown of an enormous, balding scalp. Here the creek and the tattered weed-choked bushes were visible, the bent trees growing out of the opposite bank; now and again the glint of passing automobiles came through the dusty green, from the highway beyond. There were clouds, small and insubstantial as puffs of smoke, above the trees. Alex sat down on the crest of the slope, and the girl walked a few paces down, stopped, and turned, folding her arms.

"You don't talk much."

Alex shrugged.

"Why don't we go down to the creek and put our feet in the water?" she asked.

"The water's dirty." His own voice sounded unfamiliar to him. He was suddenly oppressed in a way he could not understand, and when she, too, sat down, her back to him so that he could see only the cut-short black hair above the collar of her blouse, he almost got up and walked away. But now she looked at him. "Why do you wear long pants on a day like this?"

"I don't like shorts."

"Legs skinny?"

"Not much."

"Too white, maybe."

He was silent.

"Can't you talk? Where do you live?"

"Apartments up yonder," he said.

"We lived in an apartment." She was now staring off to where the creek ducked under a cement culvert and the wild growth at its banks closed tight, was impenetrable, full of bees and brambles and poison ivy. Her face in profile was all upturned nose. The eyebrows were dark and low, the mouth pouting and white.

"Hate damn weeds," she said. "All they do is choke everything off. Don't you think that's so?"

"Never thought about it," he said.

She sighed. "Everybody wants to go to the country. So they can pick weeds. We lived in an apartment right in the middle of the biggest city in the whole wide world. Ever been to New York?"

"No."

"You should see it."

"Seen pictures," Alex said.

She pulled at the grass. "Pictures don't do it."

"Watched the Yankees on television," he said. "They showed pictures of the whole city from a helicopter."

"Who're the Yankees?" she asked.

"Baseball." The word was out of him before his spreading sense of astonishment at her ignorance reached his tongue. "Baseball," he said again.

"Oh."

"You don't know about the Yankees."

"Yes, I do."

"Okay, who's Thurman Munson?"

"I don't know—a catcher."

He was certain that she had guessed. He thought for a moment. "Okay, what's he do?"

"He catches."

"What else?"

"Oh, then he hits it or throws it or something."

"You don't know."

She leaned back on her arms, letting her head back, as if to bathe in the sun. "Who *wants* to know."

"You lived in New York and you don't know."

"I don't live there anymore."

He pulled a spine of grass, put the tip of it into his mouth. The sun was hot on the dark cloth of his jeans, and on his face and arms.

"But I guess it's nice to come down to the country and live in the peace and quiet." She sighed, staring off at the creek again. "I guess it's all right to be out of the rat race."

The boy thought there must be more, so he waited.

"Know what a rat race is?"

He thought he knew, but when he searched for the words, nothing came.

"I don't know how to describe it either," she said.

"I could if I wanted to."

"Don't be argumentative. That's what Daddy says. 'Don't be argumentative.'" Her voice changed as she tried to imitate her father's voice. Then she sighed again. "I guess I'll be fat when I get older, like my mother."

"How old are you?" he asked.

"Old enough to do the deed."

"How old?"

"You know what the deed is?" Now she turned, hugging one knee—the other leg straight out—rocking slightly. "Well?" she smiled.

"I don't have to know," he said.

"How old are you?"

"Eleven."

"And you don't know about the deed? Not even from your little friends at school?"

"I'm as big as you are," Alex said. He held onto his knees now as if he held onto summer itself, that big space of time that freed him from having to be with others or near others, and in which the grandfather he did not quite remember might come and take him to a baseball game.

"I'm thirteen," she said simply, "so I'm older." She faced him now, letting her legs out, gazing at them as if they were prizes she had won. "I've already done the deed."

He said nothing. He chewed the blade of grass, which made a bitter froth of his own spit.

"I did it in a Laundromat with a boy named Harmon. Did you ever hear of a name like that? Harmon."

Alex merely looked at her.

"What's the matter?"

"Nothing."

"You got sweat on your forehead. Your head's shining."

He ran the back of his hand across the wet place.

"I got such pretty legs," she said. "And breasts."

He looked at her chest, but her blouse was bunched there. As if to accommodate him, she set her hands back, leaning on them again, thrusting her upper body toward him. "See?" He saw the suggestion of swelling on either side. "I have to shave under my arms," she said.

"So?"

"You want a feel?" She edged closer, lying out on her stomach, her elbows down in the grass. "Want a little?"

"Get out," he said.

"You don't even know what I'm talking about."

"Yes, I do."

"Okay then—what?"

"I know," he said, "but I don't have to say."

She gave a sigh, made a smacking sound with her lips. "I'm talking about S-E-X." She spelled the word slowly, twirling a lock of her hair between index finger and thumb.

"I know," he said. Then, almost under his breath: "Fuck."

"The deed!" She laughed, rolling over on her back, her head resting on her hands, just below him now, so that if he wanted to, he could have reached out and touched her. "Anyway, it's not all it's cracked up to be," she said. "We did it on somebody's laundry. It was warm from the dryer."

For a moment they were quiet. Somewhere there was the whining of an engine, and a slight breeze stirred the tops of the trees.

"Let's go down to the creek," she said.

He made no answer.

"Or let's do *something*."

Now air seemed to lift out of the grass, a hot wind that carried the odor of the stagnant creek, then was still. A truck horn sounded—insistent, troubled, and there was the hiss and shudder of air brakes. The boy thought of pipes, smoke, tires big as cars.

"Or you could take me as a guest to the swimming pool."

"I don't go to the swimming pool," he said.

"Well—what then?"

He wanted to tell her to go away; yet he also wanted to touch her. So he kept silent, staring down into the shadowed creases in his lap.

"I'm going," she said, rising. He watched her walk down the slope. She turned, momentarily, lifted one hand as if to motion for him to follow, but then apparently decided against it. The hand made a little waving movement, dismissing him, and she went down, through the thick growth, to the water's edge. The water, he knew, was only a brown trickle over mossy stones, and he thought she would turn around and come back. But she went on, after pausing to examine something there, went over the creek and up the steep bank on the other side, toward the highway.

In a moment he got up and walked into the shade, lay down and closed his eyes, planning what he might do today: He might sneak over to the high school and watch them practice. He imagined the future pro, James, who was so tall and fast and who hit the ball a mile and could throw a real curve ball. And then, idly, he pictured the major leaguers as he saw them on television, the real players, their tan or black arms rippling in the sun, their names floating on the air in the lazy tones of the sportscasters during the stillnesses between pitches, while somebody danced away from the bag at first, taunting the pitcher, threatening a steal, or while the umpire casually brushed the fine red dirt away from the plate. It was that voice he loved, that sense of the game's sweet calm, though he could not have expressed this. Often he lay awake at night whispering in that voice, a game he imagined, hearing in the hum of the air conditioner the sound of thousands of voices at rest, waiting for something to happen. . . .

He had nearly fallen asleep. He sat up, realizing that he had drifted, and searched for the girl in the field, his eyes burning in the light. She was gone. She would not come back here. He decided to go over to the high school, just for a little while.

III ❦

AGAIN SHE COULD NOT SLEEP. She lay listening to Brinhart's snoring and was resentful of his sleep and his noise. Brinhart never had any trouble sleeping: he slept through thunder, sirens, screams of nightmares, her tossing and turning. When she prodded him with her foot or shook him, begging him to turn over on his side, to stop his fluting and his sighing and his sudden spasms of panting, he groaned, was quiet for a moment—a little space during which she only waited for him to begin again. He always did so: it was always the same—she got out of bed after nights like this with a sense of having hauled something quite heavy across the distance between dusk and dawn.

The air now was still, freighted with the humid odor of his body and her body. She tried to breathe deeply, slowly, imagining what went into her lungs. The air conditioner had broken down again, and though it had been slightly cooler during the day there had been no lifting of the haze. If she closed her eyes, she felt immediately strangled, so she kept them open, looking at the dark. Brinhart snored, moaned, sighed. The curtain at the window was still, nothing moved anywhere. When she was like this, she lost time: there was only the idea of the dragging sameness of the rest of her life, all one, as if held before her in a photograph: all like this, awake, nerves buzzing with fear, something dead in her. Brinhart snoring at her side, a lump breathing and sighing, a sobbing, open-mouthed face, dead. The boy in his room, also dead.

In the hallway, where she seemed to come down, aware of her feet on the floor, she turned the light on, looked at a dark spot on the wood along the baseboard. She held on to the wall. The angles of ceiling and doorjamb and wall went awry. For a long time she stood there, holding on, hearing Brinhart's snoring in the room behind her. But then he stopped snoring, and she was afraid he had awakened— she was afraid he would see her shadow in the doorway. She went down the hall, through the living room, into the kitchen. It was quiet. Then there was a night wind, sweeping down through the trees, a long whisper, and she gazed out at the moon, a white shape through a moving haze, a smoke; it cast no shadows. The tennis court was there in ghostly light; the swing set, the parked cars, the apartments opposite. She could make out the cloudlike configuration of treetops shaking, the wind coming heavier, gusting; a single piece of paper—newspaper, she saw—was lifted past the window, dropped as the wind dropped, thrown on the grass, was lifted again.

She turned another light on—the fluorescent lamp over the oven, which sputtered and hissed like a live thing. It was worse this time; it had never been this bad.

It always passes

And if it doesn't then I guess that's it I won't spend the rest of my life

There was a game, a secret game she played when it was bad. It involved two people: Katherine, and the Other. The Other was the frightened one, the one afraid to close her eyes, who had no love or feeling or hope. She played the game consciously, reasonably, watching the Other. And she could only play it when she admitted that the Other was crazy, was not Katherine, but only something Katherine might become if Katherine did not play the game and charm the Other out of existence, out of the world. There were any number of ways to play the game, and sometimes she was not completely aware that it had begun, that she had started playing, but before it was over, she was always perfectly conscious of it. Sometimes she stood in front of a mirror and pleaded with the face there, watching the face plead; sometimes she paced in a circle or walked out in the night, breathing into her fists; once or twice she had watched the Other flirt with suicide, with death, and she knew the Other was as afraid to die as Katherine was—later she always knew the game was something Katherine played, or that fear played with Katherine, and that there was no Other—only fear. Yet now something told her that this was not really it, not the fear that would really begin soon if she didn't head it off, climb out, stop it.

"Stop it," she said, standing in the middle of the kitchen and clenching her fists. She went to the sink, stood there gazing down into the drain hole. She thought it might begin to look like an eye but it was merely itself: aluminum, functional, perfect. Concentrating on it, or trying to, she was calming down, breathing slowly and deeply, not thinking, and then she heard a sound in the hallway. She turned the tap on loud, reached for a glass in the cabinet above her. And here was Brinhart, eyes puffy with sleep, hair in a wild brown tangle. He wore his terry-cloth robe, his hands in the deep pockets; the drawstring lay over his wrists.

"Couldn't sleep," he said, without looking at her. He opened the refrigerator, stood gazing into it. "I kept dreaming the old man was here, and I had to keep pretending that selling insurance had been my goal in life." She waited, standing by the sink with the glass. Then she filled it with water she did not want, turned the tap off. It was quiet. He stood there looking into the refrigerator. "Funny," he said. "My Aunt Beth was with him. You remember the story about Aunt Beth?"

"No," Katherine said.

"You remember—Aunt Beth. Remember?" He closed the refrigerator, moved to the table, ran his hand over the surface, still not letting his eyes settle on her. "Just couldn't sleep," he said.

"You were snoring," Katherine said. "*I* couldn't sleep."

He looked at her, scratched the side of his head above the ear with one finger. There was delicacy in the motion, as though the hair were combed and he did not want to disturb it.

"You were loud," she said, and took a sip of the water.

"Maybe we'll have a midnight snack together."

"I'm not hungry."

"I am—but then I don't want anything I see."

"I don't even want this water." She poured it into the sink.

"Still . . . upset?" His voice was gentle.

"I just couldn't sleep." The drain rattled and dripped. Water went down pipes everywhere, steel pipes or flesh pipes.

"It'll pass, honey."

"I'm all right," she said, "I just couldn't sleep."

"It always passes."

"Yes."

He turned, looked at the clock, leaned toward it. She watched him, her arms folded across her chest. "One thirty," he said. Then he pulled a chair out from the table, sat down—one arm on the chair back, the other on the table—leaning against the wall. When he looked at her his lips began to spread in what she thought would be a smile, but then he seemed to study her. "Let's talk. Want to?"

"No."

"Talk, Katherine. Come on. Let's plan what we'll do if the old man comes up."

"He won't come—it's a waste to plan anything until we know for sure whether he'll come."

"All right. Tell me what you did today and I'll tell you what I did today."

"Please, Gordon—stop it."

"Honey, why won't you let me help you get sleepy?"

She said nothing. She looked at the window. The wind was rising again.

"Was the boy—did Alex—apart from the high school—"

"I told you at dinner. He has a new friend. He went over to the high school today, and I made him stay in his room for it. He stayed in his room and drugged himself on baseball."

"This new friend—a girl. That's something, isn't it?"

"Oh, Gordon, please stop. Please quit forcing it."

"I think that's something. I'm just saying so. Katherine this is me, remember? Gordo. We've been through all this before—neither of us can sleep, so let's talk."

"But you keep putting it that way—'Let's talk.' That's like putting a microphone in someone's face and saying 'Go ahead, say something funny.'"

"I'll lead," he said. "Let me take the lead."

"Oh, Christ."

"The girl is older than he is, isn't she."

Katherine sighed. "I told you. Her mother says she's thirteen. Gordon, I need to be able to do this by myself—"

"Why? You don't live alone, honey. Tell me more. You said she was very heavy and her name was Blanche. How did she come to see Alex at the high school? You never told me that."

"She went over there to register her daughter."

"The new friend."

"Yes."

"And she saw Alex there."

"Yes, Gordon. She thought she'd stop and say hello to him and he saw her and ran away and then she saw him later playing on the patio out back—throwing that damn tennis ball against the wall and catching it—and she came over to say hello to me, and it all came out. She had her daughter with her. They were going to pick flowers or something."

"Hard to imagine a fat woman picking flowers," Brinhart said. Then he was quiet; he was thinking, she could see that he was searching for a way to carry the conversation. "Alex likes the girl, huh?" he said.

"Alex is a zombie, Alex is buried in batting averages. The girl likes *him*—or so her mother said. Blanche."

"Now I can't imagine going through life with a name like Blanche."

"A name wouldn't help her much."

"She's that heavy, huh?" He laughed, wiped his nose with the back of his index finger. "You know it just means 'white'? Imagine that. White Smith, White Jones, White *White*."

"She was friendly," Katherine said.

"Think you'll be friends?"

"Maybe we'll be lovers, Gordon."

"I just asked."

"She talks too loud. She makes me nervous."

"She was probably nervous—she's new and everything."

"She'd been living in New York."

"Does that preclude nervousness?"

"I don't know."

"Probably predicts it."

Katherine was silent.

"Come on, we're going good."

"Oh, for Christ's sake—you sound like a doctor." She started out of the room, but he reached out and took her arm.

"Honey," he said. "Tell me—talk it out. It always helps."

"Gordon, if you'd just quit looking at me and treating me like you expect me to *crack up* any minute I'd be all right."

"I never looked at you that way—never. I worry—"

"Well stop worrying. Let me alone, *please.*"

They did not speak for a moment. He let go of her arm. The refrigerator made a loud clicking noise, then began to hum. Katherine realized now that she did not want to be alone: the apartment at night, while she walked it awake, was like the home of a stranger whose possessions offered her only their separateness.

"Is it—like the other times?" he asked.

"It's never like before." She walked to the sink, turned to face him. The light was on her shoulders and she crossed her arms, lay her hands on the sharp bones as though the light were a cold splashing of water. "Every time it's different—or it feels different. And it's like it never went away and will never go away, and I'll feel like this for the rest of my life—and then you watch me and wait for me. You're always waiting for me to start it all over again."

"No," he said. "No."

She leaned on the sink, was quiet.

"At twilight sometimes," he said, "sometimes I get this feeling—like a jump, sort of, a scare. Just around twilight —the only time it ever happens—this unexplained . . . this fear. It's natural to feel like it'll always be that way."

"I don't want to talk about it anymore," she said.

"But everybody—everybody has those feelings—"

"I said, I don't want to anymore—let's go to bed, please."

"Now don't you—do you feel better?" The gentleness in his voice. She wanted him angry, and why wouldn't he get angry and shout at her and call her an idiot?

"I'm fine," she said.

"Sure, honey. It passes. The old man will come up, and we'll have a vacation at the beach. You won't have any trouble sleeping there—and I won't. We'll have a nice summer."

"Fine."

"You're better—right?"

"Yes," she said. She looked at the pattern of flowers in the tiled floor, saw a face; the flowers made a face. If she could just get to morning. If she could just go to sleep.

"Good," he was saying. "That's good."

Then they were quiet again. There wasn't anything else to talk about. The sounds of the night began to come, and Katherine realized that the refrigerator had clicked off. There was the faintest suspiration at the window: a fluttering of wings or a motion of the air.

"A nice trip to the beach," Brinhart said. "We'll do that, honey. This time we'll really do it."

She shrugged. The refrigerator clicked on again, like an irritating third person in the room. She saw herself lying awake, and Brinhart asleep at her side.

"I know I've said that before," he said. "But I mean it. I'm not going to sit around this summer. We'll do it. We'll do all sorts of things together—picnics, maybe some hiking. We'll go up to Skyline Drive and have a picnic and shop in the roadside stores. Remember the one that sells tapestries? We'll go there. We'll take the old man with us."

"You don't have to do all that just for me," she said.

"No. For me too. Me and the boy and you. We'll have some fun, and we won't be sitting around in the fall wondering what the hell happened to the summer—"

"You'll be busy, Gordon."

"That's right. We'll keep busy."

"No, your job."

"Yeah, that damn job—I'm getting to hate the job. But it won't ruin this summer. We'll have weekends."

She said nothing.

"That damn job."

"It's not what you want to do for the rest of your life."

"That's right," he said.

"I didn't mean anything by that."

"Okay—okay. The trouble is, I can't think of doing anything for the rest of my life. I mean, that's like a death sentence."

"You're not going to quit—"

"Don't worry. But we'll have a nice summer. All right?"

"All right."

He stretched, yawned, "I love you."

She may have repeated the phrase to him: she honestly did not know for sure whether she had or not. She was so tired, so tired. Indeed, she could not be certain that he had spoken the words in the first place. He got out of the chair slowly, as if compensating for injuries in his legs and back. Then he stretched again: an expansive, sleepy gesture, smiling at her as though they shared a joke.

"I love you—my sweet guitar."

"I wish you wouldn't call me that, Gordon."

"Okay," he said. "Darling. It's just a term of endearment. Darling."

Again she thought about how in a few moments he would leave her alone on the shore of wakefulness, and though she kept him from seeing, from knowing, everything came back: she thought he might see how she was falling apart, right in front of him, falling all into little pieces on the floor; but she kept it from him, put her arms around his middle, closed her eyes in the terry cloth at his shoulder.

"That's better," he said. "You feel better."

She told him she did.

"Want to make love?" His hands were on her back; she breathed the sleep-odor of his body under the cloth. "Want to?" his mouth whispered at her ear, a little gust of breath. "Sweet?"

"Gordo," she said, "don't be silly."

"Why not?" He stepped back.

"I'm so sleepy."

"I'll kiss you to sleep afterward. We'll make beautiful love."

"It's so late—"

"Come on," he said. "No time to waste. We'll lie in each other's arms and talk until we sleep—a nice, warm, sleepy lovemaking." He put the light out, was a moving shape toward her in the darkness. In the hallway there was more light, and he shut that off too. She let him lead her in to the bed, only his hand on her wrist. "Darling," she said, but he misunderstood her. And when, moments later, he trailed his lips down her belly, whispering words that were garbled by her skin, she lay her head back, eyes open, the blackness drawn tight over the room and her face, and was barely able to keep her throat closed, to hold back what clamored there, as if trapped and struggling to rise out of her mouth—a whimper or a cry, a scream.

IV 🕊

IT ALL WENT BACK to the music, and the music went back too; it was a music that came out of the gospel and the country, from Ma Rainey and Bessie Smith and ragtime and revival and jazz, from the long history of hunger— and it was the only music that screamed, that made the noise everything made—jets and combustion engines and the war that never ended and was faraway. When Brinhart met

Katherine, she was singing Chuck Berry and the Beatles and the Rolling Stones, she was playing a guitar that made his blood leap, and he watched her hands, those wonderful hands. Katherine was a talent that burned everything up, and that music was made for her and one knew it immediately, watching her play. She was not pretty; she was large-boned and rather bulky of hip, and her breasts were small; there was something hard about her eyes. Brinhart's adolescent fantasies had been crowded with buxom beauties, mindless and sex-starved, who possessed all the feminine graces a perfumed and lace-draped southern female was supposed to have then. He would not have believed Katherine was the woman he wanted—not until he saw her and did want her. This was in 1969, when he was twenty-three, and he fell in love almost instantly. Katherine was brilliant, a fantastic musician, a wonderful singer. A determined and willful professional. She'd had Alex, unoriginally enough—as she put it—by a drummer who used to play in the band. The drummer had disappeared in the vast spaces of America as soon as the baby was a fact, and Katherine had let him go, too, without as much as a sigh of regret. For he was what he was, she told Brinhart. A drummer, nothing more. Someone who could beat time anywhere, with anyone, a nameless keeper of rhythms—and would probably drum until he died, playing his life out in one club after another, all those dread honky-tonks out on the plains. Katherine had let him go, and still sang with the band, still played her marvelous guitar too loud for her own good—there was a sense in Brinhart, then, that she was destined for a more glamorous fate than she had predicted for the talentless drummer: later he was to make a remark about the drummer and his lack of talent, and she would correct him: no, the drummer was extraordinarily talented.

Brinhart, just out of the army, with pockets full of separation pay and with nowhere he particularly had to go, followed Katherine and the band through most of a summer, up and down the New England coast—one club after another.

It was an odd courtship. Katherine had big dreams, and a child—in Brockton, with her parents—the band was falling apart, secretly breaking to pieces under the surface; and Brinhart, ignorant of everything but the child, had become a sort of traveling companion, a follower, so to speak, though he liked to describe himself as an interested observer. He told people that he might like to get into the management end of popular music, but secretly entertained the idea that he was a poet. There were times, during that summer, when he thought his travels a sort of preliminary groundwork for the poems he would one day write. He thought that to be a poet was to be sensitive, to see things others did not see, and to be hurt easily by what one saw. He had seen death early—had looked upon his mother's coffin at twenty—and he thought about death a lot. This seemed to qualify him, somehow: writing the poems could come later or it could come not at all, but one could demonstrably be a poet. Katherine, when he spoke to her about these things—and he did so in an offhand way, pretending a casualness, for fear that she would laugh at him—took him as seriously as he secretly took himself. He thought he might wait ten years, might travel that long in the frenetic, throbbing, and sleepless ambience of rock 'n' roll on tour before he began to write the poems he felt obligated, if not destined, to write.

But this was the last summer for Katherine and the band. In August she reached the end of what had been a seven-year effort: the band broke up with the suddenness and the finality of death. It went apart, literally, in a welter of hot words thrown up from antagonisms long held and long suppressed, in a rage of shattered equipment and curses, hatreds whose intensity both shocked and fascinated Brinhart. It was all the result of a near decade on the road, with little real success, and of the sort of trouble that develops between people who must live as a family but who are not family. It was entirely natural and inevitable, Katherine said, though it hurt. Oh, she said to Brinhart, how it hurt. All that work, all that hard, toiling, tedious time getting up just one song, not to mention two hundred and fifty.

She went with Brinhart. The two of them stopped for a few days in Brockton—a shoemaker's town, an old, depressing place—where they picked up Katherine's child and where Brinhart met for the first time the two strange people who were her parents—and then headed south, with no settled idea of where they would go or what they would do. They wanted to get out of New England—or Katherine did, and Brinhart would take her wherever she wanted to be. He suggested Florida at one point, but only half seriously. They rode in Brinhart's Chevy—Katherine having sold the van and kept the largest share of the money, since she had been the band's leader, the one who handled the books and filled out the tax forms every year. The Chevy was new but unair-conditioned, and while the baby slept on blankets in the backseat, his little dark forehead gleaming and hair-matted from the sweltering air, Katherine planned aloud her next move, or tried to. Brinhart listened: he was already beginning to decide about Virginia, home. These were the fierce last days of August, and he didn't know whether it was the heat, or the rigors of such a journey without a decided destination, but Katherine began to lose her resolution, began to talk about quitting, giving it all up. She claimed—though he found this difficult to believe—that she had been considering the idea for some time. At any rate he did not discourage her. He was tired and hot, and the anger, the unpleasantness of the breakup (one member of the band, the bass player, a willowy, acne-scarred and gap-toothed malcontent named Bates, had hurled the rhythm player's guitar through a motel window) had done the work of convincing him that there should be an end to his travels, his future as a poet notwithstanding. There was, too, the fact that his money was almost gone. He had come to fear retribution (the motel window) and ruin (the last dollar); he had never seen human beings in such pathological and destructive relation to one another firsthand; he wanted to go home. God, it came to him on that hot highway, how I want to go home.

"Marry me," he said to Katherine.

She did not answer him directly. She said, "You know, when you first started showing up everywhere we played, I thought you might be a sickie."

"Marry me," he said. "You can play guitar for me— until we're old and gray."

"Will you want me," she sang, "when I'm mostly old. . . ." She stared out the window at the blazing noon, grass fields burning white. "Where will we live?" Before he could answer she said, "Where are we going?"

"Home," he said.

"Virginia?" She was incredulous. She said again, as though answering herself: "Virginia."

"I'm crazy in love with you," he told her.

"I thought you were such a—a groupie," she said, still remembering.

"I guess I was—I guess I am."

"You're only twenty-three."

"Yeah?"

"You're four years younger than I am."

"So?"

"You've been such fun, Gordo. Really. But four years.

Marriage. I've been sitting here thinking about getting married, but I wasn't thinking of *you.*"

"Who were you thinking of?"

"Somebody—anybody. A lawyer who can give me a big house and a yard. A suburb."

"You know any lawyers?"

She sighed. The windshield was a dazzle of light, and there wasn't enough air—just a gusty, furnacelike stream in the open windows, as if their own breathing went out of them and filled the car. Brinhart's shirt stuck to his back, and when he looked at Katherine's folded knees he saw beads of water on the stretched skin there. "Hot," he ventured.

"Hot," she said.

"Marry me," he said.

"Oh, Christ, Gordo." She seemed about to cry, and though he had wondered why she hadn't cried during the abyssal fever of the breakup, he did not want her to do so now. "Lay off it for a little while, please?" she said.

The baby awakened, cried once, settled back into a wet half-sleep, moaning from time to time. Brinhart pressed the pedal, the car whining up past seventy miles an hour. Perhaps an hour went by before Katherine spoke again. "If I marry you," she said, her voice sudden, out of what he had thought was her sleep, "I'll never play the guitar again."

"Sure, you will," he said.

"No. I mean, I'll give it up for good. On purpose."

"You can play for me and the baby on cool summer nights. You can sing us to sleep when we have nightmares."

"No, I mean it."

"Don't be an ass," he said.

"Like that. Really. Forever."

"Right," he said. He waited for her to go on, to say she would or would not marry him. But she had closed her

eyes again, and again they rode in silence for a long time.
Presently she said, "I don't know what I want to do."

"Decide."

"Is that an ultimatum?"

"It's a plea."

"I hate myself," she said abruptly. "You know what
you'd be getting? I absolutely despise myself."

"Poor baby."

"Fuck you."

He looked out at the road. They were nearing Washington. "We'll be in Virginia soon," he said. And then he
realized that she was crying, soundlessly, eyes closed, head
back against the seat. He reached over and took her hand
and she let him: her hand was so passively in his own that
he wondered for an instant if she were not crying in her
sleep. "It's all right," he said. "We're almost home."

Home was a small brick house on Mission Street in Point
Royal; the house was just north of the most famous land-
mark of the town: the Reed House, where General Lee
had stayed two nights as a young federal soldier in 1857.
The Reed place was an out-building now—with an appro-
priately gray marker (the Confederacy, Brinhart's father
was fond of saying, wore gray because they were neither
here nor there)—connected by history to the national her-
itage but by property rights to St. Paul's Episcopal Church.
Brinhart's father, who was fiercely Catholic, made jokes
about the Episcopalians, jokes which, in 1969, were no
longer topical and in any case could not entertain Katherine. It was odd, but the old man seemed anxious in the
very first minutes to give her a moderate southerner's view
of the town and its history, as though to assure her that he
was not of the South that burned crosses and wore bed-
sheets. In his effort to do so, he embarrassed Brinhart.
Then the old man let it be known that he was against

ecumenism, and he spoke to Katherine about how everything was falling apart, the world was giving up the things that really mattered, there was no discipline anymore. "Why," he said, "look at the music they play on the radio these days." He looked at Brinhart and then he looked down at his feet.

"It's terrible," Katherine said, "isn't it."

"I didn't mean to cast aspersions—"

"Cast them—I never made it on the radio. Cast them all you want. We'll cast them together."

"That's a very handsome baby," the old man said. They were all standing out in the yard, under the shade of the maples there—they had not even unpacked the car yet. "Is the father—"

"No," Katherine said, "the father is not."

There was a pause. "Well," Brinhart said, "we better get unpacked."

"Are you here for a—will you be staying with us for a while?" the old man asked Katherine.

"I don't know," she said, looking at him steadily, so that again he looked down at his feet.

"She'll stay as long as I do," Brinhart said. "I hope— and I'm planning on staying for a long, long time." He turned, stretched out his arms. "Ah, it is good to be back."

"You took a whole summer getting here," the old man said, but he laughed, reaching into the car for Katherine's suitcase. In the careful way he bent over he looked weak, and Brinhart hurried to help him.

"It's very peaceful here," Katherine said.

In the following days, Brinhart was pleasantly surprised by the sense of order he derived from being in his father's house. This was clearly what Katherine needed. He believed she had responded to the change as he had, interpreting her many hours of sleep and her attention to the flower garden in back as signs of pacification—of a quelling of those frenetic elements in her personality that had begun by fascinating him but had, in the few months he had known her, fairly exhausted him too. The days passed in a green, end-of-summer peace, warm but not uncomfortably so now, and there were excursions to the lake or to the park, long walks, hours of wandering the lawn while the baby lay sleeping on a blanket in the shade—Brinhart felt ever more deeply in love with this extraordinary woman he had managed to bring back with him. He decided that his father's growing reticence was merely the settling in of habit: he had never been a talkative man around those he lived with day to day.

But there were deeper problems.

Brinhart's mother was three years dead, and his father was still recovering from the shock. She had died suddenly, cruelly, and the old man had witnessed everything. The two of them had gone shopping together—a Saturday-afternoon ritual for more than twenty years, Brinhart's father being a man of steady and orderly habits, from the daily ration of one shot-glass of bourbon to the seven-thirty mass on Sunday morning, or this Saturday-afternoon journey with his wife—and Brinhart's mother had crossed the street to mail a letter. A truck, coming too fast around the corner—the brakes had failed—righted itself too quickly and pitched over on her. It crushed her legs, and in five very bad minutes she was dead. This had happened while Brinhart was thousands of miles away (in Tokyo on temporary duty, sleeping with a Japanese girl named Sako, who, every night, lay down as though she were about to perform one of her privy acts—cleaning or washing or voiding—and opened her legs for him, saying "Come, you fuck now"); and as Brinhart had grieved for his mother from that distance, had flown home, to stand over a white coffin in a flower-banked room and try to remember the woman who had been his mother, unable to separate her out from death, to see her as she had been when he had thought she would always be there—so his father had had to grieve in the horror of what he had witnessed, still witnessed, even now, in his sleep.

In the evenings the old man seemed to stalk the house, growing more and more restless, and he took to leaving the room whenever Katherine brought the child in. There were tense meals, with no sound but the forks and knives against the plates and the baby's occasional murmur or cry.

"I can't get used to it," he said one night—and Brinhart thought he would finally speak about the accident. But he looked at Brinhart, eyes narrowing, and went on: "To the way you have thrown out everything your mother and I have tried to teach you." This was near the end of a meal, and Katherine had taken the baby upstairs. Brinhart waited for his father to go on, but the old man pushed his chair back and left the table, sat in the living room with a newspaper open on his lap. Brinhart followed him in there, sat down across from him.

"I haven't thrown anything away, Dad," he said.

"When was the last time you went to confession?"

Brinhart said nothing.

"You remember what happened to your Aunt Beth. I wrote you about what—"

"Dad, I'm not Aunt Beth."

His father leaned toward him, the newspaper crackling in his lap, "No, but *she* is—that girl is. She's Aunt Beth to a T."

"Jesus," Brinhart said, "you can't mean that."

"You going to marry her?"

"I've asked her to. I told you that."

"How long does it take her to decide?"

"Dad—"

"You want another man's baby? How long does it take her to make up her mind—"

And then Katherine was there. "It takes me as long as it takes me," she said. "If you want me to leave, I'll leave."

The old man got out of his chair. "Tell her I'm not after her to leave," he said, and went upstairs.

Katherine slept with the baby in Brinhart's old room, and he slept on the sofa in the living room. That night, he lay in the dark, hands locked under his head. The house made its familiar sounds, and the familiar odors of the night—the southern summer nights he had partly forgotten—which now called back feasts of honeysuckle in innumerable dusks, the murmur of voices on porches and in yellow windows, and the incessant singing of insects and wind-blown leaves, made him feel quite suddenly like a boy again. He remembered his Aunt Beth, and then he remembered his mother so clearly that he thought she might walk into the room. Perhaps he had drifted toward sleep, because then he thought she *had* come in, had stood over him and whispered, "Your father is going to take you to see your Aunt Beth in the morning. Be polite." It was so real, this half-dream, that he sat up and looked at the falling shadows of the doorway. This was the first really clear image of her since her death, and as he lay back down, he thought about how the house was her house, and she was no longer in it. The forced absence of his time in the army had somehow mixed with and diluted the absence created by her death—it had been hard to remember that she was not going on as always, back in Virginia (perhaps part of his long delay about coming home had been just this, just the knowledge that sooner or later he would lie here in the dark and really feel that she was dead); now, in the breezy dark, surrounded by the signs of her having lived here—the bric-a-brac-crowded shelves and the paintings, the furniture she had cared for, doilies she had made and surfaces she had polished—he began to cry a little. He lay crying quietly for a long time, unable to imagine his own death but feeling it in front of him all the same, a cancellation of everything, all effort and desire and ambition, and he thought of Katherine, asleep upstairs, a possible wife.

Once, during the odd period of waiting for Katherine to decide (it was perhaps a week after Brinhart's long night awake with the memory of his mother), she touched the baby's chin and said, "Don't we love Gordo?"

They were outside, lying on a blanket in the soft shade of a sycamore. It was evening, a cool green twilight, the sun large and red above the edge of the field beyond the lawn. Brinhart's father had just left them to drive into Occoquan for some seafood.

"Don't we?" Katherine said to the baby. "Don't we love Gordo a lot?"

"Bor-dah," the baby said.

Katherine laughed. "That's pretty good for a year old." She sat hugging her knees, staring out at the newly cut lawn. Brinhart lay back with his hands on his chest, looking up through the leaves.

"What do you think you'll do with your life, Gordo?" she asked.

"Spend it with you," he said.

"A job, a career, Gordon."

"I don't know. I don't like to think about the rest of my life."

"There's something you don't know," she said.

"There's a lot I don't know."

"I mean about me."

"Bor-dah," the baby sang.

They laughed. A breeze whispered above them. "So tell me what I don't know," he said.

"It's kind of heavy."

"Okay." He sat up. "Go."

"I'm serious."

"Tell me."

She looked at him. "I can't have any more children."

He was silent.

"They took everything when Alex was born."

"Jesus."

She stood, lifting the baby. "Makes a difference, doesn't it."

"No," he said quickly.

"You think about it," she said, bending to pick up the baby's bottle. She walked back to the house and in, and Brinhart watched her go, the baby's head bobbing over her shoulder.

They were married less than a month later, on a chilly, late-September afternoon. Katherine insisted that she was through with the guitar forever, but this seemed unimportant at the time. They lived that winter in the house with the old man, and Brinhart tried college again. He did rather poorly. His problem was that he couldn't decide on a direction, though he felt reasonably certain that something would eventually occur to him. He took history courses, English, even a little philosophy. He tried music theory, business management, accounting. Nothing really appealed to him. He was happy, and though his father kept commenting on his lack of direction, of any definable goal in life, he was not worried about his future. Finally he looked for work, without letting either his father or Katherine know. He found a job as an attendant at an ARCO gas station, then went over to the college and dropped his courses. This was in the spring—early April—and the old man had already begun to talk about selling the house and moving to Florida. The winter had been fairly hard on everyone, though the old man insisted that his decision would have nothing to do with tensions or arguments, past or present. When Brinhart came home with the job—his schooling over, at least for the time being, or so he told his father—the old man remarked that there seemed no reason to put off selling the house. "I'll help with your education," he said, "not with your fun." There seemed in him now a great eagerness to accomplish what had so recently been only the speculation of idle moments; it was as though Brinhart had unwittingly released his father, somehow, both from the memories and from the relation that held him there. The house was sold within the space of a month, and it was Brinhart who had handled this, his father having already departed for Florida to find a condominium by the sea.

After the house was sold, Brinhart and Katherine took a small converted garage on Prince William Street; it was all they could afford on his salary, though his father had let him keep some of the money from the sale of the furniture and the paintings and the bric-a-brac. Katherine went to work for a while that summer, but she so disliked the routine of working every day, eight hours a day, that Brinhart finally convinced her to quit. This caused money troubles, of course, but then money was not a major concern of either of them. Brinhart felt he was above material ambition, and Katherine simply had none. They were quite happy in the garage. Katherine, after her long deliberation about whether or not to marry him, a deliberation that had convinced him of her reluctance, her lack of any real passion for him, astonished him with the force of her love. He returned it in kind. Many nights, after lovemaking, they lay quiet, spent, in a sweet ambience of their own odors, holding tight, as though the bed were the edge of the world and any motion away from each other might send them both tumbling into the abyss. Brinhart often remembered how his father had witnessed the death of the woman he loved, and there were times when he grieved for Katherine, as though he had already lost her. "I love you," she whispered. "Oh, how I love you, Gordo. Will you always love me?"

"Always," he said.

"And you'll never leave me for someone else?"

"Never."

"I'm not very pretty."

"I think you're the most beautiful and talented girl in the world."

"I don't play anymore. . . . That was my only talent—"

"You play *me*. Like a musical instrument. I'm your guitar."

"My sweet guitar," she said.

It was in the middle of the second year that Katherine began to exhibit the signs of trouble.

Brinhart felt helpless to do anything about it or even to try to analyze it. Katherine just went away from him, drew down into herself, though she kept coming back, kept begging him not to lose patience: it was as if her love had grown somehow desperate. When she was down inside herself, and he tried to bring her back to him by talking, by affection, or through the boy, she would fly at him, would accuse him of baiting her; and if he tried to leave her alone, to be patient, understanding, she interpreted this as indifference, as the end of his love for her. The result was several weeks of the kind of sweeping unpleasantness and emotional torpor that one associates with the end of a marriage, rather than the beginning. There was nothing he could do, finally, nothing he knew how to do. And so he had merely waited, had merely outlasted her misery, holding on to any sign, any glimmer of an indication that she might be shaking off whatever it was that had done this to her. He had somehow got from one discouraging day to the next until, gradually and painfully, she became her old self again. The fact that there were recurrences over the years had begun to form a wedge between them that neither wanted to acknowledge—the whole thing became "Katherine's trouble," like any infirmity couples acknowledge between themselves; yet Brinhart, for all this, was optimistic, was always ready to believe things would work out, Katherine's trouble would pass away and never return, and they would even, in later years, forget any of it had ever happened.

And there was the boy.

Alex was quick, learned fast, was even, in some ways, precocious. He grew to be a mild disappointment for Brinhart, nonetheless. There were moments when Brinhart, putting his arms around the boy, thought of the cells of his little body as those of the other man, the drummer, and it was hard to keep from finding an excuse to remove himself from Alex. He tried never to let Katherine see this, but Katherine's senses, when she was having trouble, seemed to take on an extra element of acuteness, a sort of radar of the emotions, and so of course she saw through his attempts to hide these feelings.

"You know," she said to him once, "it never matters who actually fathers a child—it's who acts as the father."

He wanted to say, "That's what I *am* doing—acting." But he kept silent. She looked at him with those fierce, dark eyes of her trouble.

"You wish you'd never seen either of us," she said.

"No. No, Katherine."

"Yes, I can see it in you."

Here she was wrong. What he wished was that she had never played guitar, that she had come to him without ever having given birth to a child. But he tried, kept forcing himself to forget the drummer and to learn how to know the boy. But Alex, over the years, still troubled him. He could well remember what had happened to the bookworms, mathematicians, future scientists, scholars, and choir directors of his own time in school; and Alex was one of those—a sedentary, delicate boy, a nonparticipant. There was in Brinhart—since he had tried very hard not to be that kind of boy and since he had, for the most part, succeeded—a residue of contempt for his adopted son: there was something wrong with a kid who spent so much time getting to know *anything* as well as Alex knew baseball. Such a kid was queer or he was weak or he was ugly or freakish; such a kid wore glasses or he was chubby, as Alex was.

The years had passed with these troubles. When Katherine was herself, during those periods—some of them two or three years long—of a sort of peace (what Brinhart, at any rate, imagined was the world's dole of it for almost everyone), when things were smooth enough, and life went on too fast but was much the same from day to day, with no extremes of either happiness or pain—when Katherine was herself, he was grateful, if at times cautious; he loved her, he believed, as much as he had ever loved her, perhaps more, for what it had cost them both. But Katherine, even when she *was* free of her trouble, was adamant about the guitar: that part of her life was over; there could be no going back—much as she seemed to be willing to admit (and Brinhart felt he knew) that what troubled her was the music, that it all went back to that, the dead dream, the effort and the talent that had gone for nothing.

V

ON MONDAY Katherine and Alex went alone to the school: a reception for the sixth-grade class of the coming year. Brinhart begged off to work: he had phone calls to make— ten new married couples who might need insurance. June was the month of weddings, he told Katherine, and he had to take advantage. He had the ten names on a piece of paper in his pocket, and he must make an effort to speak to everyone on the list, try to set up appointments, return calls, meetings at the office. "Besides," he said to Katherine, "isn't June a little early for that school stuff? He just got through with school."

"Why don't you call the school board about it," she said.

"No need to be sarcastic," he said. But she had turned her attention to the boy.

"Get your shoes on. Quick. One-two-three."

The two of them left without a word, either to each other or to Brinhart. "Everything's supposed to stop," he said to the empty apartment when they had gone. "Everything comes to a halt because of the P.T.A." He hated the P.T.A. and all other organizations, including the Association of Insurance Salesmen of Point Royal. He had another drink of whiskey and thought, Fuck them all. All organizations, clubs, charities, and associations. He took the receiver off the hook, walked into the living room with it, pulling the long coiled wire out to the end, and sat down on the sofa with his drink. There were push buttons in the receiver, and he called the first number—busy. He pushed the hang-up button and called the second number, sat listening to the flatulent buzzing that he knew was the ring on the other end of the line. Perhaps he would get no one tonight: then he could say he had tried. The living room was uncomfortably warm, though the air conditioner labored away, sending small puffs of cool air from the floor vents. Outside, the sun had burned the greenness out of the trees; they were whitish, as if coated with a fine dust, and not a leaf moved. From where he sat he could see through the patio door to the green slope, the gravel lot, part of the hedgerow, and the end of one mobile home. The buzzing in the line clicked, opened, and a heavy female voice said, "What?"

"Hello?" he said.

"What? Who is this?"

"Well," he began. He hated his own voice when he had to speak as a salesman to strangers. "This is Gordon Brinhart of Iowa Life Insurance—"

The other voice cut him off. "What do you *want?*"

He tried to continue. "Well, I see here by our records that you're newly married and I'm calling to congratulate you and to see if there isn't some—"

"You—" The voice sobbed at him. And now there was some disturbance in the line, as though someone had rubbed cloth over the speaker. Another female voice— lighter, weaker—said, "Why are you calling, please?"

Before he could answer, he heard the other voice say, "A goddamn *life* insurance salesman. Can you imagine that, Mother? Give me the phone. . . ." Confusion, the sound of a struggle and more sobbing, the two voices going, and then a crazy, jangling updraft of music, lifting through the whole thing like a gas.

"Wrong number," he said. "Wrong number?"

The music went away and then it was quiet, there was nothing—not even breathing. He was about to hang up. He looked at the list, the name, the wedding date. The two voices began again, an argument; they were both going at once, a blur of distraught, half-formed phrases. Then the heavy voice sobbed at him, caught itself, and screamed, "YOU WANT TO SELL LIFE INSURANCE TO US!"

Brinhart sat there with the receiver at his ear.

"TO ME AND MY HUSBAND. RIGHT?" There was another moment of confusion; apparently someone was trying to take the phone from her. Brinhart listened.

"RIGHT?" the voice bellowed.

He sat forward, said quickly, almost tenderly, "I didn't mean to get you at the wrong time. I'm so sorry."

The voice was suddenly calm. "You're sorry—"

"We call people as a courtesy—"

"My husband is—my husband *died* yesterday." The woman went on, but he didn't catch it all: something about motorcycles and how people never look for them and how he liked to run something up. Brinhart couldn't make it all out, though now, after the screaming, she gave forth a flood of words, kept going on and on about shock and how absurd and why wasn't everybody something and wasn't death, wasn't death. He tried to listen, even if it hardly mattered. Does it, the voice said. Hardly matters now . . . and how little anything mattered in the end. It went on. Brinhart couldn't hold on to his concentration: he was shaking in his bones. It was one thing to be upset by such an ugly combination of events—his phone call, at that moment, and for such a purpose—but he was more than upset. There was a sudden band of ice across his forehead, and he could feel beads of sweat drop down his back like scales fallen from his skin. He brought the drink to his lips and gulped it, hearing the voice trail off in a series of hard little sobs.

"So I'm—I'm sorry, sir."

"No," he said, nearly choking the whiskey down so he could speak; it burned his throat, made him cough. "No, *I'm* sorry. So *terribly* sorry."

"Yes, of course."

It ended in a jumble of apologies. Brinhart went into the kitchen, carrying the receiver as though it were made of some ancient and fragile and priceless material. He set it on the hook, then gulped the rest of his drink, poured himself another, quickly, aware that he was already half drunk. He didn't care. He stood at the patio door and took two large gulps, rattling the ice in the glass and looking out, past the wide rim of shadow before him, at the sun-whitened leaves of the hedgerow down to the left. In a moment his shakiness began to subside, and he tried to bring his concentration to bear on the other phone calls he had to make. But his mind began to wander toward finding another job, something less troublesome than insurance. He wondered if Katherine could stand yet another change, and then he thought of the girl and her stroller, the evening walk.

And here she was, as though by arrangement. He saw a glint of metal behind the leaves of the hedgerow, a blue cloth something gliding past the spaces, like a small flag. He watched, and when she stepped out into the lot, the baby before her in the stroller (he saw that first), when she paused to put her hands up to the back of her head, tightening the chignon she had made of her hair, he opened the door, the screen, his fingers knotty and ineffectual on the grips in the metal, hurrying, as if she might turn around before he could get out to her: he must speak to her, must tell her what had happened to him. Part of him understood that it was the whiskey, but he experienced a tremendous warm rush of fellow feeling for her, and for all human beings, and he wanted to share, to communicate. The heat, when he stepped out, was like a taste in his mouth. He paused for a moment, his eyes unused to the full glare, out of the shade. Then he stepped down off the patio, squinting at her as she began her leisurely walk. She apparently had not yet seen him.

"Hot," he said, approaching her.

She stopped, touched the back of her neck; he thought she stiffened a little as he bent down to touch the baby's head, nearly spilling his drink as he did so. The baby stared off at the stand of oaks that bordered the north end of the lot: the wide blue eyes seemed to be cataloging everything, inwardly recording the shapes, sizes, and colors. The girl was looking at Brinhart's drink.

Brinhart said, "Nice little boy," smiling, and now he thought he saw fear in the girl's eyes. "Excuse this intrusion," he said, and realized that his voice had taken that lilting, faintly ingratiating tone of the salesman—that commercial song in his throat that he so despised. "I just" —he went on, trying not to hurry or slur the words—"I just had the most awful thing—" It was crazy, it was foolish and absurd, and he could read this in her face, if he had not understood it to be so even as he spoke. He extended his free hand. "I'm sorry. I'm Gordon Brinhart. You've seen me—I've seen—I su—sit on that patio in the evenings?"

"Shirley," the girl said. He was not certain whether she had given him her name, or was agreeing with him.

"I'm sorry?" he said.

"Shirley Ann Comminger."

"Ah. And the little one?"

"That's Tommy."

"Ah," Brinhart said, as though there were great satisfaction in the sound of the name.

"Say hi, Tommy," she said, bending over the baby. "Say hi to the nice man."

The child made no sound.

"He's shy," the girl said. "He knows how to say hi. I can't get him to stop saying it usually."

A bumble bee swept toward them, its flight drunken, sleepy; it veered back, dipped as though falling toward the baby's head, lifted, and was gone. The girl had tensed when it dropped, and then she gasped as it rose. Brinhart searched his mind for something to say: why had he come bursting out here?

"I'm so scared of bees," she said.

"Bumble bees usually leave you alone."

"Sure is hot."

"Worst spell I can remember," he said. He felt suddenly almost ebullient. He sipped the drink; the baby gave a little whimper, the blond, stubbled head fell forward and then, with what looked like some effort, was lifted back. The girl moved the stroller an inch, took a step. When Brinhart didn't move, she stopped. He said, "I sell insurance." He looked off toward the opening in the hedgerow, saw a dry, cracked rut in the path there. "One of the things I have to do is call newlyweds, to help them with their planning. . . ." It was all infuriatingly stupid; he had sounded as though he were about to try a sales pitch, though he had been careful not to let his voice take the despised tone. The girl had now grown restless, shifting her weight from one tan leg to the other. "Ah, hell," Brinhart said, "I know this is really stupid, but I just had a—well, a very odd experience, and I just wanted to explain it to another human being." He went on to tell her that his wife and son were not at home, and then he rushed through the story of the unfortunate timing of his phone call and how it had unhinged him. When he finished, she shook her head and, with a look of puzzlement on her face, said, "That's something."

Perhaps she thinks I'm a drunk, he thought. He said, "Such tragedy, and to come upon it like that—"

"Must've upset you."

This was precisely what he had told her it had done. He was now vaguely irritated, and he avoided looking at her, bending down on one knee to touch the baby's puffy, dimpled hands; the fingers were tiny, seemed boneless. "Who's he take after," Brinhart wondered aloud, "his mommy or his daddy?"

"Too early to tell," the girl said simply.

He looked up at her, past the soft belly, the perfect navel, the halter. She kept looking at the glass of whiskey. Brinhart wanted to put it down, started to; it tipped, spilled a little before he could get it upright. He stood. "Bet his daddy's proud of him."

"I don't know about that," she said.

"Well," Brinhart said, "now that we've met, you must come to see us."

She moved the stroller, and he took a step back.

"Say good-bye to the nice man, Tommy."

He walked with her, in spite of this. They went in a wide arc around the lot, past his own patio, around to where he had accosted her—which was what he had done, he now told himself. But something—the whiskey or his upset over the phone call or just the plain awkwardness of breaking away or even (he must admit this) the faint urging of desire, of a species of hope for further contact, now or in the future—something kept him walking along at her side, like an embarrassed adolescent boy, except that this boy carried a glass of hard liquor he was now faintly ashamed of. As they made the turn down the path toward the trailer court, he began to understand that she was now thoroughly afraid of him. She struggled to push the stroller over the long dry rut in the path, and he resisted the impulse to try to help her. Once, he nearly lost his footing, though where he walked, it was relatively even, grass jutting out at the edge, bending dryly under his tread, like straw.

He began to ask inane questions in an attempt to reassure her, and of course he could not let her get away thinking he was to be feared. Why did she suppose they had built the gravel lot anyway? Was it connected to the trailer court or to the apartments? She didn't know. It didn't serve any purpose, did it? She couldn't say. Did she know there was a generator or something in the ground near the tree-shaded side of it? She hadn't noticed it. Perhaps it was something to do with VEPCO? She wouldn't know; she was new here. She had only been here since February. How did she like it here? It was as good a place as any, she supposed; she wasn't the choosy type.

Finally he said, "I'm sorry."

"What?" she said. They had made slow progress down the path, and now she stopped, looked at him.

"I guess I've ruined your walk."

"Oh, no."

The whiskey had brought him to the point of confession. He said "I like to watch you walk the baby in the evenings. You're very pretty."

"Thank you."

"You're so young to have a child." For an excruciating instant he was convinced that the child was her brother. But she smiled and nodded, and that was all. The baby gave an abrupt cry, and Brinhart seemed to feel the sound along his spine. He rushed on: "How old are you?" He smiled. He could feel the awkwardness of the smile in the tightening skin of his jaw; it was there, like the heat.

She said, "I'll be eighteen."

"Eighteen," he repeated.

They entered the trailer court, walking down a gravel-and-dirt street, or what passed for a street here. The sun had lost some of its intensity now, and the light was gold. The mobile homes were tightly ranked, each with its own little square of crabgrass and parched red earth. There were small wrought-iron stoops, and one or two elaborately built wooden ones with plastic awnings. Flowers bloomed in the windows, or drooped in clay pots below the stoops. Mailboxes went on in crooked procession down the row on either side, and through the spaces between the homes on the one side, other homes were visible, back windows sprouting air conditioners or dust-coated fans whose blades rattled, water tanks above tall spines of wild grass; pipes, swaying laundry, dirty screens, and now and again the glimpse of a room, crowded with furniture. Brinhart remembered Katherine's question about what sort of people lived in trailer courts, and then he remembered Katherine. He drank the rest of the whiskey.

When they came to a particularly graceless trailer, seven or eight down the row—its wrought-iron stoop spotted with rust or mud (he couldn't tell), its awning striped white and blue, corrugated, casting a transparent curtain of shade—the girl said, "Well."

"Nice," he muttered.

She gave a little laugh. He smiled, and looked back up the row. They had encountered no one, nor any sign of inhabitation other than the whirring air conditioners in the windows, and one radio voice talking about the Middle East. The girl opened and closed her mailbox.

"Never get any mail," she said. "I keep checking it. Red says I'm like a soldier away at sea or something—except there ain't nobody that would write to me except my friend Trish, and I haven't heard from her in more than a year. Well, since I left—since I went on the road."

"Is Red—" he began, but she went on.

"I mean, since I left Ankeny."

"Ankeny—where's that?"

"Iowa." She opened the peeling white picket fence, the whole length of which shook as she did so. He saw a thin, clean sidewalk, toys lying in the middle of a crude sandbox. An empty clay pot lay on the edge of the stoop away from the door. "Well, bye."

"Thanks for the—thanks for listening to me," he said.

"Okay." She bent down to lift the child out of the stroller; the child was limp, had fallen fast asleep.

"How old is he?" Brinhart asked.

She turned, held up five fingers, then one.

"Six—"

"Six months," she said.

He watched her climb the stairs. She glanced at him again and he waved, but she had looked away, had not seen this.

"Bye," he said.

As he started back up the row he saw a man come to the door and hold the screen open for her to enter: an old man with a leathery, lined face, angular, almost gaunt features: eyes buried under thick red brows, a wiry bush of copper hair descending in a widow's peak. The old man squinted at Brinhart, and Brinhart nodded politely, but there was no response; there was only a sort of lifting of the chin, as though to smell the air, and then those buried eyes were trained on the girl as she passed through. It had all taken place in less than a moment. The door closed; Brinhart walked up to the path and the end of the hedge-row, out into the lot. The air had begun to cool a little, and it filled him with a sort of random peace. He would go into the apartment and watch a little television, and when he went to work tomorrow, he would make the rest of his calls—everything would go all right: he was Gordon Brin-hart of Iowa Life; it was summer, and a man was entitled to the motions of summer in his blood.

Before Katherine and Alex returned, he drank two more whiskeys, and then got suddenly and violently ill. He knelt over the toilet and thought himself near some sort of fatal attack. But then it passed, and he went into the bedroom and lay on the bed. When he heard Katherine and the boy come in, he feigned sleep, hoping that he had left no signs of his sickness in the bathroom. Then he *was* asleep, floating on a dreamless ocean of pain, and when he opened his eyes, he saw the television screen, an old movie flickering in the darkness. He heard noises in the kitchen, realized that his head was throbbing, his mouth and throat parched, constricted. He got up and went into the bathroom and drank deeply from the running tap. Katherine met him in the hall as he came out.

"You went to bed early," she said.

"Yeah," he muttered. "I got a headache."

She preceded him into the bedroom, sat down on her side of the bed, where the television was. She turned the sound up, lighted a cigarette. "Want one?"

"No." He lay down at her side and covered his face with his hands. The cigarette smoke made him feel sick again. "I wish *you* wouldn't smoke."

"Just one."

They watched the movie for a while: Brinhart did not recognize any of the actors. He closed his eyes.

"Do you want to hear about Alex's new teacher?" she asked.

"Not now."

"We ran into his new friend and her mother at the Safeway tonight."

He rolled over in the bed, away from the light of the television. He could only think of his pain.

She sighed. "We're supposed to go over to their place for dinner tomorrow night."

"Oh, Christ," Brinhart said.

"I couldn't get out of it. Besides, I don't know that I want to."

"Please put the cigarette out, Katherine."

She did so: he heard the whisper of it in the ashtray on the night stand. "You smell like alcohol," she said.

He turned toward her. "I had one drink."

"Gordon, you had three before we left."

"I mean I had one after you left."

"And that's why you have a headache."

"Maybe—maybe. I don't know why. I could be coming down with something."

There was a pause. She was sitting up in the bed, and now she lighted another cigarette.

"Honey, I asked you not to smoke."

"One more won't hurt."

"You're smoking a *lot*," he said. He looked at her back, the suggestion of her spine through the nightgown she wore; he thought she seemed herself, but knew that if he called attention to this, it would anger her, might even set her off again. Then he was tired of worrying about it, so he closed his eyes tight, as if to lock her out.

"I think there's something wrong with that girl," she said.

He sighed. "*What* girl."

"Amy. Alex's new friend."

"You don't like her?"

"No—I mean, there's something physically wrong with her."

"Okay, what is it?"

"I don't know—her mother is very protective of her. Or, well, not so much protective as—I don't know—*forlorn.* The way she looks at her, you know? It's kind of hard to explain."

"Katherine, I really must go to sleep."

"Did you make all your calls?"

"Yes," he lied.

"Everybody was home?"

"No."

"How many?"

"*Please*, Katherine."

Then it was very quiet; the muted voices from the television, her soft sighings of smoke, came to him through a thick hush. Presently she crushed the cigarette out and lighted another, and this angered him. He could not remain still for his anger. He got out of bed, walked into the kitchen, and poured himself a drink; it was crazy—the idea of the whiskey on his tongue made his head reel in a wicked series of throbbing pains. Yet here he was, dropping an ice cube into the glass.

"That's right," Katherine said behind him. "Pour yourself another drink. That's just what you need."

"Katherine," he said, not looking at her, "I should've gone with you tonight. I'm sorry I didn't."

"And that fixes everything, and now you can go ahead and drink it?"

"Look, lay off, will you? Just fucking lay off me."

Then they were quiet, as if listening together for a sound. Brinhart set the glass on the counter in a sudden wave of dizziness, and it dawned on him that he was still drunk.

"Something terrible happened to me tonight," he said. And then he told her—though he did not say that he had spoken to the girl. Presently he said, "I wish I had gone with you. I really am sorry."

"I know you have to work," she said. And then her eyes were quite sad.

"Honey," he said.

She forced a smile. He could see that she was expending energy, smiling. "You know I thought we'd get home and find your father here. He's just the type to pull something like that. God, I hope he doesn't. I hope he gives us some warning." Brinhart went to her, put his arms around her. He led her into the bedroom, holding her by the elbow, and when he tried to make love to her, she stopped him. "Please," she said in a quavering whisper, "not now."

He told her it was all right. They lay next to each other in the meager light of the television. She had reached over and turned the sound off, and now she watched the screen: a man and woman rushing through the crowded lobby of a hotel. Brinhart put his hands behind his head and stared at the ceiling. He thought about the drink on the counter in the kitchen. He wanted that drink, that last one. Katherine reached for another cigarette, apologizing.

"They relax me, honey."

Outside, a siren seemed to climb on the dark; it wavered, and died. There was a general stirring of wind— branches bending, leaves rustling and whispering. There would be a storm, he thought, and he got up, went to the window. The moon was sere and white as polished bone; it gave a ghostly, sharp-shadowed appearance to the ground. Far-off, he could see the multicolored neon of the shopping mall and the highway beyond the field. One or two windows winked at him from that end of the trailer court.

"Katherine," he said, thinking of the girl, "I want you." He imagined that in some magical way he had by this put the girl away from himself.

"We made love Saturday night, honey."

"We did, yes."

"Please, Gordon. Just let me get ahold of myself." She crushed the cigarette out, reached for another.

"You know, between your smoking and my drinking we ought to kill ourselves pretty good in a couple of years."

She had brought the cigarette out and now reached for the matchbox. It was empty. "What did I do with my lighter?" she said, getting out of bed.

He lay down, realized that his headache had become a dull, even thing, like something wrapped tightly around the inside of his skull. He could hear her rummaging through the cabinets in the kitchen, so the lighter had not been in her purse. When she came back into the room, he saw that she trembled a little.

"I poured your drink out," she said.

He watched her look through the bureau drawers, her jewelry box; she opened the closet, stood on her toes, running her hand along the shelf under stacks of shirt boxes and envelopes full of canceled checks.

"Your lighter isn't hiding."

"I'm looking for anything now—a match, anything."

"Let it alone. We'll just go to sleep."

She came down on her heels and stood concentrating for a moment. "What did I do with the damn lighter?"

"Come on."

"I want a cigarette." Her voice was not as argumentative as it was determined; yet now she frowned at him. "*You* go to sleep. You don't have any trouble doing it, so do it." She did not wait for him to answer. In a moment she was back in the living room, noisily going through the closet there.

"Use the damn stove," he called.

She came to the door. "I'm looking for the *lighter*, now."

He fell asleep listening to the sound of her searching, and in his dreams he saw ransacked rooms, debris, her face as she had stood there in the door. When he awoke, he found her lying next to him, smoking in the dark, the coal going back and forth like a tiny yellow tracer.

"You found it?" he mumbled.

"No," she said, "I used the stove."

He heard her blowing the smoke, and then he was asleep again. Suddenly he was alone in a quiet room, his mother there, and his father, a moon in the window behind them; they smiled, turned their faces, and Brinhart saw someone else, a face he recognized, old and wet-eyed and afraid. "Just like me," the face said. "She's just like me." Brinhart's parents were nodding. "You know what will happen," the face said.

VI ☙

BRINHART'S AUNT—his father's older sister—had ended insane. That was how his father described it. Brinhart remembered her face, and in the memory she was always bending toward him, lips puckered, offering a wet, unwanted kiss. Her lips were a shimmering red. He knew from his father that Aunt Beth had been a wild young woman during the twenties, had worn the jazzy dresses and drunk

bathtub gin and raced around in an open car with a cigarette in her mouth—and had spent one notorious week in
Miami with a Harvard boy, a boy already engaged to be
married to the youngest daughter of a prominent Boston
family; and she had paid the price: the young man's career
had been badly threatened, the marriage never took place,
and Aunt Beth, after a long period of loneliness and heavy
drinking, had wound up marrying an older man, an execu-
tive of some standing with the railroads, whom she did not
love, and whose passion for her was little more than an
element of his general passion for ornaments. When he
died, he left her wealthy and alone and as unhappy as ever,
and for a few years the drinking continued; but gradually
she began to try to get hold of herself. By the time Brinhart knew her, she was graying, she no longer smoked or
drank, and she seemed vacantly sweet as any old woman
one hadn't really bothered to see: someone who was always
baking pastries and bread, or who knew how to do all sorts
of obscure things with yarn or thread or wicker—and who
was active in the church. She wore polka-dot dresses, kept
her hair in a little gray bun atop her head, and had a way of
clearing her throat with her fingers to her lips, as though
she were holding something back—words, the sound itself.
The few times Brinhart had been with his father to her
house (his mother and Aunt Beth had never gotten along
very well and his father, to keep order, had kept the old
woman at a distance: visits were rare, and then only the boy
and his father would go) he had noticed signs of a religious
devotion even more intense than the rather severe devotion
of his parents. It was as if the religion he and his parents
observed as part of the normal pattern of life had, for Aunt
Beth, lost all proportion; there was an undeniable element
of fear in it, though Brinhart was too young to name what
made it different.

The house was an enormous place, paid for by the dead

husband; there were balustrades and spires and fluted columns in front, and inside were dark, polished wood floors and wainscoting, milky glass dormers, oak furniture in high-ceilinged rooms that carried the echo of voices or footsteps. Everywhere one looked, painted or carved suppliants looked back—from the walls, from the corner of a hallway, or from the top of a bureau: martyrs, virgins, sacred hearts, and crucifixions. Brinhart had never felt really comfortable anywhere but in the kitchen, which was spacious and white and cool.

The house was in Arlington, high on a hill overlooking the Potomac. On a clear day in winter one could see, through the stark branches of her oak trees, the snowy dome of the Capitol and the odd-looking shaft of the Washington Monument in an extending perspective toward the square, moon-colored simplicity of the Lincoln Memorial; this view seemed to lay bare the whole city, as if this one aspect, this one view out of a window, were the key to understanding the puzzle of its streets—a puzzle Brinhart had experienced during two lengthy walking tours with his father and Aunt Beth. The best view, of course, was from the upstairs windows, particularly the one that looked out of Aunt Beth's sewing room.

It was while he sat at that window, one August evening in his thirteenth year, that he experienced the first innocent sense of what Aunt Beth must have been like in her youth.

The day had been spent, for the most part, in the kitchen and in the little gazebo out in back, where Aunt Beth served cold strawberries in milk—her dog, a large, matted, and dirty Airedale, yelping and barking from the far corner of the yard, out of the shade. Toward twilight Brinhart's father had begun to talk about the old days, growing up in the northern Virginia of that time, and presently Aunt Beth remembered something that had happened to her in her evil period—that was how she put it.

"It's something to think," she said to his father, "that when you were sneaking cigarettes out behind the barn in 1927, I was—well, on my way to Miami." She hesitated, and then seemed to shrug something off; it was as if a shadow had crossed inside her eyes.

"I remember when you went down there," Brinhart's father said. "Of course. I was quite jealous of you at the time."

Aunt Beth went on to tell about a flat tire, and how the young man she was traveling with—the Harvard boy, though Brinhart had to put this together later, when his father finally told him about the Miami trip—couldn't change it because of an allergy attack. They had been speeding down the peninsula (Aunt Beth's words) toward Miami; it was hot, a tropical twilight, just the most uncomfortable day of the year, and they wore bathing suits, had been drinking illegal gin (she blushed, saying this; she interrupted herself and wondered aloud why she was bothering to tell it). The flat tire occurred on a deserted stretch of highway that was raised up on a gravel roadbed; the highway was surrounded as far as the eye could see by swamp and marsh and cypress grove. The Harvard boy had come down with the allergy attack—asthmatic coughing and wheezing, running eyes and nose—and Aunt Beth had changed the tire. She told the story in vivid detail, describing the girl she had been as though she were describing a stranger. The girl was nineteen, was tipsy with gin, and the incongruousness of the situation, in contrast to her upbringing (an upbringing common to all decent girls who were Virginia-bred), the absurdity of herself in a bathing suit, changing a tire while her companion lay wheezing and complaining in the front seat, had made her laugh uncontrollably the whole time, so that her hands grew weak, and she had to pause, sitting on the road and leaning against the running board. She said she had sent peals of laughter out over the marsh, sitting there in the half-dark, the air so thick with the odor of stagnant water and of the sea that she had become seriously afraid she would suffocate if she could not stop. She laughed again, telling about it.

She said, "I can tell you, I never laughed so hard in my life, ever. Not ever before and never again, like that."

"Don't you think the gin contributed to it?" Brinhart's father said.

"Probably." And now Aunt Beth looked quite tired.

The story—coupled with this weary look on her face—had an almost physical effect on Brinhart, as though he could smell the swamp and feel the hot wet air of that particular twilight so long ago, a twilight in another country and another time that was, somehow, this twilight too. It made him restless; it filled him with obscure longings and with a kind of sadness, and he wandered into the house, up the stairs, his hands gliding along the walnut banister as though his fingers traced the shape and texture of Time itself. He went into Aunt Beth's sewing room, to the window there, and looked out at what he could see of the river through the branches of the oaks, whose leaves were a rich dark green, drooping as though drenched in the heat. The room was full of boxes, and the one chair was overcome with stacks of patterns, scraps of cloth, two wicker baskets of thread and needles and empty spools. Along the opposite wall was an old Singer sewing machine with a wrought-iron pedal, and one of Aunt Beth's stockings lay across from it. Above the sewing machine a photograph in a gilt frame reflected the pale twilight of the window. The ever-present religion lay on the little table next to the chair where he sat—a glass rosary and a missal with several bright ribbons jutting from the pages. He looked at all this and then he gazed out at the end of the day. The dusky green air stirred, and he opened his mouth, was suddenly aware that this was the end of summer and that he would remember this twilight as Aunt Beth remembered hers. He turned from the window. On the wall above the Singer was the photograph, in shadow now, and he stood before it. It was of Aunt Beth when she was young; but he didn't recognize this at first. At first it was merely a smooth face, round and pale as the moon, ringed tightly by dark curls that were pressed down by a hat as closely fitted as a bathing cap. He gazed at the face, the dark lips—the eyebrows drawn thin and arching softly—and it dawned on him with a strange heat in his blood that this was the old woman whose voice, now, faintly, he heard below. She had come in with his father, and the two of them were talking about the river: it was dirty, Aunt Beth said, and getting dirtier all the time and no one was doing a blessed thing about it; you couldn't swim in it anymore. Brinhart imagined that the voice he was hearing came from this girl face, smiling and aware of itself and slightly naughty and aware of *that* too. It was as if he could walk down the stairs into 1927.

But he did not have to walk downstairs. Aunt Beth was climbing toward him, telling his father she would see where the boy had gone. He met her at the top of the stairs, and she seemed slightly surprised to find him there—then she seemed somehow disappointed, though Brinhart couldn't have put this into words.

"What have you been doing?" she asked.

"I was looking out the window," he said, and pointed at the long pale opening—the sewing room door. "In there."

She walked past him into the room, and looked out the window. "Can't really see anything now," she said.

It was very quiet. Brinhart stood just behind her; he was aware of the picture on the wall, and now Aunt Beth turned, looked at him.

"Why, what's the matter, honey?" she said. "You look

sort of sad. You don't want to see the end of summer, do you."

"No," he said.

She looked at the picture, and Brinhart thought she sighed, though he could not be certain—another breath of air stirred in the window. "Lord," Aunt Beth said, "look at that girl. I don't even know her."

"It's you, isn't it?" said Brinhart.

Now she did sigh. "Not anymore. Not for a long, long time now." With another sigh, she picked up the rosary on the bureau, held it in the palm of her hand, as though she were trying to remember or make up her mind what to do with it. She said, "You know, this girl is like a bad little friend I have."

Brinhart said nothing.

Aunt Beth put the rosary down, turned to him, and took his chin. "That's why I keep her here."

"How old are you, *there?*" he asked.

"Oh, I'm as old as I am now—or just about to be that old."

"When was that?"

She made a little smacking sound with her lips. "Nineteen twenty-five, I think."

Outside now, the wind was coming steadily: a summer storm getting up. Somewhere beyond the trees a dog barked, and Aunt Beth's Airedale answered from the backyard.

"Well," Aunt Beth said, and took his hand. But he did not want to leave the room yet.

"What happened to *him,* in your story?" he blurted out. "Who?"

"The one—the tire you changed—that one, who couldn't—"

"Oh," she said. "He—he went his way, you know."

Brinhart told her that he had friends who had asthma, and he thought it must be very uncomfortable but he didn't know that grown-ups got it too.

"Yes," she said, guiding him out of the room, "we can get it. And old Bernard had it bad. I remember another time—" But then she stopped, as though to correct herself, and said, "Let's go downstairs, honey." In the shadows of the room her face changed, tightened, and Brinhart did not have the courage to press her further. He did not want to, finally, and he became aware of this as they descended the stairs. The dark polished wood of the newel post as they reached bottom seemed, in the slanting shadows of the hall, so utterly itself, so mute and separate from them, that Brinhart found himself trembling. He looked at Aunt Beth's face, and thought he saw the other face superimpose itself there, like a ghost. The old woman smiled at him out of tremendous watery-blue eyes, and he saw fear now, too.

"Oooh," she said, still smiling. "Don't you hate the night?" She turned the hall light on and then she shuddered. He took her wrist, merely to hold on to something.

They went down the hall toward the kitchen, and Brinhart walked on outside, to the gazebo, where he sat for a long time in the dark, watching the storm come and go, and then watching fireflies cross the lawn, hearing the rising song of the insects.

Aunt Beth, he thought later, has become someone else. And in subsequent years, when she had moved to Florida (Brinhart wondered about the highway of her story: had she looked upon it again? And in a similar twilight?), and the phone calls had begun, her blurred voice over the miles of wire and his father, having told him about the boy from Harvard and the awful price of her irresponsibility (his father's phrase), intimating now that he thought she might be drinking again, Brinhart began to understand what he had felt that evening in her house, in that room where she had begun to tell him something and stopped herself. He believed he understood what was blooming on the other side of her slow speech on the telephone, what she was afraid of, and what everyone was afraid of, whether or not anyone admitted it to himself. And one long night in another summer he had lain in bed, huddled with terror at the thought of sinking down into darkness and never coming up again, and had spent the best part of a year afraid to go to sleep, afraid to close his eyes and let himself drift. This had passed, finally; it had gone out of him slowly, as though it leaked away, except that Aunt Beth's phone calls always threatened to bring it back.

And then one morning in winter, when the air outside was wet and cold, and even the snow that had fallen was gray, his father took him into the kitchen and told him that Aunt Beth had died. He gave no details at first, and Brinhart did not ask for any. He was too relieved to speak. This both puzzled and shamed him, and then he began to cry very hard, was astonished at the force of it, coming out of him as though of its own power and volition, as though someone else cried in him or through him. His father knelt down and told him something about things working out for the best, and then walked him in to bed. And if he had spent many hours that night, and on subsequent nights, thinking about Aunt Beth, it was only later—years later and never all at once but only in little increments in the randomness of conversation, like hints dropped without intention—that he learned the truth about Aunt Beth, what she had been and what she had suffered. Finally it had come down to the simple sentence: "Your Aunt Beth ended insane." And Brinhart had understood that all of the time during the visits—during the walking tours and the hot summer evenings out in the gazebo and the quiet meals on the screened porch off the kitchen—had been shaded by a desperation that was almost palpable, like a cloud. Because he was too young to understand it, he had merely been feeling its effects. At any rate this was what he told himself.

Aunt Beth had died babbling, alone, in the upstairs

bathroom of a man's house. The man had been a moder-
ately successful lawyer, had retired and moved to Florida
—and complained of asthma. In fact, it was an asthma
attack, the sudden recurrence of a thing he thought he
might have outgrown, that made it impossible for him to
climb the stairs and do anything for Aunt Beth. He ex-
plained this to Brinhart's father over the phone (Brinhart's
father wound up being the only one to attend the funeral,
since the boy was in his last year of high school, and since
his mother insisted that he remain behind). They had lived
as brother and sister, the man said; they were old friends.
"It's him," Brinhart's father said to his mother. "You just
bet it's him—can you imagine that?"

The single statement, "Your Aunt Beth ended insane,"
had come in a letter Brinhart received shortly after he left
the army. It was in answer to one of Brinhart's that expressed the desire to travel a bit on his way back to Virginia. He had mentioned Katherine and the band only in
passing: they were a curious sort, since the lead guitarist
was a woman, and he might follow them for a while; he
liked their music and he had spoken once or twice to the
talented young woman. He had in fact made his mind up
about Katherine, though he may not have been fully aware
of it himself.

His father's letter went like this:

Son,

I don't understand why one who has lived as you have over
the past two years—one who has been forced to travel, has
spent so little time anyplace—would want to travel a bit on
his way home. This is none of my business, of course. Since
you reached majority, I have tried not to advise you in any
way unless asked for advise, and in any case to stick to the
subject at hand no matter what foolishness I may see about
you in other matters. But I'm alone here now, with this

terrible memory, and I do miss you. So I thought to suggest
—without commenting on the strangeness of your plans
(i.e., following a rock and roll group all over the country)
that you come here first, spend some time, settle on what
you'll do either in the nature of work or school—or both—
and then take off for a few weeks. This seems to be the best
idea—after all, without meaning to lecture, you must know
that to get one's bearings first, to make all the important
decisions first, is the best idea. A man drifts, son, at his
own infinite expense. A man lives outside the rules at
tremendous risk both to himself and to those he'll be responsible for; and to drift, to go aimlessly through life, without a goal or something to strive for and without the approval
of those who are striving and who do have goals, is to break
the rules, or at least to live outside them. Your Aunt Beth
lived this way through most of her young life, and never
really recovered from the ravages of what she had done, both
to herself and to others. She tried, she tried mightily, but
your Aunt Beth ended insane. Remember that.

Your father

At the time, Brinhart had thought, *No, no, she had
courage, she was really alive. Fuck his rules and his re-
sponsibility. It was trying to follow his rules that made her
unhappy.* He had blessed the old woman, imagined her
reunited with her lover, and happy.

But he didn't know, now. There were times when he
caught himself thinking of Katherine as paying *her* price;
he hated this in himself.

He said, "You'd feel better if you gave this up." It was
early morning, and they lay facing each other across the
pillows. She looked nearly gaunt in the poor light. He had
come awake to find her staring at him, had leaned over
and kissed her, and found her lips slack, nerveless.

"Give what up," Katherine said.

"Trying to put on the rules—you've been trying so long
to put on all the rules, honey."

"What rules? What're you talking about?"

"Nothing."

Presently he said, "Why don't you get another guitar—start playing again. I'll help you get an act together—"

"Gordon, sometimes I think you've been waiting—since the beginning. Waiting for me to start up again."

"Maybe I have—I think I thought you eventually would."

"The whole thing's ridiculous—that stuff is all gone. In the past." She settled deep into the bed. "I don't want to talk about it."

"I had an awful dream last night," he said.

"Really."

"I told you about my Aunt Beth, didn't I?"

"I don't want to hear about your Aunt Beth now. I want to sleep. Go back to sleep."

"It's morning."

"I haven't been to sleep yet. Will you let me sleep?"

"Sleep," Brinhart said.

In a moment, when he saw that she had not closed her eyes, he touched her shoulder.

"Don't."

"Close your eyes."

She did so.

VII

"Two and two on the batter."

Alex lay in the shade of the hedgerow, legs spread wide, arms folded on his chest, and whispered the words of his imagined game. Lee May at bat, hitting .394, leading the league in home runs with eighteen, three ahead of Rice, who had been slumping in the first week of June. May would probably slow down during July and August, would hit thirty-four home runs perhaps, for the season; and his batting average, to be realistic, would fall to .319. Still, one of his best years. Now there were two out; no one was on base. May was looking for a fastball, high and tight.

"Low and outside, for ball three."

It was the bottom of the first. No score. But now he heard footsteps in the grass nearby, knew immediately who it was. She lay down at his side, then sat up and leaned on her arms, smiling at him.

"Hiding from my mother," she said.

He would have to remember: top of the second, Lee May at bat.

"You'd think I was made of glass," Amy said.

Alex sat up, gazed out at the field in the sun. "Want to go over to the high school?" he said.

"No."

"That's what I'm going to do."

"Go ahead." She lay back.

"What're you going to do?"

"Die, maybe." She laughed. "You know what? You're coming over to dinner tonight."

"Yeah."

"You don't sound very excited." She sat up and hugged her knees, rocked slightly. "My mother makes a great asparagus and cheese thing."

"I don't like asparagus."

"Looks like green turds," she said.

"You don't like it either."

"It's all right—I can eat anything. Absolutely anything in the whole world."

"Onions make me sick," Alex said.

"I love them—especially fried. You never had French-fried onion rings?"

"No."

"Ever French-kiss?"

"Sure."

She turned to him and let her tongue out over her lips. "Doesn't it just turn you on?"

He nodded vaguely, watched her stand up. She slapped the rear of her shorts with both hands, then knelt before him. "You been in the laundry room of the apartments?"

"Yeah," he said.

"So have I."

He said nothing.

"You want to go there with me?"

"Okay," he said.

"Come on." She took his hand, and they walked through the hedge into the courtyard. Two young women slapped a tennis ball back and forth there, calling out to each other and laughing when they missed. The sky above the rooftops was hazy, one or two clouds, like dirty flags, trailing down the grainy blue. There was no air to breathe on the asphalt, which looked as though it might melt under their feet. In one of the small lawns three babies sat with their legs straight out while a woman in a blue-flowered kimono gave them turns at a Popsicle she held; the Popsicle was melting all over her hand, and she kept wiping her fingers in the grass. At the entrance end of the row, down a shadowed stairwell, under the last building, was the laundry room; it was long and narrow, dryers along one wall, washing machines in a file down the center. A metal coin slot jutted out of each washing machine like a tongue. Amy went to the dryers, looking in each one, and Alex stood by the door, his heart pressing against the walls of his stomach. It was cool here, like the basement it was; but the odors were acrid and unpleasant: disinfectant, bleach, detergent, and mildew.

"Okay," Amy said from one of the dryers. "Close the door and lock it."

He did not know how to lock the door. The knob was smooth; there was no button that he could see. "It doesn't lock," he said.

"Hell," she said, and in a moment she was at his side. She pushed a tiny button he had not seen, on the circular plate at the base of the knob. "Now," she murmured, "we're alone."

"Suppose someone comes," Alex said.

"No one will come. Stop worrying." She touched the hair at the back of his neck. "Want to look at me?"

He nodded quickly, his eyes already trained on her hands, which were fumbling with the clasp of her shorts.

"Do you think I'm sexy?"

"Yes."

"Have you ever seen a naked girl before?"

"No."

In only a second she had stripped to the waist, white panties with yellow flowers on them showing like a lining inside the bunched red cloth of the shorts. She stepped out of it all with a matter-of-factness that stunned him and at the same time shut him entirely into the room, sealed him there with her, making him aware of the walls, the low ceiling, the world outside that must not find them.

"Do you like me?" she said. Then she pranced away from him, swinging her hips; her small buttocks were surprisingly white. She turned, walked back. He saw sparse hair at the top of her legs, looked quickly at her face. She was not smiling now. "Well?" she said.

He could only nod.

"Come on." She led him around to the dryer she had picked out; there were clothes lying in it, and she reached in and pulled them out—a warm handful, which she held to her lower body, closing her eyes and pressing with her fingers. "Oooh" she said. "Sex." Then she put the clothes down on the cement floor. There were patterns of black, like burns, in the smooth cement. She lay down, opened her legs.

"Kneel down here," she said.

He did so. Her knees were on either side of him. The fingers of her left hand went down, into the hair, the index and middle finger making a scissorslike motion with the flesh there. Alex looked at a moist pink pod.

"Touch it," she said, but then reached up, took his hand, and put it there. "Give me your finger."

Everything was soft and clinging and moist.

"Move it."

He thought he heard a sound at the door, tried to pull away, but she held his wrist.

"Do you like that?" she said.

"Someone's coming."

"Let me see you," she said. She moved his hand away, sat forward, and with both hands, took his trousers down.

"Somebody's coming." He scrambled away, struggling to get his pants up. He thought he heard the sound again.

"There's nobody," she said. "You're just scared."

Then they were both listening. Perhaps thirty seconds went by.

"I heard something at the door," Alex said.

She smiled, tipped her head to one side. "Don't you think I love you or anything?"

"Love me?" he whispered. He did not believe he had heard her correctly. He watched her pull at the clothes beneath her, covering herself now. In the walls something whirred—a fan or a generator of some sort; it seemed to grow louder, as if to warn them.

"Aren't we lovers?" she said. She put the clothes back into the dryer, not looking at him. "I wouldn't do this for just anybody, you know."

He thought he should kiss her, as he had seen in the movies, but he hesitated; it was all so strange and he felt so silly and fake. Look, he wanted to say, I'm only eleven.

"Do you love me?" she said, walking over to him.

He said, "Sure."

"So I guess we'll have a kid or something eventually."

He was silent.

"I mean we'll have to think about maybe having a kid—do you like kids?"

I *am* a kid, he thought.

"Well—do you?"

"You're crazy."

"Come on," she said, "kiss me."

He closed his eyes as their lips touched, and moved his head back and forth as he had seen it done on the screen, but the kiss wasn't what he expected: it was uncomfortable; it made him conscious of his breath. Was he to breathe? Through his nose? Was she breathing? He couldn't tell, and now, though he liked the feel of her lips, he opened his eyes, was thinking of ending it, pulling away. He saw her eyes, disproportionately large, so close, a blur of glassy blue and soft lash. She was staring at him. He broke away.

"You're supposed to close your eyes."

"I know," she said. "I was checking you."

"Close your eyes." He put his hand at the back of her neck.

"I don't want to anymore," she said, and put her hand out. Her hand came down hard on his chest. "Jesus Christ Almighty—"

"What is it?" Alex said.

She walked away from him, stood by one of the machines and bowed her head, leaning with both hands. "Shit-fuck-piss."

"What's the matter?"

She turned around, arranged her hair. "You ever have a hospital disease?"

"What's that," he said.

"Shit—a disease where you have to go to the hospital."

"I've never been in a hospital."

"I was. I know everything about it. I was in one a long time when I was seven."

"How come?"

She looked at the ceiling, sighed. "With a disease. A hospital disease. Something I don't want to talk about." She put her shorts back on, stood there breathing slowly, and then she moved toward the door. "We better open the door now."

He nodded, was relieved.

"We'll be steadies—okay?" she said.

"Okay," he said.

As she opened the door there was a clap of thunder that made them both shrink back for a moment. Amy took his hand.

"Say 'fuck,'" she said.

"Why? You say it."

She frowned. "I just did."

"Say it again."

"Jesus. Will you say it? That'll be a pact. It'll mean we're really in love because we can say it in front of each other."

"Fuck," he said.

"There," she said. "Fuck."

They walked down toward the tennis court and the swing set. "Want to go over to the high school and watch them practice?" he said.

"Practice what?"

"Baseball."

"No."

Presently she said, "My mother thinks I won't get into any trouble if I hang around with you. When I did this in New York, I got caught—me and this big kid—sixteen years old. He's the one that showed me how to French-kiss and what to do with his finger and all sorts of things. Do you know what ministration is?"

"No," Alex said.

"I been doing it for almost a year now."

"What is it?"

"It's when your womb cleans out—every month. So you won't have a baby. Or it means you didn't."

The tennis court was empty now, and above the buildings the sky was lowering, dark. The leaves of the maple saplings along the sidewalk were blown to a lighter green by a sudden wind, heavy and moist. It would storm. There was a high whistling in the eaves of the buildings, and as they entered the field Amy put her arm around him. He resisted the urge to make her remove it, but all the same he felt naked, exposed, watched from every window. The wind began to throw large drops of rain at them; and then, as though it were carried along by the stirring of leaves and the rush of raining air, Alex heard his name.

"That's your mother," Amy said.

The voice was broken, seemed to sob at them from the distance. Alex stepped away from her, said, "Got to get."

"I love you very much," Amy said.

He did not answer. He went through the hedgerow again, out into the courtyard, and now it was raining very hard, the asphalt liquid and shining. He was almost immediately soaked, drenched and heavy, his clothes hanging on him, and there, standing alone in the open door with her hands to her mouth and the hem of her dress getting wet, was his mother. Her eyes were enormous, the skin under them red, swollen. When she put her fingers around his arms, she squeezed so tight that he winced.

"Where were you," she said.

"The creek," he said.

"Don't lie to me—you were at the high school again. I've been calling you for twenty minutes."

"I was at the creek!" he cried.

She put her face down close to his. "The creek."

"Yes," he said. Her nails were biting into his skin. "Let go."

And now her mouth opened wide on two words: "WAKE UP!" She shook him. "Wake up wake up wake up wake up!" She yanked him inside. Water ran from him everywhere and his clothes were cold, clinging. She led him through the apartment to his room, shoved him in, and slammed the door. But her voice was booming on the other side. "You get RAINED on. Hear me? RAINED on if you don't wake up."

"Yes," he said. "Yes."

He removed his clothes, put on a dry pair of Jockey shorts, and crawled into his bed. She had gone, finally, and there was no sound anymore except the rain and his breathing.

Later, after he had heard Brinhart come home, and there had been an hour or so of listening for talking or footsteps in the hall—the boy lying quietly in his bed, dry now, and frightened and angry—Brinhart came into the room, knocked once, and entered, nodding politely. He looked tired. He wore a white shirt, open at the collar, and there were stains under the arms.

"Better get ready," he said, sitting down on the edge of the bed.

Alex looked at the wall, turning from him.

"Come on—we're supposed to have dinner with your friend, remember?"

"I don't want to go."

"Sure, you do."

"I don't."

"Well—you have to."

They listened as his mother came down the hall, past the

door. She did not look in, and they both watched her; then they were watching *for* her.

"Come on," Brinhart whispered.

"I hate her."

"Ridiculous. Oh, boy. Ridiculous. You know that's ridiculous."

The boy said nothing. He watched Brinhart run the back of his hand across his forehead, and then across his lap.

"She's just upset."

"I didn't go to the high school," Alex said. "I wanted to but I didn't."

"Come on." Brinhart stood up, opened the bureau drawer next to the bed. He brought out a clean pair of pants, a shirt, dropped them on the bed. "Put them on."

Alex began to dress, slowly, not looking at him. The window had turned to sun some time ago, and was dry. Outside was a view of the span of lawn between the hedgerow and the apartments. The leaves of the hedgerow were darker green and not drooping anymore, as though the rain had fed them. Above the low roofs of the mobile homes the sky was bright, and there were washed white clouds billowing high into the sun. Brinhart stood quiet, waiting for him.

"Maybe I'll take you over to Baltimore to watch the Orioles soon."

The boy had pulled his shirt on and was looking for a pair of socks, rummaging through the second drawer of the bureau. His mother never folded the socks anymore, never matched them.

"The hell with waiting for the old man to come up. Would you like to go?"

"I guess."

"You guess," Brinhart said. "You mean you don't know?"

"Brinhart, you've been telling me that."

"Yeah, that's right—the old man called, and I thought I'd wait for him."

"Every year—telling me and telling me."

"I'm telling you, that's right. We're going to do it too. You'll see."

"Yeah."

"Yeah, that's right. We will. Wait and see." Brinhart went out of the room, and Alex heard him in the hallway. "You don't mind if we go to the ball game soon, do you."

There was whispering. He waited in the room; he did not want to walk out there while they were doing that.

In a moment Brinhart came back in. He had a beer open. "Yeah, that's right," he said. "Your mother doesn't mind a bit. The Orioles. You and me. We'll go the next time Palmer's pitching against somebody good. A regular pitchers' duel."

"Sure."

"You want a sip of beer?"

"No."

"No thank you, Dad."

"No thank you—Dad."

Brinhart took a swallow of the beer. "Just giving you a hard time, Alex."

"Yeah. We're going to go see the Orioles."

"Like I told you."

He was dressed. He stood at the little wall mirror next to the window and combed his hair. His mother entered the room, and he saw her in the mirror. She wore her hair in a single, loosely tied braid that lay on the back of her neck. "Alex," she said, "please eat what they serve tonight and please concentrate on doing so."

"We got things in hand," Brinhart said, sipping the beer.

"Are you going to drink tonight?" she asked.

"A couple of beers," he said. "I'm laying off, really."

Alex turned from the mirror and looked at them. Brinhart had sat down on the bed and was taking another swallow of the beer. The boy's mother stood with her hands down at her sides, her hands hidden in a fold of the bell-like fan of her skirt, which was flowered, faded, too short. He was suddenly ashamed of both of them.

His mother put her hand out and touched his hair. "I'm sorry about today, Alex." She put her arms around him. "But you've just got to tell me if you're going to go off where I can't call you."

"I didn't go to the high school."

"All right."

"We're all right now," Brinhart said. He drank the last of the beer, stood up. "We better get going—we're already late."

They went out the patio door, around by the path. As they walked down the row they passed the young woman, who came in the other direction, pushing the stroller, the baby wide-eyed and attentive and quiet. The girl nodded at them, but did not stop to talk. Brinhart said, "Good evening." She nodded again, going on. Alex saw Brinhart look back at her.

"She insists on pushing that kid around the lot," his mother said. "That seems pretty stupid."

"There's really no place else to walk a kid," said Brinhart.

"Maybe she likes an audience."

They walked on in silence. On either side of them people sat on the stoops, or stood talking in the shade of the awnings. Three little girls sat in a tight circle beyond a parked station wagon, playing jacks. In one yard a small white dog barked at the end of a chain. Straight ahead the row opened into the field and the trees at the bottom of the decline, where the creek was, and Alex saw a quick swooping dark bird dip down into the top branches of one. The air was still now, cool, and he heard the confusion of sounds—the barking dog, people laughing, and the televisions and radios and record players going in the rooms. It was getting toward twilight, and the clouds he had seen earlier from his window had dispersed, were broken all along the low roofs to his left, tinged with gold.

"Is this it?" his mother said to him, "Did she say twenty-eight?"

It was the one. But before he could say so, Amy's mother came out and approached them, smiling, extending her arms. She wore a billowing pink dress that shook with her as she walked. Her hair was brushed down over her ears stiffly, and Alex noticed that she had put lipstick on, had powdered her cheeks and forehead; the powder was caked at the hairline.

"Isn't it just a perfect evening?" she said. She introduced herself to Brinhart, vigorously shaking his hand. Brinhart looked embarrassed, though he smiled and said something about the storm leaving everything so nice and clear. "Come in," Amy's mother said, and led them up the freshly swept walk. Amy stood in the door behind the screen, and when Alex looked at her, she tipped her head to the side in that odd way she had, and smiled. It was a smile that left the others out, like a secret. It meant the laundry room, and it made him nervous.

"Here we are," Stan said.

There was a confusion of introductions and hand-shakings, and Amy stood close to Alex.

"Good evening, sir," she said.

He said hello.

She leaned close, whispered, "Did you get in trouble?"

"Yes."

"So did I."

"You didn't tell—"

She put her hand on his upper arm. "No, jackass."

For a moment everyone looked at them. Amy stepped away from him, folded her arms and smiled.

"I thought he'd gone to the high school," said Alex's mother. "I was frantic."

"No," Blanche said. "They were over at the shopping center—at least that's what Amy told me."

"So you lied, Alex."

"He didn't lie," Brinhart said. "He told you he didn't go over to the high school—you didn't ask him *where* he'd gone."

"He lied, Gordon—he told me he'd been at the creek."

"And so he was. That's not lying—that's withholding information."

"He meant to deceive."

"Well—"

It became very quiet. Alex watched his mother walk into the room, and he could see that she was trying to control anger. She turned, looked at him coldly.

"Well," Stan said. "They're both safe now." He offered Brinhart a drink.

"What're you drinking?" Brinhart said.

"Beer—but I have wine and whiskey."

"Beer. I better stick with beer."

They all sat down. The room was surprisingly big. There was a light-blue shag rug, soft and thick, and the walls were a shade of blue, with darker blue flowers in patterns along the one that gave access to the kitchen. Two white bean chairs were on one side of the room, across from an enormous sofa and a black rocking chair. Along the wall under the windows was a series of white-painted wooden shelves crowded with books and magazines and record albums, and above the highest shelf, the television, a small portable, sat with its antennas pushed down.

"Nice collection of books," Brinhart said.

"Stan is very well-read," said Blanche.

Stan was in the kitchen making the drinks, but he called out, "Nobody's well-read in the face of what there is to be read." Then he stood at the entrance. "I'm making a Coke for the two kids, and I know you want wine, Blanche."

"Coke," Alex's mother said.

"Coke. Good. Three Cokes."

"That's the real thing we've been looking for in the back of our minds," Brinhart said. He laughed.

"Coke it is," Stan called from the kitchen.

"I'm having asparagus tips in Cheddar cheese, and a nice salad," Blanche said.

No one answered her.

"Amy, you know—Amy reads a lot too. She's read *Gone with the Wind* about twelve times."

"You let her read *Gone with the Wind?*"

"Sure," Brinhart said. "What's wrong with that?"

"I suppose it is a little racy," said Blanche.

Stan came in with the drinks on a metal tray, and while he walked from person to person it was quiet. "There you go," he murmured, as each drink was lifted from the tray. "There you go, there you go."

"So what do you do, Mr. Brinhart?" Blanche asked.

"I drink beer."

They laughed politely.

"No, really—I sell insurance right now."

"You thinking of getting out of it?" asked Stan. He had passed all the drinks out and was sitting in one of the bean chairs. The chair looked like a giant pillow.

Brinhart drank his beer, held one hand up, as if to say "Wait." Then he smacked his lips, "Ah, that's good. No, I'm—well, for now I'm staying put, I guess."

"Is it life insurance?" Blanche said.

"Yes."

"Do you work, Mrs. Brinhart?"

"No."

"I worked right up till this past March."

"Really."

"That's good," Brinhart said. "Two syllables. Keep trying, Katherine—maybe you can get all the way up to ten." He leaned forward, looking at Stan. "She's still mad about what these kids did today."

"Gordon, please shut up and drink your beer."

"Now there's a command I can follow with all sorts of good cheer."

There was another silence, and then Amy stood up. "We're going outside."

"Don't you two go out of the yard," said Blanche.

"We might be in-laws before we're through," Brinhart said. He stood up. "I'm out of beer already."

"Let me get you another," Stan said.

"We're going." Amy turned to Alex. "Come *on*."

He followed her out to the stoop and sat down beside her in the shade. There were people under the awnings and in the yards, and from somewhere came the odor of steak cooking on a grill.

"Well, you get asparagus," she said.

They drank from their glasses. She shook hers slightly, reached in among the ice cubes, and brought something back on her finger. "Eww." She wiped the finger against her hip. Alex looked away, saw a woman bend to spank a small boy in the next yard, and, a little farther down, two older boys getting into a convertible. Everything was confused and noisy and the Coke made him hiccup hot stinging fumes through his nose.

"So I got you in trouble anyway," Amy said.

He shrugged. He didn't care now. He was going to have to find a way to eat the asparagus, to concentrate and get it eaten as quickly as everyone else ate it.

"We should've got our stories straight."

He drank the Coke.

"What's wrong?"

"Nothing." He heard Brinhart laugh on the other side of the door, and then he thought he heard his mother's voice.

"She's fucked, isn't she?" Amy said.

"Who?"

"Your mother. I mean, she's pissed off."

"I don't know."

"Is your father always like that?"

"He's my stepfather."

"I saw her yelling at you this afternoon."

"She wasn't yelling at me."

"Okay—I just saw her and heard her. I got yelled at too, you know."

He said nothing. The windows across the way were brilliant now, like fires, and the sky above the apartment roofs, beyond the trailers and the hedgerow, was a stormy blue. The boys in the convertible down the way were gunning the engine, and a cloud of exhaust smoke rose and hovered above them.

"My mother won't let me breathe," Amy said. "Is yours like that?"

"No."

"She looks like she is."

"She's not."

"You can tell me if she is, you know. We're lovers."

"She *isn't*."

"*Okay*. What's wrong with you anyway?"

"Nothing." He did not want to talk about his parents—he did not want to talk at all, hearing Brinhart laugh again, too loud.

Presently Amy said, "Want more Coke?"

"No."

She took his glass and set it, with hers, between them, breathed a sigh, stretched her arms out, put them down in her lap. "I was real sick when I was seven, and my mother never got over it."

"What did you have?"

"I still have it—or, I mean, it can come back any time."

"What is it?"

She looked back at the door, then at him. "No. Maybe sometime. I don't like anybody to know."

"Is it bad?"

"It's terrible."

"Tell me."

"No." She shook her head with a sort of shudder. "I don't want to, now."

They were quiet for a moment.

"You ever been to Washington?" she asked.

"Sure, lots of times."

"Ever see the medical center? The one they advertise on TV?"

"I never saw any medical center. I saw the monuments and the Capitol."

"It's the one that's free if you can't pay."

"No."

"That's why we moved here. Because that's in Washington."

"Why didn't you move to Washington?"

"Too much money—and my mother had this trailer."

"Is what you have catching?" he asked.

She frowned, narrowing her eyes. "Yes, and you're going to get it and then you'll have to go there too."

"Where?"

She looked at the sky. "You *are* dense."

He did not answer.

"But you're cute. Chubby, but cute. You know, Harmon was a fat boy."

"Who is Harmon?"

"I told you. The sixteen-year-old."

Alex stared out at the opposite trailer. An old woman was coming out the door there, moving very slowly, leaning on a dark cane. Behind her another woman, with a purse dangling from her arm, held the door, leaning over the old woman's shoulder.

"I don't want to get old like that," Amy said.

He said nothing.

"Do you think I'm pretty?"

"No."

She scowled. "Do you at least think I'm cute?"

"I guess."

"Do you love me?"

It was crazy. "What was the matter with you today?" he asked.

"When?"

"You know—the laundry room. When you cussed."

"I cuss all the time."

"No," he said. "You got—you looked sick. Like you hurt."

"Oh, that. I got dizzy. I don't like to get dizzy. I thought something was happening to me, but it's not. It's just a little dizzy. I'm supposed to ministrate soon."

"Does that hurt?"

"No. It makes you dizzy. And you have cramps. Little cramps down here," she touched her lower belly, smiled at him. "Don't you know anything at all?"

"I'm not a girl," he said.

She shrugged. "Yeah, that's for sure. I wonder where dinner is?"

"I hate asparagus."

"Eat the cheese and spread the rest around the plate. The cheese is good."

"I thought you said you could eat anything in the world."

"I can. I'm just telling *you* what to do."

They were quiet again. They went a long time without speaking. Amy swung her legs and hummed a song, and the sound of her voice distracted him. He thought he had heard one of them inside say something about the Orioles. Maybe Brinhart really would take him this time.

"Does your father like baseball?" he asked.

"Nope."

"They're talking about the Orioles."

"What's a bird got to do with baseball?"

"Don't you watch television?" he said. "Don't you read the newspapers?"

"Daddy hates television, and Mother thinks newspapers are depressing."

"Your father doesn't read newspapers?"

"He just reads his books."

"Jesus."

"He's an expert on the order of insects."

"The what?"

"The kinds, the—families, you know."

"You mean like spider and bee and ant?"

"A spider is not an insect."

"What is it if it isn't?"

"A spider is a mean, evil thing."

"It's a bug."

"Well," she said, "it doesn't matter anyway."

The light began to fail rapidly now, and people went inside or drove away, or pulled in and were greeted. The sky unfolded a few weak stars.

"Something must be wrong with dinner," she said.

"I hope so."

"Want to French-kiss?"

"No—they'll see us."

"We can go around back."

He followed her through tall grass to the weed patch behind the trailer; here they faced the dark shape of the neighboring trailer, and Alex saw laundry, white and waving from a line in the next yard. There were yellow windows all around them. She held his face and kissed him, put her tongue in his mouth. This surprised him, and he had not made his mind up about it; yet it was pleasurable, it excited him. And now she stopped, her face a dim white oval in the dark.

"Now you," she said.

He put his tongue in her mouth; her mouth tasted sweet.

"Do you like it?" she said. "Isn't it just divine?"

"It's funny."

"Funny."

"It feels funny, but I like it."

She jumped. "Oh, a web." She waved her arms wildly. Then she told him how she hated spiders. "Don't you hate them?" she said. She did not give him a chance to answer. She told him that she did not even like to see pictures of spiders and when she walked through a web, it made her sick. She said she had hated them since she was seven and she had been in the hospital and they gave her something that when she slept, she dreamed spiders were all over her body. It was a horrible dream, and she had it all the time when she was in the hospital, these spiders and their sticky webs, all over her. She shuddered and asked him if he wanted to French-kiss again.

"You do it to me this time," she said.

But someone opened a window nearby, rattling aluminum, and she pulled him down in a little bare place, the grass tall and shielding all around them. He squatted there, hugging his knees; he could feel his own heart beating.

"We better get back," she said.

VIII ❧

ABOUT HALFWAY through his fifth beer, Brinhart decided that he liked Stan. Stan was fascinating about his insects, had all those brightly illustrated books with the exotic kinds, habitats, settings—the crazy names: -optera or Phylloxera. All those -opteras and the common ordinary housefly that has six thousand eyes. He was enjoying himself and he didn't mind that dinner was yet to be served or that Katherine and Blanche weren't saying much. He could see that Katherine had let go of her anger at the boy, at least for the time being: she seemed all right, she was still sipping the one Coke, which was pale now, the ice having melted into it. Blanche still had her glass of wine. The two of them were being polite, and at one point Stan said he was drunk, or getting drunk, and Katherine gave a little laugh, the softest, the most pleasant little trilling, high in her throat. She said, "Gordon is quite sober, of course." From time to time Blanche had gone into the kitchen to check the dinner, and she came back each time complaining about the stove and how one couldn't tell what heat one was getting from an electric oven, how she hated them. She kept saying she was sorry. Brinhart joked about skipping dinner and getting to the hard drinking, and they all laughed. He looked at Katherine and felt warm with love.

"I love you," he said, "boo-boo-boo." Pursing his lips.

"They're so passionate when they get a little beer in them," Blanche said.

"You've noticed that," said Katherine.

"We're always like that," Stan said. "The beer just brings it out."

Blanche stood up. Katherine looked at her. "Our two drunks," she said.

"You know," Stan said now, "Blanche only weighed ninety pounds when I met her—or ninety-five." He was sitting on a green hassock, facing Brinhart, who was on the sofa. "Doctor told her she would have trouble giving birth if she didn't put on some weight. Told her to drink one beer a day for a year. And look at her."

Blanche had gone into the kitchen again, and was coming out as he finished. "Look at who?" she said.

"I was telling Gordon what you weighed before we were married."

"That's his favorite story," Blanche said. "He likes to dream."

"I'm happy."

She sat down in the rocker. Brinhart glanced at Katherine, touched her wrist. She sipped the pale Coke.

"Katherine was in a band when I met her."

"What sort of band?" Blanche asked. "What instrument did you play?"

"Guitar," Brinhart said. "Lead guitar. It was a really good rock 'n' roll band."

Stan was impressed. "Will you play for us?"

"I don't play anymore," Katherine said. "I sold my guitar a long time ago."

"We have an old guitar around here somewhere, don't we, Blanche?"

"It's a cheapie. Nylon strings. I got it for Amy a few years ago. When she was—" Blanche paused, thinking. "We have all this somewhere. When she was ten. Right, Stan?"

"The tenth birthday. Yes. She played it for about a month and that was that. She said it was too hard."

"It is hard," Katherine said. "Very hard."

"Would you play for us if I can turn it up?" Stan asked. "No."

"Oh, come on, honey," said Brinhart.

"I haven't touched a guitar in ten years. Don't be absurd."

"Does it really leave you—the ability? The skill?" asked Blanche.

"Nah," Brinhart said. "She took a vow when she quit. A cabala with herself."

"Gordo, don't be an ass."

"It's a shame," Blanche said, "to give something like that up. If I could play music—"

"It was all a long time ago," Katherine said.

"Yes, but surely you can change your mind—you don't have to play rock 'n' roll."

Katherine's silence left a space in the conversation; it made everyone uneasy. Brinhart had finished his beer and so he got up, walked into the kitchen for more. "You want another one, Stan?"

"Sure."

"Gordon, for God's sake. We don't live here."

"I'm making myself at home—we're informal, right, Stan?"

"Right."

"What else can he say, Gordon?"

"No, really," Stan said. "Really."

"Stan can feel the same at our place," Brinhart said. He got two beers from the refrigerator. He liked these people very much, and it was going to be a nice long evening, and all of his worries were over. Everything would be all right and when he heard Katherine laugh at something Blanche had murmured, he stood in a sweet chill, opening the beers. He wanted to do everything for her.

"Honey," he called, "you want another Coke?"

"No, Gordon."

"Blanche, more wine?"

"I'm not finished this yet."

"Women don't know how to drink right," he said for them all. He felt entertaining and clownish in the best way. And he was not drunk; he had only had a few beers. He walked back into the living room, gave Stan his beer, sat down. "I'll tell you," he said, "I don't know why I ever drink whiskey."

"Whiskey'll kill you."

"To beer." Brinhart held his can up. "A toast."

"So," Stan said, "what's happened to dinner?"

"I turned it up to five hundred," Blanche said.

"Have you been to Washington yet?" Brinhart asked.

"I have," Stan said. "Looked over the medical center."

"Medical center? You planning on getting the D.T.'s?"

Stan smiled, looked down. "No. The—it's the Children's National Medical Center."

"They're free if you can't pay," Blanche said. "And God knows, we can't pay."

"You're—you—are you using it?" asked Brinhart.

"Well—yes."

There was an awkward quiet.

"For—uh, over a year now. Since I've been out of work. The trips down here—the, uh—the trips got pretty expensive, see. And since Blanche owned this trailer."

"I'd been renting it out for years," Blanche said. "It belonged to my parents when they retired, and I didn't have the heart to sell it after they were gone. My father willed it to me, poor thing. It was all he had left in the world when he died."

"He left a little insurance money too," Stan said.

"Yes. We've been using that. And unemployment."

"What do you do?" Brinhart asked the other man. He wanted to help. He thought of Amy out there on the porch with Alex.

"Well," Stan was saying, "I went to a teachers college because that was what I wanted to do. Teach. But I got laid off teaching, and there just isn't a job to be had out there."

"What was your subject?"

"Biology."

"Oh, yeah. The insects."

"It's none of my business," Katherine said, "but is something wrong with Amy?"

Apparently Stan hadn't heard the question. He said, "Do you know of a job to be had around here? Anything now. Not just teaching."

"Ever think of selling insurance?" Brinhart asked.

"I've thought about almost anything you care to name."

"Maybe I can get you something where I work."

"Oh, Gordon," Katherine said, "you're not in a position to do anything—"

"I might be able to get him something."

Katherine looked at Stan. "He can't do anything for you. It's the beer."

"It is not the beer, Katherine."

She sat forward, still looking at Stan. "Is there something—is Amy all right?"

"I can get you something, Stan."

"You can get another beer, Gordon."

It was now very quiet. Brinhart sipped the beer and stared at the books along the wall. He felt helplessly ridiculed, trapped into this silence, and he had a murderous desire to put Katherine in this position.

"Is Amy . . . ill?" Katherine said now, very gently.

Blanche cleared her throat. "Well, when—"

But her husband interrupted her. "Amy is—uh, she's rather sensitive about this. She doesn't like people to know —doesn't like to think people are talking about her or watching her."

This was Brinhart's opening. "That's the way Katherine feels about *her* problem," he said, and immediately felt the cruelty of it.

Stan hesitated, then went on. "It's just something we've had to learn how to live with. And I think it's best if we leave it at that, and let Amy decide what else we might say."

"That is very kind," said Katherine.

"We can tell the adults," Blanche said. "Can't we?"

"Do you really want to go against her wishes?" Stan said.

"Don't put it that way."

"I didn't mean anything by it—"

Blanche got up and walked across the room to the entrance of the kitchen. "You make it sound—you know I wouldn't do anything to hurt her."

"All right, honey."

She seemed to wrench herself through the opening. For a few moments, in the quiet, they all heard her taking the dinner out of the oven, the oven door creaking and then slamming, her muttered curses, a clatter of dishes and cabinet doors.

"We'd never say a word to anyone," Katherine said in a low voice.

"I know," Stan said, "I'm probably being silly. It's just that we're in limbo, see, and we don't know anything for sure, and we're trying some things—"

Blanche came into the room and stood before them. "As you can guess," she said, "I've ruined the dinner." Her chin bunched up and then, abruptly, she was crying.

"Oh, honey," Stan said, rising quickly and putting his arms around her.

"I'm sorry," she said.

"Hey," Brinhart said, "we can go get a pizza or something. Right, Stan? There's no need to be upset about dinner—"

"I'm sorry, honey," said Blanche, and her large hand went up to Stan's face.

"It's all right, sugar."

"Let's go get a pizza, Stan." Brinhart stood up. Katherine's ankle came against his ankle, and he turned. "What?"

Stan led his wife back to the rocker, held her hands while she sat down. Then he looked at Brinhart.

"What do you say?" Brinhart said. "Want to go get a pizza?"

"I'm afraid I—we don't have much appetite now."

"I think we should be leaving," Katherine said.

"I'm terribly sorry. Maybe we can try it another time."

"Yes, that would be nice. Another time."

"You all go ahead and get a pizza, Stan," Blanche said. She was drying her eyes with the tips of her fingers.

"No, I think we ought to call it a night."

"We can't send these people away hungry."

"Look," Brinhart said. "Don't worry about us." In the fog of his anger at Katherine everything had got away from him; he wanted to recover it all, somehow.

"I'm really very sorry," Stan said.

"Come on," said Katherine, rising, taking Brinhart by the arm, "We can fix something quick at home." She turned to Blanche. "We can feed Amy if you like."

"No. No, thank you."

"I hope you'll forgive us," Stan said.

Brinhart told him there was nothing to forgive.

It was very dark as they walked up the row toward the path. Katherine walked a little ahead of Brinhart, holding Alex's hand. The boy looked dejected, walking head down, kicking dirt and stones. Katherine told him in a measured voice to stop it, and he took his hand from hers. The air was very cool now and the sky was clear, faintly whitened by a milky swath of stars above the moon. In the windows on either side of them were crossing shadows, television screens giving off silver light. Locusts and crickets had set up their night racket, and the going-by of cars and trucks on the highway, far behind them, was like the distant humming of some tremendous machine. It struck a nerve of loneliness in Brinhart, stumbling home with his wife and adopted son, past the little picket fence and on up the row, a weird dissatisfaction following them, like a fourth walker, a shadow of grief and unhappiness and anger.

"Katherine," he said, "what was that?"

"I'll tell you when we get home."

"Tell me *now*." He had spoken too loud.

She walked on for a moment, but then she stopped. "Alex, you go on ahead, we'll be right home."

"I don't want to go by myself," Alex said.

"Do as I tell you."

The boy went on up to the path and out of sight behind the heavy shadow of the hedgerow.

"You want to know what that was?" Katherine said. She was still watching where the boy had gone; Brinhart gazed at the side of her face.

"I'm waiting."

"There's something very wrong with Amy."

"I got that something was wrong—"

"Well—that's what happened."

"No," he said. "The something that was wrong was there when we got there—why should it—"

"I think Amy is very sick with something."

They walked on.

"The drinking didn't help things either."

"Oh, hell. A little beer."

"You're both drunk."

"I'm—I am not drunk."

"You were embarrassingly drunk, Gordo."

"Oh, fuck."

"You offered him a job," she said. "Do you realize that?"

"I said I might be able to get him something."

They had entered the path, and now Brinhart did not want to talk anymore.

"Do you think I ought to keep him away from Amy?" Katherine asked.

"For Christ's sake, no."

"We have enough problems."

"Don't be an ass," he said.

"Well—we don't need theirs too, do we?"

He would say something to her in the morning: he did not want to talk anymore. He was tired, he could feel the beer in his stomach, and he wanted to take an aspirin and go to bed. He looked at her as they entered the lot; for an unnerving second or two he did not recognize her. It was truly as though he had never seen her before in his life.

Book Two

IX

DINNER HAD BEEN late again; it was already twilight. Katherine sat staring at her food, pork chops she had fried in flour and eggs; the pork chops were covered with fine shingles of white where the flour hadn't mixed with the eggs. Brinhart ate everything—the meat and the canned peas and the instant mashed potatoes. He drank beer with dinner and he would have one more out on the patio. It had been a relatively smooth week. Three days of rain, then intermittent showers, and he and Katherine had made love in the morning while a soft wind blew water out of the trees. He had driven to work listening to the radio, and the disc jockeys were funny. The sun had come out.

He had come home to this.

"The mashed potatoes are excellent," he said. He had meant to be funny.

Neither Katherine nor Alex looked at him. Alex had eaten some of the peas, and now held one pork chop to his mouth, nibbling at it.

"Love those mashed potatoes."

"Please," Katherine said.

"You two fight today? You haven't said a word to each other all evening."

"Do you want to tell him, Alex?" she said.

The boy put his food away from him and left the table, walked down the hall, and slammed the door to his room.

"You tell me," Brinhart said.

Katherine was silent. She did not look at him. In a moment Alex came back through the living room; he slammed the front door too.

"Wonderful," Brinhart said. "Do you want to please tell me?"

She picked up her fork, pressed it into the mashed potatoes on her plate, sighed, "I don't even like him sometimes."

"That's mutual—probably."

"Do you know what I caught him doing today?"

"Fucking Amy?"

"*Stop* it, Gordon."

"All right," he said. "Tell me."

"Why do you have to say things like that?"

"Go ahead, will you?"

She sighed again, gazed at the wall. "He was lying out under the hedgerow saying a baseball game, pitch by pitch, like an announcer or something, like he was announcing the thing over the radio."

"Yes?"

"Gordon, he wasn't even there. I had to call his name three or four times, and he didn't move until I took him by the arm."

"Katherine," he said. "It isn't anything to worry about."

"It is. You just bet it is."

"Was he with Amy today at all?"

"In the morning. She and her parents went into Washington this afternoon."

"Did you speak to them?"

"No."

"Alex told you."

She stood up, seemed about to clear the table, then walked aimlessly around the living room. "I never found my lighter, and now I can't find my cigarettes."

Brinhart said, "I'm going out on the patio."

"Good." Her voice was unfriendly, aggressive. "Alex just went out front."

"I don't know what you want me to do, Katherine."

"Go on. Did I say anything?"

"Lovie," Brinhart said. "Sweet."

"You go to hell."

"That's very good. That's wonderful."

She found the cigarettes on the floor, between the end table and the sofa, where they had fallen. "The cellophane," she said. "The cellophane is wet." She got down on her knees. "My God. We have a leak. There's water here."

"All that rain this week."

"It came through."

"I'll talk to the management."

"Suppose it's leaking in the walls—the wires. It could cause a fire."

"I'll say something to them."

"Can't you do anything now?"

"It's not raining now, and the emergency number is only for emergencies. This isn't an emergency. I'll speak to them tomorrow, I promise."

"But suppose the wires are wet now?"

"You smell smoke?" Brinhart said.

"Go out on the patio, Gordon."

"Come outside with me?"

"No."

"Come on," he said.

She came back to the table, sat down, lighted a cigarette. "You go ahead."

"Why do you want to sit here by yourself, honey?"

She looked at him, blew smoke; her hands shook. "I'm all fucked up right now, Gordo." Then she seemed to grimace, her teeth showing. "It's getting worse."

"Honey," he said.

She sobbed once, quite loud. The suddenness of it frightened him. He wanted to be anywhere, and he looked at the white knuckles of her hand over her mouth.

"Oh, sweet," he said. "Sweet poor Katherine."

"Don't," she mumbled.

"It's all right," he said. "You're all right."

Then, with a quick shuddering look she said, barely moving her lips, "I think I want to play guitar again." She had put both hands down on the table, the lighted cigarette jutting between the fingers of the one nearest Brinhart. He touched that wrist. "Sure," he said. "There you go."

"Don't—patronize." Now she crushed the cigarette in the food on her plate, and rubbed her eyes. "I'm just—I just—"

"You can do anything you want," Brinhart said.

"I'm just so scared all the time."

"You'll—you can start up right away."

"No," she said. "It's too late. I don't want to anyway. I want to be like—why can't I just be anyone, Gordo? Why is that? Look at Blanche. Look at what she must be living with. Why can't I be like that?"

He stood up. "Why do you have to be like that—Katherine, for Christ's sake. Stop doing this to yourself—"

"I'm crazy, of course."

"You only think that when you're scared."

"No."

"Ask yourself—for Christ's sake ask yourself what you're afraid of."

"You know what I'm afraid of now?" she said. "I'm afraid—I'm terrified that Amy is going to die of whatever it is that she has. I'm afraid I'll find out what it is and I

won't be able to stand it when I do. I'm afraid I'm losing
you and that I've already lost Alex—"

"That's crazy—"

"Yes," she said. "That's crazy."

"Crazy. Silly. A waste of time."

She was silent.

"Worrying over nothing."

"Ah," she said, "I have to get out of this."

"It passes, honey. It's always passed."

"It just gets worse, every time." Now she was shivering.

He put his arms around her—the solidness of her shoulders, he couldn't get under, get through. He held her face
in his hands. "It'll get better. You'll feel better in the morning."

"I never took drugs," she said, "I was never really part
of it. Just the music and the talk."

"You'll see. Worrying over nothing."

She sighed, patted the back of his hand. "Will you—
could I be alone, just for a little? Go out and bring Alex
back, okay? I want to apologize."

"Sure," he said. He was anxious to get away, to get out,
away from her and the rooms of the apartment. Briefly he
saw himself walking down that highway Aunt Beth had
described—alone, going toward his father, in a twilight—
that stretch of highway he had searched for all the way
down the peninsula on the one visit to Florida and had not
been able to find, and Katherine had kept saying, "Is this
it? I'll bet this is it," and her constant guessing had irritated
him and he had thought about it, thought about riding
down once by himself, just to see. Now he saw himself that
way, alone, in a white shirt open at the collar and his mind
placed Katherine far behind, somewhere off in the night.
He had often imagined the drummer who had fathered
Alex to be out there, gone, buried in distance, in memory:
it was frightening. It was as if he had already abandoned

Katherine and the boy, as though somehow, in that moment, he became the drummer. When he looked at Katherine's face, he saw eyes, a nose, lips, hair—and that was all: each held its separate familiarity for him, but he could not make a recognizable face out of them. And so he touched her cheek, could feel in himself the wish to be reassured of her presence, her very identity.

"All right now?" he managed to say.

She rubbed her eyes with the palms of her hands, "Ah," she said, "I'm wonderful."

"Wonderful," he said. "That's right."

"I think I'm going to get some sleeping pills. Would you mind if I got some sleeping pills?"

"Would I mind."

"Say so if you would. Really. I think, if I could just sleep."

"I'll get some for you, hell. Do I mind."

"Would you go get Alex now?" she asked.

"Sure."

"I'm going to bed."

"Want me to go get you some pills?"

She touched his hip. "Not now. Tomorrow."

He went out. He had missed the girl's walk and he had been looking forward to it. Coming home from work in the car, he had marked the clear sky and the cool sun and thought about sitting on the patio with the newspaper and Shirley Ann Comminger making her walk. He thought abruptly of the poor young woman whose tragedy he had stumbled onto over the telephone and was filled with the most confusing array of emotions, a dizzying tangle of memory and image—his father and Aunt Beth in the shade of the gazebo, Katherine shrieking into a microphone, Alex's baseball mementos, the sea off the Florida coast, Shirley, Stan's laughing face in the warm glow of too much beer. It dazed him, made him forget what he had

come to do, why he was here and not inside. He went to
the edge of the lot, stood there for a moment, trying to
remember. It was warmer now, a breeze blowing out of the
south. Lightning bugs rose out of the grass and up from the
black trunks of the trees. In the red sky crows were caw-
ing, and he saw bats, small as sparrows, fluttering against
the last light. For the first time in a long while—perhaps
since that evening at Aunt Beth's—he had an almost physical sense of the past; it all seemed to merge in him, to
become one time and place, inexplicably mixed with that
far-off highway, that raised roadbed and the groves of cypress. The sky before him was any sky; it was anyplace,
and for some reason this made him all the more aware of
Katherine sitting alone and unprotected in the apartment,
with no help anywhere; above him stars were beginning to
show. As he stepped out into the lot he remembered that
Alex was out here somewhere, so he called once. His voice
went out and came back in a soft echo, as though the
coming night were a vast chamber. He clung to the simple
order of the hedgerow and the path, the gravel road between the rows of mobile homes.

At the dilapidated picket fence he stopped, gazed at the
blue-curtained front windows, the light on the other side
showing every stitch of the cloth. And then Alex came
toward him from Amy's trailer. The boy walked slowly,
head down, and when he saw Brinhart, he stopped, seemed
about to turn around.

"Little late to be out," Brinhart said.

"They're not home," Alex said. "I waited."

"Isn't it a little late to be out?"

"What do you care."

"I care. Your mother cares. She cares too much."

"Sure."

"She loves you."

"Sure."

"Great vocabulary you have."

"All right. Okay? All right."

"We're going to have to be careful for a while, kid."

"She doesn't have to jump on me all the time," Alex said.

"She wants to apologize to you. She sent me for you."

"Sure."

"Sure, sure. Jesus, you ought to write speeches. That's wonderful."

"And you can lay off me too."

"Sure," Brinhart said.

"Just because she's—"

"Just because she's what?"

The boy kicked at a small broken pull toy at the edge of the grass. "Nothing."

"You're a smart boy," Brinhart said. "Use your brain and be nice."

Alex sniffed, ran the back of his hand across his mouth, looked to Brinhart's right. Shirley had come out, was walking across the bare lawn to stand at the fence. She smiled. "Hello."

Brinhart nodded. Alex walked past him, started up the row. "Where you going?"

"Home," the boy said. "Aren't you coming?"

"I'll—wait a minute."

Alex stood quite motionless, watching him.

"Is this your boy?" Shirley said.

"This is Alex."

"Hello, Alex."

"H'lo," Alex said, still looking at Brinhart.

"Go ahead," Brinhart told him. "I'll follow."

The boy shrugged, turned, and walked on in the gathering dark. Brinhart watched until he stepped onto the path, and then he turned to the girl. She stood with arms folded, looking at him. He cleared his throat, said "Nice night," and his voice bumped on something back of his tongue.

"That's a nice-looking boy," she said.

"He's my stepson."

"You have more?"

"No—just the one."

"You're—I don't remember your name."

"Brinhart, Gordon Brinhart."

"What's going on, Brinhart Gordon Brinhart?"

"No—just Gordon Brin—"

She laughed. "I *know*."

Then there didn't seem to be anything else to say.

"I came after Alex," he said. "You know, to bring him home."

"He seems lonely," Shirley said. "I saw him come by here earlier. He seems unhappy."

"He daydreams, really. He's all right." Brinhart glanced up at the path where the path cut through the hedgerow and knew that he should be there now, walking away; but he did not—he wasn't at all sure he could—move. The idea of the apartment, the quiet he would find, Katherine lying awake in the bed with the television on and the boy in his room, made him aware of his stomach.

"I saw you looking at my windows," Shirley said now.

"Was I?"

"What were you looking for."

"I was looking for my boy."

"I don't even know you," she said, and smiled. Then she extended her hand. "Shirley."

"Yes. Shirley." He took the hand, it was soft and limp.

"I don't usually talk to strangers, but I'm by myself tonight and I got lonely."

Brinhart was aware of how flabby he was, how much out of shape, how young *she* was. He did not know what he was doing here. The girl went on.

"Red's in town a lot in the evenings, seeing Max. Oh, you don't know Red yet. Red's a sweetheart. We hooked up in December. Traveling. We're sort of married, I guess.

I'm from Iowa and he's from here. He's an electrician but
he works where he wants to and he wanted to come here,
so I came with him. His friend Max—that's the one he
goes to see?—Max is a friend from the army. Red and
Max were in the army together and Max married Red's
sister and now Red's sister is dead and so Max doesn't have
anybody. They're great friends. I met Red on a bus, see.
We were on this bus from Saint Louis, and I'd been on the
road awhile, just sort of traveling around with some money
I got for turning eighteen. So we were on this bus and
we got to talking . . ." She went on, a musical and child-
like modulation and inflection that seemed almost too natural, as though acquired through practice. She toyed with
the collar of her blouse, a white, loosely fitting thing she
had tied at the waist; it fitted as a man's shirt would fit
her, but there were frills on the short sleeves. He tried
mightily to listen and in the effort lost the thread entirely.
". . . so with something like that I never had much real
family and never anything like a father. Red's old all right,
but he's nice to me, and so I guess you could say he sort of
fills the gap where I'm missing a father."

"Red is your husband?" he asked.

"No, no, no. No, we're not really married. I mean it just
looks that way, you know, but we're really only friends
now. I mean it's more like he's my father." She shifted her
weight, leaning toward him. "I know I'm just going on and
on. Sometimes I come out here at night and just hope
somebody'll stop and talk. It's hard talking to a six-month-
old baby. Red—when Red's here, he falls asleep a lot in
front of the television. Five minutes into a movie and
bang. Gone."

"I do that," Brinhart said.

"I hate that," she said.

"Television puts me to sleep. I try not to watch too
much of it."

"Me too," she said. She was animated now, her eyes wide and bright. "I really hate television. It depresses me. I can't watch it very long without feeling like I'm going to freak out or something."

"I watch the movies."

"Me too. The old ones."

"Yes, I like the old ones."

"You know what I wonder?" she asked. "I wonder—at the end of a movie, you know, and everybody's happy and the couple find a way to get together and the music plays so pretty, I like to think of them—the couple—years later when they're old and maybe a little unhappy. Then it's real for me, and I can believe it all."

"You're not very romantic, are you?"

She smiled. "Guess not." She was moving away. "I guess you have to get going after your boy."

"Maybe I'll see you again," he said.

"Sure," she said. "Maybe we can all get together sometime." She waved at him. "Well, bye."

"Bye."

She stepped inside quietly and shut the door. For a moment he stood gazing at the sky, thinking she might be watching him from the window. He breathed deeply, walked back up the row toward the path. The sky was clear, milky with stars, and the moon looked printed on the horizon. He thought of himself in the apartment, alone with Katherine and the boy. Then he walked back down the row, into the field and beyond, up the bank on the other side of the creek to the highway, the shopping center. There was a lounge there, a dark little place with dim red candles burning in lanternlike glass on every table. He went in and sat down and ordered a whiskey, a double, and when he was finished with that one, he ordered another. The place was not crowded. A middle-aged man sat at a piano bar in the far corner, playing ragtime. A waitress and two women stood at his shoulder. They all knew each other. Brinhart drank, and watched them. If he could just get himself calm. He thought of his father, and then tried not to think of him. Maybe Brinhart would call the old man and tell him to make up his goddamn mind, because there was the beach idea: he was still planning that. Katherine and Alex and himself. Soon. He ordered another whiskey. Three men came in who wore suits and ties—the same gray color. They were all in their forties and they all ordered beer. They sat at the table across from Brinhart's, and one of them—the tallest of the three, a man with gray hair combed high in a sweeping wave—commenced to tell a story about the CIA. He had been in the upper echelons, he said, and knew the Secret Service agent who had thrown himself onto the Kennedy car in Dallas. Brinhart listened with interest, sipping his whiskey. At one point the man raised his voice, seemed angry about something the television people had done during the emergency. He was particularly angry at somebody with CBS. Brinhart had another whiskey and still another, and he began to think of ways in which he might insinuate himself into the conversation. He thought of going to get Stan, imagined the two of them coming back to the lounge and getting a little drunk; but then he was merely numb, listening to the man go on about how badly CBS had handled things, and how the CIA really hated one reporter in particular who had gone on to become a national figure, known for his integrity and his good journalism. "The guy's a prick," the tall man said. "And now that I'm retiring, I'm going to find a way to expose him for what he is."

Brinhart stood, paid his check. He was numb, he didn't care, and so he thought he might tell the man something— all these Washington types, these gray government types, who retired and wrote government novels and who spoke with such authority and self-importance and who were so goddamn dull. He had sold life insurance to them from time to time—new options—and he had seen them at parties, the houses of people he worked with. They knew so much; they all had classified information. It was incredibly funny. Brinhart walked to the table and said, "Hello, I'm an agent for CBS. You're all under arrest."

"Who the hell are you," one of them said.

"I just told you."

"Drunk," said the tall man. "He's drunk."

"Get out of here, buddy," the third one said. He stood. "Go on, goddamn drunks."

"You're all under arrest. You have the right to keep your fucking mouths shut. . . ."

The tall one stood too now, and seemed to be reaching into his pocket. "Look here, bud. You just move on and everything will be fine."

"You have the right to make one phone call." It was just a joke. It was just a little fun to show them they weren't everything, and the world was big. That was it, Brinhart thought. The world was big and empty, and didn't they know it? Didn't they see what a stupendous joke it all was?

"The world," he said, "is just so big, boys."

The tall one moved and then Brinhart was on the floor, on his elbows, looking up at him.

"Hey!" someone yelled.

"Well get this bum away from me, will you?"

Brinhart got to his feet, walked around them, seeing them turn to watch him. He waved. The door opened to the brightness of the parking lot. Here was the 7-Eleven store, with its tight little group of lingering boys and young girls in blue jeans. They all sat around an old Lincoln, the radio was on: rock 'n' roll.

"Rock 'n' roll," Brinhart said.

"That's right, dad." A fat boy, long hair tied in back. Crooked teeth and a shirt that hung on him.

"Yeah, that's right," Brinhart said. Nothing like a 7-Eleven parking lot at night in summer.

"Try some of this, dad."

"Don't give him my good pot," said another.

"Bob Dylan," Brinhart said.

"Yeah."

"Big world."

"Right, dad. Big bottle. Right?"

"Right."

"Got any money, dad?"

"Who's your stockbroker, dad?" the fat one said.

"You got any info?" another said.

"Info," said Brinhart.

"I.T. and T."

"Whatever."

"Man, you're wasted."

"Watch out for the CIA," Brinhart said.

"Right, man. And the FBI. Right?"

"Right."

"It's a bad old world, man." The fat one raised his fist. Then he laughed. Brinhart realized that he'd staggered backward at the gesture with the fist. "You got any money, man? You act like a man with a million in his pocket. Don't he act like a man with a million in his pocket?"

"Acts like a man with a million in his pocket."

"Watch out, dad. Don't go down any dark streets."

"Bad old world," Brinhart said. He walked on. He heard them laughing and calling things to him but he did not turn around. When he reached the edge of the parking lot, he was ill, and stood leaning against the last lamppost, seeing the blur of headlights going by. Slowly he made his way across the road, stopping in the middle to let more cars pass, and then he was standing in the field, having fallen down the bank and nearly into the creek. Even so, his feet were wet. He looked up at the stars, and decided to find the Big Dipper. The good old Big Dipper that was so easy to pick out and so shapely, covering so many millions of miles out there in space. Big world, he thought. He was alone.

There was nothing anywhere but his eyes, searching for the Big Dipper. He couldn't find it. The stars were like spun webs of light all across the sky, and he couldn't find the Big Dipper. He looked at the moon, thinking to follow in a wider and wider circle out from it; but the moon floated above him like something on the surface of a pond. It was now terribly important that he find the Big Dipper, and he walked into the trailer court, still trying. He went all the way up to the path and back down to the edge of the field again, and still he couldn't make it out anywhere, though he knew it was there—he knew it was there right in front of him. At last he went up the row and stopped at Amy's trailer. There were lights on. Stan would be up, or Blanche. They'd know where to look—Stan would, for sure; Stan was a scientist. Brinhart stood in their little yard and tried one more time to find the Big Dipper, and, failing to do so, walked up the stoop and knocked on the door. He knocked three times before Stan opened it and stood looking at him.

"What in the world?" Stan said.

"Big world, Stan. Right?"

"Hello—"

"Where's the Big Dipper, Stan. I can't find it."

Stan came out on the stoop and closed the door behind him. "Look," he said. "It's late. You better be getting home."

"Yeah, right—the Big Dipper."

"You want me to take you home?"

"No—Christ, man. I live right there." Brinhart pointed. "Just show me the goddamn Big Dipper."

"You've had too much to drink," Stan said. "Go home." He opened his door, stepped inside. "You hear me? Go on home."

"Just show me the goddamn Big Dipper, and I'll go right home. Promise."

"You go right home now, all right?"

"Show me, will you?"

"There's no Big Dipper," Stan said. "There never has been."

"You sure?" Brinhart was beginning to believe this.

"Absolutely. You can only see it in the winter months."

"Oh, that's bullshit, man. You're bullshitting me."

"Go home, right now," Stan said, "or I'll call the police." He shut the door and Brinhart stood there, gazing at the sky.

X

FOR A LONG TIME he sat in a chair on the patio, leaning back, legs out straight, hands folded across his stomach. There were the crickets and the locusts, but the fireflies had gone. The traffic on the highway beyond was intermittent, like waves rolling in from the sea. It was mostly quiet. Brinhart felt as though he were the only person awake in the world. At one point he went into the apartment and searched for the cigarettes and a match, but then he changed his mind—and changed his mind about another whiskey too. He went back to the patio and sat down, and gradually the effects of what he had drunk began to wear off a little. He heard Katherine talking loud in the bedroom, and supposed that Alex was still up. He could hear the voice but he could not hear words, and he could not hear Alex. A soft, humid breeze blew. The crickets hesitated, were quiet, then began again. He got up at last and walked into the apartment, searched again for the cigarettes. He found Katherine in the bedroom, talking to her father on the extension. Brinhart had only seen the man twice since that first time in Brockton: both occasions were holidays. Katherine's parents lived in California now, but they had been there just two years: they had never lived anywhere longer than three years.

During Katherine's childhood they had owned homes in Utah, Illinois, Missouri, Louisiana—all over. It sounded like a list of the states, a roll call. And they had rented apartments in a number of other places, including one in the South of France, some years ago. Now they were in California. Katherine's father had been a troubleshooter, a quality-control man, for the federal government. He had been forty-three when Katherine was born. Now he was retired, was not about to move again, not even to visit his bad little girl, as he put it. He was unhappy about Alex's illegitimacy. During the two holiday visits—both early in the marriage and both while Katherine's parents were in transit, on their way to yet another house or apartment in yet another state—Alex had been almost totally ignored by him, though somehow this had been accomplished in a cordial way, like an oversight, nothing intentional. Brinhart hated Katherine's father, hated him all the more now, standing by the bed and watching Katherine try to make herself heard over the line, through the man's near deafness.

"Did they call us?" Brinhart asked.

"Shhhh," Katherine said. "No."

He stood watching her.

"All right," she said, "put her on."

Brinhart walked down the hall to the bathroom, drank cold water from the tap. He was beginning to feel dizzy again, and he was a little sick. He went into the living room and sat on the sofa with his head back against the cushion. So she had called them. And now she was talking to her mother. Her mother always made her miserable. If Brinhart hated the old man, he was enraged by the old man's wife, who was now fifty-nine or so, perhaps older, and who had about her husband an almost religious devotion, as though his imagined perfection reflected on her somehow. Indeed, it was as if she had molded him, created him. Well, she had, in fact: the man she looked at out of her sharp brown eyes bore little relation to the man as he actually was. If there was anything Brinhart hated with an unabstract hatred, it was this quality of the old woman's of seeing only what she wanted to see. According to Katherine's mother it was a sort of disgrace to be ill, or to fall short, or to die. Perfection was possible, if one wanted it badly enough. And what had rankled him more than anything was that this deluded way of seeing had been handed down to Katherine. Except that for Katherine it was inside out: she saw only how much things *failed* perfection, the margin by which things missed what her mother made up, and of course Katherine suffered for the difference. Oh, how she suffered for it. It had been done to her, this need—manifest somehow in her work on the guitar, striving for rightness, perfection—to have everything undistilled, pure, absolute.

One of the things Katherine used to say to him, during the sweeter moments, was that she loved him all the way, with a perfect love. It had become a sort of joke between them. He would ask her if she loved him enough to listen to him sing for ten thousand years without a break (Brinhart had never been able to sing on key, not even accidentally), and she would say she did. He would ask outlandish things like that, impossible things—would she crawl across a mile of broken glass just to glimpse him? Yes; would she walk around the world ten times just to touch his hand? Yes; would she give her soul to the devil just to hear him say good morning? Yes. It was always yes and it was all in fun, but there was always the uneasy fact that she thought it could be perfect, needed it to be so. Brinhart had never spoken to Katherine about this need, but it was there. It was there as Katherine's trouble was there in the good moments —a thing that took away as much as it gave: took away ease and spontaneity, gave intensity and the exquisite pleasure of contrast to the bad times that were always in the backs of their minds.

Now he heard Katherine hang up the telephone, and he waited for her to come to him. When she did not, he walked in to her, found her sitting cross-legged in the middle of the bed, smoking a cigarette.

"I was looking for those," he said.

"The cigarettes? You?"

"Why not?"

She shrugged.

"Why'd you call your folks?"

"Wanted to. You smell like a distillery."

"I walked over to that lounge across the way and had a couple."

"You had more than a couple."

"All right," he said, "I had a lot." He sat down on the bed, removed his shoes.

"I found my lighter."

"Good."

"Someone put it in my purse—it wasn't there when I looked before. I looked three times."

"How're the folks?"

"You don't believe me."

"How're the folks, Katherine."

She took a long drag on the cigarette, blew the smoke down into her chest. "The folks are like they always are. Fine. They're always fine."

"Why did you want to call them?"

"They're my folks."

He took his socks off, stood up, unzipped his pants.

"You didn't find it and put it there, did you?"

"The lighter?"

"You know very well—"

"No, I didn't put it there." He lay his pants down on the chair, removed his shirt. When he turned he saw that she was studying him. Her face seemed about to break around the eyes and along the cheeks.

"Alex didn't," she said.

"Christ, honey, let it alone."

"It wasn't there and then it was. I looked three times."

He lay down. "You missed it, that's all. What did you tell your folks?"

"About what?"

"About anything."

"Told them I was crazy as a loon."

"That you are," he said, "and so am I. We qualified for the funny farm a long time ago."

She crushed the cigarette out in the ashtray on the night table. "Someone came in here and put my lighter into my purse."

"Okay," he said.

"I'm serious, dammit." She lay down next to him, her arms rigidly extended at her sides.

"I love you," he said. He was already falling toward sleep, the whiskey closing him down. She sat up, and he watched her lean over the night table as though it were a small desk at her side. She picked up the pack of cigarettes there, lifted and dropped it in a rhythmic, nervous repetition. He could not see her face. "Where were you?" she asked.

"I told you."

"Alex said you stopped to talk to that girl."

"Not much."

"What's that mean? 'Not much.'"

He sighed. "It means we didn't talk long."

"What did you talk about?"

"Alex, the weather, and African dialects. Hell, I don't know. It lasted all of two minutes."

Katherine was silent. She lifted and dropped the cigarette package. "Who is she?"

"I don't know." He closed his eyes, felt sleep coming over him with a soft falling.

"You didn't get her name?"

"No."

Now there was only the sound of the cigarette pack hitting the table, a small papery tapping. It grew wide, and the room drifted. Brinhart heard a jet going home somewhere out in the night. Everything glided away, and then Katherine's voice cut through something thick, was right at his ear.

"Why are you lying?"

"Ah, Christ," he said.

"Wake up."

"Can't."

"Gordon, oh, damn you, don't. Gordon."

He dreamed she spoke to him from a great distance, across an enormous stillness, as though they were both under water; then he was asleep.

XI ❧

SHE AWOKE in dawn light with the realization that she had slept. She lay back, nestled against Brinhart's shoulder, hearing his breathing and moaning. She had read somewhere that everybody was three people inside: child, adult, parent. Fear was the child, being a child, and so one merely thought about being adult. Grown up. Rock 'n' roll was an extended childhood—Mick Jagger in his early forties acting like a fifteen-year-old, dressing and talking like a fifteen-year-old. She had never been really part of it, except for the music and some of the talk. There had never been any drugs for her—she had always been afraid of drugs. She lay quiet, listening. She was all right, sleepy; she closed her eyes and nestled. All of a sudden, just like that, by surprise, she was all right. A soft calling of birds at the window lulled her back.

Perhaps an hour later she arose and made a breakfast,

the apartment smelling like bacon, and Brinhart came in
and kissed her, complained of his hangover, swore off whiskey. Alex had eaten cereal sometime during the hour of her
morning sleep and was gone, probably over to Amy's.

Katherine told Brinhart that it was a lovely morning.

Yes, he said, a lovely morning.

Maybe he could call in sick, and they could all go somewhere, perhaps into Washington to look at the polished
shrines and stroll through the shade of the trees along the
mall. But Brinhart had to work, was behind.

"I stopped to see Stan last night," he said, eating a bacon
sandwich. "I was drunk and he didn't like it at all. I feel like
an idiot."

"You've been drinking too much," she said. She was
concerned.

"Not anymore," he said.

"Honey, I hope you mean it."

"I do mean it this time. I'm going to be like my father.
One drink, just after work, and that's it. Starting tomorrow."

"Tomorrow," Katherine said.

"Well I'm not going to have even *one* today. I think it
might kill me."

She laughed. "I was so mad at you when you conked out
on me last night. But, you know, I went right to sleep."

"Great," he said, eating the sandwich.

"Woke up this morning and then went back for some
more."

"That's great. I told you it passes, didn't I? All we ever
have to do is wait things out."

But then she did not want to talk about it. She had fixed
herself a bacon sandwich, and she sat down, forced herself
to take the first bite. Her appetite had flown out of her as
she decided she did not want to talk about waiting things
out. But she was all right; she spoke the words in her mind:
I'm all right. I'm fine. What a nice morning.

"Was Stan rude to you?"

"Threatened to call the police if I didn't get away from his door."

"You're kidding." She was fine. The bacon was good and crisp.

"You know what I was doing? I was trying to find the Big Dipper."

"He really threatened to call the police?"

"I made an ass out of myself," Brinhart said. He went to the sink, rinsed his hands. "I'm late. That sandwich helped. I don't feel so rocky. I was thinking about the beach last night. We're going, whether the old man comes or not. I mean it—let's go soon. Next couple of weeks, next weekend, or the weekend after that." He kissed her again, said: "Just us."

"Oh, Gordo," she said.

"You're all right now. I've got my Katherine back."

If only he wouldn't keep calling it up again. She remembered the sweet surprise of waking in a sleepy glow, the sun warm at the window, and the shadows of leaves moving there.

Later she sat alone in a cool stripe of shade on the patio, and sipped ice water. Across the lot, on the other side of a blazing alley of sun, the woods made a green curtain. Now and then a little breeze sent puffs of white dust off the gravel down to her left, and a blue jay dipped and swooped over the stones, as though it dodged invisible objects in midflight. The sky was soft, white-blue, cloudless; sparrows sang; there was the faint sound of water—children playing and splashing in a pool somewhere beyond the trees, in the older and more expensive part of Winston Garden. She felt happy for what seemed the first time in months. She watched a squirrel leap down out of one of the oaks; it sat on its haunches, munching something in its black fingers. Two patios up, a woman came out wearing a bathing suit, and lay down on a chaise longue, her skin oiled for the sun. She waved at Katherine, adjusted the dial of a transistor radio, lay back with eyes closed, arms at her sides. She was brown and young, and Katherine had never seen her before.

"Beautiful day," she called.

The young woman leaned up on one elbow. "Yes, it is."

"I may do some sunbathing myself," Katherine said.

"It's the day for it. I stayed home from work to do it— woke up this morning and just said, 'The hell with it.' So I took a holiday."

"That's nice."

The young woman lay back down, closing her eyes, and Katherine watched her for a while. From the radio came the friendly voice of a disc jockey; then there was music. The young woman lay quite still in the sun, and in a little while Katherine guessed that she had fallen asleep. The disc jockey played a song about learning how to dance. Katherine sipped ice water and listened, could not make out the verses, but part of the refrain said you could do it if you tried. It was all so simple. She gazed out at the squirrel, which had moved a few yards closer, and something darted out of the high grass at the edge of the woods and streaked in the squirrel's direction. It was an enormous tom, black and shining, tail whipping. She had never seen a cat so big. The squirrel flattened itself out, as if to run, lost footing, and the cat struck. Katherine put her hand to her mouth, watched the cat walk a few paces with the squirrel in his mouth. Almost gently, he laid the squirrel down, stood over it, licking the wet fur where his mouth had held the little body.

"Oh, *get!*" Katherine yelled, waving her free arm, rising. "Get!"

The cat merely gazed at her, implacable and passionless, those large agate eyes blinking lazily. He stepped away from the squirrel—perfectly slow, perfectly sure—and lay down on his belly, the tip of his tail jerking back and forth. He licked his paws, seemed, now, uninterested in the squirrel, which was as he had laid it down, its small puffed sides heaving.

"You get!" Katherine said, stepping out into the grass. And then she saw that the young woman had risen; the young woman was rubbing sleep from her eyes, sitting there on the chaise longue.

"What is it? What's happened?"

"That cat," Katherine said. "He's hit that poor squirrel."

The young woman squinted at her, then looked over at the cat. "Oh, Lord. Puffy," she said. "Puffy, you leave that squirrel alone. Come here, Puffy. Here, Puffy. Here, kitty-kitty-kitty."

The cat stared off at something in the trees.

"Is it dead?" asked the young woman.

"No," Katherine said. She stood perhaps ten feet away, was the third point in a triangle: cat, squirrel, herself.

"Puffy!"

The squirrel rose to its haunches, shaking, head-lifting; its whole body swayed back, the rodent teeth showing where the mouth had come open. It swayed, came down on the two handlike forepaws, the head still lifting, the nose quivering and testing the air.

"Get!" Katherine said to the cat. She threw the glass of water at him. The cat pranced away, tail up, circled, watching the squirrel. "Get, damn you!"

The cat lay down on his belly again, sleek and lazy in the sun, eyes half shut, staring at Katherine, utterly without fear or wariness or anything: just those listless, staring eyes. When the squirrel started to pull itself along the grass, rising unsteadily to its feet now and starting away, the cat made another rush, caught it up in his mouth again, shook it, laid it down.

"PUFFEEE!" the young woman screamed.

The cat settled down at the squirrel's head, licking the eyes, the mouth; Katherine saw the little mouth open where the cat's tongue licked, the jaw moving. Then the squirrel's snout was in the crook of the cat's jaw, the sleek black head facing Katherine and beginning to chew. There was a cracking sound, like the sound of peanut shells breaking. This was followed by the small, tongue-against-palate noise of eating and swallowing.

Katherine walked to the edge of the gravel. Everywhere the sun was soft, the air tender and warm. She bent down and spat something—it seemed to come out of the bottom of her stomach—into the innocent blue stones. She heard the sound again, or thought she heard it—the bone-cracking, the little tonguing sounds.

"Are you all right?" It was the young woman.

"Puffy," Katherine said, still bending, holding her knees. "You call that goddamn *thing*, that—that vicious thing Puffy."

"Hey, look—he's a cat. That's what cats do. It's nature."

"Then don't call him *Puffy*," Katherine said. "You do not call a creature like that Puffy. *Puffy*. Jesus Christ. Puffy."

"What do you suggest I call him? I call him that because of his fur. It's puffy and I call him—and I don't have to listen to this—"

"Call him Fang," Katherine said. "Doctor Death. King Killer. Cancer. Blood Beast."

The woman stood with her hands on her hips, studying Katherine with the objective curiosity of a scientist looking through a microscope. Katherine saw this as she straightened, and she tried to look back at her, but she could feel the fear darting toward her, sleek and black, and she was aware that her hands trembled.

"There's something wrong with you, sweetheart."

"*You're* the one who named the goddamn cat Puffy," Katherine said. "How sick is that?"

The other threw her hands up, walked away, saying, "Crazy. This is crazy. I'm arguing about naming my own goddamn cat."

And now Katherine wanted to run after her, beg forgiveness, say how silly it was. Of course. Silly. They'd laugh about it. The woman turned and said, "Stay inside if you can't stand the world."

"I'm sorry."

Nothing. The young woman hadn't heard, or would ignore it. She was already lying down again, arranging herself, turning the dial of the radio. Voices went in and out of music with static. Katherine walked up to her, stood out of her sun, tried not to see the ravening cat and his meal.

"You're right," she said loud enough to be heard over the radio.

The other shaded her eyes. "What?"

"I said, you're right."

"Oh."

"It is nature," Katherine said.

"What?"

"Nature. It is nature. You're right."

"Okay."

"Nothing but nature. Just as natural as breathing."

"Look," the young woman said, "you're upset—I'm upset. . . ."

"No, really, I'm fine. It's a beautiful morning, and I'm fine."

"You're shaking like a leaf."

"I was—I'm—it's silly, but I'm all right."

"Sure. A shock. I didn't like it either."

The cat was eating.

"I didn't like the noise the bones made when they broke," Katherine said.

"God." The young woman looked at her.

"Can we be friends?"

"Okay."

Katherine shook her hand, and then she was kneeling close to the other's face, and she couldn't quite hear her own voice, though she knew she was saying something.

"Hey, are you all right?"

". . . name—your name. I'm Katherine Brinhart and I used to be—I was a singer, a musician, when I was about your age but I gave it up. . . ."

"I'm Linda—"

". . . it was a sort of extended childhood but now, you know, I put away childish things and I really wanted to quit because I hated what it was doing to me, you know? Except that sometimes I don't know what to do, really, you know, what I should do. I keep thinking there's something I forgot to do and that gets a little scary sometimes with these, you know, these mood swings, sort of—"

"Well, yes. . . ." Linda said, looking down. Katherine had seen something in her eyes, and now she realized that at some point during this going-on of her voice, she had taken hold of the other's arm.

"Oh—I'm sorry."

Linda looked at her.

"It upset me. Anyway. Those things—these things—"

"Of course."

Katherine stood. "Yes. Well, nice meeting you, Linda."

"Nice meeting you."

"Though with this cat thing—" Katherine laughed awkwardly; she could think of nothing more to say.

XII ❧

AMY WALKED a little ahead of him along the highway, swinging her arms and talking. "So he just walked right up and banged on our door," she said. "You never saw anything like it. He was drunk like you see in the movies. I watched the whole thing from the bathroom window."

Cars went past them; glinting sun; she had to shout at him over the noise. Occasionally a truck lumbered past, rattling metal and hissing brakes. The air had been cool as they had crossed the creek and climbed the bank; but here, so close to the burning asphalt, it was ovenlike, and the sun was a blinding immensity all around them.

"You know," Amy said, "I felt kind of sorry for him. All he wanted was for somebody to show him where the Big Dipper was. I'd have showed him right off, whether he was drunk or not. I could see it from the window, right above his head." She burst through a pause in the traffic, sprinted to the other side of the road, stopping with a little jump on the red earth there. She whirled and smiled, and when he couldn't get across—the cars coming fast, tires slapping the small islands of tar where potholes had been filled—she began to wave at him, as though she were on a ship moving away from shore. He waved back.

"Now!" she screamed.

He bolted out onto the road, stumbled, nearly fell. Horns sounded, sudden as screams. For an instant he froze, saw only a swift passing of metal and blinding tongues of fire, a long black sedan swinging by him, polished and new and blaring. Then he ran again, and when he reached the other side, Amy put her hands on his chest.

"I thought you were a goner."

He could only try to draw in air, and now her arms were around him.

"Are you okay?"

"Stop that," he said.

"I'm just glad you're okay."

"Don't grab me like that."

On this side of the road was a red clay bank crowned

with weeds, which led to the edge of the shopping center parking lot. On the ground at their feet were crushed beer cans, ugly pieces of broken glass, flattened cigarette butts, and one mud-coated soda bottle. Up the road to the left they could see the Point Royal water tower, fat and shining in the sun, the lower curve of it painted in jagged black: CLASS OF '77. Beyond the water tower the sky was a dark, clear, rich blue. They climbed the bank, went through the weeds: thousands of grasshoppers flying before them, clouds of gnats rising like dust. The shopping mall seemed stretched along the whole length of the horizon. Above it a fantastic white cloud piled toward the top of the sky, billowing tier after billowing tier.

In the Woolworth's they sat at the soda fountain and ordered Cokes. The store was not crowded—the aisles had seemed deserted—but here there were many people: women loaded down with shopping bags and shiny black purses, and a few uniformed men, tan leathery faces besmirched with grease. At the end of the counter sat the young woman and her baby; next to her was a thin old man with dry, coppery hair. The baby was whining and the small, puffy blue eyes were pushing out tears. The girl bounced him on her knee, talking to the old man.

"What're you looking at?" Amy said.

Alex did not answer. Now the girl had seen him, and was giving the baby to the old man.

"Hey," Amy said.

"Shit," Alex said. "Here she comes."

"Who?"

The young woman walked right to him and touched his arm. "Hello. Remember me?"

"No," Alex said.

"Well it was getting dark. My name's Shirley. We met last night outside my trailer. Remember?"

"Yeah."

"Shirley." She extended her hand. Alex took it, dropped it, made himself smile. "Your daddy and me are friends, sort of."

Amy was noisily sucking the dregs of her Coke through a straw.

"Is this *your* friend?" Shirley asked.

"Yeah."

"And what's your name again? Your daddy's told me a hundred times I'll bet. But I always had such a bad memory for names anyway."

"His name is Alex," Amy said, turning. "And mine's Amy."

"It's nice to see that Alex has such a nice friend."

"We're friends, all right," Amy said. She smiled at Alex.

"That's very nice. Friendship is so important."

"Nothing like it," Amy said.

"Well, it's nice seeing you. Say hello to your daddy for me, okay? And your mommy too." Shirley smiled. "Bye."

Before Alex could say anything to answer her, she had gone back to her place, where she collected the baby and the old man; as they were leaving, the old man held the baby high on one shoulder, and Shirley waved at Alex.

"Well," Amy said, "that looks suspicious."

"What—"

" 'Your daddy and me are friends, sort of.' Boy. That's rich."

Alex said nothing.

"I wonder if they're having an affair or something."

"She's always walking that baby around," he said. He sipped his Coke, not tasting it, looking at his own flat reflection in the metal of a napkin dispenser on the counter.

"Is something wrong with your mother?" Amy asked.

Alex watched the reflection of his own unhappy face. "Nothing," he said.

"Think she knows?"

"Knows what?"

"About your father and—*her*."

"Don't be crazy," he said.

"If you put it together—how he got drunk and all. I'll bet something's going on."

He drank the last of the Coke.

"Think we ought to tell her?"

"Who?"

"Your mother."

"My mother was up when he got home. I heard them talking."

"Really?" Amy leaned toward him. "What did they say? Were they talking about *her*?"

"I don't know. I just heard the voices." Alex looked away, saw row upon row of dresses in a rack along the far aisle. He felt suddenly crowded and irritable, and the Coke had only left a film on his tongue; it hadn't quenched his thirst at all. He asked the waitress for some water, and she brought it to him.

"Do you think we'll still be friends after school starts?" Amy asked.

"I don't know."

"I've been kicked out of school before. Have you?"

"Yes," he lied.

"I wasn't really at fault," she said. "I'm only in seventh grade now because I lost a year." She toyed with her straw, bending it small in her hands.

"But I was always in trouble. I just don't get along with people that well. My father says it's because I'm too smart for my own good. But I just hate being crowded into a room with all those bodies and everybody smelling his smell. Did you know everybody has a different smell? Only a few people can ever tell the difference, and I'm one of them. I can breathe a bunch of air in a room and say just about exactly who's been there if there hasn't been too many." She yawned, stretched, her arms out over the counter, hands locked. Then she leaned back, turning a little, gazing out at the aisles to the left. Alex looked at the back of her neck. The waitress came toward them, check in hand.

"But I don't like it," Amy said, "being able to do that. It makes me nervous."

The waitress asked if they wanted anything else. She was a tall thin girl with a scarred face and yellow teeth. Amy paid her.

"Why does it make you nervous?" Alex asked.

"Because. I told you I don't get along with people that well. To me, people are just one big pain in the ass."

"Maybe," Alex said.

Another waitress stopped before them and asked if they were finished. She was an extraordinarily pale woman with orange hair; even her eyes were pale—an almost white-blue —and Alex imagined that she had been spawned among the metal spigots and the aluminum sinks of the fountain, that she had never been outside in the sun. He thought of the white around his mother's eyes, and Amy's pale, bluish skin.

"You know what we ought to do?" Amy said as they moved away from the counter. "We ought to run away together."

"Sure," Alex said. "Where."

"Anywhere. I want to see everything there is to see."

They walked into the sun, stood at the edge of the walk. Two cars were parked at the curb to their left, idling in the heat. The air was full of fumes.

"Sometimes I'm tired of almost everything," Amy said.

He did not speak.

"Did you know," she said, "that I have cancer?"

XIII ❧

IN THE EARLY PART of the evening there had been a brief shower, just enough to leave water spots on the patio; this had dried very quickly, and now it was clear and cool and calm. Brinhart and Katherine sat facing the lot, and they could hear Alex's radio—an Oriole game, the announcer's voice a weak murmur behind static. Katherine smoked a cigarette, drawing the smoke deep into her lungs, letting it out in slow sighs. Brinhart had made himself a whiskey and drank it very slowly, trying to think of something ordinary and harmless to say: something that had nothing to do with cancer, madness, death—the carnivorousness of cats. At dinner, after Katherine had again spoken of her horror and embarrassment of the morning, Alex had said, "Amy has cancer in her blood."

Katherine had dropped her fork, gasped out something of what she had been eating.

"Gordon," she said now, "make him turn the radio off."

"Honey," he said. "We won't hear it if we talk."

"I'm not thinking about hearing it. That static is awful. It's not good for his ears."

"Let him decide, all right?"

She blew smoke. "I guess so." She reached over and touched his arm. "I'm sorry."

"Don't be."

There was a pause.

"Pretty out this evening," he said.

She did not answer.

Presently he said, "I've got a joke."

"Go ahead."

"I heard it today at work. I think you'll like it."

"Tell it." Katherine spoke softly, quickly, and the smoke poured out of her mouth. Then she coughed, an ugly rasping from the bottom of her lungs.

"Why don't you put the cigarette out?" he said.

"Is that the joke?"

"You want cancer?"

"*That's* the joke." She laughed harshly, coughed again. She had laid her hands on his knees.

Brinhart put the drink to his lips, having made up his mind not to speak again.

"Well, are you going to tell me the joke?"

"Forget it."

"Poor Gordo."

After a moment, to his surprise, she leaned over and kissed his cheek. Oh, baby, he thought. That was right: he had wanted to tell the joke to get her mind off trouble. He took her hand. "All right, there was a nun, just out of the novitiate—"

"What's that?"

"It's a—it's something they go through for training. It's training—like school."

"A college."

"Right."

"So she's just graduated from college."

Why should he allow himself, now, to be irritated? He tried very hard to control his voice, and as he waited for it, waited for the tightness to go out of it, hemming and hawing as though he'd lost his place, he saw Shirley coming out from the hedgerow with the baby in a carrier on her back.

"Uh, let me see—"

"Gordon, tell the joke."

"Well, you keep interrupting—"

"But see? I'm talking and teasing. I'm doing all right, don't you think?"

"All right—I just wanted to tell you the joke. There was nothing behind my wanting to tell you that joke."

"So tell it."

He looked at her. It was an effort not to get up and walk away. "So—so she's getting out of the goddamn novitiate—"

"She's *coming* out or she's out?"

"Katherine. . . ."

"Well, is she a graduate?"

"Look. Forget it. Just forget it." He had lowered his voice. Shirley walked along the edge of the gravel on the other side, and she had not looked this way.

"All right," Katherine said. "I'll be good."

"No. It's nothing. Really. It's just a lousy joke."

"Now you're mad at me."

"No," he said.

"You're mad at me but you don't want me to know it. You're being careful. Because I scared the hell out of a neighbor being crazy."

"Stop it, Katherine. Goddammit, quit. Will you quit?"

She flipped the cigarette out into the grass, lighted another. He wished she would go inside: he wished she would pass through and be Katherine again. Things had seemed so hopeful early that morning, and he realized now how adept he had gotten at seizing on anything as a positive sign: he had driven to work almost shivering with relief and happiness.

"What's this?" she said now.

And he saw that Shirley was struggling up the slight incline of grass, toward them; she was bent low under the weight of the child.

"What does she want," Katherine muttered.

"Hello," Shirley said.

Brinhart stood as she reached them. "This is my wife: Katherine."

"Hello," Shirley said, breathless, reaching back and adjusting the carrier.

Katherine smiled, nodded slightly, cigarette held to her lips.

"You're—" Brinhart hesitated.

"You forgot already. You're as bad as me," Shirley said.

"Katherine, this is Shirley."

"There, you got it."

Then there was an embarrassingly long silence. Far away, a siren sounded, and the baby whined a little, as though uncertain whether or not to be frightened by the sound.

"Well," Shirley said, "isn't it a lovely evening."

Katherine blew smoke. Brinhart made a sound like humming: *Mmm-hmmm.*

There was another pause.

"That's a nice arrangement with the baby there," Brinhart said. "That's the way Indians used to carry them, isn't it?"

"I don't know. It gets pretty heavy."

"Maybe they were all very strong," Katherine said.

"I bet," Shirley said. "Anyway, I think it's interesting." She pronounced it *inneresting,* smiling at Katherine. "Do you know a lot about Indians? I always wanted to learn about them."

"I know everything about them—go ahead, ask me something about Indians. Asian or American, I know them."

"Oh," Shirley said, "I couldn't even think of what to ask."

"Ask anything, go ahead."

Brinhart thought it was time to change the subject. "Katherine, why don't you—why don't we offer Shirley a drink?"

"Yes, why don't we," Katherine said. "I think that's a perfect idea."

"Oh, no," Shirley said, apparently relieved that she did not have to think up a question about Indians, "I have to go. I just wanted to say hi."

"Hi," Katherine said.

Brinhart laughed, too loud. Shirley looked at him.

"I found this little cemetery behind the shopping mall.

Five graves. Red told me it was there, really. I mean, I didn't really find it myself." She laughed awkwardly. "You don't know Red. He's a nice man. We sort of traveled here together, and he's a lot older and everything, but he's real nice and he knows a lot about just almost anything."

"Indians?" Katherine asked.

"I bet he does. Sure."

"I'd like to talk to him some time. Wouldn't I, Gordo?"

"Oh, he's real nice to talk to. Real inneresting and everything. And anyway, see, he found these five graves behind the mall—or, I mean, he went looking back there and found them because he knew they built that mall right on top of a cemetery—did you know that? I mean, isn't that awful?"

"That's awful," Katherine said. "Just awful. Don't you think it's awful, Gordo?"

"It's awful," Brinhart muttered.

They were all quiet again.

"So," Shirley said, looking from Brinhart to Katherine and back to Brinhart again. "So there's these—these five graves and—well, they're not—they weren't in the way, so they let them go. But they were all grown over and rundown, and so I was thinking of going over there and pulling the weeds away and maybe putting some wild flowers around, sort of. I mean it's the least I could do. You see, my parents were both killed when I was two. I was in the car, you know. I don't remember if I told you that. I was in the car but I wasn't hurt and I don't remember. I mean, I don't remember anything of what happened. My uncle Raymond told me about it when I was much older, and now I don't know whether what I dream—you see, at night sometimes I dream this big crashing sound way away from me, like, like it's on the other side of the world—this crashing sound. And I don't know if that's because of what I learned from my uncle or because I do remember somewhere way inside. It doesn't bother me, really, but I never knew my parents, you know? There was just my uncle. And so I don't know, but I thought about these poor graves nobody comes to."

"Where's your uncle?" Katherine asked.

"Died. Just last year. He was going to coach me, you know, having the baby Lamaze. But he died while he was painting the house."

"Did you keep your parents' graves?"

"Well, see, that happened way up in New Hampshire, and my uncle lived in Ankeny, so I went there. He never got around to telling me just where they were buried. I mean he just said, you know, they were buried in New Hampshire. He was kind of a hard man."

"I think it's nice," Brinhart said, "that you want to do something about those graves behind the mall." He sipped his drink; the ice seemed to clatter in the glass.

"Yes," Katherine said. "It's just sweet."

Alex's radio had stopped, and now Alex was moving around in the living room behind Brinhart and Katherine. Shirley gazed into the apartment, leaning forward a little. "Hi," she said.

"H'lo," came the boy's voice.

Katherine threw her cigarette out in the grass, and Brinhart watched a blue plume of smoke rise there.

"He's a nice boy," Shirley said.

"A very nice boy," said Katherine.

Brinhart cleared his throat.

"I went over there with Red today," Shirley said. "We trimmed a little, and they look better. You want to see them? I mean, maybe we could all go over and look at them. They're really better. I'm going to put some flowers—"

"Wild flowers," Katherine said.

"Yes."

"I'd like to see them," said Brinhart and took the last of his whiskey.

"They're just across the road."

"You want to see them?" he asked Katherine.

She took a moment to answer; when she did so, she gave Brinhart a withering look. It wasn't fair. She was being needlessly unfair to the girl, and the girl was clearly no match for her. "I don't want to look at *graves*," she said. "I mean, who wants to look at graves."

"You used to like that—reading the dates."

"*You* did. Not me. I followed *you*." Now Katherine addressed Shirley. "I had to wait an hour for him one time at Harpers Ferry. He read every stone. Every stone. It was threatening to rain. There was all this thunder and lightning. It was like being in a B movie, one of those old horror flicks. Any minute I thought somebody might come out of the ground." Her voice had grown friendly. Shirley laughed, hefting the child in the carrier. Suddenly everything was cheerful.

"Come on, honey," Brinhart said to Katherine. "Let's go have a look."

"No, really. Not me."

"Well," Brinhart said, "maybe some other time then."

"If you want to go, Gordon, go."

"Perhaps another time," Shirley said, "we can all three go."

"Don't be silly," Katherine said. "There's no reason to be silly, Gordon."

"Come on, honey," he said. "Let's take a look."

"You go. I insist. I absolutely insist that you go."

Brinhart set his glass down. This was all wrong; it meant everything if he went and it meant everything if he stayed. He wished for rain. It was idiotic, but he stood there hoping for a quick storm, something to break up the moment, relieve him from having to decide.

"No," he said, finally, and sat down.

"Well, bye," Shirley said, and moved away.

He watched her go down, along the strip of grass, around the building, out of sight.

"Why didn't you go with her?" Katherine asked. "You wanted to."

"I wanted to see the graves, Katherine."

They were quiet for a while. She lighted another cigarette; he set his glass down on the chair arm.

"You only stayed because of me," she said. "You were afraid of what I'd think."

"What would you have thought?"

"Nothing."

"Shit. I was damned if I did and damned if I didn't, and you know it. Is it my fault the girl asked us to go with her and you wouldn't go?"

"Go," Katherine said, rising. "Go."

Brinhart rose, walked away from her. "Good night," he said.

He heard the screen open and then close—a shrill sliding, a bang—but he did not look back.

He went around the building, through the courtyard, and up to the entrance drive; he saw Shirley walking out by the road, and he ran to catch up. She turned as he approached, and he smiled, coming to a walk at her side. He was a little out of breath, and for a few paces they were silent.

"Changed my mind," he said.

"I see."

They stopped to cross the road. There was very little traffic—two cars at opposite ends of the highway, moving toward them, too far away to be of concern. From this prospect, the crest of a high hill, they could see the shopping mall, far across the sloping asphalt lot, which went in a wide curve around to the lower end of the field, the highway cutting through there above the creek. There was chickweed and wild vine and willow on up the other way, toward the Point Royal Hospital.

"I saw your boy at Woolworth's today," Shirley said as they were crossing. "He had a friend with him. A girl."

"That's Amy."

"It's nice that he has a girl friend."

"He's not supposed to cross the highway," Brinhart said. They had reached the other side.

Shirley stopped, adjusted the carrier, shifted the weight of the child. "I didn't get him in trouble?"

"No."

"Promise?"

"I won't even let on to him that I know."

They walked for a while down the slope next to the road, which sank steadily below the level of the ground, creating a steep red bank on the right.

"Did you know about his friend?" she asked.

"Yes. Amy. Sad."

"Sad?"

"He told us tonight that Amy has leukemia."

"Oh." She stopped again. She seemed to have lost her breath. "Oh, my God."

"I'll tell you, though, I think they're just watching her, sort of. I think she must've had it, and now they have to watch. I've met her parents. They moved down here so they could use the National Medical Center."

"Oh, God."

"You know, it's serious, but she's probably doing okay. She'd be in the hospital if she weren't."

They were walking again, more slowly this time. Brinhart had thought her baby was asleep, but when he crossed behind her to step down into the parking lot, he saw wide-open eyes, serene as the eyes of a god, following him.

"Hello," he said, and touched the small red chin; Shirley had turned, so that his arm nearly brushed her shoulder.

"He's awake," she said.

"Yes. He has quite a pair of eyes."

"They're not mine."

"He's a well-behaved child."

"As long as I keep moving. He gets restless if I stand still very long."

They were crossing the parking lot. A heavy woman in tight blue shorts that accentuated every fold of flesh around her hips and thighs bent into an open car with a bag of groceries, the paper crackling as she let it down. The air was gray now—the tall, gibbetlike lamps flickered on. A soft, steady breeze came out of the north, and the small maples—saplings in white concrete planters shaped like great aspirin tablets, the skinny trunks rising out of dirt black as a night sky—whispered and swayed. Brinhart stole a glance at Shirley's flat belly. She was wearing the halter top, the jogging shorts. The bones of her ankles showed through tan.

"You're very beautiful."

"Thank you." She might've been saying this in answer to some minor politeness—holding a door or bringing up a chair—he had not meant it that way. He had felt nearly religious, saying it. Now he felt a little foolish.

"We have to hurry," she said, "before it gets full dark."

They quickened their pace, went along the south end of the mall, entered an oil-stained service road, going around behind the buildings. Here there were loading docks, stacks of rain-gray bottle crates, piles of discarded boxes, and one long row of lumber, wrapped in aluminum bands. Brinhart saw blue Dumpsters ranked like parked trucks all the way up to the other end. The service road was bordered on the right side by a steep embankment, thick with thornbushes at the south end, where a green wall of pine and sycamore rose from the crest. Shirley led him to a place, about twenty yards up, where the embankment became grass, and then she climbed, bending under the weight of the child, and he followed, looking at the whiteness of her thighs where the shorts rode up. They went under a black willow, and he saw, dangling from one low branch, a condom. The branch was knife-thin, and the condom had obviously been forced onto the end of it. The thing drooped there.

"It's just up here," Shirley said. She went on. The baby's head lolled and bounced, and now he began to complain a little. But then they were at the top of the bank, and he was quiet again; Brinhart turned to see the tops of the Dumpsters, rain-spotted and streaked with something like oil, which shone under the lights. The graves were a few yards beyond the edge of the bank, and here the weeds had been pulled, or cut away, to a circumference of about three feet all around. The markers were mottled, besmirched with birdlime and the tracks of decaying leaves, rain and wind. They were equidistant from each other—a neat little row —and the carved names and dates had softened, looked slightly faded, as though someone had tried to erase them. Brinhart knelt down to read the first.

LOST TO US THIS YEAR 1859 OF A FEVER
SUMMER OF HER ELEVENTH YEAR

"God," he said.

"Isn't it something?" Shirley stood at his shoulder, her knees a little inch from the side of his face.

"Eighteen fifty-nine," he said. "Let's see ... that's—"

"One hundred and twenty years ago. Exactly."

"Wonder what she was like?"

"I've been thinking about her all day."

"Wonder what *they* were like," he said.

"Her parents."

"Yes. God, the grief—there's so much grief in these few words. Don't you feel it?"

"Yes."

He moved to the next: probably the girl's father, by the dates. "The father lived a long time."

"Eighty-seven years."

"I guess it all evens out, doesn't it."

"I don't get you."

"Well," he said, "look where the grief is now. I mean it all ends up here."

"That's morbid."

"Guess so."

The baby made a soft, questioning sound. Around them the tangled growth was darker, turning black. The sky, given the lineaments of the surrounding treetops, was a pale island of light.

"Well," she said, "I wanted to—" She looked around, walked to a low bush nearby, an explosion of white flowers. Brinhart was suddenly bathed in the feeling that no one else in the world existed but himself, the girl, and her baby— and now an image that he knew had Katherine in it moved under the surface of his mind. For that moment the girl *became* Katherine. He almost said the name. Shirley brought the white flowers back, laid them down, two or three at the base of each stone, while he watched. He thought of the dead who lay beneath him, of his Aunt Beth and his mother; the world was empty, there was only the most profound quiet, night coming, and now the baby let out a cry.

"There," Shirley said.

The baby cried.

"I guess we should go."

As they walked back down the bank and on out across the mall, under white buzzing lights that seemed to spill out millions of moths, like skinny fountains, and past the inevitable group of adolescents in front of the 7-Eleven, he told her how he had met Katherine. He told her in a quick flurry of words, wanting to talk now, or needing to.

"And she doesn't play anymore at all? That's sad."

Brinhart did not like the word used this way about Katherine. He said, "No, it was what she wanted."

"It's still sad."

"No," he said quickly.

They reached the road. He saw a yellow window in one of the apartments up near the entrance of Winston Garden, and felt a sudden, jarring despair.

"Want to go have a Coke?"

"I ought to get home."

They crossed the road. The sky was now black, and he could not find the moon.

"Red's waiting for me."

"I may walk around awhile." He was thinking that he would come back here, to the lounge, and have one drink. He walked along at her side, the baby beginning to complain steadily now, and in the entrance drive he thought about kissing her. How clumsy it would be to kiss a woman who carried a crying baby on her back. The air was crisp, though the wind had died down. He caught himself up: he would not kiss her: he felt nothing for her. Only a sort of unspecific longing upon which he had just now put her name. Shirley.

"Shirley," he said.

"What."

But he was speechless.

"Did you say something?"

"Thanks for—thanks for showing me the graves."

"Oh."

They were in the courtyard, and they went down, past the last building, Brinhart's front door, around to the patio. The fat man on the other patio was standing over the grill again, and the odor of sizzling steak wafted toward them. A cat shrieked, off in the woods.

"I think that guy must eat five meals a day," he whispered.

She laughed, put one hand over her mouth. The baby whined low, as from fatigue. "When I first got here, all I saw were fat people. I thought everybody was fat."

"Shhh," Brinhart said.

She smiled at him, nodded. "Bye, now."

He touched her arm. "Thanks."

"Anytime."

There was a warm moment of hesitation, the two of them smiling and looking at each other. He was certain she felt it too. The baby wailed.

"Okay, Tommy," she said, clumsily stepping off the patio. Brinhart watched her go across the lot to the dark wall of the hedgerow. She turned, blew him a kiss, and was gone.

He sat down in the chair, staring at the scattered lights of the trailer court, thinking about having the one drink. No: he knew it would be more than one. A couple, a few. He did not want to go into the apartment and for the moment he did not want to walk back to the mall either. So he sat, looking at the night sky and hearing the faint sound of the television from the bedroom. He imagined himself getting up, going in there to say he was sorry, to tell Katherine he loved her and he was sorry. But then he thought about how he had done nothing to be sorry for. He put his hands together in front of his face, tapping the fingers; he shook his head and sat forward, leaning his elbows on his knees. Above the trees on the other side of the lot, a star dropped in a trail of brilliant light. It illuminated that part of the sky as it went down, and when it was gone, the blackness there seemed deeper, like a wound. And now, to his astonishment, he saw Shirley coming back from the path. She walked right to him, smiling—he saw her smile in the darkness—and he saw that she no longer carried the baby.

"You looked sort of lonesome," she said. "And I remembered that you wanted to have a Coke."

"I'm very thirsty."

"Want to come over for one?"

He did not hesitate. "Love to."

"Think your wife would come?"

"No."

She turned. "Come on."

The chair made a scraping noise as he came to his feet. He turned around, looked at the screen. The living room was dark; there was only a tinge of light coming from the hallway. Yet he thought he saw something, a filmy shape on the kitchen wall, a moving shadow. He waited, imagined Katherine there. But nothing moved, and he heard only the sound of the television.

"Coming?" Shirley called from the lot.

He went to her, walked with her to the hedgerow, and down the path. The air was sweet with night fragrances and he took a deep, slow breath, carefully warding off the thought of what might happen now.

"You'll like Red," she said.

"Red's awake?"

"Yes."

"Such a lovely night."

"I love summer. I even like it when it's hot and muggy."

Brinhart told himself that he was going to have a harmless Coke on a summer night, that nothing was different. As they entered the trailer court he saw two people sitting in the dark of the first stoop. A man and a woman. The man wore no shirt, his belly hanging out over the top of his pants. The woman, bone-thin, with large dark eyes that moved with the quickness of a bird's, held the man's wrist. Farther down, a few people stood talking around an open car. Shirley led the way in, through the rickety gate, and when she opened the door, leaning inside for a moment to call Red's name, Brinhart felt quite out of place, breathing the odor of cooking; it was as if she had left him behind in the dark.

"Come in," she said finally.

He entered a small, crowded room, with fake-wood paneling and a threadbare carpet, walls thin as paperboard. An air conditioner hummed and clanked in one window, and the blinds in the other were broken, rust-spotted, and dusty. There was a portable television on a stand against the right wall; the stand was filled with magazines and old newspapers. The magazines—*Outdoor Life* and *Field & Stream* —were everywhere: on the worn, sprung sofa; in the one wicker chair; along the wall under the windows; and under the coffee table, which was homemade—two plyboard sheets supported by cinder blocks. Red was nowhere to be seen, though there were four or five beer bottles on the coffee table.

"Have a seat," Shirley said. "I have to check the baby." She disappeared down a thin passage, past more magazines, and what looked like shelves of paint cans. Brinhart sat on the sofa, touched the jutting spring; it rose up out of the cloth at one end as if someone had stabbed upward from beneath the cushion. Across from him was another room, the kitchen—a small portable freezer against the far wall. He sat very still, hands folded in his lap, and from the rooms came the sound of the baby's tired whining, and then voices, low, a murmur the tone of which he could not make out. Even so, he felt certain that an argument was going on, and he began to think about quietly leaving. He got up, moved toward the door, paused to look at a drugstore painting of trees and mountains and clouds and a sky more blue than any he had ever seen. The voices went on in the other room, an argument: Brinhart was now filled with an almost suffocating sense of entrapment, as though something were wrapped about him, cutting off air and circulation. He turned from the painting, took another step toward the door, heard someone coming down the passageway, and stopped, like a burglar—a man about to be discovered in a stranger's living room. Shirley walked in, smiled weakly at him, went on, into the kitchen. He heard ice clattering in glasses, stood with his hands in his pockets, listening. And now, coming from the bedrooms, wearing only an undershirt and Jockey shorts, was Red. Brinhart had not remembered that he was so tall. He filled the opening, leaned on the thin jamb, and pulled on a pair of worn gabardine slacks.

"Hello," Brinhart said.

The old man was muttering something.

"I don't mean to intrude."

"Not intruding."

"I hope we didn't wake you."

"No." Red looked at him. "Not intruding and not waking me." He stood attaching his belt—a leather one with a metal buckle, something embossed on the metal, but tarnished beyond easy recognition.

"I'm Gordon Brinhart."

"Yeah."

Shirley came in, looked at Red, then at Brinhart. "Let's sit in the kitchen—it's more comfortable."

Brinhart followed her. He could not see why the kitchen was more comfortable: it was a good ten degrees warmer; there were more beer bottles on the sink, and the cabinets above the sink were smoke-stained, shining with grease. In the ceiling a single light fixture, far too bright, was filled with dead moths, whose wing shadows mottled the wall, the table, and the floor.

"Sit down," Shirley said, putting a glass of still-foaming Coke on the table, opposite one chair. Brinhart took it, put his hands on either side of the sweating glass. He watched her pull another chair up, her eyes narrow, fixed on Red, who gently lifted still another chair from its place under a yellow wall-phone. Now they were all at the table, and Shirley was still looking at the old man. Brinhart sipped his Coke. "Good," he said.

"Didn't fix one for me," Red muttered.

"I didn't think you wanted one," Shirley said.

"Naw. Rather have another beer." He rose, moved with some difficulty to the refrigerator, opened it, leaned in. The white door gleamed in the light. "Want one?" he said.

"No," said Shirley.

He came back to the table with his beer. "Ask her that every night. Same thing. No." He sat down, removed the bottle cap, and drank. In the skin of his neck were bunched folds and deep lines, like cracks, and traces of freckles, faded somehow from the ruddy surface. The same deep lines and faint freckles were in his wrists; the backs of his hands made Brinhart think of the desert, of stone worn away by rivers.

"Max wants to come to work with me," he said to Shirley.

"Good."

"He's not getting any plumbing work."

"Max," Shirley said to Brinhart, "is that friend I was telling you about. You remember."

"My brother-in-law," Red said.

"He's been down, you know."

"Sorry to hear that," said Brinhart.

"It ain't nothing serious," Red said. "Max is healthy as me. He just hates goddamn Virginia."

"Oh, Red—don't get started."

"Don't know why I ever wanted to come back South."

"Red."

"Goddamn property taxes in this state. Goddamn car inspections. This ain't the South anymore—probably never was."

"All right."

Red looked at Brinhart. "You ever been out Culpeppah?"

"Pardon?"

"Culpeper."

"No."

"Should see it. One big goddamn shopping center going up, covering the place. Ain't nothing like it. You know I used to hunt—right over this ground right here where we're sitting?"

Brinhart nodded.

"Damndest thing I ever saw."

They all drank. Brinhart looked at an embroidered potholder above the stove, the word LOVE in dark, uneven stitching, circled by a perfect, bright red heart. "I can't get over how comfortable these trailers are," he lied.

"That's all they are, cowboy, is trailers."

"Red," Shirley said. She held her glass to her lips, staring over the rim.

The old man went on. "Me and Shirley here, we run into each other on the road—she tell you about that?"

"Yes—"

"I spent most of my life on the road. Been in every one of the states four times at least, and I been in Mexico and South America and Europe."

"Did your work require that you travel?" Brinhart asked.

"Work. Hell no, man. Work. I was never in any job long enough to call it work. I done every damn thing under the sun at least once."

"I see."

"I didn't get no—five thousand dollars when I was eighteen. Just because I turned eighteen. When I was eighteen, I had wanderlust. I wanted to see everything. Mountains and rivers and oceans and seas, and wild lions in Africa. I didn't want to sit in no apartment house; no, nor a damn trailer court neither. In those days a man could get out, you know, and see what he wanted to see. Things was wilder then, and looser. And—but they was tougher too. Why, when I was in the Depression I made six dollars a week cutting beef. That was in Chicago. Six dollars a week. I did it for about a month and then lit off again. I was twenty-eight years old, and I'd already been around the world almost."

"Red."

"I just lived one place at a time, till I was tired of it. Then I picked up and moved on."

"Mmmm," Brinhart said. He would leave as soon as he finished the Coke. If he could finish it. He wanted a whiskey.

"I'm seventy-four years old and I been everything from a cowboy to a cook."

"I always wanted to be a cowboy. I used to do a lot of horseback riding when I was in the army."

"You wasn't in any real army, cowboy. Not the army of General Patton!"

"No. I was in—I wasn't in the infantry."

"Tank corps. That's what I was in. Tank corps."

Shirley sat chewing ice now, gazing intently into her glass.

"I'm a jack-of-all-trades, master of none."

Brinhart nodded, sipped the Coke; there was plenty of ice in it, but it tasted warm.

"I was even a soldier of fortune for a while—a white hunter too."

"Africa?"

"Brazil, then Africa. That was in the late forties." Now Red's voice seemed to change; it was lower, less strident. "Hunted wild boar."

"I noticed that you—the hunting and fishing. Outdoor magazines."

"That's right."

There was a pause.

"Where's your wife, boy?"

Shirley put her glass down hard. "Red."

"Just asked a simple question."

"It's a damn stupid question."

"Excuse me," Red said, getting up slowly, the bones of his legs cracking. For the first time Brinhart caught the odor of age—old male flesh.

"You don't have to leave," Shirley said.

"Maybe I'll go to bed," said the old man. "I'm tired."

"Good night."

"Might read awhile—in the living room." Red nodded at Brinhart, but did not speak to him. He left his beer, half full, on the table.

"Don't pay any attention to him," Shirley said.

"Maybe I should go."

"You can finish your Coke."

He drank, not looking at her. A fly circled the room light, dropped down through the shadows by the stove.

"It gets lonely here, sometimes," she said.

He nodded.

"You get lonely?"

"Everybody does," he said, "sometimes."

"Red's nice."

There was nothing he could think of to tell her. He looked at the fine down on her wrists, her smooth shoulders, tan and shining in the light. He heard Red clearing his throat in the other room.

"You want more Coke?" she asked.

"Do you have anything—"

She broke in. "You want something stronger?"

"Do you have any whiskey?"

"No."

"That's all right."

"I don't drink, see. And Red just drinks beer now. You want a beer?"

"No, thank you."

"There's plenty of beer."

"Really, no." It was clear that she wanted him to stay. And he *would* stay, as long as she wished, and for whatever she wished. He smiled at her. "You're very nice to offer me beer."

"Oh, it's nothing."

"I used to say that the sign of an honest man was that if you asked him if you could buy him a drink, he said yes. I guess I'm not an honest man tonight." He was aware, as he spoke these words, of a context in which they applied rather exactly to him, and for a moment he was hot with embarrassment. He cupped his hands around the glass, gazing down into it.

"I don't know how anybody can drink beer," she said.

"Oh, it's good."

"Red drinks a ton of it."

This was easier ground. "Interesting life he's had."

"If you believe it all," she whispered through her hands, leaning close. "I pretend to."

He was looking at her lips. "Is this—" he began in a normal voice, but now he, too, whispered. "Is this his trailer?"

She nodded, whispered, "I helped him pay for it."

Brinhart nodded in return.

"We're friends," Shirley said. "Just friends."

This was an unmistakable hint, and now blood coursed toward his groin. Things had gone far enough for this night; yet he lingered, watching her eyes, the long blond lashes there. Her fingers nervously touched the V of her halter.

"What're you thinking?" he asked through a dry tightness in his throat.

"Nothing." She would not look at him.

"Shirley," he said. He wondered what her mouth would be like.

"What?"

"That's—I like the name. I like to say it."

"I hate it. It's a name for waitresses."

This struck him as quite witty and fine. He laughed. "Where'd you get that?"

"It just feels that way to me. Like I should be a waitress and chew gum and drink beer and wear my hair in a beehive. I hate it."

He laughed again, touched her wrist. She took it away. "What a funny idea," he said.

"Yeah. I come up with some funny ones sometimes. I keep Red in stitches. He says I ought to be on television."

Brinhart smiled, took another sip of his Coke. She was just a girl now, somebody who lived with an old man in a trailer and who had a child and probably hadn't finished high school. There was something of the timbre of the playground, the gymnasium—the cheerleader—in her voice now. He got up to leave.

"It was nice," she said.

She went with him out to the gate. They had passed Red, who sat in the living room with one of the magazines in his lap, apparently asleep. Outside it was like a fall night, with a northerly breeze and the odor of leaves. The sky was clear, almost white with stars along the tops of the far trees of the field. Through the opening at the other end of the row, just above the last awning there, was the moon, low and pale and circled, ringed by a glowing haze.

"Look," Shirley said.

"Yes," he murmured. She was at his elbow, and he believed that he could smell her hair. The trailer court seemed deserted now, though Brinhart, peering down toward Amy's trailer, wondered if Stan or Blanche might be watching from a window. But it was very dark here. Shirley was a white shape at his side. "I've had a nice evening," he said.

She smiled, touched his wrist.

"Thanks again," he said. And then he was drawing her toward him, his hands lightly on the backs of her elbows. She came to him readily, opened her mouth, one arm going up around his neck, the wrist touching, pressing; it was a long kiss, and before it was over, she had put her hand to his groin; he followed her lead, touched the soft place, beyond the bone, between her legs. Her mouth tasted of cola and something else, something he could not place. It was vaguely sour, like morning breath. Very gently she removed herself from him and glided away in the dark, went up the stoop and inside, without looking back. He stood there for a few moments, hearing his own breathing, and then the lights in the trailer went out.

Book Three

XIV ❧

HE FOUND KATHERINE sitting up in bed, propped on pillows, arms folded, watching television, which offered the only light. On the chair by the bed lay her clothes. From the television came the voice of a woman talking about cleanser: the cleanser was good for mildew, mold, grease, dried egg, handprints, crayon; it cleansed all surfaces equally well. Katherine's face was haggard, almost ghostly in the white light. Brinhart sat on the edge of the bed, removed his shoes, wished himself different. He had stopped in the kitchen and swallowed a glass of whiskey to steady himself; it hadn't worked. In ten years he had never been unfaithful. When Katherine leaned out of the bed to turn the television off, he almost winced, and as he wound his socks down off his feet the muscles of his upper leg tightened, nearly cramped. He straightened quickly, looked at her as she put the lamp on.

"Nice out."

"I want you to leave, Gordon." She spoke out of a sigh, put one hand to her forehead, the tips of the fingers pressing there.

"What did you say?"

"I said, I want you to leave."

"That's what I thought you said. Do you mind if I ask why?"

"*Why.*" She let her head fall against the pillows, looked at the ceiling. "I saw you, Gordon. I saw you go with her—I watched her blow you a kiss and I watched you sitting out there and I watched her come back and get you and I watched you go with her."

"I had a Coke with her and the old man she lives with."

"A Coke."

"I had a Coke with them. Jesus, Katherine, go ask them."

"You slept with her."

"For Christ's sweet sake, honey—"

"You never loved me. Never. I've seen you watching her. You slept with her in your mind if you didn't in fact."

"Listen—will you think about what you're saying?"

"I've thought about it. Believe me. It's not just this—it's everything. The way you've been drinking. We aren't going anywhere, Gordon. We've been treading water for ten years. And tonight just fixes it for good. I've been lying here thinking about how I could never let you touch me again, how I don't want you to touch me anymore. I want you to leave. It happens all the time."

He sat very still, his hands on his knees. One of her shoes lay in the husk of its own shadow on the floor.

"I knew I shouldn't have let you know I was unmarried when I had Alex. It made you think I was cheap, and I should've known that you'd do this one day. When I got older and somebody young and pretty came along and the guitar wasn't in it anymore—we've been hanging on for years. I'm going to be forty years old soon, and there's nothing anymore, and you want out, you know you do."

"Katherine," he said, "please. Listen to yourself."

"I wish I was dead. I wish I'd died at twenty-nine."

"This is crazy."

"That's right," she said. "Oh, Christ—isn't that just right."

They were silent for a moment. The quiet was like something solid between them. He stood, walked to the bureau, removed his shirt. He felt nothing: absolutely nothing. He believed he loved some version of his wife, but this woman in the bed was not his wife—there was no resemblance. He turned, made himself walk back to the bed, sat down again.

"All right," he said. "Let's clear the air a little bit, Katherine."

"No—no more." She arranged the pillows, lay with her back to him.

"Honey—"

"I don't want you," she said. "I don't want you." It was like a litany. "I don't want you, I don't want you."

He touched her shoulder.

"No. Get out. Please. Leave me alone."

"Katherine—it's your trouble. Can't you see, it's your trouble."

She was silent.

"I'll be in the living room," he said.

"Please, just go somewhere, Gordon."

He went into the hallway, dragging his shirt like a part of himself, and in the living room he stood trying to cry into it. He wanted to cry—held this abject picture of himself in his mind—but he couldn't make the tears come. He thought of Shirley, thought he could feel the kiss, still, on the skin around his mouth. It was as if he *had* slept with her, as if the defection were complete. Finally he went into the kitchen and poured a tumbler full of whiskey and drank it down, without ice, forcing it, poured himself another and then another, standing alone there in the light and then making his way into the living room, where he sat on the sofa, miserable, growing numb, the whiskey no longer burning and the room beginning to slide away from him, blurring, softening. He lay down after the third or fourth tumbler, staring into the light of the kitchen, growing more nauseous by the second. At last he was in the bathroom, loudly and violently ill, knowing that Katherine heard him, certain that she was awake. When he came out into the hall, he looked at the open door to the bedroom, waited for a while, trying to think of a way back, but he didn't know anything anymore, and everything was falling apart. He went in and lay down on the sofa, his face into the back cushion, his arm over his head, as though he were hiding there, and in only a moment he was asleep.

He had a strange dream. It was long ago and in a setting he did not recognize but which was exact in every detail—a small white clapboard porch and a lawn, with a view of mountains and a street, going down a steep hill, lined with trees and with brownstone houses set too close together. He had been on that porch, looking through a dusty window, and then he was inside, with his father, and there were girls.

His father smiled, was drinking something.

And then Brinhart had a history. He had gone out somewhere to get Katherine. It was all history, past. Brinhart and Katherine stood outside on the porch, looking through the window. It was all very familiar.

"Not my father," Brinhart said to Katherine.

Then he floated, suddenly, dizzily backward into a cold horror, and an awareness that he was sleeping, dreaming, his father not anywhere but in Florida, and with a frightening spasm of his heart he seemed to float again. He said, "Katherine, wake me up." He could hear his own voice, could feel the cushion of the sofa along his back, remembered everything.

"Katherine, wake me up."

And Katherine was in the hall. He was aware of her there

before he heard anything, and when she came a little toward him, he turned his head to look at her. But sleep was still on him; it covered his eyes like blindness itself, and he said again, "Katherine."

And now he could see her.

She approached, a shadow, utterly without sound. She stood over him.

"I'm sorry, honey." He could hear himself mumble the words. "Honey, wake me up." She only stood there. He was awake now, he thought, but he wanted her to make the motions anyway, wanted her hand on his chest. "Katherine," he said, crying. "Wake me up." He could feel the tears, the sobs in his throat and chest. "Wake me up." And she lay down on him, warm, heavy and yet without real weight, the bones of her hips on his stomach and her hair on his face.

"Wake me up."

But she stood away from him, her hands cupping his face. She was tender, soothing.

"Katherine," he said, hearing his voice in the room.

He opened his eyes on the last syllable of her name, and was astonished to find that she wasn't there. He looked at the walls, the easy chair in the far corner, the little magazine rack with its one newspaper lying folded. Katherine was not there, but for a moment the residue of the dream was so strong that he got to his feet and went into the kitchen, then back, looking for her. He went partway down the hall. Silence. The dark beyond her door, Alex's. He was alone, and in the yellow light of the living room he paced back and forth, trying to rid himself of the clammy sense of his aloneness, the whiskey still spinning in his head. He could not shake the feeling of having floated toward death, toward a darkness so vast that it held a place for everyone alone, entirely alone, and he lighted cigarette after cigarette, feeling the dizziness of that, too, and wanting Katherine to wake up, hoping she would come in and say something casual, would remark that he was smoking and wonder why. What was wrong. *Oh, honey, a terrible dream.* In a week—tomorrow—he told himself, you won't know why this scared you. He went into the kitchen and stood over the sink, afraid he might be ill again. It passed. He looked at the clock: two thirty. Certainly too late to call, but he picked up the phone anyway, and dialed the number. It rang for a long time, and when it stopped ringing, he wasn't sure of the voice that answered.

"Dad?" he said.

"Gordon?"

"Yeah."

"Good Lord—what time is it? What's wrong?"

"Dad—listen. You said you were coming up."

"It's two—it's two thirty in the morning. Good Lord."

"I called to talk to you."

"Ah, hold it. You woke me out of a sound sleep."

"I had too much to drink, I had this dream—"

"So what's the story? What's going on."

"Dad, if you'd let me just talk to you for a minute."

There was a long, slow sigh on the other end. "You had this dream. You had too much—did you say you had too much to drink?"

"And—and I needed to know if you're coming up or not. When. When you might be coming on up."

"You're calling me *now* to ask that?"

And abruptly there was interference on the wire: another phone ringing somewhere out in the night, a confusion of faint voices exchanging numbers.

"I got drunk tonight," Brinhart said. "Wanted to talk."

"What? Speak up. I can't hear you."

"Nothing," Brinhart said. "Look, I'm worried about you. I never hear from you anymore."

"We've just been talking about my coming up there."

"That's right. So when—I've made these plans—when are you coming?"

"I told you, I don't know for sure."

"Yes, but I need you to tell me when, Pop. Can you do that?"

"*Pop.* Are you drunk?"

"Yes. Goddammit, I said I had too much to drink."

"That's just wonderful."

"I'm drunk and I'm sloppy and I'm real scared, you know? I mean I'm really all fucked up. Have you ever been fucked up? Did you ever sleep around on Mom?"

"What?"

"You have a history, Pop. That's what I want to know. What's your history. Are you coming up here? Give me a day, Pop."

"You're drunk, boy. Call me back when you're sober, and we'll talk."

"No, see," Brinhart said, "you got away with it. Didn't you do it right? I mean, Aunt Beth fooling around like that when she was young—you never did any of that. You got all the way through and did it right, didn't you."

But there was only a dial tone now.

Brinhart put the receiver back on the hook and went into the living room and lay down on the sofa, closing his eyes, and when he sat up, perhaps five minutes later, he couldn't remember whether he had actually spoken to his father or not. He lay down again, drifted again, and finally he knew nothing but a slow, dreaming, suffocating despair.

XV

"KATHERINE is sliding downhill."

She seemed to whisper. She lay in a strange blue light.

"It never went away at all, and now it won't go away." She was smiling at someone, and she put the sheet aside, lay on her back with her legs apart, hands open, palms up, at her sides. Before her was an upside-down face, very white: the eyes looked at her. Katherine is sliding fast. It had been so long since she had looked at that face, and now here it was; it had always been coming back toward her, and now she was very confused and she thought perhaps this was going to be the last thing. Then she was standing by the bed, fully awake, hearing Brinhart's tortuous sleep from the living room. She went to the window, remembering only that she had been lying down in blue light. Outside a crow swooped down from the top of a tree in the field; a shimmer of dew was on the grass. For a moment she was not certain why she felt so sick inside, and then she heard Brinhart again. She went away from the window, ignored curtain loops, Brinhart's ties and belts, the wall sockets, not thinking.

In the bathroom she only glanced at the cabinet mirror, saw glazed, sleepless eyes, shadowed and frantic. There were razor blades behind the mirror, and she looked at the glass knob with which the cabinet would be opened. But there was no game now, no Other. Just Katherine. The sink was dirty, with mint-size drops of toothpaste and the milky trail of wet soap. She turned the shower on, waited for the stream of hot water, adjusted the cold tap, dropped her nightgown. Before she stepped in, she thought she heard something on the other side of the door, imagined Brinhart out there, perhaps listening, his ear against the wood. She had a cold, clean, calm sense of both her safety, here, and her wish to have him gone: it was almost like an idea of murder, this wish. When she stepped into the hot stream of water, there was a quick thrill of pain at the rush of it on her skin, and as she held her hair back under it, the idea of Brinhart's departure seemed already an accomplished fact. She was alone. Or she and the boy were alone.

How odd, she thought, *that I could forget I have an eleven-year-old child.*

She turned, let the water hit her full in the face, like waking up. Steam rose around her, thick as smoke, and she breathed it in. When the soap slipped from her fingers and dropped on her foot, she let out a little gasp of pain, thought it a justice of sorts—no, it was just that she was glad for it, like being glad with revenge. It was exactly that—a species of vengeance. She bent to pick it up, trying not to think, lathering herself furiously, the soap falling again but missing her this time.

Once, during that long year of their life with Brinhart's father, Brinhart had used the word *suicide* to describe her giving up of the guitar. It was a cold, rainy winter day, and the old man had spent most of it in the living room, brooding over the newspaper and watching television. Alex was down with the flu, and his phlegmy coughing, crying, and wheezing had driven Katherine nearly frantic with fear for his safety. Brinhart had tried to reassure her, spooning hot honey laced with bourbon down the boy's throat. That evening, the symptoms having eased, the fever broken, Katherine walked downstairs, through the living room (where the old man sat dozing in front of the television), and into the kitchen. She sat in the breakfast nook and cried, both from relief and from exhaustion. She cried for what seemed a long time and then she heard the old man say something to Brinhart. In a moment Brinhart came to her with a shot glass full of bourbon.

"Dad says to take this." He sat down across from her.

"I don't want it," Katherine said, holding a napkin to her face.

"It'll calm you down."

"Why doesn't *he* come in here and give it to me. Why do I have to feel *dispensed* to all the time."

"He'll—improve," Brinhart said. "Give him time."

"What does he want? What is it that I have to do?"

"Nothing, just give him a little time to get used to things." He put the whiskey down in front of her. "Come on, take this. It'll relax you."

She drank it fast. It seemed about to come back up; it burned all the way down, and the taste made her shudder.

"Why are you giving it up?" he asked.

"If you're talking about the music, don't. I don't want to talk about it. It's over."

"No, really—you must have a reason."

"All right. I'm tired. How about that? I got tired of it. It wasn't fun anymore. You gave up the church, I gave up the music. What's the difference."

"I had no talent for the church."

"Oh, Christ."

"You're throwing talent away."

This angered her. The anger burned through her as the whiskey had burned. "We're married now, Gordon. You're not a groupie anymore, remember?"

And he had said it, then: "You're committing a kind of suicide, aren't you."

She threw the shot glass at him, hit him in the chest with it. She had watched him cater to his father, nodding yes to his father's absurd statements about politics, religion, the world, the war—"They ought to use just one nuclear bomb on Hanoi, just one," the old man said, "and then we'll see how long the damn Communists want to hold out"—and she had watched them ride off to mass every Sunday: the boy and his father. She had tried very hard to understand Brinhart's devotion to the old man, but now he sat there judging her, and he had no right to do that. So she threw the shot glass, and it made a loud thud on his breastbone and dropped to the floor. He bent down, picked it up, holding his chest. She had not meant to hurt him: at least she had not meant to hurt him badly. But he stood there, rubbing his chest, his face twisted and white.

"I'm sorry," she said, "I'm sorry, Gordo. I didn't mean it."

"Sure," he gasped. "You fucking didn't mean it."

"It's just been such an awful day, and I knew he was getting mad because the baby—"

Brinhart hurled the glass against the sink with a furious wrenching of his body. The noise brought the old man into the room. Katherine looked at the old man's face, saw the shape of Brinhart's face. She wanted nothing to do with any Brinharts for a while. She wanted to be alone with her baby and she wanted to sleep. The old man stood erect just inside the door, his hands on his hips. Brinhart turned, looked at him, made a waving motion with his hand. "It's all right, Dad."

"I want an explanation of this outburst," the old man said. "This is my house."

Brinhart stood rubbing his chest.

"Well?"

"It's nothing—it's all right now. I broke a glass."

"All right," the old man said, turning to Katherine. "You tell me."

"I'm committing suicide," Katherine said.

"You are—"

"That's right."

"And how are you going to go about it?"

"Oh," she said, looking at Brinhart, "it's happening right now."

"Well," said Brinhart, "isn't it?"

"Will one of you please explain?" Now the old man was worried. Katherine could see it in his face, could see he was beginning to understand that what he had come in on was something over which he would have no control: not the talk of suicide, not even the idea of suicide, but this break in the order of his household, this moment itself. There was about the old man then an almost obsessive attention to cleanliness and order, to the surface of things. He believed (she had heard him say it many times to Gordon, knowing too, full well, that he intended *her* to hear and understand) that the decorum one imposed on the surface of things created decorum beneath the surface as well, that if one pretended long enough to observe the rules of orderly habit and decorous behavior, one sooner or later was transformed inwardly. That (he would say) was the basis of all law; it created honor and decency where none existed. Quiet habits bred quiet minds: and so on, and so on. To have thrown a bourbon glass, to have broken it on the sink, was to threaten the trembling surface of this life he had organized so well. Katherine knew this, and if she would later come to believe his idea of life—so much so, that she would feel her sanity balanced on it like a tottering board on a fulcrum—she only wanted to fly in the face of it now.

"You want me to explain?" she said, smiling bitterly at him.

"Katherine," Brinhart said, "let's leave it alone."

"Yes," the old man said. "Maybe that's best."

"No," said Katherine. "I want to give you all the nasty details."

"Katherine, dammit," Brinhart said.

The old man looked at him. "Do not swear in this house."

"Gordon wants me to play my wild guitar again," Katherine said. "He claims I'm committing suicide by quitting."

"Now, all right," the old man said. "Let's just—"

"Isn't that what you want, Gordo? For me to play again? And so I'm in the middle. Because Daddy Warbucks here wants me to quit my evil ways. To become sweet and polite and all that *shit*. Right?" She relished the vulgar word, watched its effect on the old man's face. "Now, that isn't really why I quit," she went on quickly, though he had opened his mouth to speak. "That isn't why at all. I quit because I was sick to death of the whole"—she paused, looking at him—"*fucking* thing. All of it. But your son seems to think there's some other reason. Some other dark, neurotic reason, you see. Like a sort of secret suicide, since I'm worth nothing to him unless I'm playing a musical instrument and screaming my brains out. Isn't that right, Gordo? I'm a trophy, right? A prize. You landed me and I stopped singing and you just can't handle that, can you?"

"She's upset because of the baby," Brinhart said to his father.

"I am not upset because of the baby."

"You calm her down," the old man said, turning from them.

"Excuse me," said Katherine. "I am still *in* the fucking room."

The elder Brinhart didn't even pause. As he pushed the door he spoke over his shoulder: "And I want the obscenity to cease as of this moment."

"Fuck *you!*" Katherine shrieked, rising so quickly she knocked her chair over. "Fuck *you!*"

Brinhart's hands were on her shoulder. The door had swung shut.

"You old purple motherfucking cock!" she shouted.

"Katherine, stop it. Stop it now." He had crushed her against his chest, and she cried into it, the idea coming up through her, from somewhere far down inside, that he had been right, that she *had* wanted to destroy it: the music and the talent and the prodigious desire, all of it that was inextricably herself.

"No," she said. "No," crying in the flannel folds of his shirt.

"It's all right," he kept saying. "All right, all right, it's all right."

Later he would say that this was when he realized he loved *her*, not her talent, regardless of what part the talent had played in his initial feelings for her. She didn't know, now, turning the shower off, whether she could stand it if he did leave her. Yet she was resolved: and there was in her resolution something of the stubborn will to be clear of everything, even at the cost of her own well-being. It was exactly the same as it had been when she gave up the music: this angry denial of everything, this feeling that was almost like petulance—would be petulance if it did not carry with it the sense of so much destruction.

"I don't care," she said aloud, looking at the water-beaded spigots before her.

And abruptly she remembered something else. It came to her like a vision. A moment, sometime well before Alex was born—she and the drummer, sitting in the sun at the edge of a swimming pool: morning, too early for bathers, and the other members of the band still asleep or drugged after a long journey south. This was Alabama, perhaps thirteen summers ago. Nineteen sixty-six. They had come through the night from Iowa, traveling along the Mississippi—the ugly trail of freight yards, dumps, and factories in the dark; dull black shapes piled up, blocking the occasional view of moon-gleaming water—and had arrived in Birmingham in the early-dawn light, checking into the motel and unpacking little, too tired and bleary-eyed to do anything but fall into their beds and sleep. Katherine, typically, had not been able to sleep, and had unpacked one of the flat-box guitars and gone out to sit at the edge of the pool—with her feet in the water—and play. It was a Monday, a fine, clear August morning, loud with birds and the hum of traffic on the highway into the hub of the city. She played quietly, singing low, aware of herself as she must appear to any of those poor tired vacationers, salesmen, or adulterers who had begun to leave their rooms to continue whatever journeys they had begun. She thought about how she had talent, and could live freely, out of the stream of lives. It was a delicious thought that went out of her toward the drummer as he approached, apparently unable to sleep himself, wearing only jeans and a bead necklace, his hair in a wild African tangle, a blond nimbus, about his head. He sat down next to her, rolled his pants legs up, dipped his feet into the water, and said, "Cold."

This was the moment she remembered. She had watched his feet break the surface of the water next to her own, had heard him say his one word, had looked out past the other end of the pool at a stupendous willow, the sky above it blue as the ocean—and she had experienced a sort of shock along the ends of her nerves: everything so clean and sharp and she was not in life, not in the steady day-to-day wearing-down of things that her parents had known or that everyone save her, Katherine, knew. As the moment passed she played a few desultory notes on the guitar, played them because she could, because she was brilliant. The drummer whistled softly, leaning back on his hands.

"God," he said finally, "look at that."

A man, probably a salesman—a slow-moving, portly, balding man in a rumpled suit, with both hands wrapped around the rim of a paper cup of something hot—was crossing the parking lot adjacent to the pool. He passed close enough for Katherine to see that his eyes were puffy and red, his expression disconsolate but determined.

"How would you like to be him?" the drummer said.

Now, lifting a towel from the rack, she thought about how only two nights ago she had watched Gordon coming up the walk from the car, looking tired and depleted from the drive home, clutching a newspaper. *How would you like to be him.*

"Fucking citizens," the drummer had said.

"My father—your father—they're all citizens."

"You hate your father and I hate my father."

"I do not hate my father," Katherine said.

"You do. You just won't admit to yourself that you do."

"Oh, boy," she said. "Why don't you go home and sleep with your mother."

"I hate her too."

"You hate everything," said Katherine.

"But me," the drummer said, smiling. "But me, but me, but me."

A little tremor of disgust ran through her as she dried herself, thinking of the drummer, those years—she did not want to think about any of that. It was all past, dead. The drummer was dead. The drummer had been dead long before Katherine knew him. She remembered when he found out she was pregnant; the coldness in his voice had made her tremble. His eyes had expressed everything: Get rid of it—get rid of the thing. It was not a child, not even a fetus; there was loathing in his face: get rid of it. She might have done so if his reaction had been even a little human. But she wanted a child, and recognized this as somehow both a concession to, and a further defiance of, the shape of life as her parents had so assiduously brought her up to see it. There was also defiance of the drummer, whom she had slept with in the meanness of a contempt he engendered, was filled with: she had never even liked him, never. Not even a little. Their coupling had been a sort of battle they played out in each other's flesh. Her proximity to him, finally, without considering their sporadic and unhappy intimacy, had bleached the bones under her skin, and left her as empty as he was. This was what she told herself. And she had Alex to make up for everything, to learn how to give love, to get the feel of the drummer off her skin: that man whose name had ceased to matter as soon as he had gone, and for whom there was only the corruption, the voluptuous decay, of himself. What despair she had known in those last months.

And now here she was, combing out her hair in the steaming bathroom, so much alone that she must remember that she had a child, a husband. How many times she had thought about that moment by the pool, in that summer she thought would not end. How much of herself she had thrown away somewhere, and how she hated all the endless days the same, the same. How she hated herself for feeling these things. She stood gazing at her reflection in the mirror, which was beginning to clear of steam; she seemed to watch herself come into being there. She leaned close to the sweating glass, and thought about getting clear again; she would quit everything and get clear.

XVI ❧

HE HEARD his mother in the bathroom, as he had heard Brinhart moaning in his sleep, and now he went quietly down the hall, through the living room—Brinhart's thrown shape on the sofa, the slow, drugged breathing—and out, closing the door soundlessly behind him. Amy had cancer—*that, too.* It was not real and he felt really nothing about it except a general sense of the bigness of the world and its terrible things to fear. He had spent most of the predawn rather desperately making up a baseball player, someone he might be when he grew tall and thin, like the boy James. This baseball player he imagined was left-handed, as Ted Williams had been, and he had incredible eyesight and quickness of wrist. Alex had seen the look on his mother's face when she found out about Amy; and then later, how she had wandered the apartment, how she had made that sound, coming down the hall past his room. He tried very hard to concentrate on the left-hander, who hit .358 as a rookie, slammed 41 home runs, and missed the triple crown by one RBI with 112. Johnny Gaddling—it had the sound of baseball—would be a great hitter, center fielder for a losing team. A last-place team. The old Senators, since that was all safely in the past, and he could stick to all the other statistics as he knew them.

He walked down through the hedgerow to the trailer court. A few people were stirring farther up—three men getting into a van, talking and laughing. One held a Styrofoam cup, another puffed on a pipe. There was nothing wrong with them; they were happy. Amy's mother came out and sat down on the stoop, perhaps ten feet away from him, though she did not see him. Her presence brought it home to him that he had come here hoping Amy would be up, that she would see him and come out.

"Can Amy come out?" he said.

Amy's mother sat with her large legs spread—her dress stretched tight—and held a yellow cloth to her face. "It's early," she said.

"Okay."

"Just a minute." She got up, with what looked like effort, and went inside, letting the aluminum door slam. In a moment she returned, with Amy, who smiled at him, coming down the stoop.

"Stay close, honey," Blanche said.

"Bye," Amy said.

"Please, now. Will you promise?"

"I promise."

Alex walked with her down to the field. They did not speak, and she did not hesitate, but took him to the creek, up the bank on the other side to the road. There was a heavy mist lying over the creek, like a fallen cloud. The grass was damp, glistened with dew; beads of water clung to their legs. They went across the road into the shopping center, and Amy led him around the buildings.

"There's graves up here," she said.

They climbed, stood quiet in the cut grass amid the white markers. Alex was glad of the light, which poured brokenly through the leaves and branches above them. There was a mist here, too, but it was dissipating fast. Amy removed her shoes and knelt before the first marker. She seemed to be engaged in some sort of ritual, as if she had been coming here for years.

"I followed that girl and your daddy here last night," she said.

He was silent.

"Did you hear me?"

"Yes."

"I thought they were going to do it, even with the baby and all—she had the baby with her, and I thought they were going to go ahead and do it."

"Do you really have cancer?" he said.

She answered without hesitation. "It's in my blood." She shrugged, stood, moved to the next grave, knelt down again. "Just think. There's somebody under here."

"How come you're not in the hospital?"

"It was in remission. When I was seven years old I had it and they thought I was going to die but I didn't and it went away and now they have to watch it and give me bone marrow tests because it came back last year. The medicines have changed. So I got this medicine." She spoke with an evenness of tone that unnerved him. She may as well have been talking about the thin moisture on the grass. "I don't really have any hair, you know." She stood again, clapped her hands as if to remove some dust or grass from her palms. "I got used to everything, I guess. It doesn't bother me now. See"—she pointed to one of the stones—"everybody who ever lived goes there." She sighed. Alex looked at her and realized how sick the whiteness of her skin was: he could not remember if it had always been as pale as it was now. She said, laughing, "My folks—it's like they have to turn their backs on something to laugh."

"Aren't you scared?" he asked.

"Plenty. And I'm mad too."

"I don't like this place," he said.

"You don't have to stay."

"Come on, let's go to Woolworth's."

"I don't have any money."

They were quiet for a while. A car horn sounded from the highway beyond the flat-roofed buildings of the mall behind them. Amy lay down on the grass, sighing, folding her arms over her chest.

"Come on," he said.

"Lay down." She smiled at him, extending one hand. "I thought of us up here last night. Come on, lay next to me."

He did not want to touch her; but he lay down.

"I love you very much," she said.

He was quiet. The confusion of leaves above him moved, and their number, so uncountable, fed his frustration.

"Don't you love me?"

"Okay," he said.

" 'Okay,' " she mimicked, and took his hand. "Do you think about dying at all?"

"No."

"I do. All the time."

He said nothing. It was not real. He looked at the chalkiness of her face. No.

"Sometimes it's pretty scary," she said.

He sat up. Before him were the roofs of the mall, a sky turning pale, the glint from an airplane high up, like something hurled from the sun.

"Well," she said, "what do you think about dying?"

"I don't want to talk about it anymore," he said. "I'm leaving."

"Don't leave."

"I want to go to Woolworth's."

"I told you, I don't have any money."

"I have," he said.

"How much?"

"Enough."

"Enough for two sundaes?"

"Maybe."

"*Maybe*. You're such a baby sometimes."

"I got fifty cents," he said. "How much will it get?"

"It won't get two sundaes, that's for sure."

Presently she said, "What do you think happens after you die?"

"I don't know."

"Do you think there's a hell?"

"Sure, I guess."

"I don't."

He waited.

"Well, I don't think there's a hell," she said, sitting up next to him and pulling at the grass. "I think we all get rewarded for living *here*."

"Your mother and father told you that."

"No," she said, "my father thinks hell is fire and screaming. Something like that, but it's only for bad men, mostly. I know he thinks hell is fire and screaming because he's Catholic, and I looked it up. Catholics believe in hell and fire and screaming if you're bad before you die. He goes to church, you know, a lot. Sometimes even during the week. He comes in to see if I'm awake because he wants to kiss me, and I always wake up and kiss him, except sometimes he looks so worried about everything, I pretend I'm asleep. I've got it so I can breathe just like people do when they're asleep. . . . Listen." She took his wrist. "Close your eyes and listen."

He closed his eyes, heard slow, sighing breath, thought about her under the ground. It was curious; it passed through him like something ordinary, and left nothing behind.

"Well?" she said. "Doesn't that sound like it?"

He thought it did, and he told her so.

"And I lay there pretending I'm asleep, and he just kisses my cheek and goes." She made a small, throaty chuckling

sound, stretched, and then casually, without even a glance
at him, took her blouse off. Beneath it she wore a bra. She
took this off too. Her breasts were very white, very small.
She put his hand there, lying back down. "Do you go to
church?"

"No."

"You never went? Ever?"

"No."

"Lay down."

He did so. He was afraid of his hand on that skin, but he
couldn't believe it: it wasn't real, the cancer in her blood.
The skin was cool and smooth, and it was all right if he
didn't think about the other.

"Will we be married in a church, do you think?"

"I don't know," he said.

"I'd like to get married on television. Like a princess or a
movie actress. Wouldn't you love to be in the movies?"

"Not especially."

"I would. But then movie actresses can't marry baseball
players."

"They can if they want to," he said.

"Maybe."

"Joe DiMaggio married one."

She came up on one elbow, looked down at him. "Want
me to tell you who played second base for the Yankees in
1961?" Carefully she removed his hand from her breast.
"Come on, ask me who it was."

"Why?"

"You don't know, do you?"

"Bobby Richardson."

"That's right." She smiled.

"You didn't really know it. You just did that so I'd tell."

"All right," she said. "I'll tell you who played first base."

He waited.

"Ready?"

"Go ahead."

"Bill"—she stared out at the trees, and he watched her pupils close—"Bill . . . Skowron. Skowron. Right?"

He thought for a moment, wasn't certain.

"You don't know," she said.

"Yes. You're right." He was pleased.

"See? Just for you. I got those names just for you—I made my dad tell them to me."

"I thought you said he didn't like baseball."

"Oh, he did when he was younger." She lay back down and put his hand on her breast again. Then she said, "Know what else he taught me?"

"What."

"Close your eyes."

He did, and she began to sing, softly, her voice high and whispery above him. He was astonished and embarrassed; it was like television, those old movies where people sang to each other in the middle of nothing, like talking.

"Take me out to the ball game," she sang, "take me out to the fair. Da-da and peanuts and Cracker Jacks. I don't care if I never get back—" She stopped. "I don't know all the words. Come on, sing with me. Da-da and peanuts and Cracker Jacks—come on."

"I can't sing."

"Da-da and da-da I never get back. Let me root, root, root for the home team. If they don't win da-da-da. For it's one, two, three strikes you're out at the old baseball—the old da-da. Oh. The old ball game. Da-*dum*." She laughed, put one leg up, kicked it out and brought it down again. "How 'bout that? I learned that just for you."

"You sing nice," he said. It was all he could think of.

"Thanks."

They lay quiet for a long time, it seemed. There was no sound in the trees, and he gazed at the sky, at the spaces between the leaves. A crow cawed nearby.

"You want to look at me?" she said.

He sat up and watched her move his hand on her breast.

"I'll take my pants off."

"Okay," he said.

She struggled out of her shorts, which were white, as her legs were white, and again he thought about what was in her blood. When she was naked, he put his hand in the hair, and she reached up and opened the zipper of his pants. He knelt above her and let her touch him, not thinking; it was perfect. It felt wonderful.

"Now we really are lovers, aren't we," she said.

He could not speak for what was happening to him.

"You're real hard," she said. "That's what happens."

And then there was a cracking noise, very near: someone on the bank, farther down, climbing through the broken pine branches there. Amy was rolling around in the grass, frantically trying to get into her clothes, and Alex knelt around the quick pulsing of his sex, astonished, trying to think of hiding, putting himself back; but what was happening would not be stopped, and when it finally did stop, he was too late—someone was rising over the edge of the bank, and Amy stood in front of him now, her back to him, blocking him from view, from whoever had come walking through the grass to where they were.

"Hello," Amy said.

Alex saw that she had her bra crumpled in her fists, behind her back.

"Hello," came the voice, a female voice he knew, but could not place right away. "So you've found my little cemetery."

"Yours?"

"Well, not really. Is that . . . Alex?" And he knew now. He saw Shirley lean to the side to look at him. He had his legs drawn up and his pants were binding on him, hurting. "Hello, Alex," said Shirley.

"Hello," he said. As he shifted his weight a little the tenderness in his groin surprised him. "Oh—ow!"

"What's wrong?" Shirley asked.

"Nothing—ow!" He had tried to stand.

"For Lord's sake, are you all right?"

"He was—" Amy said, "s-stung—he was stung by a bee."

"Oh, Lord," said Shirley. She came to his side, knelt down, and put her hand on his shoulder. "Where?"

Now he could rise, and he went out from beneath her hand. "It's all right now," he said, walking away toward the edge of the bank.

"Where are you going?"

He heard Amy say, "We have to get home," and then he was running headlong down the bank. He nearly fell as he reached the bottom. Amy came down more slowly, though she, too, was running. When she reached him, she held his arm, breathing and laughing. Her cheeks were blue. He saw, with horror, that her hair was awry; it was sitting to the side, like a cap knocked partway off. When she looked at him, she stopped, put her hands up, turning. "I told you," she said. "I told you about it."

He could say nothing. He looked away, saw the ranked Dumpsters in their mute clouds of flies.

"I knocked it loose," she said. She started walking, and he walked with her, and everything around them was a blur. So it took your hair like that, made you ugly. No, he thought. Not ugly. Amy is not ugly.

"You know that boy I told you about? That Harmon?" she asked.

"Yes," he said.

They had come around the buildings, and walked toward the Woolworth's, the shade of the mall very cool, and crowded: women with children—tired-looking and irritable —pushing shopping carts while the children ran ahead or hung from the front of the carts. Two men in blue coveralls stood leaning against the side of a beer truck at the 7-Eleven, farther down.

"What about him?" Alex said.

"I made him up." She seemed about to cry.

"That's all right," he said. "I don't care."

They stopped in front of the Woolworth's. An old man in a red baseball cap stood there, puffing on a cigar, his head wreathed in greenish smoke. He coughed, spit a long, shimmering streak that slapped the concrete before him.

"I don't want to go in now," Amy said.

"I'll buy a Coke," said Alex.

"No." She led the way out, through the sunny, burning lot, and when they crossed the road, dropping down the bank to the creek, she said, "You feel sorry for me, don't you. About my hair."

"No," he lied.

She went on ahead of him, climbing the slope of the field toward the trailer court, and because he could not bring himself to do anything else, he watched her go. Then he sat at the edge of the creek, in a single shaft of sun, watching the heavy, listless flight of bees, the hovering suddenness of dragonflies over the slow trickle of streaked water. Everything seemed to breathe around him. He concentrated on the way everything seemed to breathe.

XVII ❧

BRINHART FORCED HIMSELF to eat a piece of toast, nibbling at it, washing it down with milk. He was already late but he didn't care now. He would sit here all day, if it took that long. He would have things out with Katherine. He would straighten everything. Twice he had knocked on the bathroom door, and twice Katherine had sent him away. She had done so without rancor or sarcasm or—anything. Her voice had been devoid of feeling, and she had not called him by name. She might have been speaking to a stranger.

Now, sipping the milk, he imagined her sitting on the closed toilet seat, legs crossed, listening to his movements. He was not angry. He was too sick to feel anger. In one of the neighboring apartments a puppy cried and howled and complained. He thought the sound might drive him crazy. The memory of his dream of the night before, and then—as though part of himself willed it for the pain it would cause him—of Shirley's kiss, commingled in him with the sluggish, painful and still faintly alcoholic coursing of his blood, and left him sighing weakly, fighting off the beginning of a guilty sexual stir: morning erection, a taunt, a mockery. He stood at the window and rubbed his eyes, and in a moment the arousal gave way to a cold wave of fear, worse than nausea. *Oh, dammit, Katherine, I'm innocent.*

And here she was, wrapped in her terry-cloth robe, carrying a bath towel. She looked skeletal, her hair wet, close to the curve of her skull; the deepening sockets of her eyes in a face colorless and calm. She did not speak. She took the chair across from him, began wrapping her head in the towel.

"I'll fix you some toast," he said.

"I'm not hungry."

"You have to eat."

"I'm not hungry."

"Katherine."

She went on arranging the towel about her head. Then she sat staring at the floor.

"What were you doing in there?"

"Took a shower."

"Yes, but afterward. You were in there so long."

"I'm out now." Her voice was toneless.

"Katherine, nothing happened last night. She's just a lonely girl who wants friends."

She did not speak.

"You're imagining it all. Please, honey."

She sat back against the wall, her hands lying in her lap, her eyes expressionless and glazed.

"I'm telling you the truth," he said.

She sighed. "I'm so tired."

He went to the sink, stood there spitting a stream of the milk he had just drunk. It came up in a cough, hot and burning. He put his head under the faucet, the water cascading down the sides of his face, around his neck, loud and gushing, stinging cold. Then he stood back, gasping, holding on to the counter. His eyes stung, little piercing needles of pain shooting through the pupils. When he looked at her, he saw no pity: nothing. She was not even looking at him. He knelt in front of her, took her hands. "Honey, let's get out of here. Let's go someplace. Let's just pick up and go."

"I have to get a job," she said. "I don't know where we'll be."

"Let's drive down and see the old man. We had fun the last time. Remember. Right there by the sea."

"No." Her eyes were shining. "I quit."

He put his face down into the palms of her hands. "Jesus Christ. Nothing's changed. I love you. I love you, Katherine." He was beginning to cry now, repeating the phrase, and memory rose up at him like an odor out of a hole: Aunt Beth's photograph, the highway on the peninsula, Katherine as she had been when her ghosts slept, their loving, his father as he had appeared in the dream, and Shirley's mouth: Shirley, bending to look at the graves, coming into his arms, a gray shadow in the dark. "Jesus," he said, hating himself and his needs and the whole history of his desires and his life: what he had ever wanted. Nothing. A gliding. It dawned on him with the force of a blow to his chest that he had done this to Katherine just by being what he was and wanting what he wanted. "Honey, we can change, can't we? I can change. We love each other. I know we love each other."

"I'm tired," she said. But then she said, "Gordo."

He kissed her. Or he tried to. Her lips were lifeless, and she looked at him.

"Christ, honey," he said.

And now she did something that astonished him. He would not have believed it if he had not seen it. She yawned, tapping her lips with the tips of her fingers, and said, "Go to work," closing her mouth on the last word, with the end of the yawn.

He stood. "Katherine," he said.

"Go to work. I'm tired."

"I want to—will you let me get you some help?"

"Just go to work."

"Lots of people—" he began. "Lots of—"

"Stop it," she said. "Stop it."

"That's what we should've done a long time ago. Just got you in to see a doctor. A little help and everybody—everybody says they're like new, Katherine."

"I don't want any doctors. There's nothing wrong with me. It's wrong with you. Go to work."

"You haven't slept—"

"Let me alone, Gordon."

"Honey, I can't leave you like this."

"Ha," she said.

"Ah, Christ." He stood up.

"I forgive you."

"Forgive—"

"I forgive you for fucking that girl."

"I never—"

"You think I'm crazy because I don't melt in your fucking arms, is that it? No. I'm out. I want out."

He walked to the sink, turned, looked at her. "I don't even know you anymore," he said.

"There you are."

"I love you the best way I can, the best way I know how. What do you want me to do?"

"I told you that. I want you to leave me alone."

"For good?"

"Maybe. I don't know."

He could not tell now. A few moments ago he had been certain that she had gone completely mad. Her eyes were not so strange anymore, though there was no love or gentleness in them. He went to her again, kissed her forehead.

"You know," she said, "My mother was right. I never should've known what a C-minor seventh was when I was six. I was very precocious. She thought I'd be a concert pianist, and I fucked her up good and became a queen of rock 'n' roll."

"I'm not leaving you like this, Katherine. We have to straighten this out."

"Like what," she was saying before he had finished. "Like what? I'm talking. I'm telling you something."

He left her there, went into the bedroom, where he found his shoes. He dressed quickly, wanting to get away now. When he crossed through the living room, he saw, in the corner of his eye, her shape in the entrance to the kitchen. He did not look there, and she said nothing as he opened the door and stepped out.

There were two young men in the tennis court, volleying lazily, just trying to hit the ball to each other, back and forth. The sky was streaked with haze and there was the sound of construction somewhere. He walked to the car, leaned in, and rolled the windows down. As he put the key in the ignition, sighing loudly, the blood vessels at his temples throbbing, he experienced another wave of fear and nausea.

He could not go to work.

He stopped at a phone booth on Mission Street, just outside the hub of Point Royal, and called in sick. He made up a specific excuse, anxious to be believed: "I've been throwing up all night," he said, cupping his hand over the mouthpiece against the sound of cars on the road. "I think I got ahold of some rancid meat." Everything was cordial, and in the first moments after he made the call, he felt better. When he had hung up the phone, he stayed in the booth and looked through the yellow pages for the name of a psychologist. The names were a blur, so many, most of them in Washington or Arlington. The clinics and the professional buildings and the hours, all those names. He ran his finger down the page until he found one listed for Point Royal. A professional building on Church Street. He tore a corner of the page away, but could not find a pencil or pen. He searched his pockets, the booth. Two little bead chains dangled, empty, under the phone. He tore the whole page out of the book, folded it, put it in his back pocket. When he stepped out of the booth, the air seemed cooler, and he realized that he had been sweating heavily. He had nowhere to go, and for a long while he sat behind the wheel, shaking in the rough idling of the car, trying to think. Then he brought out the page he had torn from the book, unfolded it, looked at the address—after another search for the name among those many listed. Church Street. He lay the torn page on the seat next to him and edged out into traffic, got behind a truck with dust all over its panel door and an obscene word fingered into the dust. FUCK. Brinhart read the word for perhaps three miles, through a progression of lights that always seemed to be red. The slow traffic lulled him a little, and he sat behind the truck, wondering how one person could be culpable for the problems of another: hadn't he always been there, patient enough, understanding enough—hadn't he waited her out those other times? Hadn't he suffered at her hands as well?

At the corner of Mission Street and Church Street was a restaurant-bar, The Knight's Table—one of his father's old stopping places. He parked the car there, got out, imagining the abject picture he must make—a man in rumpled clothes, unshaved, downcast, obviously in need of sleep and rest. This was a close intersection, the buildings having been erected before the advent of the automobile. It was the old Town Hall section of Point Royal, the only part of the town that looked much as it had in the last century. The Knight's Table had been established in 1896; it was one of the oldest restaurants in the area, and for something more than thirty years Brinhart's father had come here for his one whiskey after work.

In the year or so after Brinhart had graduated from high school, when he had first tried college, he had sometimes met his father here, and the old man would buy him a beer. One beer. The old man would drink his one whiskey. The two of them would talk—or the old man would talk and Brinhart would listen. There were questions—what Brinhart wanted to do for a career, what his studies were—but for the most part, the old man told stories about his own schooling, how strict the Jesuits were at Georgetown. Brinhart came to know that his birth had ended his father's hopes for a college degree. The old man did not begrudge the matter. He would do everything exactly the same. No regrets. That was what one wanted in life: to get old without having to live with regret. After Brinhart had enlisted in the army, he and his mother had met the old man here for a farewell dinner, one of the last times Brinhart ever saw his mother. The three of them sat in a booth near the back and had a quiet meal. Brinhart's mother was upset: her only child going away. She continually dabbed her eyes with a napkin, sniffed loudly from time to time; and the old man talked and talked about the army—what to expect, and not to volunteer for anything, and make sure they knew about the college courses, because Brinhart did not want to wind up carrying a rifle through the jungle. Occasionally there was a hint of the old man's puzzlement about why Brinhart had given up the college and done this inexplicable thing—the army. Finally the old man said, "It's crazy, you know. Joining the army."

"Yes," Brinhart's mother said, sniffing. "They just bombed Hanoi Harbor." There was in her speech always the sense that one had missed part of the sentence: she made her connections inwardly and then spoke the conclusion and it always seemed out of context. She had once been pretty (there were pictures) but she had let the old man rule her and now she was boxlike, heavy-chinned, as though the years had carved her out of stone, though there was nothing stony about her at all: she was soft, pliant, giving, and when she was pressed—when the old man's wishes came too close to what would be open rule—she could be quite stubborn, as she had been about Aunt Beth and as she had been about Brinhart's decision to enter the army. But mostly, over the years, she had given in—both to Brinhart and to the old man. That evening, so long ago, Brinhart felt weak with love for her, and mixed with his love was a kind of pity. She seemed baffled: even, somehow, surprised—as though she had awakened from a profound sleep and found that life had done this to her, brought her here, to a dinner she had not been allowed to cook for a son she had never understood, to sit next to a husband in whom she had subsumed herself too long to be able to recognize where she left off and he began—and to cry softly, dabbing her eyes with the napkin. "I just know it'll happen," she said.

"You know *what* will happen?" asked Brinhart's father, patient, as always, with her way of speaking.

"Why, he'll be killed in the war."

"There's no war yet, dear," the old man said.

"He's going to double the draft. There'll be troops going over."

"I'll be all right, Mom," said Brinhart, and ordered another drink. His father looked at him. "Just one more, Dad."

"Cocktails are hard liquor, Son."

"Just one more."

"Make it a beer."

"He's doubling the draft," Brinhart's mother said.

"That's just to be ready," the old man answered. "Johnson doesn't want any war. He can't afford it."

"Well, in any case," Brinhart said, "I've already joined."

"You don't want the infantry, boy. Remember that."

"I don't want the infantry."

He had got a little drunk that night; the first time, really. It was a generally unpleasant feeling after a while, and as they walked down Church Street toward the car his father slapped him on the back and said, "Stay away from cheap women, Son, wherever the army sends you. I know a lot of guys will be going to them, and you'll have plenty of chances, but stay away. I kept myself for your mother and I've never regretted it."

Brinhart put his arm around his mother's waist, again feeling sorry for her and unable to understand quite why now. He said, "I love you, Mom." And she sniffed.

"Just remember your mother and don't do anything you wouldn't do with her in the room and you'll be all right. You won't have anything to regret later."

"What a thing to put on the boy," his mother said.

That was all so far away now—and he remembered, walking up to the entrance of The Knight's Table, that when he had come home the first time, on leave from training, having witnessed, on a red field in Georgia, the death of a skinny, half-literate and gentle black man named Washington, he had come home changed, someone who no longer believed the things his parents believed. He had gone to church with them, had done all the usual things with them; and he had tried to hide his feeling of strangeness in a house he remembered but no longer recognized. When he left to take up his assignment (it was in Mississippi, on the Gulf, where for two years he would sit behind a typewriter in a room with a large window looking out on the Sound) his mother cried as if certain that she would never see him again.

She had been nearly right.

He had missed two Christmases, and then been sent to Missouri. He had come home for a week in the last summer his mother was alive, and had spent most of that time searching out old friends, school buddies, places he had loved and needed to see again because he thought he might not return for a long time. This made his parents unhappy, and then his mother was dead, and Brinhart lived with so many regrets: as he entered The Knight's Table he thought of his father's ritual stop here over the years, and he took the same booth he had occupied with his parents on that evening long ago.

It was not yet ten o'clock in the morning, and he was miserable, but he would sit here and have a light breakfast, and perhaps he would have one whiskey to calm his nerves: he really had to get his nerves settled. When he had taken his seat, a tremor went through him, and as the waitress handed him a menu he saw her looking at his hands. She was in her late forties or early fifties, wore her hair in a pile of curls atop her head; Brinhart gazed at the heaviness of her hips, the spare tire of fat above the tight red vinyl belt she wore. The booth was made of knotty pine (he couldn't remember if it had been so *then*), and a candle burned in a bowllike glass on the table, the glass wrapped in a waxen net. Above him, on the wall, were a pair of crossed swords and a shield. It was dark. Behind the waitress, along the far wall, was the bar; two men sat at the end of it, sipping beer. They wore boating caps, T-shirts. Their faces were tan and leathery.

"Would you like a cup of coffee, sir?" the waitress asked.

The place had changed: he was thinking about how the place had changed, and he couldn't hold on to anything. Ten years ago the grill—for steaks—and a salad bar had been where the bar was now. He was certain of it. The bar, back then, had been in a small room off the main room. He looked for the passage into that room, but couldn't find it.

"Coffee?" the waitress said.

"That isn't where the bar used to be—there," he said. "Where's the old lounge?"

"I don't know," she said. "It's been this way as long as I've been here."

"How long have you been here?"

"Ten years."

"No."

"Yes, ten years. Almost exactly. I started in August of sixty-nine."

"God."

"Sir?"

"I don't want any coffee, thank you."

"Would you like to look at the menu awhile?"

"Let me see," he said. The menu, a large enameled cardboard sheet, was bordered with pictures of sumptuous dishes. These brought him to the edge of nausea again. He would calm down first. "Can I have a—" He paused, breathed. She stood over him with a pencil and a notepad, gazing at the pad as if she had already written something there and was reading it. "You know, I've been back in Virginia for ten years, and I never came in here until now.

For some reason I thought it would be the same as it was—
you know what I mean?"

"Yes." She seemed impatient.

"It's changed. It's really changed. My father used to
come here every evening on his way home from work—"

"There's a new management now," she said, looking at
something above him on the wall. "Is there anything I can
get for you now, sir?"

"I'll tell you—I'd like a cocktail. Just to—as a—a—
memory. For memory's sake. I know it's early—"

She gave him a knowing look.

"I see those guys over there drinking beer. I'll have a
cocktail."

"All right," she said. Her fingernails glinted redly at him
as she wrote. "What would you like exactly."

"What did you write?"

"My name. I write my name on every ticket."

"Oh."

She sighed. "What would you like to drink, sir?"

"A—whiskey. On the rocks. Just one."

"Any preference?"

"Bar whiskey is fine. You know, who can tell the difference?"

She went to the bar and poured the drink. He watched
her, and he watched the men sipping their beer. It was okay
for them. It was all right.

"There you are," the waitress said.

"Thank you."

"You have to pay for drinks as they're served."

Brinhart looked at her. "Is that the policy?"

"Yes."

He reached into his pocket, was momentarily horrified to
find nothing there. But then, in the other pocket, he found a
crumpled ten-dollar bill. She took it, went back to the bar.
As he lifted the glass to his lips he heard the cash drawer

ring, the squeak and slap of the little spring-held trap. The whiskey sent sharp pains through the glands under his jaw, and he sat there swallowing the rush of saliva that came.

"There you are, sir," the waitress said, handing him his change.

He drank the rest of the whiskey, folding and refolding the bills she had given him. The two men at the bar paid for their beers and left, talking and laughing. Brinhart thought he heard one of them say something about Iowa Life. He leaned back in the booth, feeling the whiskey flow toward the back of his eyes. It had begun to fill him with confidence. Nothing could really hurt him if he was careful, if he was moderate. "Miss," he said. In his mind was the half-formed idea of ordering breakfast—fleeting images of eggs, bacon, coffee. He watched her approach, pad in hand. But when she stood there, giving him that hard, knowing look, he thought: *This is a goddamn free country.* "Another whiskey," he said, and smiled.

Doctor Stewart's office, as far as Brinhart could tell, was in an old building, perhaps seven blocks up from The Knight's Table. Yes, this was the address. He couldn't quite make out the letters and numbers exactly, but he believed this was the one. He went up a flight of creaking stairs, through a newly built plate-glass-and-aluminum doorway. It was cool, musty here. Something hummed everywhere, and he had lost time somehow: the ten dollars were gone; he vaguely remembered having visited the bank, thirty more out of the checking account. There had been a period of walking, he remembered, a brief stop at another bar, where someone had refused to serve him. He remembered an alley cluttered with trash and crowded with garbage cans, empty crates, parts of automobiles—a crushed fender, tires, a brilliant chrome bumper propped against the soiled brick of one wall—where he had leaned against a wrought-iron fire escape railing like a man about to be searched by the police, and vomited dryly into an open drum of stagnant rainwater. Now he stood in the cool air-conditioned outer office of Dr. Stewart's. At least he was reasonably certain that this was the place. It was paneled, smelled of disinfectant. A prim blond girl eyed him from behind a windowlike space in the right wall. There were chairs opposite the opening, ashtrays on a table stacked with magazines in thick clear plastic covers. The girl smiled, then looked alarmed, her eyes trailing down his front as he approached.

"Hello," he said. Or he thought he had said it. Now he was certain he had found the right place, proud that he had found it; he was already imagining Katherine here, getting better.

"I have—" he began, but the words were garbled in his mouth, like a lot of loose pebbles. I have a wife, he had wanted to say. How stupid. Everybody had a wife. He laughed.

The girl stood up.

"Want an appointment," he said. "My wife."

"What?"

"An ointmen—" It was odd. He heard how badly the words came out. They were quite clear in his mind. "I . . . want—" he said, letting himself lean into the window. "An —appointment."

The girl sat down again, picked up a pencil.

"What doctor?" he said.

"Pardon?" she said.

He couldn't remember what he had meant. It was something important. Something she would understand and appreciate, perhaps laugh at.

"Who sent you?" she asked.

"Nobody. Sent myself."

She looked at him.

"My wife—somebody to talk to and find out—"

She tore a piece of paper from a little pink pad, wrote something on it in a great hurry, then excused herself, opened a door behind her, handed the note to someone, closed the door again.

"Brinhart," he said. "She's never seen a shrink before."

The girl smoothed the cloth of her skirt, sat down, paged through a ledger. Her nose was sharp, bony, large-nostriled. There was a mole, like an ink mark, on her left cheek.

"Pretty," Brinhart said. He leaned over the sill, just above her. Notepads and manila folders lay on her desk, along with index cards and metal boxes—gray and elongated and dusty. Behind her, next to the door, was a tall filing cabinet, the same color as the boxes. One drawer was open, near the top—more manila folders there, packed tight. "You got a beauty mark." She seemed not to have heard him. He drew in his breath to speak again, and something grasped him by the arm. He backed away from the window, looked at a short, burly man with tight black curls surrounding his face. The man wore a white coat with a medal of some kind pinned to the lapel.

"Doc?" Brinhart said.

"I'm Doctor Shriver."

Brinhart offered his hand. He felt extremely confident. "My wife is having trouble."

The doctor did not take his hand. "What do you want here?"

"Want to set up, uh . . ." he searched for the word. "She needs . . . you . . . all you have to do is show her—"

"Who?"

"My wife."

The doctor smiled briefly, scratched the back of his head. "You've had a little to drink, haven't you?"

Brinhart let his hand drop; it had dangled out in front of him at the end of his wrist.

"Why don't you go home."

"Talk to my *wife*. Show her. You have to show her she's all right."

"Go home, sir. Sober up."

"My wife—"

"Does your wife have an appointment for X rays? Is that it?"

"X rays." Brinhart resisted a dizzy spell that almost pitched him forward into the other's face. "Want to see Doctor—what's his name. Psychologist."

"This is a pathology lab, sir."

For a moment, Brinhart was completely puzzled. The man might as well have spoken to him in another language. "I got it from the phone book," he said, and put his finger on the man's upper chest.

"This is the Northern Virginia Pathology Lab, sir."

"No—look."

But the other had taken him by the wrist, backed him toward the door.

"I'm looking—" It was all lost to him: the name, the address, what he had to tell. He had been so certain that this was the place.

"Well?"

"An X-ray lab," Brinhart muttered.

"That's right."

"I got it in my car—" But then he remembered that he had looked at the page he had torn from the telephone book, standing outside the car, after he left The Knight's Table. He had crumpled it up and put it in his back pocket. He reached for it now, said, "Wait." When he brought it out, the other man let go of him, stood back. "See? I got it from this."

"Look, you're drunk. Go home and sleep it off."

"Look." Brinhart held the tattered page out to him.

"That doesn't matter, bud. You have the wrong place."

"It's there. Wait."

The other man had closed on him again, grasping him by the arms, was edging him out, pushing the door with his foot. "Go home. Before you get into trouble."

"Let me find it—my wife. All you have to do—"

The doctor raised his voice now: "Should I call the police?"

"No. Dammit. You don't understand—" Brinhart held the page close to his own face, breathing the odor of the paper. He was all out of breath, trying to find the name again. He couldn't remember the name: like that, it was gone forever. The blur of letters before his eyes meant nothing. "Please, just let me—"

"Jenny," the doctor said, "call the cops, will you?"

"No, *please*," said Brinhart, "please—you don't—"

"I'll just bet you'll find this doctor you're looking for after you sleep it off. Sleep it *off!*"

"Wait," Brinhart said.

Abruptly he was out on the landing, the aluminum and glass at his back like a moving wall, closing toward him, forcing him to the edge of the stairs. He turned; it all seemed to rise toward him. And now there was a world-upside-down banging of himself, head and shoulders hurting and twisting under and over his legs, which flayed everywhere, and one knee came up into his face like something thrown at him; he lay staring at a small red exit light, circled haphazardly by an enormous, bottle-green horsefly. Something wet and salty dropped from the tip of his tongue to the back of his throat, and he heard a loud thundering somewhere near.

"You all right?"

It was the doctor, leaning into the space where the exit light had been, his face beaded with perspiration, eyes wide with horror.

"All right—I'm—" Brinhart mumbled, but then something seared through his neck and shoulders. "I fell."

"Don't move," the doctor said.

There was the sound of shoes on the stairs. The exit light was visible again.

"Oh, goddamn," Brinhart said, and got to his feet. "Oh, Lord." He put his back against the wall, wiped his mouth, saw blood on the concrete and on his fingers. He couldn't breathe, wanted air and breathing because he was about to be sick again; he thought he might pass out. The enclosure and the exit sign reeled, and then his hands were spread on the door, pushing; he went down on his knees, coughing, spitting blood. At last he was out in the hot street, standing again. The doctor was there.

"Are you hurt? Wait."

Brinhart gazed at the little badge on the white coat. Absurdly he remembered how much he disliked doctors. "You," he said, walking away, "you bastards." He went toward what he thought must be Mission Street.

XVIII ☙

THERE HAD BEEN more wandering, a period of hiding, of sleep in the lee of a parking lot wall, between two oil-smelling cars. A woman had spoken to him, looking at him out of blazing sun, her eyes hidden behind mirrorlike lenses. He could not remember what he had said or what she had said, and he was not quite certain that he hadn't dreamed it. But now he had come down a sloping drive, and found himself standing under a traffic light, looking across at the facade of The Knight's Table.

There was his car, parked where he had left it, windows open. He thought it might have rained. When he crossed the street, dragging himself forward as through a thick tangle of weeds, he caught a vision of himself reflected in the windows of a passing car. He could not believe what he saw. *I am Gordon Brinhart. This is me.* The face he had seen, blood-spattered and wet, yellow-eyed, grimacing darkly, with dried blood lining the mouth—that face was unrecognizable. It was the face of so many drunks, derelicts, street sleepers, and flophouse bums he had looked upon and dismissed. When he got into the car, he held his face down in his hands for a long while, sobbing dryly, swearing to himself that he would take hold now, that his condition was not permanent. And suddenly he could not sit still, could not remain in the cramp of the seat, behind the wheel. He got out, struggled out, as though the car were on fire. Two women and a man walked down the sidewalk and they all looked at him, inclining their heads toward one another and speaking in low tones. Brinhart walked up Mission Street to an Exxon station. There were three cars in line at one of the pumps, and the attendant—a thin boy with hair down over his shoulders and oil all over his gray uniform—was busy writing on a credit card receipt. An old woman in a black dress, holding a shiny black purse, stood next to him. She looked at Brinhart and opened her mouth.

"Bathroom," Brinhart said. "The key."

Now the attendant looked at him.

"The key."

"Hanging inside the door there," the attendant said. "What happened to you?"

"Fell."

"Drunks," the boy said.

Brinhart got the key and went around the building. The key was unnecessary: the door was ajar, and an odor came out at him. There were streaks of something on the door, coagulated drops. The floor of the place was wet, dark, urinous; heavy piles of toilet paper lay under the sink and along the foot of the commode, a drenched, dissolving mass. He stood just inside the door, breathing the urine, and briefly he could not remember why he had come here. He made himself urinate in the bowl, where more drenched toilet paper lay like a water creature, something with the capacity for growth. Everything seemed swollen. And now Brinhart looked at himself in the mirror, reached for the paper-towel dispenser. It was almost empty. Someone had written FUCK YOU across the metal, over and over again, with a black Magic Marker. The sink was grease-stained and rusty near the drain, and the water would only come in a trickle, close to the porcelain, like a miniature fall. He wet a paper towel, unfolded it, slowly, not looking in the mirror. His hands wouldn't work right and he tore the paper, let it fall, reached for another. This time he opened it first, wet it, put it against his burning eyes. Then he gingerly wiped the blood from the corners of his mouth and from his chin and neck. He worked very carefully, and when, momentarily, he lost his balance and put one hand down in the grime on the sink, he wound up getting it on his cheeks somehow. So he took the last paper towel and wet it and tried to remove the grime, watched it spread out on his face as though his skin soaked it up. Finally he dried his face on the sleeve of his shirt and went back out to the attendant, who smirked at him as he offered the key. "That bathroom is filthy," Brinhart said.

"You want to clean it?" the boy said.

"Filthy."

"You clean it."

"Call the health department—"

"Fuck you."

Brinhart walked back down to the car. That was the trouble with everything: no honor, no respect. Booze and sex and money. He got into the car, put the key in the ignition. All these selves. How sick of the self he was. As he drove down Mission Street in the direction of Winston Garden, he kept glancing at the swirl of faces on either side of the road and he thought how everything was pulling apart everywhere toward these magnetic islands of self and that was why he had never stopped drifting, why he had never been able to settle in place: he had just never been willing to believe all the shit. All the appeals to greed and selfishness and cowardice: twenty years in a job that promised only more money, a pension, security, a new car every year, and profit sharing and insurance. And what he would do now—he would turn around and go back, to the office; he would tell them how he thought it was all a lot of shit. Then he would go home and tell Katherine everything. He would make her see that for ten years she had been going against her nature—her very soul.

He stopped at The Knight's Table and had one shooter, just to shore up his courage.

At the office of Iowa Life only Treadwater was there. The secretaries had gone home, and the boss, the district manager—whose name was Lewis—was in Washington for the month. Treadwater sat with hands folded at his desk, like a schoolboy waiting for class to end. He was a nervous, thoughtful little man (the secretaries always received flowers from him on holidays, birthdays, and sometimes for no occasion at all—merely that he had thought of them), who above all else was afraid of losing his job. This was a neurosis with him, something he readily admitted to, and it made him rather absurd at times. Brinhart had always felt superior to him, but he had liked him too, and now, entering the office with the vague idea of telling someone how he thought it was all a lot of shit, he looked at Treadwater and realized that such a proclamation would be unkind if it were made only to him.

"Where is everybody?" he asked.

Treadwater rose from his desk. "My God, Brinhart—"

"Yeah," Brinhart said. "As you can see, I wasn't home sick today."

"No."

"I was—*out* sick. I'm sick now."

Treadwater sat down again, fumbled with his tie. His eyes were wide and nervous, and when he had smoothed his tie, he folded his hands again. Brinhart approached him.

"I started drinking at ten o'clock this morning."

Treadwater said nothing.

"I wanted to tell everybody what a lot of shit I thought Iowa Life was. But they're all gone."

"You're going to be fired. You got to watch out."

"You heard something?"

"No. I mean—for this. Go on, before somebody comes in."

"What time is it? I don't even know what time it is."

Brinhart walked around the room, looking for a clock. One of the secretaries kept a windup alarm clock on her desk; it had stopped. "Shit." Brinhart stood holding it.

"It's past five o'clock."

"You don't have a watch?"

"No."

Brinhart put the little alarm down, walked back to the other man's desk, sat down on the edge of it, smiling at him.

"You don't want to do this," Treadwater said.

"Ah, fuck."

"Go on home. Lewis might stop in. You don't want to be here like this if he stops in."

"He won't stop in. Not that lucky."

"I won't say anything," Treadwater said.

"Don't care if you do."

"You will tomorrow."

"Sure."

"Come on, I'll close the place up and take you home."

"No."

"I'm going to close up. You can't stay here."

"Shit—I was really going to tell them."

Treadwater got out of his chair, came around the desk, took Brinhart by the arm. "Come on, Gordon."

"Don't suppose it ever strikes you what a lot of shit this is."

"Yes, it does."

"Don't you get mad?"

"Yes. Come on."

"Like to walk out of here and never come back."

"Come on." Treadwater led him to the door. "Will you come home with me?"

"Treadwater, I want to know something."

The other man looked at him.

"How come you don't go crazy?"

Treadwater did not hesitate. "Because I'd lose my job if I did."

"Jesus Christ."

They walked out to the pavement, and Treadwater locked the door. "I better take you home."

"No."

"You can't drive like this."

"No. I have to get home. Katherine—"

"I'll call her for you. Come on."

"I wanted to tell them—I wanted to say it to them. . . ."

Treadwater led him to the parking lot behind the building, to a green Volkswagen. Brinhart got in, then tried to get out, but the other man held him down. "Come on. Just until you sober up."

"I'm sober enough, goddammit." But he sat back on the seat, closed his eyes, and then he was staring at something enormous and white. It kept coming and coming at him and he flinched, ducked, cried out. Treadwater's voice came from a long way off. There was noise—car horns, sirens. In a few moments he opened his eyes, looked out the open window at a fresh-cut lawn, gold-green at the little crests of slopes in it. A small red-brick house with a screen door that slammed, and a little boy rushed out to the car. "Daddy, we're going out to dinner."

"We'll see, Son," Treadwater said. He got out, walked around, and opened Brinhart's door.

"Where are we?"

"Point Royal."

"Jesus—where?"

"Granville Avenue."

"I went to sleep."

"Five minutes."

Brinhart got out, almost fell back, holding on to the door. "I can't stay here."

"Just until I get some coffee in you."

"No, take me back, will you?"

The boy touched his father's wrist. "Daddy."

"You go on inside," Treadwater said. "Tell your mother I've brought someone home with me."

The boy went away.

"You look a mess, Brinhart."

"Listen," Brinhart said, "I don't want your help—I didn't come looking for your help."

"All the same—"

They waited, and Brinhart began to wonder what they were waiting for. In a little while a tall, plain woman came out of the house and crossed the yard. She wore a faded denim skirt, and her hands nervously toyed with the neckline of her blouse. She walked through the shadow of an English boxwood beside the driveway. Brinhart saw that she wore low-cut tennis shoes, thought of sleeping with her. It was hard to imagine her with Treadwater.

"Is there something wrong?" she said, and he realized that he had been staring at her, appraising her.

"This is Gordon Brinhart," said Treadwater.

"I'm drunk," Brinhart said. "I like your tennis shoes, honey."

"Her name is Helen."

"Yeah, Helen. I'm miserable, Helen."

"I should say you are," Helen said. She looked at her husband.

"Couldn't let him drive—like this—in this condition."

"You promised the children we'd go out this evening."

"How many kids you got?" Brinhart asked.

She looked at him but did not answer.

"I couldn't predict this," Treadwater said, "could I?"

"Look," Brinhart said, but then he had lost it. He stared at them both, seemed to see them through water. His voice went out from under his eyes and he didn't know whether it reached them or not. "Just wanted to tell them what I thought about their shit. What a lot of shit—it's not my fault, see."

They just stood watching him.

"And I didn't need your help or your help or anyone's help at all. I didn't want anybody's help, especially not your help, because I—always felt sorry for you—"

Treadwater's wife turned suddenly and walked back up to the house.

"Where's she going?"

"You're getting worse by the minute, Brinhart."

"Ah, shit—tell her I'm sorry." Had he said it? Had the words come out of him? Treadwater held his arm now and was leading him toward the house. "Treadwater," he said, "I'm lost. I don't know where I am."

"I'll take you home in a little while."

Helen opened the door and Brinhart stepped beyond her into a warm little room. There were two heavy leather armchairs, a sofa with a rumpled slipcover, a television set in an elaborate Mediterranean cabinet, and a wall of mirror-squares in which he saw himself and the Treadwaters through the dark shape of a sailing ship on cresting waves. On a shelf above the television set he saw a little homemade

shrine, a plastic Virgin standing in a circle of artificial flowers, hands held out, as if to bless the room. He thought of
Aunt Beth, and when he looked at Helen Treadwater there
were two faces, the one superimposed upon the other.

"No," he said.

"Just some coffee."

"No, get out—let me go. What the hell do you want with
me anyway?"

"We want to help you." Helen spoke through her teeth.
"We're such good Christians."

"Helen," said Treadwater.

"Did you know that good Christians are scared to death
all the time?" Helen said.

"Helen, for God's sake."

"I don't care. I have children to think of."

Brinhart pushed past Treadwater and was out on the
lawn. There were shadows everywhere, though the sky
above the houses on the other side of the street was a bright
burned orange; the clouds looked like folds of flaming
cloth. He staggered across the lawn, toward the little green
Volkswagen; it was far away. He seemed to walk through a
tunnel toward it, and was astonished when it rushed at him
and met his hands.

"You're going to pass out." Treadwater's voice at his
side.

"Take me back—my car."

"You can't drive."

"Treadwater, please. For Christ's sake."

The other man helped him into the front seat, closed the
door on him, than walked back across the lawn to exchange
a few words with his wife. From time to time both of them
looked at Brinhart, who had laid his head against the frame
of the window. At last Treadwater came back and got in
behind the wheel. The car jerked as he started it, and something splashed in Brinhart's stomach.

"I think I'm going to be sick," he said.

"Not in the car. Get out."

A moment passed.

"Brinhart."

"I'm all right—Christ, please. Just get me out of here."

"I can't understand you. What? Are you going to be sick?"

Brinhart shook his head, and then all the world shook—everything spun around him. "Get me out of here."

Treadwater opened his door.

"For Christ's sake—drive. Will you drive?"

There was another pause.

"You're ruining yourself," Treadwater said, closing the door and putting the car in gear. "You're ruining everything."

They did not speak again until they had made the turn and pulled along the curb in front of the office.

"I'll take you home, Brinhart. Lock your car."

Brinhart got out, left the door to the Volkswagen ajar, walked to his own car and got in. He couldn't find his keys.

"Brinhart!"

"Leave me alone."

"Brinhart, don't—"

He found the keys, started the car and pulled away, hearing Treadwater's voice fade in the rush of air at the window.

He let himself into the apartment, heard music. He had driven all the way to Arlington, down the GW Parkway along the Potomac: somewhere, back up in the trees that bordered the road on that side of the river, was the house Aunt Beth had lived in. He felt some obscure, but eerily persistent force drawing him there to look upon those windows, that yard, the gazebo, again. And as he had drawn near, as the view of Washington had begun to look familiar,

he felt an equally strange, equally powerful urge to get
away, to turn around and speed into the gathering summer
dark, toward home. This he had done. And now he stood in
the living room, the several odors of dinner—hamburger,
boiled potatoes, and broccoli—coming to him like assaults
on his senses. And the courage—whatever resolve he had
managed to call out of himself during the unsteady drive
home—to put on the surface of life again, to pretend things
back somehow, to forget the whole intricate tangle of the
past days, left him. He stood there in the assaulting odors,
the aching darkness of the living room. Then he stepped
out, closed the door quietly, went out to the swing-set, sat in
one of the swings, his heels on the ground out in front of
him. He touched the sore place in his mouth, was blank
for a moment; then he fell. The swing danced above his
head. It all looked like a ruin in the dark, the skinny sup-
porting posts rising up out of the ground from thick clumps
of grass. Brinhart lay on his back and stared at the crossing
bar, the chains dropping from it, moving shadows. Beyond
the shadow of the bar was a pale, moonless sky, thin clouds
sailing by on the wind. It was humid, quiet, and he listened
to himself breathe—a broken rattle deep in his throat. For
a moment or two he might have slept, but a few desultory
drops of rain on his forehead brought him to his feet. "I'm
drunk—I'm so drunk," he said. "Katherine . . . Christ." He
walked back to the apartment, stood for a long time at the
door, trying to make himself go in, and at last he went back
down, past the swing-set, on through the hedgerow into the
trailer court. Again he was knocking on Stan's door, now
with some dim notion of telling him how sad everything
was. But there was no one home; he saw light in the windows, but no one came to the door: Stan would not take
him in anyway. He should've stayed with Treadwater. Oh,
why hadn't he stayed with Treadwater? He went back to the
hedgerow, thinking of getting to a telephone, talking Tread-

water into coming to pick him up. But he didn't have the other man's number and finally, with a sense of having known all along he would do this, he walked up the row to Shirley's trailer. Her lights were on. He paused just inside the gate, weak with fear. What this would mean. It had grown darker, and the small rain was on the air, the beginning of fog. He went up the stoop, nearly falling as he did so.

"You," Shirley said, opening the door. She wore a white cotton robe, and her hair was in curlers, lightly encased by a scarf.

He did not believe he had knocked. "Let me in."

"You—you're—my God, what happened to you?"

"Let me in."

She pushed the screen door toward him and he took it, held on. The room behind her was dim, red, crooked somehow.

"You're drunk."

"No."

"I can smell it. Oh, God, look at you." She guided him to the sofa, where he lay back with his feet over on the floor. He closed his eyes.

"What in the world," she said. Her voice was above him. "Have you been in a fight?"

"No."

"Jesus."

"Shirley," he said, "I'm all in pieces—"

"What are you doing here?"

He looked at her, noticed for the first time a mole at the base of her neck, just above the collarbone. "Nothing—I can't—I can't go home."

She went into the kitchen, ran water, returned with a wet rag, which she put on his forehead in a fold.

"Thank you," he said.

"You smell awful."

"I fell down. I—I've been sick—"

"You can't stay here." She went over to the wicker chair, pushed the stack of magazines on it to the floor, sat down, kicking them aside with one sandaled foot. "Red won't stand for it."

"Were you going out—"

"For a walk." She removed the scarf. Then, glancing at him, she put it back on.

"Where's Red?"

"Seeing Max."

"Shirley," he said, sighing, "my whole life—"

"Tell me." There was sarcasm in her voice.

"Katherine—" he began. "Katherine thinks we're—"

"We're what?"

"She's—she thinks I slept with you—"

"Jesus, you're a mess. I don't like . . . messes. I don't want another mess. You tell her the truth. What happened last night—I mean, you tell her—"

"It's all broken up, Shirley."

"Listen here," she said. "You're not going to blame that on *me*."

"I'm not. Forget it. I'm not."

They were quiet for a few moments, and then there was a blankness, a falling-slow, that was abruptly broken by her voice. "You aren't going to sleep, are you?"

"No," he said.

"You can't stay here."

There was another quiet, and again he went off in a floating. He saw alleys and metal drums and lights, and then he seemed to stand at the edge of a fast-running river; he entered, watched the water course around his ankles. There was a soft tapping somewhere, like rain on windows. He opened his eyes once, saw her fingers dropping on the rough wicker in a rhythmic, nervous motion, and then he was gone.

He awoke to Red's coughing. The wicker chair was empty, and Brinhart had dreamed voices. Now Red came out of the kitchen, running one gnarled hand through the shock of hair.

"Where is she?" Brinhart said.

"She's asleep."

"I didn't mean to—"

"Like everybody, cowboy. It's late."

"Ah, Jesus. . . ." Brinhart was soaked with sweat. His head began to register the deep pain of hangover, and he closed his eyes. "I'm dead."

"You were like the dead. I tried and she tried to wake you."

"What time is it?" He looked at the crimson of his own closed lids, through which danced odd shapes of lavender and violet light, colors that sent little eddies of sickness through him.

"It's almost five thirty in the A.M."

"Ah." He coughed, sat up quickly, held the palms of his hands over his mouth.

"You going to upchuck?"

"*Ah*—no."

"You been on a real binge, ain't you."

"Never in my life—"

"Want some coffee?"

"No."

"Sure you ain't going to upchuck?"

"No. Don't talk about it."

"I suppose you'll hang around until she gets up."

"Please."

"Yeah—please."

There was a pause.

"Never again," Brinhart said.

Red laughed: "Yeah, that's the most broken vow, ain't it."

Brinhart was silent.

"That one gets broke more than ten thousand marriage vows."

"Ah—I hate this."

"Speaking of marriage vows—you getting set to break that too?"

"No."

"Yeah, sure."

"Just . . . please—" Then he heard the old man moving around in the kitchen. He didn't know how much time might have gone by; at some point he had propped his head on the arm of the sofa and pressed his fists to his forehead. Then he was facing the blank cushion, and it was quiet, very quiet. He opened his eyes into light that hurt.

"Waking up?"

It was Red, sitting in the wicker chair, sipping coffee. He had a white shirt on and his hair was combed back, wet, looking a few shades darker.

"God, I was asleep again."

"Yeah," Red said. "Ought to stick to beer, cowboy." He made a hawking sound in his throat. "I used to drink the corn. Got so I could take the stuff like water, and I figure about eight or nine times in my life I got to where I was on a binge, what you might call a binge. I'd go two, three days straight without eating or doing anything but pouring that shit down my throat. And then I'd come out of it, sick as hell—as *you*—seeing things, crazy and scared and spitting and wishing I'd die. Must of been about thirty years ago now. Ain't had a touch of it in all that time. Just beer. I can drink beer any time of the night or day and as long as I want to and I never even get close to drunk. Guess it's just the way my system's made or something."

Brinhart tried to think of something to ask him, something to make him go on: if he could just get through the next minute or two. And now he was suddenly aware of an unbelievable thirst. "I have to—I need some water."

"Get it yourself," Red said.

"Oh, come on, man."

"Shit."

He closed his eyes, and there was another space. He saw Katherine. She lay reading a magazine: the simple picture of any one of a thousand unimportant moments, the passage of years by this accumulation of bendings and sighings and habits and small uttered sounds in sleep: it terrified him now, and with a jolt he lifted his head. The whole thing couldn't have taken more than a minute, but the room was full of morning light, Red was gone, and a glass of water stood in a pool of condensation on the coffee table.

He sat up, drank the water, swallowing, swallowing; it was sweet, cold, the most exquisite thing that had ever passed his lips. He put his feet on the floor, resting his elbows on his knees. When he had finished the water, he lay back, stretching his legs out on the floor under the coffee table. The cushion was soft, and he was thinking about what he must do: he must go over to the apartment and talk to Katherine before it was too late. It was probably already too late. But he would try this time: he would tell her the truth, all of it. He would tell her how he had lost a day of his life, drunk, wandering the streets of Point Royal. He would ask for her forgiveness, beg her to forgive him, and she was losing her mind, and nothing he could do, nothing. His stomach moved, burned. The water. He seemed to rise in an effortless unwinding of himself; he was putting something over his head, something warm and soft, like wool. He moved through the room without sound, gazing out the window at children running under bright sharp shafts of sunlight. There was somewhere he had to be. And then he was kissing Shirley's belly, feeling cold air on his back. Shirley said, "Oh."

He spoke the word back to her. "Oh."

"I thought you'd leave when Red did."

He opened his eyes again. So he had slept still more. Shirley sat back in the chair, her hands on the arms, her legs crossed. She wore the white robe, and it parted over her knees. Her hair was down, combed and brushed to a fine luster. She looked clean, freshly bathed and powdered.

"God," he said, "I can't wake up."

"You have to now."

"I am."

"I can't let you stay here all day."

"What time is it?"

"After seven."

"Where's Red?"

"Left—to town. He's a qualified electrician and he takes a job now and then." She put one hand to her chin. "Then he's going over to see Max."

Brinhart was now aware—it came to him in a hot flow of embarrassment—that he had awakened with an erection. He thought she glanced at him there, and he put one leg up.

"Are you . . . better?"

"Not much."

"You were drunked up like I've never seen anybody."

"I want you." He heard himself say it, and some part of him coldly waited for her response.

"I don't want you," she said. "I don't want a drunk."

He sighed. "I'm not a drunk."

"You sure put on a pretty good act."

He said nothing.

Presently she said, "You were drinking the first time I saw you."

"I'm not a drunk."

"Nobody ever admits it."

They were quiet for a time. Brinhart lay looking at her. The backs of his legs had grown stiff from this last sleep, and he massaged them, sitting up now.

"I'll bet you think I'd jump into bed with anybody," she said.

"No."

"I wouldn't, you know. I mean I only went to bed with—with Tommy's father."

"I never thought that of you."

"We weren't even in a bed," she muttered. "We were in his car."

"I never thought anything like that about you—that you jumped into bed with anybody."

"You going to tell me you love me now? Is that it?"

"No," he said.

"At least you're honest."

"You don't love me, do you?" he asked.

"I used to think—I don't know you. I wanted somebody, you know?"

"Yes."

"Red is nice . . . but."

They were quiet again. He was thinking that he wanted her and that he did not care anymore about anything but that. He seemed to witness these thoughts in his own mind. "Ten years," he said.

"What?"

"Nothing." Lots of marriages broke up, for any reason, every day. The idea veered toward him like a black current of air. He had never called Katherine his old lady; he had never spoken of her in the casual derogatory tones other men used when they talked about their wives.

"Suppose I did let you," Shirley said. "Then what?"

"Oh, Jesus," he said. "I don't know."

"Are you going to split up? You and your—and her?"

"I don't know—I tell you, I don't know anything anymore. There's not one thing in this world I'm sure of except my name, and that I'm miserable."

"Don't give me that," she said. "I'm not going for that unhappy husband stuff, so you might as well quit that."

"I didn't mean anything by it."

"I can be pretty mature when I have to, you know."

"Yes, yes. I know." He gazed at the floor.

"What I was thinking," she said, "was that if you *are*—splitting up, I mean—then maybe we could do it."

His blood jumped.

"I mean—maybe you could move in here." She was sitting at the edge of the chair now, biting the nail of her right index finger: she spoke through the biting. "I don't think Red would care much."

"I think he would," Brinhart said.

She sat back again. "Maybe—this is all maybe. Red sort of understands. I took up with him, you know, because I needed somebody. He's sort of just a friend now."

"Did you—" He did not know why it was important that he know the answer to the question, but just as it became impossible to ask it, it became important.

She asked it. "Did I sleep with him?"

"Well . . . yes."

"That's really none of your business, is it."

"No."

"The answer is, I did."

"You didn't have to answer it."

"Does it make any difference?"

"No, I said you didn't have to answer it."

"Then why'd you want to ask in the first place?"

"I don't know—forget it."

She touched the front of the robe. "We did it twice—maybe three times."

"All right, all right."

"At the beginning."

"I said okay."

"So I did go to bed with somebody besides Tommy's father."

He was silent.

"I lied."

"All right."

"Red was a very tender lover."

"What are you doing this for?" he asked.

"I decided to tell you the truth."

"Are you baiting me?"

"I don't know what that means."

"Never mind."

There was a pause. She looked at the bitten nail of her finger, one leg swinging across her knee.

"I'm sorry," Brinhart said.

"For what?"

"For everything."

"Don't be."

He heard the baby stirring in the other room.

"You want to know the rest?" she asked.

"It's up to you."

"Some things work and some don't. Red's like my father. It didn't seem right to sleep with my father."

"I see."

"But I get so miserable sometimes—with just me and Tommy."

"Yes."

"So," she said, sitting forward again, "you think you might move in?"

"I really don't know." This was a lie; he knew it was a lie, and he thought he could see in her face that *she* knew it too. "I don't think that will happen," he said.

"You want to keep me around, is that it? To come to when things get rough at home?"

"No—that isn't it."

"Well," she said, "this is just talking anyway." And then he saw that she was about to cry. It astonished him and thrilled him at the same time. In the wish to say the right thing, wanting only to ease her embarrassment (she shook her head now, looked away from him), wanting to put away the crude talk of what he would or would not do, the ugliness of this negotiation of her, he said, "I only know I desire you, Shirley. Any man would."

"Sure."

He had failed to understand her loneliness, her feelings. And now, realizing this, he thought he felt something like love climb up inside him. "I don't want anything from you," he said, "except to have you believe that."

"You sound like a counselor. Forget it."

"Shirley."

She got out of the chair, walked over, and sat down next to him, putting her hands on either side of his face. The robe had opened, and her breasts were exposed. They were large-nippled, white; the fullness of nursing was upon them.

"I don't care anymore," she said.

The words sounded unnatural to him in his surprise. She bent toward him slowly, put her mouth to his chin, then up to his nose. She unbuttoned his shirt, lay her hands on his chest, massaging warmly. Then she kissed him, arranged herself above him.

"Oh," he said into her mouth.

"What's wrong?"

He put his arms around her, held tight.

"What's the matter?"

"Someone's coming."

They waited.

"No," she said, rolled to his side against the cushions. She fumbled with his belt buckle, and he touched her cheek, unable to believe himself or any of this; and the baby cried in the other room.

"You're not—" she said. "You're soft."

"I'm sorry." He kissed her on the forehead, again on the mouth, slow and careful, thinking of her as though she were miles away.

"You're not even excited," she said.

"No," he sighed. "There's too much—I had too much. I'm weak. The baby's crying."

"You want to blame it on the *baby*?"

"No. Everything."

"Come on," she said. "Love up to me." She snuggled close, put one breast to his lips. "Come on."

"Sweet," he said, trying. "So sweet."

But the baby cried loud now, a shrill, endless syllable on the other side of the wall.

"Oh, damn," Shirley said, and in a moment she was up, the robe wrapped tightly around her. "This goddamn life. I absolutely hate Virginia."

Then she was in the other room, cooing and warbling over the child, and Brinhart, quietly, almost surreptitiously, let himself out into the hot brightness of a day he lacked all courage for.

XIX

KATHERINE AWOKE at dawn, after a long sleep. She had lain down for a few empty hours during the previous day, had somehow managed to fix a lunch and a dinner for Alex; but early after dinner she went into the bedroom, leaving him in front of the TV—a static-ridden baseball game on a Baltimore station.

"Good night," she said. "Go to bed when that's over."

Alex said nothing.

She lay down in the bed and stared at the ceiling for a while, and then she got up, went back in to him. "You'll never be a baseball player," she said. "You know that."

"I don't want to be," Alex said.

"You'll never be anything."

"I don't want to be anything."

"That's good—because you won't."

"Where's Brinhart?"

"I don't know and I don't care," Katherine said. "I don't care if he never walks through that door again."

"Then why are you crying?"

At that moment she hated him, hated how he looked like the drummer and how he loved his baseball and how he asked why she was crying. She was not crying. She could not cry, and the terrible thing was that she wanted to—she wanted to with all of her mind and heart and memory.

"I'm not crying."

"You're upset."

"Aren't we all," Katherine said.

Alex watched the game.

"There's something wrong with you," Katherine said.

He never took his eyes from the screen.

"You hear me?"

"Yes."

"Then why don't you say something."

And all at once the boy was crying; it burst out of him in a deep sob that startled Katherine. He was still looking at the screen, and she knelt at his side and put her arms around him.

"I'm sorry," she said. "I'm so sorry."

He sobbed again, but he did not speak.

"So, so sorry."

"Don't," he said.

"I didn't know what I was doing, Alex."

"It's all right." Now he did look at her, his full, rounded features smoothing out from the clenched look they'd had when he cried. He wiped his eyes with the backs of his hands, and she held him tight. She felt almost nothing. She had to work to feel anything at all.

"You watch your game," she said.

"Okay."

"Come in and cuddle with me if you want."

"I'll watch the game."

She went back into the bedroom and looked out the window—a brief glance, as though to reassure herself that the world lay out there as it always had. Then she undressed and got into bed, thinking about how she would not be able to sleep. She was already exhausted from the idea of wakefulness. In a moment she rose, put a clean pair of slacks on, and a blouse. She went back into the living room.

"I'm going to run to K mart," she said. "Will you be okay alone?"

"Can I go with you?"

"No—I'll only be gone a minute. You watch your game." She sat on the sofa and pulled sandals on.

He seemed reluctant. "Okay."

She stood, smiled, touched the top of his head. "You don't want to miss your game. I'll be right back." Though this was all true, she felt as though it were a lie. But then she knew the lie was in pretending that there was nothing wrong. She did not stop to examine this thought: she reacted to it, hurrying through her purse to be certain that she had enough money, combing out her hair in the mirror above the bookcase.

As she walked up toward the entrance to Winston Garden, she felt momentarily free, relieved, full of possibility. It was amazing. At the entrance she stopped and recounted the money: one dollar and thirty-five cents. She thought that ought to be enough. She would sleep tonight, and it was perfectly all right to take a sleeping pill if you couldn't sleep; it was a national habit. She crossed the highway, entered the parking lot. There was a drugstore at one end of the mall, but they would charge too much: she would find what she needed at the K mart, much as she hated that store. She walked across the lot, and a soft gust of wind came down out of the sky. It was not yet twilight, the sun burning in the windows before her, but it was already twilight-cool: a perfect summer evening. Cars moved through the lot like animals searching for a safe place to lie down; they paused, turned, circled, came back. The mall was crowded. At one end of it some promotional thing was going on, a clown dancing and honking a hand horn in a circle of shouting children. The K mart, an ugly long blue building, was at the north end of the lot, and as usual it was packed with people who looked tired and harried and unhappy, who pushed shopping carts or shepherded children from aisle to aisle. Katherine saw them all from the window before she entered. Just inside, a short bald man with a lumpy face—a face grotesquely out of balance, like a Halloween mask—stood at a small podium under a sign that read CHECK ALL PACKAGES. He gazed at her as she passed, as though to memorize her face; she would have no trouble remembering his. This thought made her smile, and she became aware almost immediately that she had done so. She went down the aisle without looking at what lay in such florid color on either side of her. Twice she had to stop and wait for someone to cross in front of her, but she could already feel the urgency to get what she had come for and then get out.

A loudspeaker somewhere harangued everyone about what savings there were at K mart and how pleasant it was to shop there. When the voice stopped, a perversely bad song repeated everything the voice had said; it did so three times, like a broken record, and then the voice came through again: a blue-light special in aisle number four. Katherine saw that she was in aisle number four and she stopped, looked around. Two girls in bright summer dresses and robelike store jackets pushed an oblong cart toward her; atop the cart, at the tip of an aluminum pole, the blue light flashed. She thought of ambulances, stepped out of the way. The two girls went by without looking at her. Katherine almost spoke to them, and for some reason this fact terrified her. She had to get out of here but she could not find her way. It was all so big and busy and spiritless; it was like hell. She moved down the aisle, found the sleeping pills. One large bottle left: three dollars and fifty-seven cents. She would have to write a check. Frantically she searched her purse for the checkbook, found it, was relieved, as though she had been suddenly assured that she was all right, sane, herself.

She took the bottle and walked back toward the front of the store, saw long lines at every checkout counter, and realized that she must get to a bathroom. She must find a bathroom first, and holding on, feeling everything drop down in her, she rushed toward the soda fountain. She did not think she would make it. People milled around in her path, or crossed in front of her, or came toward her in groups too large to negotiate quickly, and she somehow managed to pull part of a display down. It was a pile of boxes at her feet before she saw that in the boxes were wineglasses, and that one of the glasses had shattered. She went on, came to the counter, and found no sign, no indication of a rest room.

"Where's the rest room?" she asked a waitress.

But the waitress hadn't heard her.

"The rest room," Katherine said.

Two old woman who sat drinking milk shakes looked at her. One turned to the other and frowned. "I don't believe they have one here," she said, "do you?"

"I don't know," the other said.

"Miss!" Katherine said to the waitress.

The waitress looked at her out of dull green eyes. "I'll get to you in a minute."

"I need the rest room."

The waitress pointed. "Around there, through the double doors."

Katherine pushed through the doors and found a long hallway piled high with boxes. The whole place smelled of cardboard. She went down to the end of the hall and came upon a dead end: a metal door that would not open. The knob wouldn't even turn. She crouched there, her shoulder against the metal, and groaned, trying to hold on, cramps coming now. She felt cold all over, and yet there was sweat on her forehead. Gradually, painfully, the cramps subsided, and she went back toward the double doors, searching in among the piled boxes now for the rest room. And here it was, behind five large cartons of paper towels stacked one atop the other like heavy stones to make a wall. She tipped the whole thing over and went in, and again, just as she sat down, she was doubled over with cramps. Sitting there while it all ran out of her, she began to feel the terror again. It came so fast; it went all over her and she would never be rid of it, never. Something about the absurdity of her position made her laugh, suddenly, crazily, and then she saw that the toilet paper dispenser was empty. She did not hesitate, nor did she think. She went out into the hall, her slacks around her ankles, and tore open one of the boxes of paper towels. In the bathroom again, she had another severe cramp, but nothing came, and when she had cleaned herself, she left the roll of paper towels on the floor and went out, past the green-eyed waitress and the old women and a crowd of children carrying balloons, toward the customer-service counter, where she knew all checks had to be okayed.

There was a line, a long line. People stood there docilely waiting to be photographed and looked over and questioned by a tall, thin, slow girl with stringy hair and—again —dull green eyes. Two other girls stood at the far end of the counter, talking and smoking cigarettes; one of them sipped coffee. The line did not move, though the girl who was working sent people away with their checks marked

OKAY and her slow initials written beneath the names. She worked methodically, but she was so achingly slow. Katherine stood watching her, the line not moving, getting longer all the time. This was the one place in the store where no one spoke, or at least no one seemed to want to speak. Yet there were no complaints; there wasn't even a sign of impatience on any of the faces here. It was incredible. Katherine thought how incredible it was, warding off another spasm of random terror. She watched a man come between two people at the front of the line. He wore a store jacket, was more animated than anyone she had looked at among these others. He reached down over the counter and brought out a big, silver microphone, turned, so that she could see his face, and with gleaming teeth smiled into the beaded mike-head. "K mart shoppers, there's a blue-light special now in aisle number seven, aisle number seven," his voice sang. "Ladies' purses. Thank you for shopping at K mart."

It was too much: Katherine watched him set the microphone back in its place and walk away, still smiling, edging through the crowd and disappearing behind an enormous tobacco display.

She said, "This is the minute." Then she almost laughed —this hysterical rising laughter in her throat. A black man in a sweat-stained blue cap looked at her, but she pushed by him, saying no more, not even excusing herself when she bumped shoulders or touched elbows. She went straight to the counter, looked down at the microphone, which had a circular base, and was sitting atop a stack of receipt booklets or ledgers. The girl with the stringy hair and the green eyes looked at her, but did not move. Katherine picked up the microphone and clicked it on, watching the girl's mouth open. "Hello, K mart shoppers," she said, pressing her lips against the cold little screen, her voice booming out all around her. "I'm standing in the goddamn check line. I've been standing here for twenty minutes with all the rest of these robots, and I just wanted to say what fun it is to come to this store and shop. And oh, when you have to take a sudden shit, now that is really fun. Isn't this a good human sweet lovely uplifting place to—" Someone gently removed the microphone, or reached in and clicked it off, and then removed it. Katherine's voice fell back to her mouth, and she was so surprised by this that she let go. She saw a large, light green back, full of bone and muscle, turning, the microphone disappearing somewhere. A voice boomed, "K mart shoppers, let me apologize for that outburst, I assure you that steps are being taken to correct the situation." Katherine walked in this voice, through the parting, staring faces, and no one spoke to her, no one tried to detain her. She felt supremely superior to them all, walking out into the mall and the parking lot, with the bottle of pills in her pocket. She walked straight home, and found the television off, Alex in his room, muttering to himself. A plate with bread crumbs and a smear of peanut butter on it lay next to him.

"Where were you?" he said.

"You know how that K mart is." She touched his shoulder. "I fed you tonight. Hungry so soon?"

For a moment he did not answer. The light was dying at the window, and she went there, opened it, breathed deeply. "I did something really crazy over there," she said.

"Where's Brinhart?" the boy asked.

She turned; she was suddenly very weak. She thought the slightest disturbance might cause her head to open up like a cracked shell. "I don't know," she said as casually as she could. "He said he'd be home early."

Alex was silent.

"Well," Katherine said, "good night. I'm going to bed."

"What did you get at K mart?"

"I got some sleeping pills. I'm going to take one and

really sleep. So if you have a nightmare just come get in with me. I probably won't hear you."

The boy just stared at her. She caught herself wondering how much he knew. But she only wanted to sleep one night, just one night straight through, and if only they would stop looking at her as if they knew. For an instant she wanted to be free of Alex as much as she had earlier wanted to be free of Brinhart. "Don't stare," she said. "It's impolite."

"I want Brinhart to come home," said Alex.

Katherine kissed him quickly on the cheek, said good night again, went into the bedroom, and closed the door. The thought of locking it crossed her mind, but she decided it was better to lock herself away in sleep. She undressed, took three of the pills, lay down, and in only a moment she was deeply, profoundly, asleep.

Now, having awakened, she felt no sense of having rested or slept. In fact she was more exhausted than she had been before she lay down. Slowly the night's long blankness came back to her, and she closed her eyes, wanting to go back. Immediately she opened them again, realizing that Brinhart was not there. For perhaps fifteen minutes she lay trembling, thinking the apartment empty of everyone but herself: Brinhart had come in the night and taken Alex away. This struck her with the force of something already known, and she got out of the bed, calling, "Alex? Gordon?" She went into the hall, stood outside the boy's room. It was nightmarishly quiet. She opened the door, saw him lying in a crumpled mass of sheet, his feet jutting out over the edge of the bed. Carefully, so as not to wake him, she closed the door and went on tiptoe into the living room, where she thought she would find Brinhart. But Brinhart was not there, and it began to dawn on her that he had not been there, that he was gone. "Gordon," she said. She went into the bathroom, stood in front of the mirror, and gazed at a face she no longer seemed to know. "I have to get dressed," she said to the face. But she did not move for a long time, and finally she was back in the living room. She stood at the open door, looking at a misty dawn. There, in its place, was the car. She walked down to it.

"Gordon?"

Then she knew where he must be, and she opened her mouth and let something out. It might have been a scream: she did not know for sure. But she knew she did not want to be seen here, and she rushed back inside, closed the door, and put her face against the wood.

She wrote the boy a note:

Be good today. You're a big boy

But then she crumpled this up in her fist and dropped it into the trash. In the bedroom she arranged the sheets on the bed, closed the blinds, sat in the chair by the window, waiting for something to happen, anything to happen. She would not think until then, not at all, until something took place.

XX ❧

HE WAS DREAMING about Amy. A cloudy talking, and her presence. And then his mother stood over him.

"Come on, get up."

"What is it?"

"You were talking—I thought someone had come in here." She lifted the sheet from his shoulder. "Get up."

"Mom—"

"I have to—I'm going out. I'm going to get a job—something to do." She was opening drawers, setting clothes out for him, as if this were a school day. "Your father has left us."

Alex did not understand.

"Your father has left us."

"Brinhart—"

"Get up."

She dressed him, her hands quick and ungentle. He could not clear his mind of sleep.

"You'll have to fix your own breakfast," she said. "You like to fix cereal for yourself anyway."

"Am I going with you?"

She held his chin, brushing his hair. The spines of the brush hurt his scalp. When he looked at her face, he saw what he thought must be wrong with her: *My mother's crazy now.* He remembered the sound she had made in the hallway the night before last.

"Am I going with you, Mama?"

"No."

"Mama?" he said. "Mama?"

"Be quiet."

"Why are you dressing me up?"

"I want you to go over to Amy's as soon as you eat breakfast."

"Can't I go with you?"

Her hands went down to his wrists and held him, as though she were afraid he might try to run away. "You will cooperate today. You have to, Alex."

"I'll be good—let me come with you."

It was as if she hadn't heard him. She brought a bow tie with a little silver clip out of one of the drawers and put it on him. Then she led him into the living room and sat him down on the sofa.

"I'm going to go get a job, so we can stay here." She smiled, but her gaze seemed to miss him; it went off over his head. "Because it's just going to be us from now on. Brinhart is gone and he's not coming back. Do you understand? It's only you and me now."

"Where is he?"

"Gone. That's all that matters to us. Gone for good."
Again she smiled. It was all wrong and it terrified him and
without wanting to, further terrified because he could not
control himself, he began to cry. Nothing in him was strong
enough to hold it back.

"Stop it," she said. "Alex, you stop that right now."

"Don't go," he said. "Don't leave me here. Please."

"Will you quit it?" She knelt before him, smiling again.
"What is there to be so upset about? We don't need him, do
we?"

"I want it like before," Alex said, wiping his eyes. "I
want to go back like before."

"Stop it now. Just quit." She stood, put her hands on her
hips.

"Why can't it be like before?"

"When are you going to learn that it can't ever be like
before—not one second after anything happens, not one
little second later, *before* is gone forever every minute."

This made no sense to him. Again he saw that her eyes
were going past him, past everything.

"You have to learn that," she said.

"I want Brinhart," he muttered.

"Brinhart is gone. And I can't worry about you now. I
have to worry about me. I have to go out there and get
started. We'll talk about everything later."

He watched her go into the hallway and after a while, he
heard her closing doors. She closed every door, and when
she returned, she bent down and kissed him, stood fumbling
with her purse. "I don't want to stay here," he said.

"I know I can trust you to take care of yourself."

He was silent.

"We'll fix everything up."

"What if Brinhart comes back?" he asked.

"No." She shook her head. "No." She brought her leather
key purse forth, and it seemed to leap from her fingers; it

landed in his lap. "We'll lock the door. We won't let him in."

My mother is crazy now.

"You'll be good today, won't you," she said. "You'll go over to Amy's. Spend the day with Amy."

"I want to go with you." He was beginning to cry again.

"Just be good," she said. "Come on, see me off."

He let her take his hand. She led him to the door, opened it, stood aside for him to pass through. Then she was in front of him again, pulling him along to the car. He looked for Brinhart. "Where is Brinhart?"

"I told you," she said.

"No, you didn't. Where is he?"

"Gone."

"Where, Mom?" He was crying. She didn't seem to notice.

"Never mind where. It's nothing that concerns you." She had got into the car, closed the door. Her eyes were bright and wide and she rolled the window down, leaned out to kiss him.

"Let me come too," he said.

"You can't. Go over to Amy's like I said."

"I'm scared," he cried. "Please—Mama?"

"I've got to find something," she said. "Don't you see? I've got to find something." She backed the car out, and he moved with the window where she sat. She did not see him now—or if she did, she gave no sign. Alex stood and watched the window glide away from him, and then there was just the car, reflecting sun, gathering speed as it climbed toward the entrance, past the tennis court and through the long morning shadows. When it was gone, when he could believe this had happened, he raced back into the apartment as if something pursued him. He thought it had never been so quiet or so empty, and for a long while he sat on the sofa, gazing at the room, which slowly filled

with sunlight. Finally he went into his own room, took off
the clothes his mother had dressed him in, and got into bed,
pulling the sheet and the spread up around his face. But
then he was too frightened to lie still, so he got up, put on a
pair of jeans and a T-shirt, with his tennis shoes, and
walked through the apartment, opening doors, looking at
everything as if for the last time. None of it had changed. It
was all exactly as it had been yesterday, the day before.
Brinhart's things still hung in the closet. Nothing had
changed. And with a wordless sense of impending disaster
he hurried outside, down through the hedgerow and into
the trailer court. There was nothing else to do. He went
straight to Amy's trailer, stood out in the dirt-and-gravel
road, waiting for some sign of life behind the windows. The
door was closed, the curtains drawn. He waited for a long
time before he started up the walk. When he reached the
stoop, he turned, had changed his mind, had thought about
going back to the apartment so he could be there in case
Brinhart showed up. The sun was blinding here, hot and
bigger than anything else; it burned all across the sky, and
through that white glare he saw Brinhart.

Brinhart was coming out of Shirley's trailer.

Alex watched him come out to the gate, lean on it a
moment, wipe his face with part of his shirt. It was Brinhart
and the sun was on his shoulders. And now he had seen
Alex.

"Alex?" he called, holding one hand like a visor over his
eyes.

Alex had been about to run to him, but now everything
swarmed at him; he watched Brinhart lean into the sun.

"Alex."

The boy went out Amy's gate, kicked gravel as though he
kicked something he had cared for, felt himself small and
crooked and dumb inside.

"Alex!"

"You"—he whirled around, saw Brinhart trying to tuck his shirt in—"you fucker!" he screamed.

"Alex, wait."

He ran. He ran blindly into the field, down the slope, falling once, rising, entering the thick growth at the edge of the creek and falling again, one foot slipping through muck into the tepid water. He could hear Brinhart shouting, out of breath, and when he glanced back, he saw the shirt flashing down the hill. "You fucker!" He clawed and scrambled up to the highway and across it, not even looking for cars, on into the mall, around the buildings, and up into the trees, exhausted now, barely able to remain on his feet. He lay under a tangle of honeysuckle, trying to hold his breath, while Brinhart's voice grew nearer. When he could, he crawled farther into the sheltering undergrowth, lay on his stomach, facedown on a damp blanket of moss and decaying leaves; and for many minutes he heard Brinhart, who wandered along the bank and through the brush that surrounded the graves, calling his name.

XXI

WHEN BRINHART GOT BACK to the apartment and saw that Katherine had taken the car, he called in sick again. Treadwater answered the phone.

"I'm sick again today," Brinhart said.

"Brinhart," said Treadwater.

"Sick. You got it? I'm sick. I won't be in today."

"Lewis is here this morning."

"Tell him for me."

Silence on the other end of the line.

"Will you do that?"

"I guess."

"I'm not drinking, Treadwater. Really."

"All right."

"And I'm sorry about yesterday."

"Sure," Treadwater said.

"Man, I can't tell you how much I'm sorry about yesterday and everything else—every goddamn thing else."

"I can't talk now."

"Did you say anything about—did you tell anyone—"

"Don't worry about that," Treadwater said. "Worry about yourself."

"Yeah."

"And get in to work." Now Treadwater was whispering. "He knows you weren't here and he thinks he might've seen you in town."

"Jesus."

"So if you're not coming in, stay home for God's sake."

"I told you. I'm sick."

"I hope you are—for your sake."

"You're so kind, Treadwater."

"Just remember—" The other man broke off suddenly. "Lewis is in the room with you now."

"Uh—yes, sir."

"Tell him I said I might try to make it this afternoon if I feel better. Tell him it's a stomach virus."

Treadwater hung up.

"Tell him to fire me if he wants to, and that I said, fuck him."

Here he was, speaking to a dead line. He put the phone down and sat at the kitchen table, his head in his hands, the surface of his scalp hurting, like a raw, exposed nerve. It was hard to imagine he would ever feel other than this. Once or twice he made a low, guttural sound of torment. Outside someone started a lawn mower—some functionary of Winston Garden about to set the grounds in order. Birds sang under the window, four or five blue jays browsing in the grass. Brinhart watched them for a moment, then he got up and looked through the cabinets for whiskey—had he drunk it all? He found one small airline quarter-pint, drank it off with a desolate, willful urgency as though it were poison. Then he filled his mouth with water from the tap, gargled, spit into the drain. Now and again his tongue went over the scabrous inside of his cheek, as if to remind him of his wounds. His knee was barked, raw, tender; his elbows had begun to ache dully, and the bones of his back seemed about to break through the skin. Every thought made him sick, so he tried to put everything out of his mind. But it was as though his physical pains and throbbings were connected by some single nerve to all the scenes of the past two days, like extensions of an electrical wire; each ache, each jolt of pain in his bones and in his skin, lighted up another scene. He sat miserably, in a chilly sweat of fever and diarrhea, on the toilet, elbows hurting where they rested on his hurting knees, hands clasped in an anxious, half-praying knot.

Jesus Christ.

He stepped into the shower, still wearing his clothes, turned it on cold, faced the stream of water, and opened his mouth and drank. Then he undressed, walked into the bedroom, and lay facedown on the bed. A strand of Katherine's hair lay across the other pillow and he picked it up, held it gingerly, as though afraid he might break it; then he stretched it out, lay over on his back, looking at it. "Aw, God," he said.

And then he thought of his father.

If the old man had come, perhaps none of this would have happened. But why? Why would that have changed anything—why did he feel that it might have done so, might have kept things straight? At least the surface of things. Treadwater had said he did not go crazy working for Iowa Life because he would lose his job if he did. *That* was crazy.

Yet here was the idea of an old man like Brinhart's father holding everything together by his presence. The old man and his order and his habit and his honor and decency and moderation. Oh, it was all crazy and there was nothing that didn't hurt to think about, and Brinhart lay on the bed, naked, because he could no longer make up any idea about what he should do—or what he could do.

At last he pulled a clean pair of pants on and went into the kitchen and dialed the number. He had only meant to get out of the bedroom, but now he listened to the faint sound in the line, imagining the old man coming in from the beach to answer the phone. He waited a long time. Finally the line opened.

"Yeah."

"Dad."

"Gordon?"

"Are you coming up here or not."

"You sober now?"

"I'm sober. Are you coming."

"What was with you anyway, boy?"

"Nothing—nothing. You said you were coming up."

Silence.

"Well?"

"You sound like somebody's mother."

"Are you coming up or not?"

"Well, it's pretty rough right now, Son. I'm sort of tied up for the next few weeks. What's the trouble? Why don't you all come down here?"

"You did this to me," Brinhart said.

"What?"

"Ah, nothing. Forget it."

"Why don't you just take a week and all of you come down?"

Brinhart pictured him in his sea-green bathing trunks, sand on his feet, water and sun on him like health. That was how Brinhart had last seen him—almost six years ago. The old man had become a sort of beachcomber, studied marine life on his own, an amateur biologist who recited, like a kind of poetry, the names of sea creatures Brinhart never knew existed: heteropods, ctenophores, arrowworms, sapphirine gurnards, salpas. He knew their shapes and where they were to be found and how long they had been at home in the sea, and he seemed to have forgotten everything else. Brinhart spoke of some of the changes that had taken place in Point Royal, and the old man did not even know anymore what difference the changes made: he claimed that he couldn't picture anything of the town he had left, though he had, for the most part, grown up there. He was brown—a deep, rich, lasting brown—and during the entire week of the visit he never wore anything but the sea-green bathing trunks. Brinhart had assumed that he and his father would go to mass together on Sunday, but the old man never mentioned it. Sunday morning came, and he cooked a big breakfast and walked Alex out to the shoreline and in the early afternoon he took a nap on the beach, and he never got out of the bathing suit. Brinhart went to church alone, and when he returned, Katherine chided him for keeping up an appearance that meant nothing anymore. It was true; it was all true. And then that night, the old man took them all for a walk along the beach, his arm around Katherine, talking jovially about the various forms of weather and about the tides, his voice going out from him like a proclamation of his new health, his new way of living. In contrast to the old way Brinhart thought he seemed nearly excessive. Brinhart walked along behind Katherine, and held Alex's hand, while the old man went on about sand sharks and surf fishing; he felt out of place, somehow, as though he had stumbled into a group of people he did not know, who knew each other and who were eager to talk about themselves. The sea that night was a spectacular vision under the moon; the waves crashed, and the wind seemed to come from their crashing. Katherine, at one point, laughing at something the old man said, turned and embraced him. The old man returned the embrace, and they stood there.

"It's so beautiful," said Katherine.

"Don't know why I stayed up in Point Royal so long," Brinhart's father said.

Katherine lay her head down on the old man's shoulder. "Thank you. Thank you for a beautiful week."

"Nothing to it." He turned to Brinhart. "This is a lovely woman you got, Son."

"I know," Brinhart said, and felt banked, wordless.

The old man extended an arm toward the sea. "Consider the order and harmony of the waves; they've been rolling in here like that for millions, literally millions of years—ages before the first man walked the earth."

"What a poetic thought," Katherine said.

She had cried when they parted the next morning. And they had not gone three miles up the coast before she turned to Brinhart in the car and said "What a wonderful week. He has really blossomed here."

"Maybe," Brinhart said. "But then we don't know what he's like to live with now."

"Oh, Gordon—you always find something wrong in everything."

"I'm just saying what I think."

"I think it was a wonderful time." Katherine seemed to be forcing it—as though to compensate for something.

"He's accepted you," Brinhart said. "I like that."

"It was a marvelous week."

"Yes."

Then she seemed to sulk.

"It was fun," Brinhart said.

"It was *perfect*."

He was silent. They drove on, and the road took them out of sight of the sea.

"I'm going to miss it so," Katherine said.

But she had never allowed him to convince her to return. The following year, the year after, he had planned other trips, and each time she found reasons for staying in Virginia. Once it was because she was having her trouble again, and another time they had just moved, and she did not feel like the long drive. Finally Brinhart began to think she wanted to keep the memory of that one week, that one perfect week, intact.

Now, holding the receiver tight against his ear, listening to his father say again, "Why don't all of you come down?" Brinhart tried very hard to arrange things in his head: how much money it would take, how he might get Katherine to come with him, whether or not he could take a week from Iowa Life without losing his job.

"Gordon?"

"I'm trying to think."

"Well, I gotta go. Give me a call if you think you can."

"Then you're not coming up here?"

"No, I didn't say that. That's still a possibility. Look—I meant to tell you. I've met a lady, see. And if I come, I'd be bringing her with me. Is that all right?"

"That's all right."

"What happened was—we broke up, sort of, and I got to thinking of you and Kathy—Katherine. Not that I didn't think of you before, of course. But I haven't seen you in so long or heard from you and I was pretty lonesome there for a while. But we straightened things out, see. And then I got sort of busy with this biology thing. I'm taking a course at the community college down here. I mean, *we're* taking it. And anyway, you know, things got busy again. But maybe we can swing something later on in the summer—"

Brinhart blurted into the phone "Dad, for Christ's sake. We've got trouble up here. I thought you were coming up."

"What trouble? Tell me what trouble, Son. It's not the drinking, is it? Is that what that was all about the other night?"

"No, no, no, no, no. It's just that—well, Katherine and I are having some problem."

"You splitting up or something? What? What is it?"

"No," Brinhart said. "Forget it. It's not that."

"The kid? Something's wrong with the kid."

"No. Look, forget it. Just—well, come up if you say you're going to."

"I fully intended to, Son."

"All right—good. Maybe we'll come down there."

"Well, now, listen. You give me some warning now. Don't just pop up here or anything. I got a few things I want to get straight before you show."

"Yes, all right." Brinhart's voice broke.

"Hey, look—are you all right?"

"Dad, Christ—"

"Are you drunk—is that—"

"No, I am not drunk."

"Well, I don't know what's wrong, boy. You tell me what's wrong, and then I won't ask stupid questions."

Brinhart breathed everything in. "Yeah. It's okay. You're not coming, and maybe we will."

"All right, one way or the other—and I'm not going to ask another question. I mean, you're an adult now and I assume you can handle things. I'll assume that, Gordon. If not, well then, you'll tell me exactly what the hell is the matter."

Brinhart was silent.

"There comes a time when you have to stand on your own, Son."

"That is not the point."

"Well, now I'm really in the dark. What in the world are you talking about?"

"Nothing. That's just not the point. It never was the point."

"Okay, it's not. Let's say the point is that you either give me something direct and *to the point* or we forget the whole thing. How's that?"

"Katherine is having trouble."

"What kind of trouble."

"I thought I might explain that to you in person."

"Then come down."

"Right."

"There's nothing keeping you from coming down, is there? I'll send you the money to come down."

Brinhart was silent.

"Do you want me to send you the money?"

"I'll let you know. I think we can make it."

"Good."

"So maybe—maybe we'll be down."

"That's perfect. Give me a call sometime next week—let me know for sure."

"Okay."

"We'll straighten everything out down here."

"Absolutely," Brinhart said.

Later he wandered the field, looking for Alex; but there was no sign of him, and of course he had not expected to find any. Yet it angered him. "I'm your goddamn parent," he said aloud. He called the name once or twice, but his voice was weak; he doubted if it reached past the creek. Finally he walked back into the trailer court, saw Amy sitting on a crate in the lawn outside her trailer.

"Where's Alex?" he asked her.

"Don't know," she said. Her voice was very small; it barely reached him.

"Are you crying?"

"No." She gazed toward the field. Blanche came out of the trailer, moving slowly. She wore a light blue dress and high heels, and at first she did not see Brinhart.

"I'm looking for my boy," he said.

Blanche seemed startled. "No." Stan was in the door, looking lost, out of breath, his eyes puffy and swollen. He carried a small red suitcase. Blanche stood over Amy and touched the girl's shoulder.

"Don't," Amy said.

"Ah, Blanche," said Stan. He had come out, had put the suitcase down and was wringing his hands.

"Close the door," Blanche said. "You left the door open."

Brinhart began to move away, but Amy got up and approached him. Her eyes were brilliant, dry; they seemed to look through him. "I got something for you to tell Alex," she said.

"I can't find him, Amy."

"You tell him."

"Amy," said Blanche, "you can tell him yourself in a few days."

"Sure, honey," Stan said.

"I got it again," Amy said. "You tell him."

"Amy, for God in heaven's sake," said Blanche.

Amy nodded at Brinhart, then went to her mother and took her heavy wrist. "Tell him," she said again.

Stan put the suitcase into the van. He had only glanced at Brinhart. He helped Blanche get in, then held Amy's hand while she followed. It was all very gentle; it all looked exceedingly polite. And now Stan walked over to Brinhart.

"I'm sorry," Brinhart said.

"Tell your boy that Amy had to go away—for a while."

"Yes."

"But she'll be back. She licked it before."

"Yes—I know."

"You *know*—"

"She told Alex, and Alex told us."

"Nothing we can do," Stan said, his voice rising on the last word. "Just what they tell us. You know? We're just—helpless. Helpless."

"They know what's best," Brinhart said.

"Yeah. Bone marrow transplant. It looks like now . . ."

"I'm so—"

". . . it—they said it gets to a point sometimes where nothing . . ."

". . . sorry."

". . . nothing—helps."

"Maybe it'll turn out—" Brinhart began. He wanted to touch the other man's face. "Maybe—"

"Tell your boy she'll try to come back. They got to be such good friends." Stan took Brinhart's arm, let it go. "I'm sorry we weren't . . . more friendly."

"Things got all mixed up."

"She'll be back. She's got a lot of spirit."

"Yes."

"She's all we have."

Brinhart extended his hand. The other man clasped it, then gazed at the van. Clearly he did not want to go near it. Brinhart saw the little shadow of the girl in there, which seemed part of the massive shape of Blanche, whose shoulders took up most of the back window.

"Thank you," Stan said, and walked, with agonizing slowness, to the driver's side, and got in.

Then they were gone.

Brinhart went into the field again. He wanted to talk to Alex, tell him. But then too, he wanted not to have to talk to anyone, see anyone, just now. There was milkweed in the field, and wild celandine, and he thought he could hear everything growing. He watched a storm come—had walked down to the creek to sit there on the bank for a time, the shade coming down over his shoulders. The wind swept toward him and after a while he went back up to the crest of the hill and waited for the rain to start. It came in great cold drops. Brinhart put his head back, mouth open, as though he would bathe in the rain. His headache, his physical anguish, was almost gone. He went back up the row, past Amy's trailer, and stood at Shirley's gate. There was thunder and lightning now, and he went through the sweeping rain to the stoop, under the awning. The door was open, and there was music inside. He looked in, his nose on the thin webbing of the screen, and heard the baby cry sleepily in one of the rooms.

"Shirley?" he said.

But Red came from the kitchen, shirtless, beer in hand. "What do you want now?"

"You're home—"

"That's right. And I wish *you* were too."

"Shirley—is Shirley—"

"She's asleep, cowboy. You kept her up late, worrying about you."

Brinhart turned, sat down on the stoop. The rain came straight down now, but without force. The thunder had rumbled away, passing toward the mountains. Lightning flickered behind the heavy clouds.

"You been locked out or something?" The voice was not unkind.

"No."

The old man came out and sat down next to him, sipping the beer. "You and your wife—you breaking up—"

"I don't know," Brinhart said.

Red gulped the beer. "Want one?" He held it up.

"No."

"Going straight, huh. Hung over."

Brinhart didn't answer.

"Be a shame if she let a little thing like a bender get to her."

"Please, let it alone."

"None of my business."

"That's right."

"But this little gal *is* my business."

They watched the rain. Across the way a yellow taxi had pulled to a stop, and two women rushed out of one of the trailers, bumping each other under one umbrella, laughing. They got into the taxi, with some difficulty, and then the taxi backed out, was gone. For some reason Brinhart felt its absence acutely.

"Listen," Red said. "I want to tell you something about her."

"About Shirley."

"Yeah." The old man had leaned toward him, all beer odor and talcum. Brinhart breathed through his mouth, averting his eyes.

"I don't know where my wife went," he said. "Everything's falling apart."

"Listen," Red said. "About Shirley. Now she ain't all that bright—I guess you noticed that."

"No, I didn't notice that."

"Aw, come on, cowboy. Don't play games with me."

"What are you getting at?"

"She's just a—she's a girl, see. She's not all the way growed up yet in her head."

"I don't know anybody who is, man."

"Yeah, well you can say that. You know what I'm talking about."

"Go ahead," Brinhart said.

"Well, that's it. I just don't want her to get hurt. You get my meaning? I ain't going to sit by and watch her get used."

"She isn't—she won't get used."

"How you figure she won't?"

"Look, what're you telling me."

"You know damn well what I'm telling you, cowboy."

"I just—I'm just—I wanted to talk to somebody. I'm in trouble. Have you ever been in trouble and needed to talk to somebody?"

The old man stood, took a long drink of the beer. Then

he sniffed, hawked, spit into the gathering pool of rainwater below the stoop. "You got a wife, cowboy. And a kid. You talk to them and maybe you won't have no trouble. Now, I don't figure much in Shirley's plans—maybe I never did. But she's like my own child, see, and I never had any kids. Like my kid, this girl. And I don't like what's happening. You get my meaning? She ain't just a—a lay. She ain't like that at all."

Brinhart walked out to the gate, and then he turned. "I never wanted to hurt anybody," he said.

The old man just looked at him.

"Not once in my life. Ever."

"Yeah, well, just remember what I said."

"Maybe you ought to think about it too," Brinhart muttered, moving away. He did not look back.

He went straight to the apartment and lay down on his bed, in the wet clothes, wanting sleep more than he had ever wanted anything in his life. In only a moment he was gone; but then it was all fierce, shaking, nightmarish, and he awoke, buried his face in a fold of pillow, only half aware of himself. For perhaps ten minutes he lay there like that. Then he was gone again.

XXII ☙

ALEX SAT ON THE BANK, just below the little row of graves, and watched a scrap of paper blow across the oil-stained asphalt below. The sky was beginning to darken to the east, and the wind was cool and moist. He had come out of the woods after a long wait, had gradually assured himself that Brinhart was gone. Then he had hurled stones at the grave markers, expending himself in a cold fury, tearing at the flowers Shirley had laid over the graves, hating Brinhart and everyone and everything. He wished Brinhart would die and he wished Brinhart would come looking for him again so he could tell him. Finally he had come to the bank, and sat looking out at the loading docks and the Dumpsters, crying a little, and now he was merely watching the clouds come. Up the way, three men were unloading a truck; they were small, so far away, and the truck idled, sent little puffs of smoke into the air from an exhaust pipe that jutted above the cab: the exhaust pipe looked like a burning stick.

He saw the van pull around into the drive, move slowly toward him, past the first Dumpster. It stopped, and Amy got out. She waved, walked to him. It took her a long time. When she reached him, she was out of breath.

"I made them bring me here," she said. "I knew—I knew you'd be here." She began to cry.

"What is it?" Alex asked.

"It's like the movies," she said. "It's like lovers in the movies. I knew you'd be here and you *are* here."

"Why'd you come with *them*," he said.

"I have to go away. I have to get aspirations in my hip. I got it again, the—you know."

Alex stood up and walked across the edge of the bank, then in to the row of graves. She stepped to his side and took his arm. "Will you always remember me?" she asked.

"Jesus," he said.

"I'm probably going to die now."

He did not answer, could not look at her. He felt a queer combination of embarrassment and shame for her. It was not real; he could not get it real inside his head. None of it: Amy, his mother, Brinhart. None of it was as real as a Johnny Gaddling home run anymore.

"It isn't better," she said. "And that's what worries them."

"Amy!" her mother called. She stood outside the van and

waved a handkerchief; they could only see the top half of her body from where they stood.

"I got to go," Amy said.

And now Alex was crying. He was crying for it all, for everything, and Amy kissed him on the cheek. "Don't cry," she said. "I don't care. I don't care a lick anymore." She held his shoulders. "Come on, say you don't care a lick either. We'll be close always, forever, and you'll remember me saying I don't care a single lick."

Her mother had climbed the bank, was there now, her large hands gently closing over Amy's shoulders.

"And then when I get back," Amy said, "it'll be like a happy ending in a movie."

"We have to go, honey," her mother said.

Amy put her arms around her mother. Alex looked away, heard Blanche say, " 'Happy ending in a movie'— you are a romantic, sweetheart. Of course it'll be a happy ending. We're just going to get you fixed right up. We're going to get her fixed up like new again, Alex."

"I don't care if I die," Amy said, "because everybody will anyway."

"Don't talk silly," Blanche said. "Nobody's going to die. You'll see. This is going to work, and you'll be all right. I just know it'll be okay."

Alex couldn't look at them. He wanted it to be yesterday, the day before. Last year. The sky was growing dark now, swollen and black; far over the roofs of the mall he saw a gray curtain dropping down from the tattered undersides of the clouds.

"Good-bye, Alex," Amy said.

He watched her go down the bank, under her mother's arm. As the van pulled away he waved, or he held his hand up as if to wave. It wasn't real, and he did not believe it, and he did not even know her. He had thought about how he did not even know her as he watched her head bob above her mother's forearm when they had gone down the bank. Now, as the van went out of sight, the rain began, and he ran down to one of the loading platforms, in the lee of the enclosure, against a metal corrugated door. The rain came pouring out of the sky, and he watched it, not thinking—not feeling. The rain gathered at his feet.

Book Four

XXIII ☙

THE ANDREW JOHNSON HOTEL is one of the oldest buildings in Point Royal. It is seven stories high and, though it was once fashionable and exclusive, it has for some time now been on the verge of insolvency. A sign overhangs the sidewalk outside its doors: THIS ROAD ONLY LEADS TO HIGHER PRICES FREE COFFEE. The sign is pathetic, as the building itself is pathetic, and yet at the time that Katherine checked in, asking for a room on the top floor, it was still patronized by the occasional family of tourists who could not afford a hotel in Washington or Dulles, and by the few transients who were interested in it for its age and history, who craved its atmosphere and were willing to bear the poor ventilation and the lack of television or swimming pool or lounge (the cocktail lounge had been closed in 1972) for the sense of place and time it offered and for the knowledge that it would all soon be gone forever. These people were mostly young, mostly from the North—students, some of them, come to look at the historical places, the markers of war and Confederacy: Manassas, Fredericksburg, Fairfax Station (the little church where Clara Barton instituted the Red Cross). Katherine passed four such people in the hall on her way to the room: seventh floor, overlooking Grandville Avenue. She had parked the car on Mission Street, adjacent to the overhanging sign, and walked into the lobby with a cold sense of wonder, looking at the dark walnut furniture, the threadbare patterns in the rug—chandeliers in the high, cherub-painted ceiling, yellow as old teeth. The desk clerk, a short, square, heavy-shouldered man, gruffly asked her what floor.

"Seventh," she said.

"Nothing on that floor."

"Why not?"

"I'm not talking to you."

Katherine saw now that he had a telephone receiver propped between one shoulder and his ear. "I want the seventh floor."

He gave her a key, turned, spoke into the telephone. "No, it's the third, sixth, and part of the seventh. Just get it to me soon. I got somebody who can take care of it."

"Excuse me," Katherine said.

He looked at her. "Yeah?"

"Thank you. Should I sign something?"

He turned away again. To his left a light blinked in the switchboard and something buzzed intermittently, like an alarm. It seemed quite loud.

"I got another call," the man said into the phone. "Just hurry and get it here, the place is beginning to stink."

"Excuse me," Katherine said. "Where's the elevator?"

"Down there." The man pointed.

"Thank you."

She went down the corridor, thinking about how the man had noticed nothing in her face. It was strange that one couldn't see, couldn't tell. She thought how little the face gives up, for all its possible expressions. But those were lies, those expressions, and as she approached the elevator she let her fingers touch the wall, gliding along the smooth surface. It was all so hard to believe. Here she was, standing at the elevator door, holding a key. She looked back through the lobby, the windows in the door through which she had come. There was the sunny street. Cars flashed by, looking as though they were aflame. And now the elevator doors rattled open, slowly, slowly, giving forth an odor of disinfectant that stung her nostrils. When the doors closed on her, she stood very still, feeling the cables pull her skyward, hearing them strike the sides of the shaft. She thought of the shaft, dark and empty below her. On the seventh floor she stepped out into an evil-smelling and dim hallway, thickly carpeted and hot. The room doors were dark wood, and there were gold numbers on them. A few feet away, against the wall, a canvas laundry-cart stood; it was overflowing with rumpled sheets and pillowcases, and looked like a ransacked drawer. Katherine walked along the one side, reading the numbers on the doors. She heard a low, murmurous female laugh somewhere and she thought she could hear singing too now: a door opened, closed. She turned around, saw a slender black woman with a mop and a bucket—wild African hair and long, willowy arms. The woman put the bucket down and bent over it, singing, her dark fingers wringing the mop, a gray fall of water splashing too loud out of the mop head. The mop handle went off at an odd angle from the bent back. Katherine turned, walked on. The four young tourists came out of a room just before her, marveling aloud at the age of the place. They were loaded down with cameras and tripods and maps, and they spoke with thick New England accents. One of them, the only girl—who could not have been more than twenty years old —looked right at Katherine. "Hi," she said.

Katherine said hello.

"Where do we go first?" said one of the others. They passed down the hall. Katherine went to her room, put the key into the slot. But she did not go in right away. She looked back down the hall, and saw, in a sort of tableau, the whole group watching her: the girl and her three companions, the black woman standing over the bucket, mop in hand, like a rifle. It seemed that they were all waiting for her to say something to them. But then the black woman set the mop down just inside the room at that end, and the tourists stirred toward the elevator, which emitted a little starved *ding* as it opened again.

Katherine went into her room and closed the door, put the chain in the lock, stood leaning against the inside wall, gazing at the one bed with its lumpy mattress, the bureau and the bed lamp and the radiator. Above the radiator was the window, but she did not look at it. She could see its light, square shape as she took in the room, and now she would not allow herself to be where she saw even that. She went into the bathroom, to her left, and closed the door. The bathroom was all white tile, white curtains, white porcelain. The floor was white, though there were a thousand gray stains along the edges of these smaller tiles. She took her clothes off, folding them carefully and setting them on the closed toilet seat, and when she was naked, she looked at herself in the mirror. Her eyes trailed down to the waist and back up, to the small breasts, the shoulders, the suggestion of bones just below her neck: what the body was draped on, just bones, so many bones under the folds of flesh. She swallowed twice, stared at her face until the features began to change: the eyes merging, the cheeks floating, falling away. There seemed at last to be nothing but the eyes, large and round and overlapping, and she made them look down at the sink, everything turning suddenly white, suddenly clear. She washed her hands, was surprised to find herself doing so. She dried them on a white towel and went out to the bed and lay down for a few moments, without letting the muscles of her arms and legs relax. She put her hands down along her hips, her ankles together, toes down;

it was all gravity—gravity was everywhere. She lay there imagining how it pulled, how everything went banging against the earth and nothing ever fell. There was no such thing as falling but only the great pull of the magnetic field that made the needle of a compass point north, north. And perhaps she really would, perhaps she really would. *Really would what.* Really would go where she must be going. She wondered how late it was; and then she did not care, pushing the thought from her mind like a temptation.

On the bed stand, just within her reach, was a radio with one knob missing and with a broken slat among the hundred plastic slats over the speaker. She turned it on. When she moved the dial, there was nothing, so she turned it off, lay back again, feeling a stir of air from the window which, she saw now—she was looking at it now—was open at the top. She thought she heard someone screaming far away, but the sound died, and there was only the murmur of engines below, the rustling of the curtains here. The curtains were white, transparent, fresh-looking. Presently she got up, walked past the mirror opposite the bed—she was a shape in it out of the corner of her eye—to the window. Quietly, carefully, she parted the curtain, opened the lower frame, pushed the top frame into place, and leaned out. Below, washed in shadow, was the street; it was almost empty, dry now in the afternoon sun. On this side a few people straggled toward Church Street, which crossed Mission Street and went on, past the new housing development up that way. Beyond the buildings across from her she saw rich green willow, oak, and cedar. Above the trees the sky was clear now, with one puffy blue-white cloud in the center. It had turned into a beautiful afternoon, and she thought about all the people who must be happy on such a day as this. She stood gazing down at the shadows of the street.

Very soon after she'd come to town, it had started to rain. She had parked the car in a municipal parking lot on Prince

Street, and walked close to the buildings; for the most part the wind carried the rain away from her. But then the wind had shifted, and she stepped in under the awning of a clothing store to wait it out. A bronze-colored woman with a shopping bag was already there, looking out at the wet street from the hoodlike cover of a blue scarf. Her arms were round, large, smooth as a baby's, and her breasts, tightly held by a faded red tank-top, were like melons. Everything about her suggested plenty, surfeit, quantity. She turned to Katherine—those black eyes, opaque as buttons, in yellow sclera—and said, "Lawd, hit's some kind of rainin', ain't it?"

Katherine nodded.

"You almost got wet."

"A little."

"Not a cloud in the sky earlier this mawnin'."

"No."

"Look lak a tornado at fust. You ever see a twister?"

"No," Katherine said.

"I have. Thomasboro, Illinois, in 1967. Took a trailer court right off the map. You never see such a gawd-awful mess as that was. Scared my sister right back into the church." She laughed. "Front row every Sundee from that day right on to this one too. That trailer court went away lak it 'us paper: let no man contradict that."

There was a single, deafening clap of thunder, and a flash of lightning that suffused the street in a ghostly green light.

"Lawd."

Katherine realized that she had cried out.

"Scared me too, honey."

"Yes."

"You a sight now, look lak you done seen a ghost. You cold? You shaking like a leaf, girl."

"Cold," Katherine said, looking at her. Any moment she might touch the woman's arm and ask her to put it around her. Hold me, she wanted to say. The black eyes were gentle and friendly and smiling.

"You all right, honey?"

"Yes," Katherine said. "Yes."

"Honey, you crying to beat the band." The woman put one brown hand on Katherine's shoulder. "Ain't nothin' but a little storm, honey."

"I know. Yes." Yet it felt like laughing. It felt like this uncontrollable laughing coming up out of her chest. She had to calm down—she was going to get a job, and it was just the boy and her now, and that was all right. She had to make sure to keep it in her mind that it was all right.

"Hey, now," the woman said, frowning, gently patting her shoulder. "Hey, now, hit's all right."

"No," Katherine said. "It's not the storm—not that."

"What you saying, honey?"

"Nothing—let me be."

"Hey, you got grief? You suffering something?" The woman leaned close, and Katherine could smell her breath; it was sweet. She was about to tell everything, only she couldn't find the words. And then a young man stepped out of the store and stood very near, his hands in his pockets, an impatient, hurried look on his face. He watched the rain. He had long blond hair and blue eyes and a wen on his right cheek, a chalky lump that looked hard as bone.

"It's grief got you, ain't it, honey," the woman said.

"No—that's right," Katherine said quickly. "The storm."

"I hate the rain," said the young man. "It should only rain between the hours of midnight and four A.M."

"That would be all right," the woman said. Apparently she understood that the young man's presence had changed things. She gave Katherine's shoulder a little squeeze, then let go. "Seems lak ever' time I come to town, hit got to up and rain on me."

The young man laughed. "A dark cloud follows you around."

"Dat's right. She does."

"I wish you'd send a bulletin out when you're coming into town to shop."

"Sho' is the truth." The woman laughed.

It was all what people might say to each other under an awning in the rain, and Katherine wondered how they got from one day to the next, what it was in them that kept them going, made them strong enough to accept fatness and age and ugly growths in the skin.

"I left the windows of my car open," the young man said. "So I have a choice—or I had one. Wet car or wet *me*. I think I've decided on a wet car."

"Ain't no use in both gettin' wet."

"Right."

Katherine leaned against the plate-glass window of a display: shoes all in a row, every size and shape. Two manikins, stylishly dressed, elegantly posed, with dead gazes and slender necks, stood on satin-covered pedestals above the shoes. She wanted to get inside the window and lie down in the bright, airless security there.

The rain let up, and soon she was alone. The bronze woman had said something to her about God, but she hadn't heard it—though she nodded as though she had. She went out in the drizzle and walked for a while, past shops and restaurants and offices, trying to see in the plethora of signs some direction in which she might go. She had come here to find work; but that was just a word, and now she found it very hard to think.

She went into a restaurant and filled out an application, and the questions made her mind swim. Her hand was unsteady, and she could not keep what she wrote on the lines, the words slanting down toward the bottom of the page and out of the spaces provided. She did not know how to be brief, how to describe past employment; she wrote "I don't know" in answer to a question about why she sought work with the restaurant. None of it made any sense. And finally she sat in a chair on the other side of the manager's desk while he went over what she had written. The manager was a pale man, who smiled at her with only his mouth. He had scalelike wrinkles under brown eyes, and when he'd given her the form to fill out, he'd winked at her: "It just so happens that we *do* have an opening."

"I don't understand this," he said now, "where you say 'Undecided' about your marital status. Uh, are you— married?"

"Yes," Katherine said.

"I don't, uh—"

"I'm leaving my husband."

"But you haven't decided for sure?"

"I don't see what that has to do with being a waitress," Katherine said. "So I put 'Undecided.' "

"I see." He reached across the desk and picked up a pair of horn-rim glasses, put them on, gazed at the form again. "This here, where you say 'Rock and roll queen.' Uh, what is that."

"It's what it says."

"Yes, but you see, I don't understand. Is it a joke?"

"No," Katherine said.

"You're serious." The man looked at her.

"I played guitar in a rock 'n' roll band for seven years."

"When was that?"

"It's right there—on the form."

He looked at the form again. "You say, you don't know why you want work with us."

"That's the truth," Katherine said.

"You've never waited tables before?" he asked.

"No."

"You don't know why you want to wait tables now?"

"Yes, because I need a job."

"What about the guitar?"

"What about it?"

"Miss, I just can't make this out."

"How much training does it take to wait tables," Katherine said.

"Yes," the man said, "but you don't appear to really want the job."

"I'm not—I don't desire the job. Do you know anybody who does?"

He said nothing.

"Do you know anybody with a life ambition to be a waitress?" she asked.

"Look," he said, "if this is a joke—"

"It's not a joke. I want the job. I'm telling you the truth."

He put the form aside, folded his hands, leaning his elbows on the desk. "Well, I'm afraid you might not like the job, anyway. You know what I mean? A person has to have some—has to want something here. Even if it's . . . well." He sat back in his chair.

"I just told you the truth," Katherine said.

"Yes, well—we'll call you if we think we can use you."

"You have an opening for a waitress. I need work. I'll do a good job."

"We'll call you."

"You're not going to hire me, are you?" Katherine said.

"Mrs., uh, Brinhart." He had lifted his glasses and glanced at the form. "When you put things like 'School of horror'—my God, School of horror—when you put things like that down on a form that is quite seriously designed for you to be able to best describe your background and qualifications—I mean, what am I supposed to do with that?"

"Where did I put that down?"

"Under 'Education.'"

"No," Katherine said. "That's my writing. I didn't put that."

"Then what does it say?"

"It says 'School of *honor*.' I'm sorry, I couldn't get it straight. I was an honor student."

"Oh."

There was a pause.

"Still," he said. "These other answers. I just don't think you'd be right for us now."

"You said you'd call me."

"Well—"

"You lied."

"Mrs.—Brinhart—"

"I told the truth and you don't want me and now you're lying. Is that it? You want me to lie?" Katherine stood up. "I desire to waitress here with a sexual desire. I mean, I am about to have an orgasm just thinking about coming to work here."

"All right now," the man said. "I think that will be all today."

"That's not good enough? All right, how about this—I have a deep and profound religious feeling about working in this goddamn place."

"Good day," the man said. He left her there, standing alone in the office with the big window that looked out on the dim tables of the restaurant. She saw him pass among the tables, and she saw him stop to speak to a young woman who sat near the door. The young woman rose, walked back toward the office. Katherine waited.

"Is there anything else?" the young woman said, standing in the door.

"That's such an important question," Katherine said, and she smiled.

"Will that be all, Miss?"

Katherine walked past her. The manager stood near the booths along the far wall, his back to the door. He glanced over his shoulder as Katherine crossed the room.

"You'll call me," she said. "Right?"

He did not answer.

"If you need me. If you should develop a craving for me."

Outside the sun had come burning back, hotter than it had been before the rain. Cars went by her, shimmering with water, and the puddles in the street were brilliant. She walked up the block, past a recruiting station, to a music store. There were guitars in the window, and she had often glanced at them as she had passed down this street, a passenger in Brinhart's car: it seemed to her now that, even when she drove that car, she was his passenger. Now she stood gazing at the guitars in the window; they were hung in a tight row, above a glimmering display of horns. She looked past them at the store itself—long shelves of sheet music, more guitars, hung in another row farther back. The place looked empty—but the door was open. A little bell tinkled above her as she entered. Before her, on the other side of a glass enclosure, were five pianos, arranged like furniture, on a wide beige carpet. Here the carpet was blue, soft, marked by cigarette burns and small tears; and the steady tread of thousands of shoes had made a threadbare path along the glass counter to the left, in which harmonicas, capos, flutes, and microphones were displayed. The air smelled of paper, rosewood, wax. Behind the counter were still more guitars. Katherine walked down the center aisle, between the piano enclosure and the counter, to a row of Gibson electrics. And then she was aware of music, played tentatively, like a form of tuning, in a room off the end of the counter. As she reached up to lift down one of the Gibsons, a girl stepped out of the room and smiled at her. "Help you?"

"Just looking," Katherine said. She sat down on the wood-paneled base of the display case, held the guitar, letting the fingers of her left hand touch the strings—a C-sharp-minor chord in the twentieth fret.

"You play?" the girl asked.

"I have."

The girl stood very close. She smelled of guitar wax—or perhaps the guitar smelled that way. Katherine wondered how her senses had sharpened: they gave her everything in the extreme. She thought she could hear the cilia moving in the girl's air passages. The girl was quite thin, with straight black hair and a narrow face. She wore faded jeans and a white T-shirt that showed her breasts—two great aureoles atop two tiny mounds.

"That's my favorite instrument," the girl said.

Katherine ran her palm up and down the sheen of the guitar neck, the cold, smooth wood.

"That one has twenty-four frets."

"I see that."

"It's the very best."

Her guitar had been just like this, only not as heavy. It had been the same burgundy color. When she had sold it, she had done so quickly, for five hundred dollars, and had felt relieved, somehow—almost healed, forgiven. She remembered this with wonder.

"Let me show you," the girl said, and gently lifted the guitar out of Katherine's hands. "See, it has three pickups."

"Yes."

The girl put the strap over her head and began to play. Without amplification the strings only whispered—a small, metallic sound. This brought back to Katherine all the endless hours of her practicing, alone in the basement of a house in Georgia, and then in Missouri. She was seventeen again, just starting, just finding out her hands were uniquely fitted to the task, her fingers long enough to reach any chord, any formation—her sense of rhythm so natural, so easy. Like breathing. Two times on any riff and she had it; and then she could make them up, she could bend and stretch the ones she knew, she could go anywhere on the neck and have music, knew where every possible note was, so that when she listened to a song, if she could remember the tune in her mind, she could play the tune on her guitar: oh, it was like that. And here, now, this girl's lumplike fingers faltered, rattled the strings, muted them when they should ring, ruined the notes.

"See?" the girl said. "Doesn't it make playing easy? Absolutely anyone can play it with practice." She made a thumping bar-formation and bumped brokenly up the neck, smiling, certain of herself. The high E, Katherine heard, was a halfstep off, and as she watched the girl play a blues riff, she thought of stopping her to tell her. But she kept silent. The girl played the rest of the progression too hard, and the sound died in effort.

"See?"

"Yes."

"And I've only been playing for three years."

Yes, Katherine thought, she would look good to someone who didn't know better. "Only three years," she said.

"Now," the girl said, pulling the strap over her head, "you try it." She laid the guitar down in Katherine's lap. "You can see for yourself how easy it is to get sound."

"I don't want sound," Katherine said. "I want music."

"Of course. That's what I mean. Here, put your fingers . . ." she took Katherine's hand.

"No, look," Katherine said. "I'm—I've played before." And now, suddenly, she was angry. "I know where every note is on this guitar, honey."

"Oh?" The girl looked doubtful.

Katherine was about to show her. Oh, she would show her. But as she touched the strings—two quick harmonic notes—and then tuned the E string, she thought it would be petty, wrong. She sighed, the neck of the guitar lying in her left palm. "I played this model for seven years in a band. I was a lead guitarist."

"Really."

"I should've told you. I didn't mean not to—didn't mean to let you go on like that. I'm not here to buy a guitar."

"You said you were just looking," the girl said. "Maybe I should've minded my own business."

"That's very kind of you."

The girl studied her. "You must've been really good, huh?"

"I was wondering—"

"You played lead."

"Yes."

"Wow."

"And I was wondering if you—I'm looking for work. . . ."

"I don't know any bands around here," the girl said.

"No," said Katherine. "No."

"You mean here? Work here? In the store?"

"Yes."

"We don't have a thing now."

There was an awkward silence. Katherine realized that she had been letting her fingers caress a few slow, bluesy notes. Then she seemed to watch herself trail down the neck in a C progression.

"Jesus, you do play."

Katherine stood, put the guitar in its place. "I could sell them for you—"

"Well," the girl said, "I'm not the manager, see. He comes in on Wednesdays and Fridays."

"Maybe I can come back."

"But I'm sure there won't be any openings. I mean, I'd know if there were."

"Would he talk to me?"

"Well, I don't see why not."

"Probably wouldn't do any good if he did," Katherine said. "I just had one interview."

"Are you all right?"

"I'm wonderful."

"Maybe if you go on into Washington."

"Yes."

"But you ought to look for work playing that thing," the girl said. "Really."

"Maybe I'll go on into Washington," said Katherine.

"There's a lot of places to play in Washington. You can hook up with a band."

"Yes," Katherine said. "Maybe."

She had not gone any farther than the Andrew Johnson Hotel, though she'd filled out applications in two other places. A furniture outlet on Grandville Avenue, and another, smaller music store on Manassas Boulevard. The other music store was interested, though Katherine had not played for them: they needed a salesperson, and she knew about guitars—she told them she had worked in a music store in Illinois in 1966. So she probably had a job, and yet she stopped at the hotel, pulled over out of a stream of traffic and nearly caused an accident to get there, under the pathetic sign. As she entered the hotel lobby she felt the ghosts of the guitar strings on the ends of her fingers; at first, this was a pleasant sensation. Then it struck her like a blow to the face that all the music was gone, so far in the past; she thought about how Brinhart, who had come with her from there, from those years of her dream, had left her, really left her. It was as though she grieved for him. "Oh, Gordo," she whispered, "we didn't make it. I'm sorry, Gordo. I couldn't help it."

She went up to the desk clerk and his telephone.

And now she stepped naked out onto the ledge—a thin white strip of concrete, which glistened with what looked like salt. She held on to the window, and the air blew at her. She shivered, felt a deep, painful throb of shame, let go. Teetered for a moment, grabbed at the window again, one hand flattening out against the brick side of the building: somehow she had got to the right of the window: she did not know how she had made it this far over and she had no memory of having done so. And then a voice was calling. The voice floated toward her from somewhere. "Hey!" It grew loud, echoing in the fallen shade below and across from her. "Hey! You!" She peered at the sun-bright roof tiles of the other building. Someone stood there, directly across from her.

"What the hell—lady!"

Katherine was still. It was all pulling. No one ever fell, but only kissed back to earth from the force of the pulling.

"Get back! Get back in there!"

And now someone screamed, far below. Katherine looked down, saw no one. She waited. Car horns sounded. There was a high rush of wind.

"You! Goddamn!"

The other had come to the edge of his roof now, and she could see him. He was a small shadow there. He was partly shadow, but now she could make out the features of his face. She saw his wide, white eyes on her, and suddenly her nakedness frightened her. She had come this far, this close to the last thing: that thing that now, she thought, must have been waiting for her all along. Yes. But the voice kept calling to her. It would not let her decide, and then, so suddenly and with such horror that she almost fell, she came to see what this was, what she had been about to do. And in this cruel moment she wanted to go through with it more than anything in the world. But that voice.

"No!" she screamed—a long, tearing sound out of her throat. She let herself down to her knees, crawled back through the window, gasping; a song she had sung as a child went through her mind: *Bye, baby bunting,/Daddy's gone a-hunting.* It was all mixed up, everything, and she stood with her arms crossed over her breasts, looking at herself in

the mirror, dry-eyed, and breathing as if she had been running. Then she began to laugh. She laughed hysterically at
her face laughing there in the mirror: two people laughing.
Everybody naked, laughing. This went on for what seemed
a long time. But gradually she became aware that someone
would be coming for her. She felt cunning flow toward her
from somewhere: she would outsmart them; because she
had come this close. Now she knew. And she told herself
this as she dressed, carefully, quickly, efficiently; it was all
easy now, brilliant: she was Katherine Brinhart and she
knew what she could do to stop it all from torturing her so:
she could be cunning. She could escape. She stood before
the bathroom mirror and began to gasp again. *So this is it
This is being crazy*

She must get out: get away. She tried to arrange her hair,
still gasping, feeling dizzy now. She was certain she could
hear the sound of running footsteps outside the door.

But the hallway was empty.

She stood just outside her room, gazing up and down the
long dim corridor, and when the elevator made a sound—
the cables knocking against the shaft—she ran to the exit
door, into the stairwell and down, moving swiftly, but as
quietly as she could. The stifling air here choked her. Twice
she had to stop to catch her breath. She stood wearily
against the moist wall, watching the doors on the landings.
When she reached the lobby door, she peered through the
wired glass, saw two men walking hurriedly past, toward
the elevator; she thought one of them was the man she had
seen on the roof of the other building. She waited. The two
men got on the elevator; the doors closed on them. Still, she
waited. The lobby looked empty. She could see a glass ta-
bletop on metal legs, with magazines stacked beneath it. A
dark entrance directly across from her gave forth a sudden
light; but it had come from a glint in the windows, there:
one of the cars out on the street. Slowly she opened the
door, stepped into the cooler air. There was the desk clerk.

He glanced at her. A policeman rushed in from the street and went past them both. Katherine sat in a red chair near the glass-top table and paged through a magazine. The desk clerk stared at her. Finally he walked around the desk and approached her.

"How you like your room?" he said.

"Fine." She tried to turn the pages calmly.

"You rented on the seventh floor, didn't you?"

"Seventh floor? I guess."

"Yeah, it was you."

She stared at a whiskey ad in the glossy surface of one page of the magazine. "I'm waiting for my husband—he was supposed to be here quite a while ago."

"It's you."

"I don't understand."

"You're the only one. The others went out. You were the only one up there."

Katherine stood. "Well, I wish I knew what you were getting at." Her voice was steady. She would just walk out and disappear. She had been cunning enough not to sign the register, and he had been too busy to ask her to—with his phone call and his order for something from someone that would make the place not stink. She remembered this, and looked right at him. "It stinks on the seventh floor. When we come back, I want a room on the first floor." Then she merely walked away from him.

"Lady," he said.

She did not turn around, and as she approached the door she walked faster.

"Lady," the desk clerk said, "you're the suicide, ain't you."

She was outside, she was walking down the street in the hot sun, her eyes trained to the glinting sidewalk. There were voices all around her, and again she heard the word *suicide*.

So they said suicide So they said

She crossed the street and walked up the block to the corner, past four or five knots of people who searched the upper windows of the Andrew Johnson Hotel, looking for someone like her.

XXIV ❧

ONCE, after a gig, Katherine had gone alone to a truck stop to drink some coffee, and to get away from the petty squabbling of the band. This was in the winter of 1967. They were playing the Worcester Inn, Katherine was pregnant and knew it, but she had told no one about it. Massachusetts, that year, was all snow and blowing wind, though on this night there was only a powdery dust; it was too cold for snow. Katherine sat alone in a booth next to the window, and the waitress—a prim young woman with thin, elegant fingers and a yellow smile—talked to her about working all night, how she hated it and liked it, the advantages and disadvantages. The waitress liked to sleep, and she slept most of the day, and it wasn't so bad in winter, since the days were so ugly. The nights were ugly too, but you didn't mind working then; it wasn't as if you were missing anything. She went on, and Katherine sipped coffee, thinking about being pregnant. Finally the waitress asked her what she was doing so late at night (was she traveling?), and Katherine told her about the band. The waitress was enthralled. She sat down in the booth across from Katherine and asked what sort of a life it was: she thought it must be very exciting.

"Yes," Katherine said, "very." She was tired, sick to her stomach; she smoked one cigarette after another, talking to the waitress. Perhaps fifteen minutes after she had first sat down, a disc jockey she knew walked in. He had a woman with him, whom he introduced as his lover. The waitress got out of the way and the disc jockey sat down with his lover, and Katherine began to think of finding another place to go. The disc jockey's name was Clag and he had made a trademark out of the name: he used it for any of a hundred different rhymes, and his talent was that he could come up with these rhymes almost at will. His radio voice was one of the fastest, one of the loudest; he screamed at you about Shag the Clag and Bag of Clag, and he screamed over the music. Katherine knew him because he was active in booking acts in Worcester, and because he sometimes did his radio show from the halls in which she had performed with the band. She had not seen him this trip, and she was unhappily surprised to see him now. His lover, a stylish woman who claimed to be twenty but looked forty, was named Beverly, and she was a dancer, or so she said. Clag introduced her, and then he said, "Beverly, honey, you are looking at one of the best lead guitarists I've ever seen."

"That's just wonderful," Beverly said.

Katherine began to excuse herself, rising, but Clag took her wrist and insisted that she have a cup of coffee with them. "Hey, sugar," he said, "don't be a bugar."

Katherine sat down.

Beverly told her about being a dancer. "I dance go-go, you know," she said.

"Good," Katherine said. "You rhyme too."

They laughed.

"So how's this trip been?" Clag asked.

"Like the others," Katherine said.

"Clag's into making recordings now," said Beverly. "Maybe you should talk to him."

"Just fifteen dollars an hour," Clag said. "I got a studio set up in my basement now. You should see it."

"Maybe we will," Katherine said.

"Maybe."

"This is a busy week."

"You still hoping somebody'll come waltzing in from New York."

"Maybe. We're just playing where we can play."

"New York is pork. Dreams."

"What instrument do you play?" Beverly asked.

"I told you, honey, lead guitar."

"Oh."

"You know what happened to me last month?" Clag asked.

"What."

"I got drafted."

"Isn't that a scream," Beverly said.

"That's a scream all right," said Katherine.

"I got out of it though," Clag said. "I pretended I was crazy. They took me to three different doctors, and I told them I was Jesus Christ incarnate, that I was using the radio to bring young people back to God. It was my mission, my calling. You should have seen me. I did the rhyming bit, talked like I was doing a gig. So the last doctor—I think it was the last one—he asks me what I think I'm doing. Yeah, the last one, because I got out of there after this. He asks me what I'm doing, and I say 'I'm getting out of the fucking army.'"

Beverly laughed.

"Now I ask you, how is that for a command performance."

"That's wonderful," Beverly said.

Katherine looked out the window. The war was going on way off in the dark. She knew so little about it; there was only the music and the traveling and the fact that she was pregnant. She couldn't manage it. As she lighted another cigarette Beverly reached over and touched her wrist.

"You'll get cancer."

"Bev's interested in health."

"I'm studying health. That's my major."

"She's putting herself through college."

"That's good," Katherine said.

"It's a waste of time," Clag said. "Just like what you're doing."

"Okay."

"You agree that you're wasting your time?"

"If you say so." She took a drag of the cigarette, and the waitress came by to ask if they needed anything.

"Not a thing," Clag said. "But tell me—who's your favorite group?"

"The Beatles," said the waitress.

"Who's the lead guitarist."

"Oh, I don't know about that stuff."

He dismissed her with a gesture, leaning toward Katherine. "Lead guitarist is a male role. You can't break that."

"Shut up, Clag, will you?" Katherine said.

"I'm telling you—good as you are, you'll never make it."

"All right, so I'll never make it."

"How old are you?"

"You know how old I am."

He looked at Beverly. "She's twenty-five. Age, too. I'd say you got about another year or two, and then it'll be too late."

"What do you want me to do?" Katherine said.

"Just laying it out there. You ought to come over and use my studio and get yourself a record. A demonstration album or something."

"It's really a very good studio," Beverly said.

"Wonderful—I'll bet it's a wonderful studio."

"Fifteen dollars an hour. A lot better than you ever got at any New York studio."

"It's all padded," said Beverly. "Like a crazy room."

They went on to describe the studio, interrupting each

other. Katherine stopped listening. She gazed out the window at the film of snowy dust in the parking lot. She was pregnant: she was determined not to let anything stop her from playing in the band, from going on until something broke, and yet she was so tired. Oddly she remembered falling asleep once in a room in Georgia, her parents talking idly on the other side of the wall, and she remembered waking on another morning—as though it were the next morning—in New York, her father bringing her out of sleep and taking her to a window to look out at the tops of buildings. She had felt the street so far below, as though she sailed in a weightless balloon of plaster and glass. It had terrified her. And now, as some of that terror came reeling up from the bottom of her mind, she heard Clag say something about how the mob controlled popular music. She wanted to go home, but there wasn't anyplace like that: home. Her parents were in Brockton, only sixty-five miles away, but there wasn't anyplace that was home. Clag went on about the Syndicate, how difficult it was for any band to work outside their sphere of influence. And she loathed him, without warning or reason; it was like a chemical entering her blood.

"I have to go," she said, "I have to get some sleep."

"Well, it was nice meeting you," Beverly said. Clag got up, and now they were all leaving. There was a confusion of good-byes, Beverly asking that Katherine take her number, in case she was ever in Worcester again. No one had a pencil. The waitress let them use hers. It was all more than Katherine could stand. But finally she stood out in the parking lot and watched Clag and Beverly pull away in a Dodge Charger, and when they were gone, she went back into the restaurant. The waitress looked up from a crossword puzzle.

"Forget something?"

"I'm pregnant," Katherine said.

"What?"

"I'm pregnant."

The waitress looked at her.

"What do you want to do with your life?" Katherine asked.

"I don't know—get married. Have—have kids."

"You want a kid?"

"Yours?"

"No. You want children."

"Yes, I guess I do. Someday."

"You want a house and a garage and a car and a husband."

"What is this?"

"You wait," Katherine said. "I am going to be famous." Then she went out to the van and got in and drove down the highway, fish-tailing in the dust of snow. She imagined the baby, or tried to: it was only a bald doll in her mind. She couldn't make it come alive, and she wanted to, wanted to look at this baby as though it were an argument against her hopes. No, it was not hope; it was need—it was something she needed in an almost physiological way. And nothing, nothing, she told herself, would stop her.

She saw a pair of headlights in the road ahead, and realized that they were stationary, the beams going off into the darkness beside the road. She stopped the van, perhaps fifty feet away, and got out. The wind cut at her face, so she held her hands up to her eyes, peering through the crooked light. There was a low buzzing sound, like wires arcing, and she smelled something burning. She closed the door of the van and walked cautiously toward the headlights, which illuminated tall stalks of wild grass and wet tree trunks along the shoulder of the road to her right. It was terribly quiet now except for the wind, and her own tentative footsteps. The headlights belonged to a station wagon, one side of which was caved in. She saw a pool of spreading liquid beneath it, and then she saw still another car a few yards up the road, lying over on its roof. With a kind of wonder, she touched the taillight of the first car. When she stepped around it, she came upon someone lying in the road. It was a man, a very robust man, lying on his back with one leg up inside the car, his hands folded over his chest as though he had chosen to lie there like that. Katherine saw white cuffs, a small-knotted tie, a face that merely looked at her; there was no blood.

"Ahhhh," the face said.

And Katherine gave something like a muffled cry. She knelt down, put a shivering hand on his forehead. "I'm going to get help," she said. "I have blankets in the van."

"I'm so drunk," he said.

She touched his mouth. "Don't move."

Now other cars had stopped—a milk truck, and a Volkswagen. Everything grew bright. There was still another car. Katherine had walked out to the middle of the road and she spoke to the running shadows. "Get help—someone is hurt here." She heard other voices, and then she heard a scream. A man screamed. She turned, saw him running from the other car.

"Two people in there," he said, going past her.

Everything was confusion now. Someone had lighted flares. There didn't seem to be anything for Katherine to do. Yet she walked back to the man lying in the road, hearing the voices and the running footsteps, and knelt down to look at him again.

"Drunk too much," he said. "My wife."

She got up, wandered over to the other car. It was a Dodge Charger—all that windshield. Beverly's face looked at her from the broken glass; Beverly's face was upside down, looking at her; it was almost violet in the spreading glare.

"Beverly," Katherine said.

Beverly was dead. Katherine could see without wanting to that Beverly was most certainly dead. She crouched down in the road, her hands over her ears, the wind soughing through the lighted trees and raking her across the back of the neck. It seemed to be driving her down into the asphalt. Then someone lifted her, long fingers around her arms. She said, "Hold me."

"You have to get out of the road."

It was a policeman.

"Yes," Katherine said.

"Are you all right?"

She did not answer him. She walked through a crowd of people who wore night robes; they all stood in the road like an absurd gathering of sleepwalkers: they had come from the houses back in the trees, where now a flood of yellow light on that side made shadows everywhere. Then she remembered Clag, and she turned around. The policeman was peering into the overturned car. He stood back, shook his head, turned, looked past Katherine. "I got two dead," he called, "over here." And a voice from behind her said, "This one seems all right. A few broken ribs, maybe." She went on, past the other policeman, through the lights and the gathering crowd. As she got into the van she saw an ambulance come from the other direction, around everything, pausing in the road, its flashing cold blue rooflights casting an ugly beam around like something spilled.

It was that night—that predawn—that she had sent the drummer packing. She had done so merely by telling him that she was pregnant. And when he was gone, she went to the rhythm guitarist's room, woke him, told him about the accident, and finally got into bed with him. The rhythm guitarist's name was Bailey. He was very fat, twenty-six years old, and he looked like an adolescent—his skin so fair that he almost never had to shave—and there was about him the sense that one day he would lose all the fat and become a man, full-grown. He was the brunt of much teasing from other members of the band, and as a result was mostly moody, quiet—a presence that rarely announced itself. Katherine had never felt comfortable with him, yet as dawn came that morning she got into his bed. There was something about the idea of lying beneath him, that great bulk and weight, that made her want this. Yet she lay loathing him and herself while he strained, and she thought about the drummer, who had done this to her. The drummer had said only two things when she told him she was pregnant.

He said, "This doesn't fit into my plans."

She said, "I didn't think it would."

"Get an abortion—or it's bye-bye," the drummer said.

"Bye-bye," said Katherine. And she had watched him pack what he owned—he did not own the drums—and walk down the road toward Worcester, like a hobo, his few belongings in a sack he carried over his shoulder. She had watched him go until she couldn't see him anymore, and then, as the light began to come over the tops of the trees (the motel sign fading—VACANCY—though it still blinked and buzzed: VACANCY. VACANCY. VACANCY), she thought about how she was carrying the beginning of his baby.

Later, with the fat, boy-body straining over her, she seemed to feel the exact lineaments of her pain and her despair. And when it was over, she quietly told him to forget what had happened, to entertain no hopes that it might happen again. This angered him—hurt him, as she knew it would.

"What are you?" he said. "What are you?"

"Just please forget it."

"Believe me," he said. "It was forgettable."

"Don't be mad."

"Look, what did you come here for? What did you think —what—" He began to cry. This astonished her.

"I'm sorry," she said. She lay in the bed, the blanket pulled up to her chin. He stood by the window, the sun coming through the blinds on him—the heavy folds of his body. She had always shuddered at the idea of that flesh touching hers, and she began to see what she had done, how far her fear of what was ahead—the magic future receding, as though it ran ahead of her and she would never catch it now—had taken her. It seemed now that everything was failing, that it had been slowly failing for a long time. She sat up in the bed and told the rhythm guitarist that she was pregnant.

He looked at her. "That figures."

"You knew?"

"No. But it figures."

She lay back down, watched him cross the room, picking up his clothes. He began to dress. "I sent him packing," she said.

"Yeah, that figures too."

"We no longer have a drummer."

He was silent.

"We'll have to get one quick."

"You're not going to quit?" he asked.

She was surprised by the quickness of his understanding now, his ability to deal with the facts and to let go of his anger. "No. I'll never quit. I'm too good to quit."

"What'll you do?"

"Play until I have to stop. Then give the baby to my parents."

"They'll take it?"

"They take anything I give them. Always have."

"Jesus."

Presently he said, "Why don't you get rid of it?"

"No." She would have it and she would make herself love it: you had to *will* love, you had to make it happen in yourself. "No," she said to Bailey. "I'm going to have it."

"You really loved him, didn't you?"

"No," she said.

"Yeah." He pulled his belt through the loops in his pants. "You were ga-ga. We all saw it. We knew you were sleeping together. We thought it was stupid for him to sneak out of the room every night, like we didn't know. Or Bates thought it was stupid." Bailey smiled now: for the past year Bates and the drummer had gotten a room to themselves, forcing Bailey to room alone; he seemed now to be acknowledging to Katherine his own sense of isolation and loneliness. He went on: "I couldn't figure it—I mean, I thought for a minute that you were just like them, that you'd been visiting them all that time maybe in secret, and leaving me out. Like maybe it was all a big joke, and Bates would tell me today how he's got pictures and everything. And then you started acting like fucking me was some kind of punishment you wanted to inflict on yourself. That's a wonderful thing to know. And that *was* it, wasn't it."

"No," Katherine said.

"Yeah, sure."

She was silent.

"You better get dressed and get out of here before Bates wakes up and starts looking for everybody."

"Yes," Katherine said, rising. "I'm sorry."

"You were upset by the accident."

"Yes."

"Come see me next time you're upset. Next time you get pregnant from a perfect son of a bitch."

"All right," Katherine said. "Please."

She had spent the last three months of her pregnancy and the first month of Alex's life with her parents in Brockton. Bates and Bailey and the new drummer waited for her, took odd jobs and even panhandled a little until she was ready to return. Katherine was that good on the guitar, they told her parents: she was worth the wait. The new drummer was a thin, red-faced boy only nineteen years old, and he was a good drummer. He worked hard. But he was not nearly as good as the other had been, and of course Katherine, who could hear the difference, began to know again that nothing would come of the work and the miles of travel. She put it way in the back of her mind; she entertained every hope, every illusion. And when her parents begged her to give it up, to raise her child, to find a husband, she only felt all the more determined.

"It's satanic," her mother said, "that's what it is. How can you do this to us? How can you persist in this craziness?"

"Let her be," said her father.

They were all at the table. Katherine was to be leaving in the morning. She watched her mother put a forkful of peas in her mouth and thought about leaving the child to grow up with these people. Yet she wanted their approval, wanted to feel that they were with her, not just giving her what she wanted, but with her.

"Mother," she said.

"You go out there," her father said, "and we don't see you for months, and then you come home pregnant. How are we supposed to feel?"

"What do you want me to do, Daddy."

"I want you to stay home where you belong. Get married."

"Do you have anybody in mind?"

"You know what I mean—settle down."

"Settle down in this house."

"In this town."

"I hate this town."

"All right," her father said. "I just mean you don't have to live *with* us."

"No, but even if I do—what happens? You want me home and you write me and say, come home, you miss me. So I come home and you sit on the sofa and watch television, and mother sits in the bedroom and does crossword puzzles. What is that? What is it that makes you want me here so much, just so I can sit under the same roof, while you go on like I'm not even *here*."

"Katherine," her mother said, "that is unfair. That is the most unfair thing you ever said."

"It's the truth, and you know it's the truth. Look, you love each other and that's wonderful, but it leaves me out. It always left me out. Do you understand? I can't remember once ever feeling like I was home, *at* home. Like I was anything but a—but something to be tolerated or spoiled or made busy so you could be alone. So you could have everything—you could have each other to yourselves."

"You're so wrong," her father said. "We had you late in life, I'll admit. It was hard to make the adjustment—"

"Yes, well I didn't feel—I felt what I'm telling you."

"Don't you think any child feels that?" her mother asked.

"Maybe. But maybe I needed a little more than *any* child."

Her father stood. "We gave you what was in us to give you. I don't want to discuss it further."

"After all," her mother said, "we're still giving you what you ask for. We're taking your child so you can go off on this crazy pipe dream of yours."

"Kick you in the ass," her father was saying. "They grow up and kick you in the ass."

In the morning there was a tense parting: Katherine kissed her father's cheek. At breakfast he had again tried to get her to seek child-support from the drummer. She refused: she would make it on her own, though her father's expression when she said this made her see how little he thought of her idea of self-sufficiency. He did not say what she knew he must have wanted to say, which was that *he* was being coerced into the position that should have been the drummer's where child-support was concerned. She touched his hand, said, "I'll pay for everything. I'll send you money every week while I'm gone. You won't have to spend a dime."

"Well," he said, "just don't say that about making it on your own. You've had plenty of help. We've given you all the help in the world."

"Thank you," Katherine said.

They hadn't spoken a word from that moment to the time of her parting. And then her father had hugged her, a clumsy, tentative thing that made her brace herself, as though they might both topple over. Her mother only touched her shoulder, and kissed her cheek—a distant, cold, politeness.

"I'll be back in a couple of months," Katherine said, and walked away from them.

She did not return until Christmas of that year, and by that time she was already making up her mind to quit. She was tired, she did not know her own child; yet she lay in bed at night, hearing the Christmas music that her father played all night on the stereo (a stack of records thick as a tire) because he needed to hear it to feel like Christmas, to believe it was Christmas, and she caught herself wishing the baby would sigh out its life, die in its sleep, relieve her from having to start. She asked herself, *Having to start what?* The life her parents led.

But even if she had never thought of quitting, she could not have stopped the band from flying apart.

During those last months, in the time just before and shortly after Brinhart's arrival on the scene, she had slept with Bailey off and on—a sort of tacit agreement between the two of them that she would decide when and where, and that neither of them would speak about it to the others. She also slept with the new drummer, and with Bates once. Nobody said anything, though she supposed they all understood, all knew.

"Why do you do this anyway," Bailey asked her one night, "when you hate it so?"

"I don't hate it," Katherine said. "I don't."

This was after Brinhart had begun to follow them around. Bailey stood at a motel window in Connecticut and said, "You hate it with me. Don't say you don't hate it with me."

Katherine lay in his bed and felt as though the blankets clung to her like mold.

"What about our groupie?" Bailey said.

"What about him?"

"He's pie-eyed about you. He thinks you're peachy-keen, squeaky-clean."

"Don't say that."

"It's true."

"He's a boy. He's four years—he's a hundred years younger than I am."

"You're so fucked up."

"Come fuck me," said Katherine. There was a sort of excitement in the loathing she knew she would feel. It fed her passion somehow. She lay back and Bailey came to her and she took him to herself, thinking of her parents in a room, reading a magazine together, her father sitting on the arm of a chair over her mother, who sat with legs crossed primly, as though she had never lain this way with anyone. Katherine lay gazing over Bailey's heavy shoulder at this picture of her parents. Bailey finished, lay over on his side and slept, and she thought of herself as somebody lost, afloat somewhere high above the ground, not yet plummeting.

Everything was falling apart.

And Brinhart showed up at every gig, stared at her as though she were an idea of something generous and good. She couldn't stand it. She was quite rude to him in the beginning. He told his stories or spoke about her talent, and she looked away, pretended not to be listening. The other members of the band scoffed at him behind his back, and she remained silent, or she laughed as they laughed, at Brinhart's expense. Still, he turned up at every gig, and afterward he waited patiently for them to tear down the equipment—sometimes he even helped. It grew hard not to like him, though he tended to drink more than he should, and there seemed to be something missing in him: Katherine felt certain that something essential was missing. He would follow them all to the next town, would sit with them and listen to the talk around the table when they sat up late, in one truck stop or another. He paid his own way, and he was very solicitous of Katherine. And one evening it dawned on her that he was not as inexperienced as she had thought: he had been on the other side of the world, and he knew things. He had a very good sense of humor, and there was—in spite of the something missing—a solidness about him, a species of coherence, that appealed to her. She stopped sleeping with Bailey, and Bailey—poor, used, overgrown boy that he was—understood.

"You need somebody like him," Bailey said one night. "Somebody straight and true, just like him."

They were sitting on two boxes in the hallway behind a stage, at a high school in Vermont. It was summer, and the band was about to break apart. The hallway was thin and dirty, and there were chalk drawings all over the walls, of the parts of women, the spread legs of dreamed copulation and of homosexual tauntings, pricks the size of broom shafts and crude as the figures on the walls of caves.

"The guy's a walking advertisement for husbands."

"Meaning what," Katherine said.

"Oh," he said, "meaning marry him, go off and raise kids, have a house and a yard. That's what he's got to offer you. He's a husband. A born husband."

"Maybe he is," Katherine said. "What's wrong with that?"

"Not a fucking thing, sweetheart."

She was silent. The hallway filled up with noise: a crowd of teen-agers at the far end, where the wings of the stage were. Katherine thought of Brinhart out there, waiting for the band with the others—waiting for *her*.

"Look," she said to Bailey, "let me tell him about—everything."

"I'm discreet," Bailey said. "You know that about me at least."

She thanked him, kissed him, and then Bates came by and they all went out into the lights, and she played her guitar with an idea of Brinhart's eyes on her fingers, her mouth as she sang. And somewhere during the first song, she made up her mind that she would see what Brinhart might do for her, that she would find out what there might be in him that she could hope for: she would see if his love would happen.

When it began to happen, and Brinhart had made his proclamation in the car, traveling south, her disbelief that he could actually feel that way about her made her hesitate. It frightened her, finally, so she waited for him to change his mind. She waited, and he was constant, and she began to believe she loved him, and then everything turned upside down: she could not bear the idea that he might change his mind, that his love for her might be merely a fascination with her talent. Even so, this didn't matter, couldn't matter: he had become essential to her: it was only in his presence that she felt herself of any value at all, and so she began to want only to be with him, only to have a life with him, some kind of a life. She entertained the vague idea of the garden and the house, of the boy growing up, Katherine and Brinhart in a rough approximation of Katherine's parents, so devoted to each other, so without needs beyond each other. Somehow she would make it there, no matter what—and, no matter what, she would tell Brinhart nothing about this time in her life.

In ten years she had not broken this promise to herself.

Now she drove up Prince William Street, trying to decide where to go. She thought of the way the street had looked from the seventh floor, those curtains of shade thrown down by the buildings—the building she almost jumped from. It was all wrong, all so wrong: she felt a thrill, imagining herself falling through to somewhere. *To where? Where am I going?* She had wanted—she had needed—to be famous. There. That was it. She had needed people humming her songs and whispering her name and going to sleep to her voice. Droves of people. Radios, juke boxes, record players, television—the whole preposterous gamut of the nation's appetite and attention. Yet she remembered her mother saying that the music was sexual and wrong. *Only a whore would play that music.* When was that? The last time, the time with Brinhart. She had told her parents about the breakup, and her mother had said *good.* So emphatically. *Good. It should've stopped a long time ago. Only a whore would play that music. That music is sexual and wrong.* And Katherine had indeed felt the thrill of sexual arousal, playing feedback, governing it as she faced the amplifier, the scream of an electronic law pulsing along her nerves: face the amplifier, it shrieks; play the notes, the shriek is music: you didn't even need your right hand on the strings. She had felt like a priestess of some forbidden rite, and she had reveled in it, had done things to enhance it.

But no, Brinhart had said to her mother, *all music is sexual.*

Not like that—like African tribes or something.

That's a bit racist, Brinhart had said.

And Katherine had told them to leave it alone, she was probably going to quit anyway. There was no place to go now; the band was dead, and couldn't they let it alone at last?

But now *she* couldn't let it alone. Ten years, and she still couldn't do it—she was beginning to understand that she would never be able to do it.

She turned the car around, drove east for a few miles. She might try something in Washington. So a part of her still made plans, remembered Alex, imagined tomorrow and the next day and the next—or, rather, assumed these things. She would go to Alex, and the two of them . . . but she couldn't complete the idea. She remembered the peace she had felt at the ocean—the visit with Brinhart's father. She had spent each morning of that week on the balcony of the old man's place, looking out over the sea. There had been trouble *that* summer: and the trouble had all gone out of her, there, so far away from everything; it was not the sea so much as it was distance, freedom, as though her trouble —the steady piling up of days she could find no adequate way to fill—lay behind her, up North.

She drove fast. She pressed the pedal to the floor and the car sailed over dips and swells in the road. The sun poured out of the maples on either side, the dappled blue surface of the road coming crazily at her.

So they said suicide

She slowed down. There was a crossing street, a light. Before her was a boundless landscape of asphalt lots and stores and motel signs and restaurants; a profusion of clashing color and insane cartoon figures vying for her eye— McDonald's, Burger King, Bob's Big Boy, the Exxon Tiger, the Michelin Tire doll. Everything smiled, everything. Lunatic faces. Faces that seemed to be straining to say there was no death.

XXV ❧

BRINHART LAY SPRAWLED on his bed, and Alex stood in the entrance of the room, watching him snore, moan, swallow. It was now late afternoon, and the boy had spent most of the past few hours at the high school, though no one practiced there and the field was wet. He sat at the very top of the bleachers, watched the cars go by on the road out beyond the left-field fence. He had imagined himself, Johnny Gaddling, tall and left-handed, a line-drive hitter, great center fielder—Golden Glove, batting champion, Most Valuable Player. Now he walked back into the living room, gazed out the front door. The sun had come out; puddles of water were drying in the tennis court. Nothing moved anywhere. He imagined people thrown across beds behind all the windows, and now more than anything he wanted to see winter come—school, much as he had hated school. He remembered sitting alone in his classroom during the recess after lunch—all the other children out running in the playground—that time the sixth-grade teacher, Mr. Morgan, that man who had been a Marine captain, came in and found him making up a list of batting averages, the highest ones, beginning with Ty Cobb's .424. Mr. Morgan was a thick man: thick neck, thick shoulders, thick arms and chest and legs.

"Why aren't you out with the others?" he said.

Alex told him he didn't feel well.

"You been to the nurse?"

"No, sir."

Mr. Morgan stood at Alex's shoulder and looked at what he had written. Then he smiled. "For Lord's sake," he said.

Alex tried to cover the page.

"Summer's on the way, kid," Mr. Morgan said. "It'll be

here before you know it." He reached down, took the page from beneath the boy's hand, folded it, put it in his shirt pocket. "Now get on out there with everybody else."

Alex had walked out of the room with the man at his back, and he had thought about summer, which would never arrive: he longed for it so. Now, closing the front door, as though he were shutting summer out, he walked back into the bedroom, stood over Brinhart, who looked dead, was not breathing or moaning or swallowing anymore. Brinhart opened his eyes, looked at Alex, closed them again. "Where the hell did you go," he said.

"Nowhere," Alex said.

"Where's your mother."

Alex told him.

"Jesus."

"She said you left us. That you wouldn't be back."

"I didn't leave you. I'm here." Brinhart opened his eyes again, pushed up on his hands, and came to a sitting position. It was odd; it was as though he had never been away. He rubbed his eyes, yawned. "Ah," he said. "What time is it?"

"Afternoon," the boy said.

"Where the hell did you go."

"Told you, nowhere."

"Don't be smart. We don't need for you to be smart right now."

"I saw you," Alex said, "I saw you with her."

"Jesus Christ," Brinhart said. "You don't know what the hell—"

"Why don't you *get*," Alex said.

"Yeah, why don't I."

But then the boy was confused: he did not want Brinhart to go. He could feel himself getting ready to cry and he turned away from Brinhart, hating him and hating every single thing in the world.

"Hey," Brinhart said, "come on, we're going to work it out."

"Sure, Brinhart, sure."

"Things happen, kid. It isn't the end of the world. Not yet."

"*You* say."

Brinhart got out of the bed and went into the bathroom. But he came right out. "So she's looking for work."

Alex was silent.

"She didn't—Jesus."

"I want my mother," Alex said. He was not crying; he was managing it.

Brinhart put his hands on the boy's shoulders. "Look, what was she like? You know what I mean. What was she —how did she seem."

"Crazy."

"No, come on. Jesus."

"She *was*. She was crazy, Brinhart."

"Jesus."

"She's going to do something, isn't she," Alex said.

"No, now wait. You're getting ahead of everything. Just hold on."

"And it's because of *you*." Alex tore himself out from beneath his hands, walked into the living room. Brinhart followed. Neither of them spoke. They sat across from each other, and Alex toyed with the arm of his chair. It was very quiet, and the sun poured through the patio door, a wide beam through which dust floated down like a miniature snowstorm.

"I love your mother," Brinhart said finally.

"Tell *her* that."

"Yeah. And I love you too. There are things even a smart kid like you wouldn't understand."

"Yeah."

"Yeah. You bet. Yeah."

They waited a while longer, and then Brinhart got up and went into the kitchen. Alex heard him pick up the phone.

"What're you going to do?" he called.

"I don't know. I'm a little—I'm nervous. Just like you are. I want to know where she is. Thought I might call the police and see if any—if there've been any accidents."

"She has a job," Alex said. "She's at work."

"Exactly." Brinhart stood in the entrance of the kitchen and pushed the buttons in the receiver. Alex went to the door.

"Where're you going?"

"Nowhere."

"Don't start that—that 'nowhere' business."

Alex was silent.

"Amy's not home, Son. Don't—just stay here, will you—"

"I'll be out here." Alex stepped out before Brinhart could say anything else. He was afraid now, the same fear that had been in him all day mounting to the surface; it was something he remembered, that he did not want to remember: this cold fear. He walked up to the entrance, stood at the edge of the highway watching the cars, the approaching shapes, each of which became someone else's car, a car with a stranger at the wheel, whipping by him or slowing to make the turn into Winston Garden. No one looked at him: the faces were all as they had always been atop the shoulders; nothing had changed, everything where it was supposed to be. The sun came down out of the high cliffs of white clouds, and the wind blew yellow dust up from the shoulder of the road. Somewhere out there under the sun his mother lived and moved. He could feel her everywhere. He remembered Amy—that she had gone away and would not be back. He would never see her again. And in a moment she had become confused with his mother: this one,

this *she*, who would never return. He watched the oncoming
cars, the strangers; they were all going home.

XXVI ❧

BRINHART CALLED his father again. There was no answer.
He let it ring many times, standing alone in the kitchen
while the boy moved farther and farther away in his mind,
going off, escaping again to his nowhere. He could not
imagine that Katherine would come home, or that—if she
did—he would be able to fix the broken places between
them. He hung the telephone up, moved to the sink,
reached into the cabinet above it, brought out a tumbler.
He searched for some whiskey, vodka, anything. Then he
remembered that it was all gone, nothing was left, and he
hurried out to the front of the apartment, called Alex. The
boy was gone. He went back inside to the bedroom, still
carrying the glass. He sat on the bed, stared at the wall
opposite him. Four photographs hung there, of Katherine
and the boy and himself, the three of them standing in sun
—trees and clouds and sky behind them: a picnic at Harpers Ferry, three years ago. Katherine looked happy. Alex
squinted into the camera. Who had taken that picture?
Mildred Schapp. A friend who had lived three doors away
at the old apartment, the last one before Winston Garden.
Brinhart had desired Mildred Schapp. He had fantasized
that he and Mildred Schapp lay on Mildred's sofa, and Mildred only wanted to offer him the gift of herself: not to hurt
Katherine. Brinhart in his dreams had slept with thousands
of women.
    Now he stood, holding the glass very tight. He looked at
his knuckles, the bones there, where he held the glass. It
was all none of his fault, any more than it was anyone's

fault. He put the glass down on the cabinet in the bathroom and went back into the kitchen. There was the telephone. He tried his father again, and then he tried Katherine's father. No answer anywhere. He went to the living room, sat down, and folded his legs beneath him, then stretched them out, leaning against the arm. There was nothing to do but wait. He got up and turned the television on and then he sat down on the sofa again, elbows resting on knees. The sound was too low, and for a while he strained to hear. A woman and a girl were in a hospital room, talking over the sleeping body of a man. Brinhart got up again, turned the sound up just in time for the screen to go blank. Nothing. He waited. The screen opened to a vista of red fields, and a man spoke about working a hard day with the cattle and now it was time for a beer. The beer poured as from a divine fountain into a frosted glass, and the music played. Brinhart walked into the bedroom and opened the closet and put the cloth of one of Katherine's nightgowns against his face. He stood there for some time, breathing the odor of the cloth— bleach and the closet naphtha, and, faintly, Katherine's body—and at last he found himself in the living room again, sitting on the sofa, watching the television. There was nothing on. Soap operas, reruns. He turned the channel selector around four or five times. Nothing. He struck the television, struck the little switch, shutting it off, and then he stood by the front door and struck the wall. Finally he went outside again, walked through the warm sun down to the field, where he shouted Alex's name, looked for him in the choked gulley of the creek, which was a little swollen from the morning's rain. For a long while he sat on the bank, tearing stalks of weed, and imagining that the boy watched him from whatever hiding place. "You're like all the Alans and Normans I ever knew," he said aloud. "Making up the new number systems, it's just the same. Just like keeping tabs on the fucking baseball." He thought the boy was nearby; he could feel his presence, the way Alex had always watched him. The boy was always in hiding. He hid inside his body, behind his face. "Why don't you *play* the damn game. Do something. You're a fucking sissy. Sissy."

Here he was, a man sitting on the bank of a creek at the end of a marriage, talking about baseball to nobody—to the drooping branches and the mud and the streaked water. A man being petulant and unreasonable and loud, like an angry boy.

"Alex," he said, "dammit. Alex. She has to find us together."

Nothing.

A bird sang above him and a high jet roared over the bird. Flies landed and then took off from his arms, landed and took off, never settling. One perched on the toe of his shoe, wrung its hands—a little green distraught thing that he drove away with a twitch of his leg. Brinhart wept for a little while, and then he walked back up to the hedgerow, where he saw Katherine and Alex going up the sidewalk in front of the apartment. He ran to catch up with them.

"Hey!" he called.

Katherine turned, looked at him, then went on, holding the boy's hand. She had opened the door by the time he got to her, and now he simply stood there while she held the door for Alex.

"Mom," Alex said.

"I was looking for you, boy," said Brinhart.

Katherine stepped inside, and he followed. She and Alex embraced, and he watched this, closing the door.

"Honey?" he said.

She held the boy's face against her chest. "No," she said.

"I was looking all over for him. Where'd you find him?"

"No."

"I was—worried about you. We have to talk."

"No."

"Honey, look—"

"We don't need anyone," she said to Alex, bending to look into his eyes, "do we?"

The boy said, "No, Mama," but it was with a tearful voice, and Brinhart couldn't tell how he meant it: he might have been pleading with his mother.

"Katherine," he said, "it's your trouble. We always made it through before—"

"I'm home," she said to Alex, "and it's just us now. Just the two of us. It's going to be all right."

"Katherine, god-*damn*."

And now she did look at him. She spoke dispassionately, quietly. "I'm quitting. Nothing you can say will change my mind. Will you please get out now, and leave me and my child alone."

Brinhart looked at the bones just under her neck and felt himself recoil, something unbelievably hot burning up toward his eyes and down toward his throat. "You're crazy," he said. "You've lost it '

She turned and walked the boy into the hallway, and he heard her close a door.

"You're insane!" he screamed.

He broke a lamp. He lifted it out of its place, the wire tearing from the wall, and broke it in the middle of the room. Then he swept his hand across the television set, knocking everything—a stand-up photo of Alex at three years old, two figurines, and a terrarium—over onto the floor. He stood looking at his hands. Everything in the room seemed alive, watching: what would he break next. But he was done now, his hands falling to his sides. He went into the hallway, heard Katherine's voice murmuring behind the door to Alex's room. For a little while he stood with his ear against the wood, listening.

". . . or we could go there too. They have a nice school too, and it's in the country. But here, look. Look at that. Look at that white sand."

"I don't want to go there."

"It's so beautiful. You know it's beautiful. It's a perfect place."

"What about Amy—"

"She's gone, Alex. Make up your mind. I don't want to see Blanche or Stan."

Brinhart thought the boy was crying. He opened the door; the latch clicked. Katherine turned at the sound. She was sitting on Alex's bed, her purse in her lap. The boy knelt on the floor before her, and at his knees were seven or eight bright folders, open, like maps. Brinhart saw color photographs of bright green lawns, mountains, shimmering seas edged by shading palms and sand white as sugar.

"I thought you were gone," Katherine said, "and I heard you breaking things."

"I'm taking the car," he said.

"We're going overseas."

"You're crazy."

"We're going to have a wonderful life together overseas."

Brinhart looked at the boy. "If you want to come with me, you're welcome. I'll be at the trailer court."

"Oh," Katherine said, rising, "goddamn you, damn you, damn you."

"Stop it," Alex said. Then he screamed, "STOP IT!"

Katherine knelt at his side, clumsily, her arms reaching around him. "There," she said, "don't let him ruin it for us. We won't let him ruin it for us."

"I'll be over for my things later," Brinhart said. He didn't know if either of them had heard him. It didn't matter. He went out again, to the car, and for a moment he stood gazing at the sky above the rooftops of Winston Garden. It looked almost green, and there was another wind blowing, the sign of another storm; it was unreal. The clouds, darkening to the west, were shaped like the monstrous features of some animal face: a monkey, or a snout-faced man. Unreal. The shape and texture of the car door-handle surprised him; it was so solid, so clean. It made a little clicking noise as he opened the door and got into the car and put his hands on the wheel—it kept clicking. Then it stopped, and he realized that the sound had come from the next apartment: a baby there playing with a toy gun. In the doorway he saw a woman, very old, with a black net in her hair and with long blond whiskers on her cheeks. She nodded at him, and he returned the nod, started the car, and backed out into the lot. When he looked at the door again, she was gone, the child was alone, playing in the grass, yet he felt the presence of the old woman in an excruciating moment of rising grief and love. He waved at the child and then he drove out to the highway and around, through the red drying puddles and the sailing cloud shadows to the trailer court.

Shirley sat on the stoop, and he saw that she watched him come down the row. He parked in Red's place, as though he had been doing so for months.

"That's Red's place," she said as he got out of the car.

"Where is he?"

"*You* know."

"With Max."

She nodded. He walked up to her, stood under the shade of the awning. "Where did you go this morning?" she asked.

"I—went home. Back to the apartment."

She said nothing.

"Where's the baby?"

"Napping."

"Can I come in?"

"Nobody's in," she said, "but the baby—and the baby's asleep. You can sit here if you want to." She moved over and he sat down. For a few moments neither of them spoke. Brinhart looked at the shadows forming across the street, and then he looked at her flattened thighs.

"Well?" she said.

"I'm sorry about this morning."

"Forget it."

"I should've been able to—I should've considered—"

"It happens," she said.

"No, I mean—about what we talked—what I said."

She smiled briefly, looked beyond him, biting the nail of her index finger. Then she examined it, went over it gingerly with the end of her thumb. "I thought it might storm again. I love to watch it storm. I don't think there's anything more exciting than watching lightning . . ."

"I think—my wife and I are splitting—"

". . . of course, it's scary to most people."

He was silent.

"So," she said presently, "you're splitting up."

"Looks like it."

"You still love her."

"Ah, Christ," Brinhart said. "I'm washed out. I just don't know anything anymore."

"Poor baby." She turned to him and frowned. "Poor, poor baby."

"Yeah," he said. "All right."

They were quiet again.

"Red won't like it that you came back."

"I saw Red this morning—later this morning."

"Where?"

"Here."

"You were here again?"

"Yes."

"He didn't tell me. I slept until almost two o'clock."

"He said you were asleep."

"So what else did he say?" she asked.

"Not much."

"He took care of the baby."

Brinhart made no answer.

"Tell me what he said."

"It wasn't anything—we didn't get along too well."

"Tell me, will you?"

He told her.

"God," she said. "Poor Red. He's so worried."

"Maybe I should go," said Brinhart.

"Do you want to go?"

"No."

"Then don't."

After a few moments she said, "Do you want to be with me now?"

"Oh," he said, "yes."

She took his hand and led him inside.

They lay in her bed, under the cover sheet, not touching now. The window let in the faint greenish light of dusk, which shone on the paneled walls, and made soft shadows from the raised picture frames there. The pictures were mostly of animals—drugstore prints of horses and cats, wild deer, three tan puppies huddled together in sleep. It was a small room and the pictures were everywhere. There was a single bureau, a dressing table, a puffy wing chair with cotton jutting from its arms. On the bureau a few books were stacked, spines out, so that Brinhart could have read the titles in better light. The bed itself was lumpy, the headboard coated with a fine dust. He lay with his hands behind his head and looked at the closed door. Red had come home a few moments ago, and now was moving around in the adjoining room. Once or twice Brinhart had heard him cough. Now he closed his eyes, wondered what Katherine and Alex were doing: they seemed thousands of miles away now; and now, with all his heart, he came to know that he could not leave them, that he would have to go back to them. He lay quiet, knowing this, and Shirley stirred next to him, sighing stale breath.

She had been strangely diffident in their love making;

Brinhart had gone inside her with a sense of falling, of her depths, this woman he did not really know, who only allowed him here, and who hadn't met him or his desire with anything but compliance. He had come quickly, with shame, apologizing into her hair-covered ear; and then he had fallen asleep. The sleep had been shallow, half wakeful, crowded with brief dreams of Katherine and Alex and— oddly enough—Red, who wandered among the rooms, disapproving, grumpily swigging his beer and muttering curse words under his breath. Brinhart awoke once, his stomach throbbing with hunger, and saw Shirley pacing the room, naked, the baby held up over her shoulder. For an instant he had lost time: it was 1969 and a woman he loved walked the room with someone else's baby. He turned, buried his face in a pillow whose cover smelled alien, and shut his eyes tight, aware that he had slept and that he would probably not be able to go back to sleep, that he was hungrier than he had ever been in his life, and that above all else, just then, he must go back to sleep, he must hide. Now, lying in the near dark, finally and irrevocably awake, he heard Red clear his throat on the other side of the door. He turned to Shirley, who lay staring at the ceiling. His motion made her stir, and she propped herself on one elbow, looked down at him, her face expressionless, calm, revealing nothing.

"Red's home," he whispered.

"We really slept. We won't be able to sleep tonight."

"He's outside the door."

"He . . . knows. I talked to him. He knows."

"What did he say?"

She lay back down. "Nothing."

"How long did I sleep?"

"A couple of hours. You moaned and groaned a lot."

"Ah, God." Brinhart held his stomach. "I haven't eaten—"

"I'll fix you something."

"I can do it—maybe we should go out." But he did not want to go out. He did not want to move, though the idea of the night, here, was now very much a part of the increasing discomfort in his stomach. He glanced at the three tan puppies on the wall, and she traced, with one finger, the line of his jaw. In this light she looked haggard and vaguely corrupt, and again he buried his face in the pillow.

"What's wrong with you?"

"Nothing."

"You seem so unhappy. Poor Brinhart."

"God." He lay over on his back again, gazed at the door. She put her hand down and cupped it over his groin, and then she kissed him. Her tongue tasted of sleep, and when she offered him her breast, he felt such a sharp pang of hunger—the briny flavor of her skin—that he almost cried out. Again she was quiet; she lay open for him in a passiveness that increased as his passion grew. It made him feel swallowed, drowned; again it was over very quickly.

"I'm sorry," he said.

"Why?" She got up, reached for a roll of toilet paper by the bed. "It was good. Really." Then she left him alone. She closed the door quietly, as though not to wake him, and he lay hearing the baby and Red's low, muttering voice. He dressed quickly, and when he opened the door to go out, his hunger made him gag: but it was nervousness too. Red was out there, waiting for him like a judge. Brinhart stepped out of the room and was suddenly transported, as though through some trick of the camera in a movie, to a moment more than ten years ago: that moment of the numbness of knowing his mother was dead, of understanding the words and not feeling them, feeling really nothing at all, when he stood outside the Japanese girl's apartment, still covered with the odors and juices of her body, and there was the long flight home ahead of him. All of the years ahead undone, not happened; Katherine somewhere across the world, playing her music. He stood very still in the narrow hallway of the trailer, one hand on the wall, like a blind man looking for the shape of what lay before him. Slowly, gathering the present and his own history to himself, worried that he might pass out any moment for hunger and for the broken state of his nerves, he went down the hall and into the living room, which was empty. The air conditioner hummed weakly in the window, and the cover page of a magazine on the floor was suspended in the current of cooler air. A single lamp was on by the sofa, and he sat down there, put the magazine on his lap. *Sports Afield.* A man in a hunting jacket aimed a rifle, snow-covered mountains above his shoulder and tall pines off to the right. Brinhart opened the magazine to the table of contents, and now he smelled food, heard the beginning of a crackling of grease. He looked up in time to see Red come scowling from the kitchen.

"Well, cowboy."

"Hello, Red."

The old man sat down in the wicker chair, crossed his legs. He wore a white shirt and brown slacks. "She's making hamburger. Can you eat?"

"Yes."

"Bet you can."

Brinhart turned the pages.

"You want a beer?"

"No, thank you."

"You're on the wagon, huh."

"Yes."

The old man frowned, plucked a piece of lint from the front of his shirt. The shirt was well starched, open at the collar. "You know, I paid for the hamburger."

Brinhart waited.

"You get my point?"

"I'll pay you for it."

"Good."

Shirley came in, cradling the baby in one arm. She lay the baby on a blanket, facedown on the sofa, next to Brinhart. Then she sat on the floor, patted the diapered rear end. The baby looked heavily, drowsily, around the room.

"The hamburger will be ready in a little bit," Shirley said. "Frozen French fries too."

"I was letting cowboy, here, know that I didn't want to support him too."

"I heard," she said, simply. "If he stays, he'll help out."

"Shit," Red muttered. "You can both go to hell." He got up, with some difficulty, and made his way to the front door.

"You're not going to eat?" she asked.

"Shit." He went out and slammed the door behind him. For a moment it was very quiet.

"He'll adjust to it," Shirley said.

"There's no way he'll stand for me living here."

She looked at him. "Where will we move?" The baby began to cry, and she picked him up, patted the small shoulders, crooned softly off-tune, rocking gently.

Brinhart watched this, and thought about how he didn't even know her.

"You're white as a sheet of paper," she said and laid the baby down. She went into the kitchen. He touched the child's head, laid his hand on the little back. No. He could not force it, could not call any feeling out of himself. It was still as though he would leave here and go home and Katherine would be waiting up for him. He sat back on the sofa and opened the magazine to the middle pages and tried very hard to concentrate on the columns of print; but the words ran down off the page and out of the world, and he realized that he was crying. He wiped his eyes on his shirt, got up, went into the bathroom, and turned the light on, looking at himself in the mirror over the sink. The bathroom smelled of shaving cream and talc, and faintly of something else. It was a moment before he recognized the peculiar odor of the old man—beer and starch and aging flesh. And flowers: he saw now that there were flowers in a vase atop the toilet; roses whose petals had dropped and lay scattered around the vase like the pieces of a torn doily. He picked up one petal, held it to his nose. And then he put his head down under the running faucet, bumping the sides of the sink, the water coming clean and cold around his eyes. He turned the water off, buried his face in a hand towel, heard Shirley call, "Ready," from the living room.

He did not know if he could gather the strength to go out there and look at her. He arranged his hair as best he could with his fingers—he did not want to use the old man's brush, which lay on a shelf above the toilet and was ruddy with hair—and stepped out into the hall again. Her bedroom was faintly visible through the open door across from him—the rumpled sheet in moony light there. He went into the living room and sat on the sofa again. She had put his plate on the coffee table, and was in the kitchen, opening and closing cabinets. "I can't find any salt," she said. "Do you need salt?"

XXVII

DAWN LIGHT came through the window and made a sheen out of the brochures. Katherine sat gazing at them where they lay on the kitchen table; she was smoking the last of a pack of cigarettes. After Brinhart had left, she had felt tremendous relief; she had embraced Alex and soothed away his tears, talking gaily to him about where they might go together. She fed him eggs and bacon for dinner, talking to him. She could not believe she had ever felt so unqualifiedly cheerful and full of hope. She kept Alex up very late, telling him about the wonderful possibilities. She told him and told him, everything coming to her full and complete, as though already accomplished.

And then she realized, with alarm, that he was exhausted and barely able to keep his eyes open. She laid him down in her bed, telling him, and he insisted on going to his own bed. He couldn't sleep anywhere else. He wanted his bed, he told her, and then she heard him. It dawned on her that she had been talking, talking. She couldn't shut up, and that wasn't right. She closed her mouth. But then she was trying to talk him out of going to his own bed. She spoke about how they must cling together now, just the two of them. Wasn't that really wonderful? And Alex insisted again.

"Go ahead, damn you!" she screamed.

And she watched him walk slowly and disconsolately out of the room. Oh, she had thought things were right now. She had come so close to stepping into the windy sky of the seventh floor: but she had not. She had thought of this plan: the sea, travel. Going away. But the boy had gone to his room, and she was so terribly lonely now, and she lighted a cigarette, walked into her bedroom, turned on the portable television, lay back, and let the sound fill her mind, or tried to: People were speaking about a somebody who apparently had died mysteriously years ago and nobody ever knew why. It all seemed to run together, as though the voices spoke one long word, another language. Katherine got out of the bed, walked through the dark hallway to the kitchen. The dinner dishes were still on the table, four or five of her smoked cigarettes in the ashtray on the counter. The window was a faint blue, and when she turned the fluorescent light on over the oven, the room jumped to light; she had not realized how little light got in here from the living room. When she looked at the clock, she saw that it was nearly five o'clock in the morning.

For some reason this filled her with horror.

"God," she said, moaning, and she went quickly into Alex's room, turned the light on there. He did not stir. He lay in a ball at the foot of the bed, both hands between his upraised knees. He seemed not to be breathing. She touched his shoulder. "Alex," she said. He groaned, rolled over on his back, his eyes opening for an instant, like the reverse of a blink. "Alex."

"No," he mumbled, and turned to the wall.

On the floor next to the bed was one of the brochures. The rest were in the living room. Katherine gathered them all up, arranged them carefully in one hand, and then she went back into the kitchen, cleared away the dishes, and laid the brochures out on the table before her with a pack of cigarettes, her lighter, the ashtray. She gazed at each photograph for a long time, trying to imagine how it would be to live there, be someone else there. She tried to think clearly enough to plan everything out, to choose the right place and then make certain of it. But she lost herself in the pictures and soon all of it—the band and the seven crazed years, the despair, the sense of her own willful destruction of an elemental part of herself, the dream dying out of her like blood, and the dead face of Beverly: everything came back to her, as though it had happened only minutes ago. It all coursed in a stream until it reached Brinhart, the quiet boy who turned out to be a talker; part of her liking for him then had been the surprise of finding this out: a storyteller. Anecdotes about life in the army that made everyone laugh and made the army seem like something whose absurdity sponsored such fun, spawned it. Brinhart, her hope, her lover, and the one who had brought her through so much pain and fear, and who had understood her enough to let her be herself, even when she had no idea who or what that was anymore. Brinhart stood in her mind like someone that had died, and now all of herself went out to him: ten years, ten years, and she had loved him so. Oh, yes. She had been in love with him and what he had done. She thought about what he had done. The memory of the past three days swept at her like a covey of fearful ghosts, and she gathered herself around what seemed a single knot of pain under her throat.

She finished the last cigarette, got out of the chair, aching from the long time she had spent in one position. Beyond the wall there was a sound, and she thought the boy must have awakened. As she started out of the kitchen she heard the low dull whine of machinery outside; a droning Jet Liner dragged its roar across the waking world. Everything stirred all at once. She turned, looked at the brochures— those beaches, those skies. They all seemed painfully insubstantial in this clear morning light; they were agonizingly far-off and dreamy. She went into the bathroom and turned the shower on, and then she turned it off, stood quiet a moment, waited. The thousand day-to-day things people did —showering, voiding, sleeping; bending and walking and kneeling and making love and cleaning—they did right up to the day they died, and then they stopped. She opened the cabinet, looked at the bottle of sleeping pills among Brinhart's shaving equipment and the cologne he had never used. She had been flying last night: flying.

Alex opened the door, peeked in. "Someone's here."

"Go see," Katherine said.

He went down the hall slowly, still half asleep.

"Hurry," Katherine said. She went into the bedroom and stood looking at the clothes in the closet. But she lacked the energy to change. She closed the closet door, and Alex came down the hall.

"It's her," he said.

"What."

"Amy's mother."

"Get in your room."

The boy went in and closed the door, and as Katherine

went toward the living room she heard a quavering, almost
animal sound there. She hurried toward it. On the sofa,
crumpled over fat knees and crying into her hands, was
Blanche.

Katherine felt nothing for her.

"What do you want?"

Blanche shook her head. "I'm so"—she began—"so
very—"

Katherine shifted her weight. Blanche looked at her out
of eyes swollen and bloodshot.

"My little girl—"

"Alex told me," Katherine said.

"Just such a shock—even when they tell you not to get
your hopes up—"

Katherine stood over her.

"Didn't—I know it's early," Blanche said. She wiped her
eyes with the backs of her hands. "But I couldn't stand it
over there with Stan right now. He just sits there and stares
into space. He's been doing that since three o'clock this
morning. I'll—it's like the end of the world. I can't get him
to—" She sniffed, ran her hands over her mouth now, looking across the room. "Ahhh. You see, my little girl—" And
her face seemed to fall apart, the tears rolling out and dropping down her cheeks, so that Katherine thought, *I can't
stand it. Be quiet. Go away.* "My child," Blanche went on.
"I know I'm a mess." She tried to gather herself. "Do you
have cigarettes? Could I please have a cigarette?"

"I'm out of cigarettes," Katherine said.

"Ahhh. Last night. A little before midnight. So quick.
Like a sigh. Nothing worked. We went all over the place
then. Stan and me. Just—riding. You see, there wasn't anything we could *do.*" And now the large head went down
into the palms, the shoulders heaving—a great sobbing bel-
low that must have come from the bottom of her lungs.

Katherine knelt before her, briefly touched her hair,
brought her hand away as if it had been burned. Then she

saw her own arms go out, around the wide shoulders.
"There," she said, because she knew that was what she was
supposed to say, "there now. There. There."

"I'm sorry," Blanche said, sitting back. "Just let me get
ahold of myself a little."

"It's too bad," Katherine said. But she couldn't feel it.
She touched the woman's knee, and something moved at
her side. Alex. "Alex," she said.

"Amy is dead," Alex said.

"My poor little girl," said Blanche, composing herself
now, "just sighed away like a breath of air."

Alex went to the door, put his hand on the knob. Katherine saw this, and something stopped her voice: something
inside her said, *Let him go. Wherever he wants. Let him.*
She watched him go out. He left the door open.

"I don't have any Kleenex," Blanche said.

Katherine rose, went to the door, stood in the frame, and
watched Alex disappear beyond the hedgerow. Behind her
Blanche murmured and sniffed, said something about the
poor boy. Katherine thought the other woman said, "That
poor little boy."

"No," she whirled around. "No."

"I can't think," Blanche said. "I can't remember what
we're supposed to do next."

Katherine put her hands over her ears. "Please. Leave
me alone now. Please."

Blanche hadn't heard her. Again she had lowered her
head into her hands, sobbing. "I kept it all back with Stan. I
can't let him see me like this—I bore it for him without
stint. . . ."

The strangeness of this expression made Katherine think
of leaving her here. She said, "You have to leave me alone
now."

"Oh, yes. Yes. I'm sorry."

"You have to go away."

"You'll come over . . . please. Would you please come over? Stan—"

"I have to decide," Katherine said.

Blanche struggled out the door. "I don't know what I'll do about Stan. We don't have any family. The end of the world—"

"You go home," Katherine said.

The other woman gave her a puzzled, helpless expression. "You go ahead now. You'll be all right."

"Yes," Blanche said, nearly falling from the edge of the sidewalk. She looked down, then back up at Katherine, walking away. Katherine closed the door quietly and went into the kitchen and put the phone off the hook. There was so little time. There was too much time to think, and it was important to hurry. She went into the bathroom, brought the sleeping pills out of the cabinet. She thought Alex should be with her, to guide her into sleep. But it was only a thought. You had your family around you in the bad year, the awful time. You had your family in the cold. They helped you on toward death. She would not let it go, would not let anything come into her mind, and she was all the way down at the end now but she would do this, just as anyone bent down to pick up a fallen piece of clothing or cleaned one's teeth. She sat on the bed and took the first pill. It went down easily. She took another. Then another, another. They all went down easily. She took one more, and again one more. She waited, waited, shaking a little; she would not let herself think beyond this next one. And this, and this, and this.

XXVIII ❧

ALEX WENT to the graves and sat leaning against one of the stones. Here were the dead. They were where Amy was. No, that was not right. Amy was where they were. He was out of breath, though he had stopped running before he crossed the highway: he had walked here. He was not crying. He put his hand down in the grass. Not real. He just couldn't hold it in his mind. Dead. He tore at the grass, then laid it down, and the wind blew it away. The sun poured down through the leaves above him, dappling his shoulders, and the whole world seemed to have let sound go out of it, off into space. Across from him, on the lower branch of a sycamore, a squirrel darted back and forth, as if confused. Alex found himself crouching, and then he was holding his hand out, clucking his lips, stepping cautiously closer. The squirrel seemed not to be aware of him, but then, as he was almost upon it, one quick eye settled on him, and the animal froze.

"Look," Alex murmured, "something to eat." He carefully bent down, searched the grass and the pine-needle-and-dead-leaf-covered ground at the base of the tree for a stone or a fallen branch. There was nothing. "Here," he said, holding out his hand. The squirrel made a few darting movements on the branch, then scampered up the trunk of the tree, turned, head down, watching him. Alex crept into the deep shade, found a piece of windfall, almost too heavy for one hand. Then he went back to the tree, but the squirrel was no longer there. He waited a few moments, being very quiet, listening, still as a hunter deep in the woods. Then he dropped the stick, club, putting his hands to his face, breathing the odor of the bark on his dirty fingers.

"Goddamn fucking squirrel," he said.

He walked down the steep bank, almost falling, and as he went across the wide parking lot, the sun getting hot here, the air thick and redolent of exhaust, he became certain of Amy's death, and felt very sad for what she would never do or see or know. He had only a sense of *her* loss, and when he traversed the road, running before cars that sped blindly at him out of the sun, a little thrill of elation went through him: he was alive, his mother and Brinhart and everybody he knew were alive. It would get all right. Yes, he thought· it would all be fixed and be all right again.

The apartment was quiet In the kitchen were the brochures, and the ashtray, full. He wandered into the bedroom, saw his mother lying asleep on the bed; he thought of leaving her there, knowing without having to think about it that she needed sleep, rest. But then he was too much alone, the quiet was too big around him, and so he went to the bed and lay down at her side, put his head on her shoulder. She did not stir.

"Mom?" he said, and touched her face. "Mama?"

Then he shook her. And then he shook her and shook her, and something came out of his mouth—he did not know what he said—and now he pushed her shoulders down into the mattress, screaming. His mother's mouth opened, then, a sound like whistling came, and he was running wildly down the hall, out, screaming across the parking lot. Two people were in the tennis court, and James, the older boy, the baseball player, was sitting in a lawn chair outside his apartment. Alex stood in the middle of the asphalt lot and screamed, and now there were faces all around him. He looked at the boy, James, and he tried to say *help*. The boy went up the sidewalk and into the apartment, followed by a young woman in a bathing suit and a tall, bent man with one arm. One of the tennis players, a blond woman with a dark spot on her cheek, held Alex by the shoulders.

"Tell us," she said.

But he couldn't make any words come, couldn't draw in air. The woman struck him on the back. There was a swirl of faces and bodies; he saw James again, saw him holding up, for everyone to see, the pill bottle. It was not empty.

Alex saw that it was not empty and he was now being pulled from the lot, the woman drawing him away.

"It's all right," she said. "It's going to be all right."

Alex fought her, and then someone else was holding him. He was all anger now, and they wouldn't let him go: if it was all right, why wouldn't they let him see? He was lifted, swept off the ground, raging and kicking, and he tried to look at who carried him; the blond woman's face floated before him, but he couldn't see whose arm held him under his own flailing arms. Finally he was set down again, though he still fought to free himself, the arms still holding him. He turned, or was turned, and the baseball player's face, contorted with fear and anger—and something else too: pity or respect or both—looked at him and said, "Hey! We got an ambulance coming. Stop it now. It's all right. We got her on her feet."

Alex struck the face.

"You little—"

Someone else held his arms again.

"Crazy—"

"Let him alone," the blond woman said: Alex heard her voice and under her voice there was another sound. Someone crying. He looked through the baseball player's legs, realized that he had fallen to his knees. A few feet away an old woman stood with a wide-brimmed straw hat in her hands, crying. She cried and whimpered and stared off into space, and her fingers toyed with the brim of the hat.

"Get her out of here." The blond woman's voice.

"That's my grandmother," the baseball player said. "She's upset."

Alex tried to break free again, but his strength had left him. He lay back, or fell, and the blond woman carried him. He saw so many faces, and then he closed his eyes, hearing the steady murmur of the voices. "I hate you," he said. But he did not know whom he meant. "I hate you, I hate you," he said. The image of his mother's face swam before his closed eyes, and he said, "I hate you." Then he was crying, a steady flow of it all out of him.

"Hate you, hate you, hate you. . . ."

XXIX

BRINHART AWOKE that morning and thought he was in his own bed. He sat up, looked at the room, at Shirley, who lay with her back to him, naked, her hair brittle and unkempt on the pillow. There were two moles on the point of her right shoulder blade; looking at them made him acutely aware of her strangeness—her otherness from Katherine. Shirley sighed, turned over on her stomach, hands cupped to her face; then she was leaning on her elbows, gazing at him.

"Red's home," he said.

"Always, that's the first thing you say." She rolled over, locked her hands above her head, stretching. "I heard him when he came in."

"I have to go to work today," he said.

"Yeah." She reached for him, one hand over his hip. He lay on top of her. In the red world of his closed eyes there was a nameless dread, and he tried to put it away from himself: this was what had happened in his life, this girl. Quickly, efficiently, and with a casualness that left him alone somehow, she guided him into her, lay under his striving almost as though asleep, her eyes closed, her hips barely moving to accept him. He buried his face in the pillow above her shoulder, tried to go very slow, and then couldn't —and again he lay sorrowful and half sick, at the end of himself, while she let her hands come down on his back.

"Nice," she murmured into his ear.

He moved from her, lay on his back. She put her head on his shoulder, one leg over his groin.

"Nice?" she said.

"Yes."

She snuggled.

"The baby's crying," he said.

"Didn't stop you this time."

"No."

"He's all right—it's good for his lungs."

"I have to go to work," he said again.

"Call in sick."

"I've done that two days running."

"If they fire you, we can go somewhere else."

"There isn't anywhere else to go, I'm afraid."

"What's the matter?" she asked.

"Nothing."

"Are you happy?" she snuggled again.

"How can you expect me to be happy? No."

She did not speak for a moment.

"I'm sorry," he said.

"Forget it."

"I just have to get used to things."

"Sure." She patted him on the chest. Then she got out of the bed, crossed the room, and brought a Kleenex out of the bureau. She stood there, ministering to herself. He looked away, heard Red hawking again, this time on the other side of the wall. The baby was not crying now, though from time to time Brinhart heard the little voice, angry or playful, he couldn't tell. Shirley put a robe on and faced him.

"You know, I don't have any protection," she said.

Brinhart sat up. "*What?*"

"I might have another baby."

"You *what?*"

She laughed, turned, began to brush her hair with her fingers, the one hand clawing through the tangles. "Just kidding."

"Jesus Christ, don't do that—" He couldn't catch his breath for a moment.

"Scared the hell out of you, huh."

"Just—don't do that. Don't play jokes."

She smiled at him, and then left the room. Immediately he was up, getting dressed. He heard Red go out, waited a moment, then went into the bathroom and used the other man's razor; he took the old blade out and rinsed the razor thoroughly: the thought of Red's whiskers made him queasy. When he returned from the bathroom, she was in the kitchen, so he stood by the window and looked out at the row of trailers across the street. Down the row he saw Blanche struggling alone toward her trailer from the field, her face twisted and white and ugly. He watched her go into the trailer and then he turned, remembering the whole dizzy progress of yesterday: Amy's illness had slipped his mind. He had not thought about anything but his own trouble all this time. He looked at Shirley's baby, and a great pity rose out of him toward it. The baby lay back and sucked the milk from the bottle. Brinhart went into the kitchen, found Shirley sitting at the small table, sipping coffee. Another cup and saucer, and the pot of coffee, lay across from her. He sat down, poured some for himself, watched her push a thick lock of hair back from her forehead. She was crying.

"Oh, no," he said.

She sipped the coffee, shook her head slightly, setting the cup down.

"What is it?" he said.

"Nothing."

"Shirley, Jesus—"

"Nothing," she said. "I don't know. Isn't this crazy?"

"Did I—I didn't mean to hurt your feelings—" This was lame, he knew. "I'm sorry," he said.

"It's not you. What makes you think that? Sometimes I get tired. You know? It doesn't have anything to do with you." She wiped her eyes. "Oh, boy, you think it's because of you. That's a laugh."

"I'm sorry you're unhappy," he said.

She ignored this. "You know, I've been thinking about getting out of here. Going someplace. West again, maybe."

There was nothing he could think of to say.

"I'd like to get out—you know what I mean?"

"I think so," he said.

"Maybe you might go with me."

"I can't leave here. Can't leave my job."

She put her hands to her face. "I'm—I've been so messed up lately. I mean, I don't know what I want anymore."

"It'll work out," he said.

"Oh, shut up, will you? I don't *need* that stuff."

"I'm sorry—"

"That's all you ever say." She went into the living room, picked the baby up, held his face in the hollow of her shoulder. He watched this from where he sat, and when she came back, not looking at him, he reached out and touched her arm. "Could you leave me alone, for a while," she said. "Please?"

"I have to—okay."

She went out again, and he heard the bedroom door close.

Outside, though it was not yet seven o'clock, the sun shone like a torch through the low branches of the trees bordering the field. There were crows high above the trees, and birds chattered everywhere, as though disturbed by some stealthy, threatful presence among the thick blossoms of crab apple and mimosa and honeysuckle that grew between the trailer court and the far road west of the highway. The air was moist and heavy—another photochemical inversion, the haze settling down over Point Royal like fine blue dust. Brinhart got into the car and drove down toward the field, but then he stopped, turned around. The trailer court lay before him in a bright bath of sun, and a lone dog crossed from one row to the other, head down. He drove past Shirley's trailer and on, around to the highway, toward the center of town. He tried not to let anything into his mind because, as he sped on, the idea of a single whiskey—just one to even him out a little and give him the nerve to make it through the day—came to him like a sort of lust. He turned the radio on loud, put the knob all the way around, and twice he nearly went through stoplights. When he parked the car in his space, he imagined what Treadwater would say—what they would all say. Somehow he must look and act like a man who had no trouble.

Treadwater was at his desk, talking over the telephone. He smiled at Brinhart, who stood in the doorway for a moment, his courage having failed as he opened the door. Brinhart walked to his own desk, sat down, folded his hands over the papers there: a few phone messages, a letter from the United States Insurance Association. Across from him, staring into a compact open on her desk, was one of the secretaries—Mrs. Berg. She was a pathetically skinny girl with bulging, dark, starved eyes, and she was as meticulous about her makeup as she was sloppy about her dress. This morning she wore a white skirt, a sleeveless blue blouse. She looked at Brinhart and shook her head.

"What's wrong?" he asked.

"Lewis's mad at you."

"Is he coming in today?"

"Don't know."

"Why's he mad at me?"

She shrugged. "Thought you'd know."

Treadwater hung up the phone. "Brinhart," he said.

"Lewis is mad at me?"

"He's not happy."

Brinhart leaned back in his chair and folded his hands across his chest: he wanted to appear casual and unworried, but he could feel the blood gathering under the skin of his cheeks. "I can't help it if he is," he said. "I can't help it if I get sick."

"We hear you weren't really sick," the secretary said.

Brinhart looked at Treadwater, who shook his head. "I was sick." In a moment he pretended to be very busy—a conscientious man trying to catch up with his work.

It was almost noon before the phone call came through. Treadwater was the one who answered it, confirmed aloud that Gordon Brinhart worked there, *was* there. Brinhart partly heard this. He was talking with a client: an expensively dressed woman with ugly, flowering burn scars across her lower face. She had a problem with a claim; she was unhappy, and her unhappiness flowed out of her toward Brinhart like radio waves. He couldn't stand it; and now Treadwater sat holding the receiver, obviously afraid to interrupt the woman, who fumbled with the straps of her purse and went on and on about what she had lost. Brinhart turned to him and said, "Is that for me?"

Treadwater nodded.

"Excuse me," he said to the woman.

"They're holding," Treadwater said.

Brinhart stood, took the receiver from him. "Yes?"

The voice on the other end, an even, professional voice, seemed to say everything in a dreamy repetition, a memorized, familiar monologue.

"My God," Brinhart said. "My God." He might have said, "I knew it, I knew it." He hung the phone up, turned to the woman, who gazed at him unconcernedly—a bleak, deadpan, scarred face, waiting to go on complaining about the lost loved one and the failures of insurance. Treadwater took his wrist with surprising force.

"What is it? What's happened?"

Brinhart looked at him: the features of his face were not

clear; they seemed to be pulling apart. "My wife—I have to leave."

"An accident? Did she have an accident?"

"No."

"Are you going to be able to help me?" the woman said.

"Not now," said Brinhart, pulling away from Treadwater. "Ah, Jesus."

"You go on," Treadwater said, standing now, holding a pencil in his fist; and now the woman was standing too.

"An emergency?" she asked. But Brinhart went past her and out, running across the lot to the car. There, getting out of *his* car, was Lewis, bald pate shining in the sun.

"You," Lewis said. "I want to talk to you."

Brinhart may have muttered, "Not now." He was in behind the wheel and Lewis had come around to stand at the open window with his hands on his hips.

"Brinhart, I said I wanted to talk to you."

"Not *now*, dammit."

"You're fired, Brinhart. That's what I wanted to say."

"Fired." He had started the car, and as he put it in gear he saw the other's massive shadow; the sun burned above Lewis's head.

"I saw you, Brinhart—I saw you staggering around in front of The Knight's Table."

Gordon Brinhart put his head down on the steering wheel.

"I've got a check in my car for two weeks severance pay. That's fair enough. Wait here and I'll get it."

"Keep it," Brinhart said. "Shove it up your fat ass." He backed out of his place, the other man jumping to get out of the way, and pulled around to the entrance of the lot with such speed that the tires squealed. As he surged into the road he saw Lewis running toward him, a fat, waddling, outraged man, shouting and holding up his fist.

✦

The Point Royal Hospital was actually a few thousand yards outside the town limits; it was close to Winston Garden. It lay sprawled, all one floor, on a spacious, willow-shaded, and grassy lawn, beyond a tall wrought-iron fence. The road that led to it crossed the highway above Winston Garden; the road was a narrow blue strip through an over-hanging tangle of branches from the oaks and maples that lined it, and the entrance to the hospital was marked by a red-brick monolith with raised white letters. This was not immediately visible from the road as you came around the curve, and so Brinhart missed it, sped past it, and braked—nearly losing control of the car—when he saw the low build-ing through the fence, and the willows to the left. For a moment he sat with his head on the wheel and breathed, hearing birds above and around him: they seemed to shout at him. Another car came from the opposite direction, veered at the last moment, and, blaring its horn, sped away. Brinhart went slowly back up to the entrance and in, care-ful to signal the turn, though the road was empty now. He drove up a dappled lane into a wide, circular asphalt lot, past two slow-walking nuns, who looked at him with sad eyes, as though offering a sort of blind consolation to any-one in their path. He parked the car and walked toward the double glass doors of the emergency entrance, going slowly now, for fear of what awaited him. Until now he had been a blank vessel of alarm; but here, so close to the moment when he would stand in a room and look upon his wife, it came to him that Katherine was already dead. He had en-tered the lobby. He stopped, held both hands to his stom-ach. To his left, against the wall, a row of soft chairs seemed to yield up Alex, flanked by a woman and a teen-age boy. Brinhart stood looking at Alex's face, and now Alex saw him. He did not speak, nor did he give any sign that he knew Brinhart. The woman patted Alex's shoulder and murmured something to him. Brinhart approached, a hard little lump forming just above his heart. "Alex," he said.

The blond woman stood up, took his arm, and said, "Are you Mr. Brinhart?"

"Yes."

"I'm Sue Morgan."

"My wife—"

"No news. We're waiting."

"Jesus Christ."

"Your son found her," Sue Morgan said.

"Not my father," said Alex.

"Stepfather," Brinhart mumbled. Then they were all quiet. He sat down, and Sue Morgan sat down, and Alex cried, but would not allow Brinhart to touch him.

"Upset," the teen-age boy said.

They waited a long time. People came and went. One man walked in with a bad cut on his arm; he held a blood-soaked handkerchief over the cut: A fortunate man with a wound. Brinhart paced, finally, back and forth, and when a man in a blue smock called his name, he gasped.

"Over here," Sue Morgan said.

The doctor approached them—there was nothing in his face. It was an ordinary face, and there was nothing in it: the eyes were narrow, blue, and cold. "Mr. Brinhart," he said.

"Yes." Brinhart looked at the other's lips.

"She's still in some danger, sir. But it looks like she may pull out of it. Will you come with me?"

"Oh, please," Brinhart said, following the blue smock. "Please, please, please, please."

"We'll wait here," Sue Morgan called.

He turned, was surprised to see that she was wearing a tennis outfit: he hadn't noticed it before. "Thank you," he said. Then he was following the blue smock again. On either side of him were open doors, beds with people in them, rooms with obscure metal equipment hanging from the ceilings. A confusion of voices spilled out of the intercom, and from one room came the sound of a radio; it all tore at his nerves. At the end of the hall the blue smock turned. An orderly went by, pushing a metal cart full of bottles. The bottles made a tinkling sound, like tiny bells, and the orderly gave him a bored, dissatisfied look. The blue smock turned again, stopped. "Wait here, Mr. Brinhart."

"Yes, of course." He was anxious to be cooperative, as though this might somehow influence the outcome. "Yes, sir."

The doctor went through a swinging door. To the left of the door was a long, wired glass window, but the nurse's station, which was across the hall, was empty. Brinhart walked over to the counter and waited. He had never believed a hospital could be this quiet. It was now unbearably quiet, and he thought of morgues, death rooms, the little graveyard behind the mall. The orderly who had passed him earlier came by, pushing the cart, which was now empty. The orderly whistled, and Brinhart felt a kind of wonder, watching him—this boy who walked daily through injury, illness, and death, and who seemed so oblivious to it, ambling down the hall and out of sight. He put his hands to his mouth: it was so quiet here because Katherine was dead. Katherine had got to the bottom of her sleep and was gone.

"No," he said.

Then he heard the squeak of the rubber soles on the floor, looked up, saw a round face, a blue nurse's cap. The swinging door gave forth the blue smock now too.

"You can come in," the doctor said. The nurse stood at his shoulder and then was gone; she carried a clipboard and a pencil. Brinhart followed the doctor through the swinging door, and when they were on the other side, the doctor turned around, put one finger up to his nose. He had dark black hair on his arms, and Brinhart saw, as the hand dropped back to a pocket in the blue smock, a bloom of dark curls in the *V* of the neck. "There'll be some questions we'll have to ask you, Mr. Brinhart. I suppose you know that this was an attempted suicide."

"Oh, please," Brinhart said.

"I'm sorry. She's starting to come around now."

"Will she live?"

"This time—yes."

Brinhart went back against the wall, breathing. "Ahhh," he gasped. "Oh, God." He held on. "Jesus." The walls moved, and he had begun to cry.

"It's all right now, hold on," the doctor said.

"Oh."

"She's still in the woods, as it were. I mean, this is a serious problem. I think you realize what all of this means."

"Can I see her?"

The doctor considered a moment.

"Can I just look at her?"

"You must be—you'll have to have the psychiatric people here examine her."

"I know. All right."

"Now, of course, you wanted to see her. Come with me."

It was all so cold and dispassionate; it was as if the doctor felt disdain for this work, for Brinhart, and for Katherine. Brinhart followed him down another corridor, narrower, shorter than the other. He thought about how they were going deeper into the hospital, and how if Katherine were too deep, she might never come out, might never find her way out of the maze of hallways. The doctor walked, cold and efficient, ahead of him, to a wide white door.

"Right in there, Mr. Brinhart."

"Thank you."

"There's a nurse in there with her."

"Yes, sir. Thank you." Brinhart's voice shook. He opened the door. The nurse and the bed and Katherine were shadows before a large, sunny window; they made, actually, one shadow—a sort of tableau of the Healer and the Sick. The room was bathed in sun, and it was surprisingly big. He saw grass on the other side of the window as he walked toward it. The nurse, who was Oriental, had Katherine sitting up in bed, and was feeding her a clear liquid. Katherine seemed not to see anything; but she looked better than he had thought she would. There was color in her cheeks. She turned her head, seemed to look past him; but then she murmured, "Gordo—I couldn't do it."

"I'll leave you alone," the nurse said.

Brinhart experienced a moment of panic at the thought of being alone with his wife. He gave no sign of this. He smiled, watched the nurse go out; the door closed on a whisper of air, slowly.

"I couldn't do it, Gordo."

He sat down on the bed and put his arms around her. She lay her head on his shoulder, but her arms were crossed in her lap as if dead.

"Honey," he said. "Sweetheart. I'm here."

"We fucked everything up. I'm so sorry, Gordo."

"No. I know. I'm sorry. Don't talk about it."

"Gordo—" She began to cry.

"It's all right," he said. "All right. It's going to be all right." But he did not believe himself, and he thought his heart might break. He rocked her, gently, like a little girl, in his arms.

XXX ❧

THE DOCTOR was kind enough to come back and tell Alex that his mother would be all right. Shortly after he did so, Alex told Sue Morgan that he wanted to go home.

"Honey, don't you want to wait for your father?" she asked.

"No," Alex said, "and he's not my father. He's my step-father."

"He's your father, then. He's the one—well. I think, anyway, that you ought to wait for him, don't you? I don't mind waiting, really. And you know, you shouldn't say 'stepfather' like that."

"I want to go home," Alex said. And then, understanding what he must say to get what he wanted, he added, "I can wait for him there."

"You can wait with us—"

"I can take care of myself," he said. "They left me alone plenty of times."

"I'll bet they did," she muttered.

"I can take him home," the baseball player James said. He had been paging through a magazine, and now he dropped it in the chair next to him and stood up.

"I really think I ought to stay here," Sue Morgan said, "for a while anyway." She looked at Alex. "I think you should too."

"I want to go home," Alex said.

"Come on," said James. "I'll walk you."

"Is the apartment open? Can you get in?" she asked.

Alex told her he could.

"No," Sue Morgan said. "Let me take you." She reached for her purse.

"I want to walk with *him*," Alex said.

She paused, studied him for a moment. "Well, all right then—it's really up to you, I guess. Isn't it."

"Come on," James said.

They moved away from her.

"I'll tell your father you're waiting for him at home," she said.

James led the way out. They walked across the grass to the road, and Alex kept looking at the older boy's arms, the veins that stood out there, roped over the wrists and forking up to the elbow. James led him through a small red gully beside the road, and then they were walking along the shoulder. The shade was deep, the stones spotted with flecks of sun that moved as the leaves moved above them; the configurations of shadow in the road were like stains. The road curved, angled downward in a slanting fall toward a break in the leaves; it all seemed to end in the sky, though Alex could see the glint of traffic in the bright space. He had walked fast, to keep up with the faster stride of the other boy, and he was a little out of breath.

"I'm sorry I hit you," he said.

But James apparently hadn't heard him. They walked on.

"I said, I'm sorry I hit you."

"I heard you," James said.

Alex bent down and picked up a stone, held it between his thumb and forefinger. It was a piece of slate, blue as the sky, and he remembered how his mother—once, long ago—had brought him a piece of blue rock from Skyline Drive. "See," she had said, "that's why they're called the Blue Ridge Mountains." And Alex had dreamed of mountains made of blue stone, and his mother had been like anyone else then.

"You ever been to the mountains?" he asked James.

"Nope."

He was thinking that he and this boy might go there together, might run away and become the best of friends. He thought of Amy. He imagined himself and Amy and this boy running among the great blue boulders.

"You never been to the Blue Ridge?"

"Shit," James said, "those ain't mountains."

"They are too."

"Yeah, well they *call* them mountains. You ever see a picture of the Rockies or the Alps?"

"Sure, lots of times."

"*That's* mountains."

Alex kept silent for a moment. A fugitive gust of wind shook the leaves above them, then passed, rolling over the tops of the trees. It was still again. They were nearing the highway. Birds called among the branches, and a lone butterfly made its erratic way across the road in front of them, the sun igniting its wings with the intermittency of blinking light.

"I watched you play," Alex said.

"Yeah, I seen you watching."

"Know what Williams hit lifetime?"

"Williams."

"Yeah, Ted Williams."

"Who's he?"

"You don't know who Ted Williams is?"

"Why don't you tell me."

"He was just the greatest hitter who ever lived."

"Oh, *that*," James said, "I don't know any of that stuff. I just play the game. I never liked watching it much."

"How can you play if you don't watch it?"

"That's silly. You either play or you watch."

They walked on.

"It's more fun to play it," James said.

"More fun to watch," said Alex. He tried to throw the piece of slate a long way into the woods. It hit a tree, dropped in the undergrowth with a thud.

"You got to learn to play it," James said. "It's no good just to watch."

They had reached the place where the road widened toward the highway. A Jeep went by them, full of girls, and they all waved and called at James, who waved back. Alex watched them go into the shade—flailing white arms and flying hair.

"Who're they?" he asked.

James laughed. "Girl friends."

"I had a girl friend."

"Sure."

"I did. She died last night. We found out this morning."

"You're bullshitting me, kid."

"No. Last night. Her name was Amy."

James looked at him. "Really?"

"It's the truth."

"Ah, I don't believe it."

"For real," Alex said. He had never felt so full of pride. But then it all went out of him like a breath, and it hurt. Everything hurt then.

"That's hellacious," James said, "if it's true."

They reached the highway, crossed it, walked down to the apartments. The sun was everywhere now, as though the world had opened wide around them. High up, two bursts of cloud, white and grainy as sugar, climbed toward the light; one cloud left a trailing tatter of almost transparent mist, like the tail of a kite. The highway, where it disappeared in the distance, was a hazy blue.

They entered Winston Garden, walked in the glare of parked automobiles.

"Why'd your mother—" James began. "Uh, why do you think your mother—" He hesitated. "What made her crazy?"

Alex ran out ahead of the other boy, then turned. "None of your fucking business."

"Hey, look, kid."

"None of your fucking business," Alex said. He ran on, down to the apartment, heard James calling for him to wait. He thought he could still hear it as he reached the grass and angled toward the door; but abruptly he was caught and held, the stronger hands locked around his arms.

"Wait a minute, damn you."

"Leave me alone," he cried.

"What's got into you, for Christ's sake."

"Get *off!*"

"Aw, shit—" James pushed him, and he nearly fell. For a moment they stood glaring at each other. "Loony little bastard."

"Fuck you," Alex said. The other boy struck, once. Alex didn't even see it coming and he lay with his face in the grass, and his nose seemed to expand.

"Little shit," James said, and walked across to his apartment, without looking back.

The apartment was locked. Alex sat on the front step and watched the blood collect at his feet. It had dawned on him as he tried the door that he did not want to be here when Brinhart returned. He did not want to hear what Brinhart would have to tell him. The blood dropped from him, and he thought about how Brinhart would see this and know that he had been fighting. He was glad of the blood. But after a while it stopped, and Brinhart hadn't come, so he got up and wandered over to the trailer court. Bees flew at him. He retreated toward the field, circled, came back to Amy's trailer and knocked on the door. No one there. He peered through one window, saw the empty living room with the soft rug and the many books. Then he went back out to the drive, gazing up the row at the rickety fence. The whole court seemed deserted, though there was the faint noise of the air conditioners in the windows. Four or five trailers up on this side, a dog barked. Somewhere a screen door slammed. He squatted in the dirt, drew a line in the fine dust the sun had made; beneath the dust the ground was moist. He sat down, watched a hornet trail along the sill of the window he had looked in. The glass there was rain-spotted, filmy from this angle; it looked sealed. Twice the hornet knocked against the sill.

If only Amy's father and mother would come home.

There was something he wanted very badly to say to them, though he could not put it together in his mind. He thought if they came soon, he might look at them, and then what he wanted to say would come. He took a fistful of the dust and hurled it into the first breath of wind.

XXXI ꗝ

BRINHART SAW THE BLOOD and thought it must be Katherine's. It made him ill, but he steadied himself, leaning against the door. After a moment he let himself in, walked through the quiet rooms, seeing really nothing. He went into the kitchen and picked up the phone. Again no answer. He imagined his father standing at the edge of the sea, arms extended. No answer. He walked outside, thinking to find Alex. Sue Morgan had told him the boy insisted on going home. Brinhart had walked away from her, and she had called after him, "How is your wife?"

He turned. There was this woman he did not know, who wore a tennis outfit and who looked naked and out of place. "She's fine," he said. "Fine. Fine."

Now he went down to the field, the creek. No sign of the boy. He went back to the apartment, thinking to wait. Thinking, in spite of himself, that he knew where Alex was, and that he did not want to have to face him yet. There were things to do, and so again he went to the phone. This time he called Katherine's parents. He stood listening to the far-off buzz, waiting, and he was about to hang up when Katherine's father answered. "Yes?"

"This is Gordon—"

"Yes?" The voice was tentative, weak.

"Katherine is ill, sir."

"Yes?"

"Did you hear what I said?"

"Who is this?"

Brinhart muttered, "Jesus Christ." Then he shouted into the breathing on the other end. "This is Gordon. Long-distance. Katherine is ill."

"Oh," said her father. "Oh, Lord. Is it bad?"

"It's very serious," Brinhart said.

"Is she *sick*?"

"Yes. Sick."

"Oh, my Lord, no."

"She's been hospitalized."

"Lord, oh, Lord—"

"Can you come out here? Can you take the boy?"

"What? Will she—she isn't dead."

"No. Listen to me. Put your wife on."

"Oh, no. Oh, Lord." The old man was crying. It dawned on Brinhart that he was crying, and so he said, very loud, that there was nothing to worry about. The voice bawled into the line. "Oh, Lord. My Lord."

"PUT YOUR WIFE ON!" Brinhart screamed.

"She's not here."

"Christ."

"Oh, Lord. How is she. How did it happen. What is it—"

"She's had a nervous breakdown."

"Nervous—oh, Lord. The nervous system?"

"Look," Brinhart said, "can you come out here? I got an eleven-year-old boy I don't know what to do with. I've lost my job, and Katherine will be in the hospital for a while—"

"Is it cancer?"

Brinhart said nothing.

"Those cigarettes. Oh, Lord."

"Look—forget it."

"What?"

"It's *not* cancer. We're all right."

"But what *is* it?"

"Nervous breakdown."

"Nervous what?"

"Christ! Nervous. She got—she has a nervous stomach."

"You said nervous breakdown."

"That's right. Jesus."

"I knew it. I always knew it. I swear to God."

"Can you come *out* here?" Brinhart asked.

"She knew what the pancreas was when she was eight years old. She was always nervous like that. I knew it."

"CAN YOU COME OUT HERE!" Brinhart screamed.

"We can't drive anymore," Katherine's father said, crying. "We don't have the money to fly."

"Katherine tried to kill herself," Brinhart said. He was now shaking all over with rage, and he realized that he, too, was crying. He wiped his eyes with the back of his hand. "Goddammit."

"Oh, Lord. Lord. Lord."

"I'll be back in touch with you," Brinhart said. "Can you take the boy?"

"The boy—oh, no. Lord, no. We wouldn't be any good—"

"I'll call you back."

". . . it's that music," Katherine's father said. "It's that music, isn't it."

"No," Brinhart said. "No. I'll call you back."

"I don't know what her mother will say. She can't take these kind of shocks."

"I'll call back," Brinhart said. He hung the phone up and stood there with his fists clenched at his sides. He hated them all—his father, Katherine's parents, all of them—for their lives and their order and their peace. For their meticulous attention to those things that had driven Katherine to her despair. He thought of Aunt Beth, babbling alone in a toilet, all the good energy of that face in the photograph on the sewing-room wall—that vitality driven down and made into self-hatred merely because it was what it was.

He wandered the rooms of the apartment, coming to

know that Katherine would take a long, long time healing, if she ever did really heal. He entered Alex's room, with its bright banners and its color photos of the gods of baseball. He stood in the doorway of his own room—his and Katherine's—which was musty with the odor of fear and drunkenness and sorrow. He sobbed into his hands, turning, a man who would have to start over again, from the very beginning.

When he had got control of himself, he went over to the trailer court, walked out the patio door and across the lot to the path. He remembered the first awkward conversation with Shirley—that night he had made himself sick with whiskey; it seemed to have happened somewhere faraway, years away: it wasn't even a month ago.

When he came down the drive, wiping the places under his eyes where tears had dried, he saw Alex walking over the far crest of the field. He did not call out to him. He wanted to spare the boy from having to run away from him again; yet, as he watched the head bob down out of sight, he felt as though the boy and himself were alone on an empty planet—the boy leaving him here to put most of an uninhabited world between them.

At Shirley's trailer he saw Red's truck. Shirley came to the door as he opened the gate. She smiled at him, stepped out, met him on the sidewalk. She wore one of the halter tops and a pair of red-flowered culottes. Her hair was pinned back, and she squinted at him in the sun, held one hand like a visor over her eyes.

"Shirley—" he began. He wanted to say good-bye.

She interrupted him. "Red and me and Max are going to California." She touched his shoulder. "I get to spend some money on myself too. We're going to San Francisco and live by the Golden Gate."

"That's—that's wonderful," Brinhart said. He kissed her once, lightly, on the cheek. "I'm happy for you. Really."

"You're staying here," she said, "right?"

He said, "Yes."

"Red'll be glad of that."

"I'm happy for Red."

There was an unpleasant pause. The baby whined, then sang, in one of the windows. A cloud rolled past the sun, and briefly everything was gray. She bent down and picked a toy up from the grass, blew a stray stem from it. He looked at her hips, then looked away, saw sunlight slip down the side of the trailer; the awning gave shade again, dark yet glittering with the dust on the air.

"Shirley," he said, "I wanted you to know—"

Again she interrupted him. "I mean, I really do hate Virginia, you know? And I'm sure I'll love it in San Francisco."

"Yes. It's a beautiful city."

"You been there?" She smiled.

"Once. Long ago. I was in the army. On leave."

She nodded, went up on her toes, and kissed him on the mouth. "You were nice," she said.

"You too."

A dog was barking somewhere, and again the baby cried. Red moved past the doorway; he did not look out.

"That Red," said Shirley. Then she walked back up onto the stoop, went inside, bringing the door back to the jamb without sound. She stood gazing through the screen at Brinhart. "Well," she said, "bye,"

"I'll think of you often," Brinhart said.

She smiled, turned, was gone.

He heard her crooning to the baby as he walked away, down the row in the brightness.

XXXII ❧

THE CREEK WATER trickled in a green-slick stream over moss, and nearby a frog croaked. Dragonflies hovered, changed direction, made square flight-patterns just above the water. Alex watched this without interest, and when he looked at the other bank, the fallen pine cones and the piled-up needles, Amy was there. She lay back as she had on that first day, her elbows propping her up, her chin on her chest. It was Amy. He studied the dirt and pine needles and maple shade, saw the curve of a stone jutting up through the moss at the water's edge. It was Amy. She was chewing a piece of grass.

"Can't talk to a friend," she said. "We're lovers."

He was very still, very quiet.

"Too good to talk," she said. "All you can do is lay around."

Alex closed his eyes. She was there.

"I know your mother," she said. "I hate baseball." She sang, "I don't care if I da-da-da-dum." She lay back and gazed at the sun.

"I hate baseball," Alex said.

"You love it more than ever."

And she was gone.

He opened his eyes, and there was only the green water and the dragonflies, the solid moss and the pine cones and the moist shade. He put his head down on his hands, and something moved behind him. He turned, saw Brinhart, and nearly cried out.

"Didn't mean to scare you," Brinhart said.

Alex looked back at the creek. When Brinhart sat down next to him, he edged closer to the water, away from him.

"Your mother's fine now."

"I heard. The doctor told me."

"Look, don't run away, all right? I want to talk to you."

The boy was silent.

"Doubt if I could catch you if you ran off again. I'm sort of beat." Brinhart sighed, picked up a pebble, and threw it into the water. "We can make it, Alex."

He would not speak to Brinhart. He stared at the opposite bank, where Amy had been.

"The three of us. We can work it out."

The boy spit into the ground between his knees.

"We can try anyway," Brinhart said. "We have to try."

For a long time neither of them spoke. Brinhart threw another pebble into the water. Alex moved still farther away.

"You know," Brinhart said, trying to laugh, "I wanted to pawn you off on your mother's folks. See, I've been fired." He threw yet another pebble. "Anyway, we're stuck, for now."

"Yeah," Alex said. "*You're* stuck."

"Okay. I'm stuck—you got blood on your chin. You've been bleeding. What happened to you—"

"What do you care," Alex said. "I got in a fight."

"I care. I love you. I love your mother."

"Some love."

"It's all I got, kid. You know? Maybe it's the only damn kind there is. It's screwy, I know. But there you are."

"Too bad."

"Yeah, it is. Isn't it."

Alex kept looking at the other bank.

"I ever tell you about my Aunt Beth?" Brinhart said. "Sad story. We all make sad stories. For instance, your mother. You know your mother is a lot like my Aunt Beth. See, some people just have a hard time fitting in. And what we have to do, we have to help each other out. Because it's just—it's no use unless we try as best we can to—help each other out. God knows, I have messed things up, Alex. I mean, both of us—I mean, all three of us did. Now, I don't know, but it seems to me that we ought to be trying to pull together a little bit. I'm sitting here without a job and with —with my wife in the hospital, you know? This is a—this is a real bad time. But—I mean, we're lucky too. We had a little girl die that we both know—of course that's—that's really sad, you know. But your mother is going to be all right. See, and so we're stuck. We don't fit in anywhere and we're hurting. I am hurting, let me tell you. I mean, I don't even know what I'm going to do. But I'm going to try and make it up—I mean, we're still alive and we have to try. Because there just isn't anybody else now."

There was another pause. Brinhart sighed, cleared his throat.

"You're just a lot of shit," Alex said.

"Right."

"A lot of shit."

"But I'm all you've got—we're all we've got," Brinhart said. "You hear me? I'm telling you the truth. I was scared as shit to talk to you."

An airplane went across the very top of the sky, and there was the long thunder of its engines. The frog had ceased, and as the roar of the jet passed on out of the world, everything seemed at once hushed and fragrant, odors springing up out of the grass all around them.

"Your mother is going to need all the—need everything we can give her. We just have to give her something."

"Like what."

"Maybe we'll get out of here and go somewhere. Someplace where we can feel like we're—well, like we fit. I don't know what we'll do."

"You're just a—a drunk."

Brinhart was silent a moment. "Well . . . yes. That's— that seems to be the unfortunate truth."

"Yeah," Alex said, tearing at the grass. "Yeah."

"But listen," said Brinhart. "One thing we have to do—we have to stop tearing our own guts out. You know?"

"That's just shit."

Now Brinhart tore at the grass; he put a stalk to his lips. "Yeah." He said, "Well—what're you going to do, then?"

"I don't know," Alex said. "But it won't be with *you*."

"Yeah, well—we're pretty fucked up, aren't we?"

"You think that makes it all right, talking that shit to me—that man-to-man shit. I'm not going for it, Brinhart."

"Used to know this kid," Brinhart said. "Man, this kid—back when I was about your age. In school. He'd come to the cafeteria every day and say, 'Goddammit, peanut butter.' Every day he'd do this. 'Goddammit, peanut butter.' I used to sit next to him and watch this, and finally one day I said to him, 'Look, why don't you have your mother make something other than peanut butter.' And you know what he said?"

"No," Alex said. "And I don't care either. Why don't you just leave me alone."

"Because," said Brinhart, "whether you like it or not, I'm your father. Legally responsible for every damn thing you do. Now listen to me. I mean, you have to listen for now." His voice shook, and Alex looked at his eyes. Brinhart's eyes were glazed over. He rubbed his nose with the back of his hand. "You know what this kid said? The one who hated peanut butter and I asked him why he didn't have his mother fix something else? He said—I'll never forget this—" Alex thought Brinhart might cry now; this astonished him. Brinhart went on. "He said, 'Oh, I make my lunches. My mother never makes them.' You—you see what I'm getting at?"

"No," Alex said. He was telling the truth.

"Well," said Brinhart, "think about it."

"My mother," Alex said, and then he was crying. He

couldn't help it. He would've done or said or suffered anything but this: crying in front of Brinhart. "My mother, goddamn you."

Brinhart moved closer, and the boy felt his arm come over his back. "I know. I know—go on and cry. I'm just running my mouth to keep from crying myself. I've been blubbering all day."

"Get away from me!" Alex said. He had done so out of a sense of suffocation. He had not meant it in anger. But as he strove to free himself Brinhart's arm tightened around him, and he fought free, or was let go; he stood with one foot in the water and the other on the bank. The water was warm and sluggish; it filled his shoe. He stood there and watched Brinhart rise.

"Okay," Brinhart said. "I'm too tired and worried and sick to fight you." He climbed the bank, was in the field, walking toward the crest of the slope. He went very slowly, his white shirt clinging to his back, showing the faint ghost of his backbone. Then he stopped, went down on his knees; it was hard to tell if he had fallen or just sunk down that way, and then Alex saw that he had become ill. He looked pathetic there in the sun. Alex averted his eyes, felt a tremendous surge of pity for him—and a sort of protectiveness. He saw the branches of the crooked trees, the mossy water; the shade seemed to change, then; it was all a green blur. The whole world grew loud and hurrying and threatening: a confusion of animal and mechanical sound. The leaves trembled here, everywhere, on every branch, as he trembled. He looked back at Brinhart—a small, struggling figure far away in the field. Brinhart had got to his feet, was walking away.

"Wait," Alex said. Then he almost shouted it. Instead, he went up the bank, clawing at the long wild grass to pull himself forward. Brinhart was going on, had almost reached the crest. Alex watched him for a moment, and again the sounds rose around him, a clamor of birds and traffic and his own breathing. "Shit," he said. And then he did shout. "Brinhart!" He walked up the slope. "Brinhart! Wait!" Brinhart had got so far away so quickly. He was so small and exposed there, at the crest, with the roofs of Winston Garden rising behind him. "Wait!" Alex called, and began the climb toward him.

He did not hurry, because Brinhart had turned, and was waiting.

$\mathcal{V}$OICES OF THE $\mathcal{S}$OUTH